the American governess

Kay Bell

the American governess

Kay Bell

CAMPANILE
PUBLISHING

Published by Campanile Publishing
www.twlawless.com

Cover design by Golden Orb Creative

Cover photograph by Masson, used under licence from
    Shutterstock.com (photo ID: 76487269).

Text design and production by Golden Orb Creative: www.goldenorbcreative.com

A National Library of Australia Cataloguing-in-Publication entry has been created for this title:

    ISBN 9780994265180 (paperback)

    ISBN 9780994265197 (ebook)

Dick Bell with the 15-foot crocodile he shot on the Burdekin River, North Queensland, in July 1946

CHAPTER ONE

BARKERS HILL was just another outback town.

It was an hour too far from the Coral Sea to glimpse a coastal breeze, and the wind that beat the backs of the rock wallabies high on the hill, rarely bothered to sweep the streets below. The town rose from an imperfect amphitheatre, trodden down at one end, spilling out onto a vast, scrubby plain dotted with spinifex and brigalow which stretched east as far as the Great Dividing Range. Between downpours, the town was stained with guano from the squadrons of flying foxes that blackened the sky each sunset. There was whimsy in its faded grace, but, these days, hopelessness nestled against every undulation like a sheltering child.

It hadn't always been like that.

A hundred and fifty years ago, someone had found gold, and buildings as grand as wedding cakes sprouted like weeds. But prosperity reached slack water after fifty years and then began to ebb, imperceptibly at first. Once the gold ran out, there was nothing left to do. Few moved away; most remained from lassitude rather than optimism. They had nowhere to go and, even if they did, they had no means to get there.

The mullock heaps encircling Barkers Hill leached cyanide and mercury into the river for decades, although no one seemed to mind. Eventually they were cleared, so that the children couldn't run up and down them any longer, and the mine shafts were covered over. The landscape they left behind was pockmarked and empty. Since people still needed to eat, the cattle industry persisted, even when almost every house and business in town was for sale.

The Diggers Arms Hotel was no exception. Outside, the advertising hoardings—like its façade—were faded and crumbling, and the rot continued inside. Aside from an old man bent over his beer, a barman with a bloated, claret face, and a dog tied by a frayed rope to the stretcher of an empty stool, the pub was deserted. Misery draped itself over the public bar and yet, despite all of that, a young man ducked under a spider on a web suspended across the top of the doorway, and out of the burning spring sun.

As he walked towards the counter, the soles of his shoes bonded to the floor like limpets. He lifted his feet—a Russian soldier in the May Day parade—but nobody noticed. God only knew what had spilled onto that floor and had never been cleaned away. Eventually, he dragged out a stool and sat by the counter. By then, his eyes had adjusted to the dimness. He looked around. There wasn't much to see.

Exactly whose dog it was, wasn't clear—the old man leaned too far the other way to suggest any bond with the animal, and the barman was oblivious to it. Above the shiny beer taps, about halfway along the counter, were bottles of spirits, upended on their dispensers, and covered in a fine, red dust. The same dust had been the young man's persistent companion since he had left the coast. It had infiltrated his clothes and coated his hair until it felt dry and steely. The scent of stale beer reached his nostrils and lingered, but there was something else hanging in the air, something acrid and bestial. Perhaps it was just the dog he could smell.

Behind the beer taps stood rows of German steins on narrow shelves reaching up nearly to the ceiling. A long time ago, someone had decorated the bar with an alpine theme, never mind that this was the dry tropics, and central Europe was a hemisphere away. He turned his back to the bar and glanced at the web again, watching it quiver with the rising heat. The spider rode the gossamer, inert until a sudden gust of wind tore the web in half and sent it flapping like a flag in a gale. The spider broke free and surfed the waning breeze to the floor. The dog glimpsed it as it fell, let out a groan and stretched just enough for his tongue to reach it. He gathered it up in his mouth and looked blissful for a moment.

Minutes passed and still nobody noticed the young man. The barman's eyes were fixed to the flat-screen TV on the wall, as he polished the lip of the same glass over and over. Every so often, the dog sighed. The young man swivelled back towards the counter again. He gripped its edge and pulled himself and the stool forward. It was either his sweat or the accumulated filth that stuck the skin of his palm to the bar's surface and held it fast until he eased it free. Above his head, a tired electric fan carved ellipses into the air, threatening to wobble off its bracket and scoot across the ceiling. The noise it made, *fwop, fwop, fwop*, was part squeal, part sweep of a broom, yet the draught—if there was any—never seemed to touch him. He thought about leaving, and he would have left, except for the heat shimmering off the bitumen outside like a miasma, and the dryness that had glued his tongue to the roof of his mouth.

He cleared his throat, but no one noticed. He moved his stool again, until the steel feet scraped against the floor. The dog's ears flitted back and forward, and the barman winced at the noise but didn't move. Eventually, the barman's eyes shifted away from the screen, in time with a break in the transmission of a cricket match being played somewhere cooler. He put down the glass and glanced at the young man. His eyes fell to his backpack, lifted to his t-shirt, and then returned to the young man's face. He appeared diffident, as if debating whether walking a few metres to the left to serve a stranger would be worth his while.

The young man shifted in his seat, but he wasn't going anywhere and, for a while, neither was the barman. Just when desperation was about to erode his resolve, the young man won.

The barman sidled over glumly. It had taken a monumental effort for him just to move. His eyes were watering and he was almost panting. 'G'day, wadkanagetcha?' he asked, his voice strangulated, pausing to wipe the bar with the same cloth he'd used to polish the glass.

'Excuse me?'

The barman huffed. The young man pressing against his bar was worse than a stranger: he was a foreigner, and so he repeated his question slowly, his intonation mirroring his exasperation, over and over until the young man made some sense of the words and demanded a cold beer.

'Potskoonarorppine?' The barman spoke like a ventriloquist. He rolled his eyes, conveying the height of each glass with fleshy hands.

The young man pushed ten dollars across the bar. The barman grunted and reached for the note. He shuffled away, returning moments later with a beer and some loose change, which he dropped in a small pile next to the glass.

It would have required more energy than the young man had to count it, so he tossed the coins straight into his pocket. He picked up the glass and let it cool his fingers, then he put it to his lips and drew in the froth. The icy bitterness skipped across his tongue and down his throat in an exquisite rush. He drained it with a few sharp gulps. His tongue had found freedom. 'Bartender! One more!' He pulled out the change, and added a note.

The barman brightened. He flashed his teeth. It passed for a smile. He poured the pint and tottered over. He sized the young man up. 'You're not from around here, ay?'

The young man's ear was tuned in to the man's accent now, and to the locals' habit of adding 'ay' to the end of every other sentence. He sipped the foam before he answered. 'No, I'm not.' His voice was clipped; in the outback, politeness was excessive.

The barman's face settled into a sneer. He was still making up his mind about the stranger. His eyes narrowed. 'So, you're American, then, ay?'

'Chase Miller.' He extended his hand.

The barman grinned. He had solved the riddle of the sphinx. He shook Chase's hand but did not introduce himself. 'So, what are you doing out here, then?'

Chase liked it better when the barman had been taciturn. 'I'm backpacking around Australia.'

'Well, you picked the best place to visit. Yep,' he remarked, glancing around, 'this is paradise on earth right here. Once you get to know us, you'll never want to leave.'

Chase nodded vaguely and gazed out of the grimy window to his right. The sunlight, the buildings and the dirt were all graduating shades of beige. The breeze had whipped up little eddies of ochre dust and gathered together all the stray bits of litter. He watched the detritus sweep along the footpath and tumble into the deep gutters, where it settled.

Having taken so long to arrive, the barman now seemed reluctant to move away. 'You planning on staying here for a while?'

'That depends.'

'Yeah?' said the barman. 'On what?'

'On whether I can find work,' he returned, sipping his beer.

The barman sucked in his breath through a gap in his molars until his cheeks popped. 'Plenty of work about on the stations.'

Chase frowned. 'The railroad?'

The barman snorted. 'Not the railroad, the cattle stations. There's a lot of them around here. It's hard bloody work, but, ay.'

'You mean, work on a cattle ranch?'

'Well, they're cattle stations around here.' He picked up his polishing cloth and folded it. 'Most of them are on the internet, but there's also a community board beside the post office, and a lot of them post jobs there.' He began to shuffle away when he stopped again. 'I just had a thought. You know, there's an old American lady runs cattle out at Glen Eira station. Keeps mostly to herself, but she's always looking for someone to do odd bits of work around the place. Jack Hughes'll be by in about an hour. He goes out that way on the mail run. You could always get a ride with him and try your luck there. She might take you on, seeing as you're an American too, ay.'

Chase smiled a little. 'You know her name?'

'Hmm,' he hesitated. 'People around here call her Mrs Mac, but that's not her real name. Now let me think...' He scratched his head. 'Nup. Can't remember her name. Never mind. All you need to remember is Glen Eira station, ay.'

'Thanks,' he returned. 'I'll think about it.'

*

While Jack Hughes loaded mail, parcels and crates onto a trailer hitched to his Land Cruiser, Chase sat on a bench in the shade outside the post office and phoned Glen Eira station. The number was on an advertisement stuck to the notice board, exactly as the barman had described.

Mrs Mac was either away from the homestead, or she didn't take calls, so he spoke to someone who called himself the manager. Chase could only surmise how a manager on a cattle station spent his time, and Ian Stewart gave very little away. Still, he sounded pleasant enough, telling Chase that they could always do with another pair of hands, and agreeing to try him out for a month on a wage half of what Chase had hoped for, with food and board thrown in. Since he'd only ever earned minimum wage and tips, if he saved everything, he still might make a dent in his college loan.

Hughes agreed to give Chase a ride as far as Glen Eira. He finished securing the load with a tarp and a series of ratchet tie-downs, and sat in the passenger's seat with the door wide open, rolling a cigarette. He looked under the weather. His eyes peered out of his scoured face like tail-lights on a foggy day.

It was a ritual he never hurried: the filter stuck to his bottom lip, a single rectangle of Tally-ho paper running along his left index finger until he'd pinched out enough tobacco and put the pouch away. Then he teased out the threads along the length of the paper, furled and unfurled the cigarette with his thumbs a few times, tightening the loose strands a little more with every roll. He positioned the filter at one end, before lifting the cigarette to his mouth, licking the long edge of the paper, and rolling it up one last time. Finally, he tamped the loose end with his match and lit it.

He sucked in the smoke and held it in his lungs for so long, that Chase wondered if he'd absorbed it into his body. Coolly, and without any sign of a splutter, Hughes eventually let the smoke curl out of his nostrils. His fingers moved along the shaft of the cigarette as it burned down, until there was barely enough left to grip it even with the very tip of his yellowed nails. He took one last puff, butted it out on the running board and let it fall into the gutter. With an incline of his head, he signalled to Chase that he was finally ready to leave.

Hughes left the passenger door ajar for him, and settled into the driver's seat. He turned the engine over and it fired up with a throaty grumble. He leaned across and fiddled with the switches on the dashboard. Chase wedged his backpack in the back between boxes too fragile to survive a trip under the tarp, climbed in alongside Hughes and buckled his seat belt. He was grateful for the chill blasting out of the vent. Hughes shifted into gear. Two clicks of the indicator and they were off.

The heritage buildings lining the main road were already shrinking behind them. A right turn, and the buildings disappeared entirely.

Less than a kilometre later, the only evidence that Barkers Hill even existed remained only in a road sign facing the other way. Chase turned his head and chuckled. *Welcome to Barkers Hill*, the sign had once said, although someone had painted over part of the letters, and clarified their new meaning with a diagram. They flew past two men in high visibility vests sent to repair it. One of the men was laughing while the other daubed the sign with white paint, but Hughes hadn't noticed a thing. He was already somewhere else.

The road stretched out ahead like a thin, grey ribbon, rising and falling under a cloudless sky, skirting parchment fields and desiccated grasslands. As Hughes toed the accelerator, Chase settled back into his seat and closed his eyes just for a moment, but the whirr of the wheels on the bitumen and the lingering alcohol lured him away. For an hour or so, he was elsewhere as well.

A sudden thump jarred Chase back into the Land Cruiser. The tyres no longer hummed. He shifted about, stretched out his neck and rubbed his eyes. His corneas felt gritty. He prised his eyes open and gazed out the window. The scrub was exactly as dry and unprepossessing as it had been when he'd drifted away: nothing had changed except that the road was no longer sealed.

About three kilometres along, Hughes pulled up to deliver mail to a series of roadside letterboxes as outrageous as a Thanksgiving Day parade. Chase climbed out to stretch his legs. A cloud had momentarily strayed in front of the sun, but he still felt the furnace blast of an oven door left ajar.

The delivery done, Hughes turned away and relieved himself by the side of the road. From under his sheltering hand, Chase glimpsed an immense sky, the land falling away to the horizon like the leaf of an open book. After a moment, he returned to the car, pulled out his water bottle and drank.

Hughes climbed back into the cabin and flung him a glance. 'Good thing you're awake. You'd have missed the best bit,' he said, firing up the engine.

'Really?' He'd already crossed almost half the continent, and was adjusting to its empty desolation. There were no monuments to the great or the good. Right then, it was more Dante's hell than Milton's heaven. 'It all looks the same to me,' he mumbled.

'You're joking, right?' Hughes shifted down a gear, and the Land Cruiser descended a gentle, drawn-out slope. 'There's beauty all around us,' he continued. 'So, what are you doing out here, anyway?'

Chase suppressed a laugh. 'Not much. Just seeing the world, I guess.'

Hughes blew out his breath as they freewheeled down the rest of the bank. 'I just don't get cities.' He loosened his grip on the steering wheel. As the water splashed the windscreen, he pointed to a natural dam upstream. 'Ibis there,' he commented. 'There's a blue-winged kookaburra up in that tree, and woodswallows over on that branch. You don't get that in cities. There's plenty to look at in the bush, if you've got eyes to see. It's a bloody bird-lover's paradise.' The car jolted left and right as they crossed the creek, and momentum took them almost to the top of the opposite bank before Hughes accelerated out.

Chase wasn't much of a naturalist beyond a roast chicken dinner. His eyes followed Hughes's finger to a half dozen or so downy woodswallows sitting huddled along the limb of the tree like catkins on the branch of a pussy willow, and for the briefest time he was homesick.

They stopped twice more to make deliveries, while Hughes kept the motor running as he dashed in and out. Other times, he might have paused along the way for tea. 'Can't stop,' he grumbled. 'Got a bloody American tourist.'

Just over an hour later, they turned onto a secondary road, leaving behind the corrugations that had dominated the last couple of kilometres. Gripping the handhold had numbed Chase's fingers. As the road flattened out, he let go and shook the buzz out of his hands. Hughes slowed down and picked his way past a pothole, and then a gate left partly open. A faded sign wired to the gate announced their arrival at Glen Eira. They coasted down a driveway flanked by ghost gums, at the end of which stood a homestead and, with a grind of the handbrake, they pulled up.

The homestead had seen better days: paint had become curling paperbark, shedding off the timber that clad the top half of the west-facing wall. Two of the verandah posts were rotten where they met the deck, and the roof above them gently bowed. The turned newels hinted at a house that had once been loved. Now, with decay nipping at its foundations, it simply looked neglected.

Chase clambered out of the car and reached for his backpack, while Hughes unloaded boxes and bags, and stacked them on the verandah. Moments later, a wiry, gap-legged figure sauntered towards them.

'G'day, Jack,' the man called out as he approached.

Hughes put down the crate he was carrying and shook the man's hand. 'G'day, Ian,' he replied.

Ian Stewart turned to Chase. 'You must be the lad who rang up about a job, ay?'

'Chase Miller,' he responded, accepting Stewart's enormous sandpaper palm.

'Welcome to Glen Eira station,' said Stewart. He motioned towards the deliveries. 'That everything?'

'Yep,' Hughes replied. 'Even managed to get you a box of new season mangoes.'

'Right. Good. Nellie'll be happy about that. You got time to stop for a drink?'

Hughes glimpsed at the deliveries left in the trailer, lifted his hat and scratched his head. 'Yeah,' he returned. 'Nothing left in there that can't wait for a bit.'

'Come on, son,' said Stewart to Chase with a pat on the shoulder. 'Might as well get you working straight away. I'll show you where this lot goes.'

As Chase carried the deliveries inside and sorted out the boxes, Stewart brewed a pot of tea. Adjacent to the kitchen, Hughes sat with his legs dangling off the back verandah, smoking another cigarette. When he had finished squaring away the deliveries, Chase joined the two men by the back door. Aside from the three of them, no one seemed to be around.

'So,' said Stewart, handing out mugs of tea, 'what do you know about cattle?'

'Not a lot,' Chase replied. He gazed out past the outhouses. The post-and-rail fencing was casting a lengthening shadow across an empty cattle yard. 'As a kid, I taught myself how to lasso chairs.'

Hughes swallowed a chuckle.

'Did I hear you say you could ride?' Stewart continued.

Chase was already shaking his head. He hadn't said anything about horseback riding; he was pretty sure he hadn't been asked. He had never ridden one that wasn't attached to a carousel.

Hughes raised his brows and traded looks with Stewart again.

'Pity that. We're a bit old-fashioned around here. We use horses to muster the cattle,' said Stewart. 'A lot less stressful for the stock.'

'More station hand than stockman if you ask me, Ian,' Hughes remarked.

Chase watched his chance of employment fade with the daylight. 'Well, I can build most anything,' he said, 'and I'm pretty handy with technology.'

Stewart rubbed his chin. 'Yep, that could be handy. These days, you need someone who knows about computers.'

Chase settled back again, listening to the men discussing the rising price of beer and the state of the Queensland economy, and then Stewart stood up and stretched. He gathered up the empty mugs in one hand and said to Chase, 'Right, what about I show you around, and then you can get yourself cleaned up before dinner, ay?' He turned to Hughes. 'You driving out to Glenstrae now?'

Hughes glanced at his watch. 'Geez, I better get going!' He leapt up. 'I want to get most of the trip done before it gets dark. I'll be staying there the night, and then I'll be off again first thing.'

'Right-o,' Stewart replied. 'How about I catch up with you in a couple of days, then, Jack, ay?'

Stewart watched Hughes clamber down from the verandah and head back towards his Land Cruiser. Then he turned his attention to Chase, sizing him up as he would a colt in a saleyard. The lad was a bit taller than him, but he seemed too slight and too pale to be sturdy. 'Let's get you settled in,' he said.

As he showed Chase the way to the ringers' quarters, Stewart couldn't help but wonder if the American would see it past his first day. He seemed eager to work, and there was never any lack of jobs on the station. He watched Chase shoulder his backpack, and there was something in his swagger Stewart found reassuring.

He would give Chase a chance to prove his hunch wrong.

*

The sounds of dawn on the station were as alien to Chase's ears as a gecko's chirp. He had been too exhausted to hear any of the strange noises the bush made at night, and he slept without moving a muscle until a shaft of bright sunlight abruptly turned the inside of his eyelids brilliant orange. He had even been too tired to dream. He drew the sheet over his head but the stuffiness made it insufferable. Defeated, he opened his eyes, glimpsed the clock on the opposite wall and groaned. It wasn't quite five. Beyond the walls of the hut, there was already a hum of life that had been totally absent when he arrived.

It was only when he sat up that he realised that he was not alone in the ringers' quarters. Three out of the remaining five camp beds were now occupied, although who they were and when they had arrived was a mystery. He hadn't noticed the drone of their snoring before, yet it threatened to drown out the clatter of pans and running water in the kitchen, and the murmur of distant conversations.

Chase swung his legs out of the bed and opened up the old wooden cupboard where he had stowed his clothes the night before. He debated momentarily what he should wear, although his limited wardrobe, and the reality that almost everything he owned needed washing, settled matters. He pulled out a pair of clean jeans and a shirt. His last and his best. They would have to do.

Nobody stirred as he dressed and sat on the edge of his bed, watching a cane toad traverse the floor with a series of indiscriminate, half-hearted flops. He had learned from experience to shake out his boots every morning before putting them on. The toad was enormous, and resembled the politician he'd glimpsed on the cover of the local paper. He suspected that neither it nor the politician had a destination in mind beyond the next jump, but they were both entrenched and the next generation simply carried on where the last left off.

He straightened out his bedding and contemplated the day ahead, while his stomach lurched. The corrugated iron that clad the ringers' quarters was already warming up, and he could sense the heat radiating from the eastern wall adjacent to his bed. As he folded up the sleeves of his shirt, the door to the hut swung open, sending a cool sigh down the length of the hut. It had gone five-fifteen, and no one else had moved.

'Wake up!' growled Stewart. He nodded at Chase, eyes narrowed, approving. One of the men, a stockman he called Wally, rolled onto his back and farted. 'Get up!' Stewart resumed, his lip curling. 'Now! Come on, I'm not your flipping mother, fellas!'

Wally yawned and opened his eyes. Gingerly, he pulled back his blanket and sat up. Stewart watched him for a moment, his hands in his pockets. Then he glared at the outlines of the sleeping men, and darted out of the hut.

Wally glimpsed Chase from the corner of his eye, but didn't say anything.

Chase had no idea of the protocol, although a morning greeting was a morning greeting. While Wally scratched his head, he introduced himself. 'Good morning,' he said, his voice clanging in his ears like a door-knocking evangelist.

The man looked away. Perhaps, Chase thought, his enthusiasm troubled him.

'Morning,' he muttered finally, and Chase didn't press him any further.

Stewart returned, buckets rocking like clock pendulums from the end of each arm. Silently, he strode over and stood between the two still-occupied beds. He put one of the buckets down, lifted the other to shoulder height, and pitched the contents over one of the sleeping men. While the man shot up with a blast of expletives, Stewart picked up the second bucket, pivoted and threw it over the other man.

The second man fell out of the bed and onto the floor. He was sopping. 'Fucking cunt bastard! I'll kill the cunt that did that!'

Stewart laughed. 'Steady on there, Thommo, you won't be killing anybody. Not today, at least.' He turned to Chase. With a point of his finger and a cock of his thumb, he growled, 'You. With me.'

Chase followed Stewart out of the hut, grateful to leave the staleness of sweaty bodies behind.

'The cook'll sound the triangle when breakfast's ready in the ringers' dining room next to the kitchen. I'll catch up with everyone there, and tell you what's planned for today,' he said.

Chase nodded and watched him recede. He could hear the men swearing inside the hut, and he could still hear them all the way to the lavatory. By the time he returned to his quarters to take his clothes to the laundry, it was silent. The water had been mopped up, and the sodden bedding hung out on the clothes line. He hadn't heard a bell or a triangle but his clothes were in the machine, and he had nothing more to do.

The dining room was empty when he arrived. A fresh pot of tea and another of coffee stood on straw coasters on the sideboard, together with milk, sugar, mugs and plates, and the beginning of a buffet breakfast. He helped himself to coffee and cereal and sat down. The door to the dining room opened and an old woman in an apron charged in, carrying bacon, sausages, beans, eggs and toast on platters stacked up each arm.

Chase rushed forward. 'Can I help you there, ma'am?'

The woman smiled. 'No,' she began, 'I'm right.' She put down the platters, glanced at Chase and caught her breath. 'Thank you,' she added, her velvet eyes fixed on his. 'I haven't seen you before. You're new here.'

'Yes, ma'am,' Chase replied as he glanced at the series of raised, dark welts on the woman's forearms. As she spoke, he listened for a twang, a roll of an *r*, or a soft *a* in her speech, but he had not detected any accent beyond Australian. 'Chase Miller,' he said.

'You're not…Mrs Mac, are you?'

The woman crossed her arms in front of her belly, gripped the points of her elbows and laughed. 'Me? Mrs Mac? No fear. I'm Nellie Turner, the cook.' She was still chuckling as she straightened up the platters, and placed a serving fork and spoon on each. 'Just so you know, there's no Mrs Mac here. I call her Miss Becky, but she's Miss Golding, or Boss Lady, to the ringers.'

He liked Nellie the way a child likes a grandparent. She was unfathomable; there was a depth to her dark eyes. All of a sudden, she glimpsed her watch, flustered, and said, 'I'd better let everyone know that breakfast's ready before there's a riot. Now, you help yourself to the food.' She ran her eyes over him. 'You look like you could do with a feed, ay.'

Seconds passed between Nellie beating the triangle in the yard and the men entering the dining room. Where there had been silence and order, abruptly there was chaos, the clack of boots on the floor, the jostle of hunger in the presence of food. Chase learned that, besides the three ringers, there was a station hand and an electrician, all of whom had bedded down in the quarters overnight, without Chase noticing.

The men circled the sideboard, heaping food onto dinner plates as if they had been starved for days. The platters emptied, chairs scraped against the flagstone floor and the dull clank of cutlery replaced the chatter. Chase sat next to a man named Pete, and tried to make conversation, but when there was no response to any of his usual ice-breakers he also fell silent.

Thommo, who had dried off since his early morning encounter with the bucket, was in better spirits. He sat on the other side of Chase, put down his fork and nudged him in the ribs. 'Waste of time talking to him,' he opined. 'He's a gimp.'

The exchange sent Chase back to the first day of school. He weighed up the value of replying and decided against it. He nodded vaguely instead, and kept buttering his toast, drawing the spread out to the crust, slowly, purposefully, avoiding Thommo's gaze.

He bit off a corner. The food looked much the same as back home, but the taste was foreign. He sipped the coffee and let it flood his mouth, but even then he couldn't discern a flavour much beyond sawdust. While the others were wiping their plates clean, he left most of his meal behind.

Thommo chewed with his mouth ajar. He was cocksure of himself. He solicited an introduction and then sniggered. 'Chase? I just don't get people who give their kids weird names,' he said. He reached across the table, picked up the red plastic squeeze bottle and masked his sausages with tomato sauce. 'So,' he resumed, 'where are you from, Chase?' He drew the word out, smothering it with attention.

The last time Chase had heard anyone say his name that way was in grade school. He chose not to respond.

Thommo drove a whole sausage into his gaping mouth. 'Where did you say?'

Eventually he replied, 'A town. Nowhere anybody here has ever been, or is likely to ever go.'

'Yeah?' Thommo continued, picking his teeth with the tine of his fork. 'So, what are you doing here, then?'

A wiry man with an electric shock of ginger hair, called Westie, leaned in to listen to the answer.

Chase was sure it wasn't Thommo's or anyone else's business why he was there, but he answered the question as he had done dozens of times before. 'Backpacking across Australia. A working holiday.'

Westie returned to his original position, satisfied with the reply, although Thommo narrowed his eyes, working through Chase's response. He followed up with, 'So, what do you think of Australia?'

'It's great. Love it.' His delivery was emotionless.

Thommo's eyes widened. He smiled. 'Too fucking right, mate! Best country on earth. You see,' he continued, appeased, tilting towards Chase, 'the difference between us Aussies and everyone else is we're genuine. Honest, friendly and down-to-earth, we are.

Just ask anyone. It's all because of our history, you see. Us Aussies, we're all equal, even Aboriginals like Wally here, as long as they don't get on the piss. Yeah, everybody's the same in this country, no worries.'

By the time he'd stopped speaking, Chase's expression had changed, but Thommo hadn't noticed.

CHAPTER TWO

BIGOTS AND BULLIES were everywhere—Chase knew that—but it didn't make sharing space with them in such an intimate way any more palatable. He was relieved when breakfast was over. He was beginning to appreciate the cattle station as a shared cage.

Necessity required him to have shelter and food, and when both were supplied for free along with a job that paid real money, everything else became white noise. He wasn't there to make friends. When Stewart told him that he and Pete would be working together for the whole day repairing fences, he felt reassured. At least Pete was taciturn.

He shoved Thommo's myopic world vision to the rear of his thoughts, collected the tools and materials for the day, and stowed them in the back of an old utility vehicle, exactly as instructed. He and Pete climbed into the ute and drove a few hundred metres to the first paddock past the house yard. A gentle breeze tickled the paddock from time to time, drawing with it a curtain of dirt. There was an unfamiliar pungency to each gust. Except for the dirt and an egret, the paddock was empty.

While Pete walked the perimeter one way, Chase walked the other. Several strands of wire had snapped and curled back on themselves like springs. At the bottom of the paddock, a few of the star pickets had toppled over. Heat and humidity aside, it would take no great effort to fix.

As he strode, he glimpsed a battle-line of ragged, wine-stained clouds gathering on the horizon. The air was heavy in a way he hadn't noticed earlier. 'Looks like rain,' Chase remarked to Pete when they met up again. He lifted the roll of number eight wire from the tray of the ute, carried it over to the fence, and set it on a spinner.

Pete didn't answer, but shook his head instead.

'Well,' he glanced again at the sky, 'it looks like rain to me.' It didn't yet smell like rain. Wispy fingers of blue-grey fractus projected out of the cloud wall, and pointed downwards. At any moment, he expected to hear the rumble of thunder.

Pete's mouth contorted, but he struggled to find words to fill it. 'N-n-n-not yet,' he eventually replied. 'L-l-later.'

'Yeah? Well, I guess you should know,' Chase remarked.

They worked in silence, until Pete motioned that it was time for a break halfway through the morning. He called it a *smoko*, although neither of them smoked. They returned to the homestead for apple streusel cake, and more coffee that tasted like dishwater.

As he walked back towards the paddock, Chase overheard Westie mention that the wet was about to arrive, and that it was lucky that, except for a few strays, the muster was pretty much done. He also let slip that he and Thommo would be moving on to another station, once the rain set in. Next to him, Pete grinned.

Back in the paddock, while Chase welcomed the cleansing of the wet season and looked to the skies for an impending deluge, the ringers brought more cattle down from the distant yards to tag and drench.

By five in the afternoon, the workday had ended. Chase felt a gnawing void, but he wasn't sure if it was hunger or something else. A piece of cloth brushed against his left forearm, and he twisted his shirt sleeve around and inspected the cuff. It appeared that he had snagged it on some jagged wire, and ripped it almost clean off. His grandmother's words resounded: he ought to have known better than to wear his best shirt fencing.

After work, he sat near the ringers on the back verandah, and sipped the beer that Stewart had handed around. The cold, smooth bottle soothed his aching hands. He was spent. Nothing in the world could have tasted any better.

He drained the bottle, stood up and stretched out his back. He showered and took in the washing he had left drying all day on the line. It was dry and fresh enough, in spite of the wetness in the air, and only barely wrinkled. Ironing anything was a step too far, but at least he would have something clean to wear to dinner. As he stowed his soiled clothes to wash later, he examined the rip in his shirt. The cuff hung by a thread. He doubted he could mend it.

At dinner, as Nellie brought in the food, he asked her if he could borrow a needle and some thread.

'You ever sewn anything before?' she asked, sizing him up.

'No, ma'am.' he replied sheepishly, 'but it's my best shirt, so I guess I could learn.'

'Huh. You'll probably just make a mess of it. You'd better give it to me,' she sighed.

'Well, I could pay you after I get my first pay,' he said earnestly. 'I mean, I wouldn't want you to do it for nothing.'

Nellie shook her head. 'I don't know what it is about you, Chase. Maybe it's your accent, or the fact that you are one of the politest people I've met in a very long time, but I like you. As long as you don't tell anyone else, I'll mend it for you tonight. For nothing.'

'But I'll have to wash it first. It's dirty.'

She guffawed. 'Wash it? What for? You reckon I never smelled a man's sweat before? I had a husband once, and I brought up a family. You just bring me that shirt straight after dinner. I'll be in the kitchen doing the dishes.'

'Thank you, ma'am, I appreciate it.'

Before she left the dining room, Nellie cuffed him gently behind the ear. 'That's for wearing your best shirt while you were fencing, and that,' she cuffed his ear again, 'is for calling me ma'am instead of Nellie.'

*

After dinner, Chase returned to the hut to retrieve the shirt he'd rolled into a ball, and he stuffed it into a crumpled plastic shopping bag. Pete was sitting on the edge of his bed, playing a game on his tablet, while Westie and Thommo drank beers and shuffled cards outside. Stewart's three-stubby limit was more suggestion than rule: the contract stockmen mostly did exactly as they wanted to. Cigarette butts, like the bottles, were lined up next to them like soldiers on parade.

It was well after seven, yet the sunlight lingered, and it was brighter then than it had been at midday. The clouds that Chase had believed would bring a storm had passed, although the suffocating clamminess remained. From the yard, he could see Nellie standing at the sink, illuminated by the kitchen lights, singing and swaying to the rhythm of music blaring from a radio. Despite her fine, tanned skin, he figured she had to be at least seventy and as broad as a whisky barrel, but there was a lingering grace in her movement.

She heard the smack of the screen door, and turned to see who had entered. 'You got your shirt there, Chase?' she said. She wiped her hands on her apron and opened up the bag. She spread the creased shirt out on the table with spidery fingers, and examined the tear. 'Hmm. I can do something with that.' She slapped the shirt back in the bag, hung it off the back of a chair, and resumed her work.

There was familiarity in the slap of the water, the clatter of cutlery in the bowels of the sink, and the faintly stale odour of the kitchen.

'Is it okay with you if I sit here a while, Nellie?' he asked. 'I'll dry.'

'Stay if you like,' she said. 'But you don't have to dry. I'm paid to do that.'

'I don't mind.' He picked up the towel and wiped each piece carefully, leaving them on the table for Nellie to put away.

'So,' she said, glimpsing his fastidiousness and grinning. 'You got a story to you, Chase?'

He smiled. 'Doesn't everybody?'

'Well, maybe they do and maybe they don't. I reckon the people with the most to tell say the least, and the people with the least—well, they're always gasbagging about themselves, and you can't shut them up.'

'I suppose you're right.'

'You're a long way from home. There a reason you ran away?'

He chuckled. She was all about the motivation and not the destination: she didn't care why he was there, why Australia, why the outback, only why he had left home in the first place. 'I just graduated college and I needed to experience something different. This is just about as different as it gets.'

'Yeah? So why did you need that experience? You bored at home, or something?'

'Not bored. I guess I was numb. Home is safe. Here is anything but safe. Besides,' he continued, 'I studied psychology. There's a whole world out there for me to explore. I figure that if I want to understand others, I'm going to need to understand myself first.' He dried the last plate and folded the towel. 'Take Miss Golding, for example. I mean, what makes a woman leave America to run a cattle station half a world away? Now, to me that makes an interesting story.'

'Huh,' said Nellie. 'You reckon there's a story in that?'

'I do,' he replied.

'I don't think Miss Becky's going to want to tell you her story, Chase. I think it would be a waste of time, you asking her.'

'Asking her? I haven't even met her. How would I ask her? I'm starting to think she doesn't even exist.'

Nellie picked up a few of the dried plates and began stowing them away. 'Oh, she exists all right,' she muttered, puffing gently as she stretched to reach the overhead cupboard. 'So, you want to meet her? Well, I'm just about to brew up some coffee. Why don't you stay here and keep me company while I do that?'

He wanted to tell her that her coffee was awful, and he'd sooner drink the remnants of the water in her sink, but he didn't dare.

'Would you like me to make the coffee for you?'

Nellie spun around. 'No. Why would I?' She eyed him suspiciously. 'I get it: you think you can make better coffee.'

'But at breakfast…'

'At breakfast I serve instant because the men prefer it, but after dinner I brew Miss Becky a pot of real, American-style coffee.'

Chase brightened. 'Real coffee?' He could almost taste it.

'That's right. But don't you go asking her any questions tonight. You let me take the lead, okay?'

'Fine.'

'We go back decades, me and her. You let me work on her and maybe, just maybe, she'll tell you her story.'

'Agreed.'

'But there are no guarantees. Miss Becky is her own woman. Understood?'

Chase nodded.

He was a young man and Nellie knew that all young men wanted the world, but, even if nothing came of it, he seemed content enough just to look forward to his first decent cup of coffee.

*

It was a while before the door creaked again. Chase took a sharp breath in, and let it tumble out noisily. For the last few minutes, he had been sitting at the table, drifting along on the scent of percolating coffee. Now that the stovetop sputtering had nearly stopped, he was just another addict hungering for a fix.

He heard a woman's voice say *You can pour me that coffee now, Nellie*, before he realised that Miss Golding had walked into the kitchen. Her pace was soft and irregular, as if she was shuffling with a limp. Her accent was unmistakably New York, debased, but still distinct. His head swivelled.

She spotted him and stopped dead. 'Who are you?' she asked. 'Who is that, Nellie? And what is he doing in my kitchen?'

He studied the tiny woman standing over him. 'Chase Miller, ma'am,' he replied.

'Chase Miller,' she repeated. 'I don't believe I know you, Chase Miller. You're an American. Do I know Miller, Nellie?'

'No you don't, Miss Becky. He's just started. He's the new station hand. And right now, he's giving me a help with the washing up.'

He extended his hand. 'Pleased to meet you…' he began.

Miss Golding glanced at Nellie instead. 'The new station hand? An American? Strange, I don't recall Mr Stewart ever mentioning it.' She returned his gaze for a moment, and then looked away again. 'Or maybe he mentioned it and I forgot. *Pfft*. Memory gone. That's what happens when you're old, you know. Or when you don't choose to remember.' She paused to sit and her face contorted. 'I am Rebecca Golding, owner for the time-being, caretaker for future generations, guardian and trustee—however you wish to describe me—of Glen Eira station. It's far too soon for me to know if it's a pleasure to meet you or not.'

Nellie placed a mug of coffee in front of Miss Golding and motioned to Chase to keep quiet.

'Poor Nellie's never developed a taste for coffee, but won't you join me?' said Miss Golding. 'Coffee, Miller?'

'Please,' Chase returned, watching Nellie pour out his coffee, and set a bowl of sugar and a creamer on the table. He took a draught of the brew and exhaled. It was dark, heady and delicious.

'Ah, you miss the coffee, too? So did I, to begin with. I've been here, what, fifty years, and I still can't get used to what they call coffee out here.'

'It's fine in town,' he said.

'I wouldn't know, I never go there,' she replied. She took a sip. 'So, Miller, what's an American doing in the arse-end of the world, as a former prime minister of these parts put it?'

'I might ask you the same question, ma'am,' he replied.

'You might, but I figure you to be a man of discretion and politeness, so you won't. I wouldn't tell you anyway, even if I could remember why I came here. It was such a long time ago.' She caught him trading looks with Nellie. 'And don't you go asking her, she's a dreadful gossip, but her memory's even worse than mine. She's likely to make it all up and sell it to you as the truth. So,' she continued, 'was it murder? You look too young for it to have been embezzlement. Did you kill someone stateside, and then come here to evade the authorities? What evil has brought you here?'

'No evil, ma'am. A thirst for adventure and…'

Miss Golding cleared her throat. 'And you can peddle that nonsense elsewhere, young man. Forgetful I may be, but stupid I am not. We all have our nasty little secrets, do we not? Nellie here is veritably riddled with them. She and I could be sisters, except she is part-Aboriginal and I'm… Well, I am whatever I am.' She glanced at Nellie. 'Ah, that's right, I forgot. We don't say part-Aboriginal, half-caste or full blood any more. It's not politically correct. You will soon learn, Miller, that, while I am always right, I am never correct, politically or otherwise. I am a difficult, nasty, vengeful old spinster. Words fly out of me like excrement out of a Bangkok sewer.' She drained her cup and accepted a refill. 'Do I frighten you?'

'Not at all,' he replied.

'Pity.'

'Do I?' he asked.

'Perhaps.' She stood up. 'I'll take this back to bed with me, Nellie,' she said. 'You, Miller,' she added, 'have gumption. I don't know if I like that.'

He and Nellie watched Miss Golding shuffle away from the table and out the door. When she was out of earshot, he muttered, 'I thought you were going to take the lead. I was waiting for you to.'

'I didn't get the chance to, did I?' Nellie replied. 'She gets this way, sometimes, at night. It's the medication she takes to stop the pain. Maybe she'll be clearer tomorrow. She liked you, I can tell.'

'She has a strange way of showing it, if she did.'

'People like her aren't open books, Chase. You have to work at it. What's the use of telling a story anyone can hear?'

'Everyone knows the story of Cinderella, don't they, and yet it's still a favourite. A story's worth telling if it's a good one, not only because it's an unavailable one. I don't know if Miss Golding's is going to be worth all the effort.'

'Oh,' Nellie replied, 'just come back to collect your shirt tomorrow night. Sit down, drink your coffee and listen. Eventually, she might talk and, if she does, you can tell me if it was worth the effort.'

*

The appearance of a young man from America had unsettled Miss Golding. Despite the countless backpackers looking for work who had passed through Glen Eira station over the years, it had been a while since any of them had originated from the United States. Most of the itinerant workers she had hosted had been continental European, and she generally avoided interacting with them. It was futile to trade stories and convey subtleties to someone with only barely functional English.

When she did interact with them, it seemed to Miss Golding that they had all left their over-illuminated and over-heated cities, to chase an illusion of danger and excitement. In a risk-averse world, with the exception of warzones, the bush seemed to be the last treacherous frontier. Mr Stewart always warned them that, despite all the safety measures, a cattle station was still a very hazardous place. For the uninitiated, the unsuspecting and the unlucky, life could be extinguished in the blink of an eye.

Most of the backpackers who arrived at Glen Eira were uncommitted; in an unfamiliar ocean, they kept close to shore and merely paddled in the shallows. In little time, the routine of tending stock, checking dams and mending fences became tedium: the work was hard, thankless and unending, the climate stifling, and many left, disillusioned, back to the ease of the city. They were children raised in safety and sterility, looking for a chance to play for a while in someone else's mud.

For Miss Golding, such people were obvious. They held no mystique.

Americans, on the other hand, were enigmatic.

She imagined that, although there were no expansive vistas left in the European countryside, clean air, seclusion and peace remained abundant in the plains of Nebraska and the Dakotas, even in the twenty-first century. Australia and America had so much in common: both countries were filled with wildlife which attacked even if unprovoked, and Americans didn't have to come all the way to Australia just to experience work on a cattle ranch. So, there had to be another reason why they came. When young men like Chase did drop in, they became a puzzle for her to solve.

She didn't go to bed with her coffee, but sat in an armchair in the living room instead, her mind drifting to other times and other places. The sun slipped away as it always did at that latitude, quickly and with no fanfare. Despite the darkness, she couldn't be bothered standing up again and turning on the light: her hips ached when she moved. She had only just turned seventy-two, yet with each gesture, her body protested the passage of time, and she resented it. She had not anticipated that old age would arrive quite as quickly or as savagely as it had.

She searched her mind. What was it that she had been thinking about? She remembered. *God bless the United States of America.* She was at once connected and disconnected to her heritage, although she hadn't craved either the familiarity of Brooklyn or the excitement of Manhattan in decades. She had been in the outback for so long, that she had all but forgotten the frenetic pace of city life. There were many delights in Manhattan for the young, but for the old and from afar, Manhattan seemed frightening and unbending. Glen Eira was comfortably familiar. It was silent as the tomb. It had become her universe, and it was enough.

CHAPTER THREE

THE FIRST TIME Becky Golding saw a red kangaroo was the day George Lumley hit one with his truck. There weren't any where she came from, not even in the Bronx Zoo. One moment the road was wide and empty, and the next it was hidden behind a fleeting shadow six feet tall and weighing a hundred and sixty pounds.

She had been watching the scrubby undergrowth to her left wax and wane as the Bedford truck she was riding in bounced along a road, a hundred miles or so inland from the North Queensland coast. It wasn't really a road, at least not in the sense that most New Yorkers understood a road to be. In the outback, she'd come to understand that things became greater than the sum of their parts: a solitary fuel pump in the wilderness became a gas station, two tables and eight chairs a café, and a track became a road even when it bore no similarity to one.

This *road* she and George were travelling on wasn't made of concrete or asphalt; it had no pavement, no gutter, no grate spewing clouds of steam. It was a country lane carved from dusty, grey-brown, silty sand that blew up as they passed and billowed out behind them like a wedding veil. It was a country lane that ran for hundreds of miles without a single highlight. After over three hours of bone-rattling, Becky suspected that this country lane was leading her nowhere.

She had suspended daydreaming and had just begun wondering how anything could survive here, when the kangaroo bounded out of the softwood gnarl by the side of the road. Even though she'd been watching the ironbark gums recede into grassland and then advance towards the road again, she hadn't seen any warning that it was there. There wasn't any ripple in the undergrowth, nothing at all.

'Whoa,' George said, slamming his foot on the brake as it leapt into the truck's path. 'Whoa!' he repeated as he pumped the pedal.

Becky gripped the dashboard to stop her head from hitting the windscreen and the rest of her from sliding into the footwell. A foot or two away from her, the kangaroo dazzled: its face was as fine as a gazelle's, its eyes the shape of almonds, velvet-brown and fringed with exquisitely long, feathery lashes. She didn't expect it to be as beautiful or as graceful. Then, as quickly as it had appeared, the kangaroo smacked against the truck and disappeared. She thought it was under the wheels and her heart sank until she saw it leap into the copse of low, shrubby wattles on the other side of the road.

George kept the engine idling and put on the brake. He jumped out of the cabin only to climb back in again a minute later. 'No harm done. Must have just hit the bull bar,' he said, shaking his head. 'He was a big boy.'

Becky strained to catch a last glimpse of the kangaroo but it was gone.

'A roo that size could have smashed the windscreen and put a great big dent in the truck,' he continued, 'and, out here, that would've been bad. Very bad indeed.'

'Will he be alright?' she asked, still looking in the direction it had gone.

'The roo? Honestly, I don't know, but I wouldn't get too sentimental over it if I was you. Around here, roos are a bit like blowies: they're everywhere and they're bloody annoying.'

His last comment was only partly intelligible but she'd caught his drift. She thought it was heartless. She knew there was no point in saying so.

George swivelled to look through the rear window to check that Her Majesty's mail hadn't been disturbed by his sudden braking. He seemed satisfied that it hadn't. He shifted the gear stick back into first, disengaged the brake and, with a loud, reverberating whine, the truck began to move again.

It was hot as hell in the cabin, and although the back of Becky's thighs were glued to the vinyl, she still sensed a rivulet of sweat run down her calf. She imagined it would puddle in her sneaker, but it was so hot that the sweat evaporated long before it reached her ankle. She stretched her arm out of the open window, looking to the rush of passing air to provide some relief, but there was none.

George glanced across at Becky's beetroot face. 'If you're thirsty, there's a water bottle over there.' He pointed to a large, squat, blue polystyrene jug with a white lid.

'I'm fine, thank you for asking,' she replied. 'Is it much farther?'

'Another hour or so.'

'Oh.'

She had long since stopped counting the distance they'd travelled in miles, and settled in for another suffocating hour. The truck pitched and rolled with the changing surface and camber of the road, its engine screeching its way up each incline as if it was climbing Everest and then groaning its way down again. Each screech and groan signalled to her that they were at least making progress and there would be an end to the journey *in an hour or so*. It was comforting.

It was so comforting in fact, that she fell asleep in spite of the flies buzzing along the bottom edge of the windscreen and the stink of George's armpit. She rested her head in the crook of her arm, closed her eyes and let herself drift home, where there was snow by dawn this time of year, and grey slush by lunchtime. In that moment, she was climbing the steps of the family brownstone and rapping on the door. *Mom, I'm home...* She was dreaming about something—nothing—when the absence of engine noise shook her out of her sleep and hurled her back to the tropics, the heat, the Bedford truck, the stench and George Lumley's cursing.

'Shitty effen piece of shit!'

Becky stretched and yawned as the pins and needles chased away the numbness in her arm. 'What's wrong?' she asked, flexing her wrist.

'Oh, I'm sorry, miss, I hope you didn't hear that!'

'Hear what?' she asked.

George looked relieved. No matter what, a man never swore in front of a woman: his mother had beaten that rule into him. 'The truck's packed it in. Engine's overheated. Bought it brand new in 1960. You'd think you'd get more than seven years out of the rotten thing.'

He was still grumbling as he swung open the door and hopped out. He propped open the hood and let fly another stream, minus the expletives. A minute later he returned to the cabin and pulled out some tools and an old Johnnie Walker bottle, empty of any whisky but full of a colourless liquid Becky supposed was water.

'Piece of rubbish!' he repeated as he disappeared under the hood again.

Becky opened the door to circulate the stuffy cabin air, and listened to the clanging of the spanner hitting metal.

Moments later, George returned to the cabin. 'That's cooked Mrs MacGregor's shopping well and truly.'

'Is there something wrong with the truck?'

'Nah, love, I thought we'd just stop here a while to admire the view.' He guffawed. 'Of course there's something wrong with this piece of garbage truck and unless you've got a spare radiator in your handbag, we're well and truly stuffed.'

'Oh.'

Becky looked around. They might as well have been going in circles for all the difference the last hour's travel had made to the landscape. It was flat all the way to the horizon. A few skeletal gums, some bendee trees and the occasional misshapen termite mound punctuated endless tussocks of spear grass. From somewhere, a crow started to scoff. George was scowling.

'Are we very far from the homestead?' she ventured.

'Not very far. About three or four mile, I reckon. Five at the most.'

'Couldn't we walk it?'

He looked Becky up and down. 'I could, no worries, but I'm not too sure about you. You're already red as a berry. Don't reckon you're used to this kind of heat, ay?'

'It gets pretty hot in New York in summer. Only, it's winter there now…'

'Best you stay with the truck. I'll go get us some help. It'll be faster if I go alone.'

He took the water container, filled up the whisky bottle and handed it to her. 'That's clean water, in case you're thirsty. Drink some now and I'll fill it back up again before I leave. I'll take the rest of the water and the pistol, and I'll leave you the rifle.'

Becky blanched and put down the bottle. 'Rifle?' she said. 'What would I need a rifle for? Anyway, I can't shoot.'

George laughed. 'Of course you can't. Not much of a cowgirl, are you?' He leaned in and continued as he exhaled, 'There's a whole lot of things here just waiting to kill, and they love foreigners, especially young ladies from New York like you.' He leaned out of the window and blew a fly out of his nostril. 'So you don't know how to shoot, ay?'

She shook her head.

'Then I guess I'll have to teach you.' He reached across and pulled out a .303 rifle hidden under a blanket on the parcel shelf behind her head.

She followed George out of the truck and watched him as he explained the bolt action mechanism and how to line up the sight.

'You're small but you look pretty strong…for a girl,' he said. 'I don't think the recoil should trouble you too much. Now, let's set you up.' He handed her the rifle. 'See that tree over there?' He pointed to a dead wattle a few dozen yards away. 'Get that in your sight and let one go when you're ready.'

The rifle was heavier than Becky had imagined. She lifted the butt, worn smooth from generations of hands, and tucked it firmly into her shoulder. Then she pointed the gun at the tree, lined the post up in the ramp sight, and squeezed the trigger. The force of the recoil knocked the barrel upwards and her backwards, as George watched and chuckled from behind.

He lit up a cigarette and inhaled. 'Well, it's something like that,' he said.

She stood up and patted the dust off her shorts. She held out the rifle. 'I don't think I need this all the same. You can take it.'

George blew out a smoke ring. 'You might feel differently if you see a wild pig. They've got tusks as sharp as razors, they charge and they're enormous. And then there are the snakes, the dingoes and not to mention the crocs.'

'The crocs?'

'Crocodiles? Man-eaters?' He smiled. 'You would of heard of them, ay? Twenty foot long, some of them. Big as a car.'

'Crocodiles? Here?' Becky looked around as if she wanted to run, but had no idea in which direction to head.

George guffawed. 'Nah, not here, not really. Too far from the river, here, for the crocs. I just thought I'd have some fun with you.'

She still looked worried.

'Honestly, love, there are no crocs here, but all the rest is fair dinkum,' he added. 'Best you keep the rifle, hey?'

'Okay,' she agreed reluctantly. 'And you?'

'I've got my pistol. I'm used to the bush; it doesn't worry me. Now that the midday sun's passed, I'll head off. I'll be back as soon as I can. You should be safe near the truck. Sip your water, stay in the shade and keep as still as you can. Oh, and by the way, if you do have to shoot something, make bloody certain it's not yourself, all right?' George wedged his hat on, slung the water container over his shoulder, lit up another cigarette and strode away.

She felt like an abandoned child. She desperately wanted to call him back, so they could wait for a passing car together, even though she knew there might not be one for days. He was her lifeline; she might as well have arrived on Mars. She watched him walk away, spindly knees, skin brown and leathery from too much sun, socks halfway up his calves, until he disappeared over the horizon, and then she pined for home.

*

Miss Golding awoke in the early hours of the morning, still sitting in her armchair in the gloom, the empty coffee mug dangling from the end of her finger. She was no longer wherever it was that the minds of the unconscious travelled to when they were resting, and the pain in her hip—her constant waking companion—had returned, this time like a lightning bolt. Normally, she would have supplemented her medication at around ten, just before her bedtime, but she had slept through. Not only had she slept through, but she had slept seated in her armchair, and the searing, throbbing, eighteen-out-of-ten ache was her punishment for it.

She had either been reliving the past or she had been dreaming, and it did not matter to her which. She hadn't thought about George Lumley in decades: he had been dead for the last four of them. For a while at least, she had been young and lithe and innocent again. The memory brought back the thrill of first encounters, and if she could have, she would have stayed in that place forever. There was no darkness in her soul back then, no bitterness borne of harsh experience. That came in the ensuing years.

She hardly slept these days, but when she slept, the pain abated; yet it always returned the second she awoke. At that moment, it had returned with such ferocity that it took away her breath. She twisted as far as she could and clicked on the Tiffany lamp. Her fingers crept along the top of the occasional table, searching for something. Filled with pills as bright and diverse as bonbons, a Webster pack lay on that table, alongside a glass of water covered by a crocheted doily which was weighed down by orange beads, and at that moment she needed both. The pills offered her some relief, imperfect as it was. Her fingers finally reached the Webster pack and she sighed.

She placed the pack of medication on her lap. Most of the blisters were empty, but there were enough doses remaining, four times a day for the next three days of the week. She pierced the card with her thumbnail and pushed out the contents labelled *Thursday evening*, and fed the pills one at a time into her mouth. Then she lifted the glass and swallowed. The water was tepid and stale, and she scowled.

There were moments when she contemplated swallowing the entire contents, blister after blister, in the hope of reaching blissful oblivion. She thought about it regularly, but could never bring herself to do it. There was something that transcended the discomfort, and kept her engaged. Perhaps, because of her age, living had just become a habit. Perhaps, it was the last remnants of a hope that she had simply never lost, despite what she told herself, and despite her age. Whatever it was, it kept her alive.

She knew that she couldn't stay in the chair much longer, but she decided to wait for the pain to ease just a little, so she could stand up and go to bed. After a few minutes, her impatience won out. She simply couldn't wait. It took the next five minutes and resolute will for her to rise up and shuffle out of the room and down the hallway, to her bedroom.

In the comfort of her bed at last, with the medication dulling the pain, she shut her eyes and prayed to return to that other time.

*

Everything fabulous and shiny and wondrous happened first in New York; the rest of the world was a millpond waiting for a ripple.

Brooklyn wasn't exactly Manhattan, but it wasn't a million miles behind, either. A short subway ride from the family brownstone in Brooklyn Heights took Becky downtown, and from there it was a quick stroll to Greenwich Village. New York was alive and well and its beating heart was making music beside the fountain in Washington Square Park.

'Mom,' she said one Sunday in 1961, as her mother was baking Toll House cookies, 'would it be okay if I went over to Suzanne's house to study?'

Sylvia Golding looked at her daughter sitting on a stool by the bench, swinging her legs. 'Suzanne? Suzanne? Have I met her? Have I met her mother?'

Becky pinched off a piece of dough and nibbled. The chocolate melted on her tongue. 'Oh, you remember Suzanne Young, don't you?' she said nonchalantly. 'From grade school?'

'I don't… Wait… You mean Jack and Adele's daughter? The Youngs on Hicks?'

'That's her.'

'But aren't they in Chicago? I thought they had to go to Chicago for Jack's work.'

'They did, but now they're back.'

Sylvia pressed down on the mound of dough until it resembled a thick, rough, speckled platter and then dusted it with flour. 'How long would you be?'

'Oh, I don't know. I have a lot of homework. I'd be home way before dinner.'

'Did you ask your father?'

'I'm asking you.'

The rolling pin thudded as Sylvia thought.

'Mom?'

She rolled the pin over the dough, backwards and forwards, backwards and forwards until it was a half inch thick and at least a foot long. Then she picked up the metal cutter, turned to Becky and huffed.

'Mom!'

'Fine. Go. But don't you want to wait until the cookies are baked?'

Becky slid off the stool and kissed her mother on the cheek. 'Thanks. You're the hippest!'

'And be home by five. A minute past and you're grounded, miss!'

'Promise!'

Five minutes later, Becky had changed her clothes, grabbed her purse and slammed the door behind her. She dashed down Henry Street towards the subway, happy to feel the insipid spring sun on her face. She met up with Suzanne at Eighth Street station, on Broadway. 'So, are you up for a walk in the park?' she asked.

Suzanne shrugged and pulled up the lapels of her coat. 'I don't know.' She looked at Becky's black Capri pants and bare ankles. 'I'm no beatnik. You know I like Elvis.'

'Elvis the Pelvis is dead and buried. You'll love this. I promise.'

'So, where are we going, exactly?' asked Suzanne as she struggled to keep up with Becky.

'Oh, Suzanne, I forgot you're not from here anymore. It's not far. Two more blocks and we're there.'

They turned the corner onto Waverly Place and caught sight of a crowd drifting in the same direction. That stopped Suzanne in her tracks. 'What is going on?'

'I'm not sure,' Becky replied, looking around. Ahead of them were at least a hundred people, mostly men in overcoats, all heading towards the park. 'I've been here a few times but it's never been like this.'

Suzanne's feet were glued to the pavement. 'I can't, Becky. My folks are going to kill me. I'm going home.'

'Don't go home, Suzanne, not yet. Let's see what's happening.'

She was already shaking her head. 'I don't want to see what's happening. I'm sorry, really I am, but this isn't a Sunday afternoon stroll in the park. I'm going home.'

'Well, you're going to miss out, but if you're sure...'

'I'm sure.'

Becky watched Suzanne turn back towards Eighth Street and then she followed the crowd into the park. She had drifted there once or twice before to listen to the music and observe the passing parade, after which she'd rushed home, filled with the spirit of a day spent listening to Bob Dylan's lyrics, his guitar and his harmonica. She had been just twelve when she first heard Joan Baez and Pete Seeger sing about peace, love and human angst.

But this was different.

This time, there were thousands of people. She heard the singing before she could really see what was happening.

We shall not, we shall not be moved…

She shuffled towards the fountain, but her small stature was an impediment. Everyone around her seemed ten feet tall and she felt as if she was crawling on her knees. She heard a horse whinny.

Just like a tree planted by the waters…

A police officer, his billystick in his hand, pushed past her. The brass buttons on his uniform were gleaming. 'Sir,' she said tapping him on the arm, 'what's going on here?'

'Huh? What?' He fixed his eyes on Becky. 'Go home, kid. This is no place for a little girl.'

'Why? What's going on?'

'Go home, I said! Now!'

Becky tried to turn away as the words of the 'Star Spangled Banner' rang in her ears.

Does that star-spangled banner yet wave o'er the land of the free and the home of the brave…

She tried to push against the crowd and, when her strength failed her, she called out but no one seemed to hear or, if they heard, they didn't care. There wasn't to be any peace and love today. She was aware of being carried on a human wave, heading inexorably towards the fountain. She wasn't scared exactly, but the suffocation of the crowd and the terrible noise and the awful confusion made her head spin. Faces propelled towards her, like *It Came from Outer Space* in 3-D glasses. She felt herself pushed against the flank of a horse and her knees buckled underneath her.

A moment later, her world grew dim and faded away.

*

'Do you know what day it is?'

'Of course. Why,' said Becky, shielding her eyes, 'don't you?'

'Stop being impertinent,' someone remarked. The voice sounded a bit like her father's. 'Answer the question.'

Becky blinked against the brilliance of the light on the doctor's head. Or at least she assumed from his white coat and the stethoscope slung around his neck that he was the doctor. But why on God's holy earth was he asking her such stupid questions? Her head ached and her mouth was dry.

'So, Becky, what day is it, dear?' asked the nurse.

'Why, it's...' She was sure she knew it a moment ago. 'Why, it's...' she began again, 'it's Thursday?'

'Are you asking us or telling us?'

'I don't know. Am I in school? Is this a pop quiz? Did I get the answer right?'

The nurse huffed.

Becky felt like Alice. She had fallen head-first down the rabbit hole, and now it throbbed like crazy. At any moment, the Mad Hatter and the Queen of Hearts were likely to appear. She looked around. Perhaps they were already there. 'I think I'll go back to sleep now,' she announced. 'I'm really tired and my head aches and I want you all to go away.'

'No dear, don't do that. We have some more questions to ask you. Do you know where you are?'

'A hospital?'

'That's right.'

'And do you recognise the people standing behind me?'

Becky hadn't noticed anyone else in the room but now that the doctor shut off the light and her eyes were slowly adjusting to the dimness, she realised that she and the medical staff weren't alone.

'Mom? Pop? Are you sick too?'

'No, Becky. You were injured, don't you remember?'

She didn't recall a thing. She tried to search her mind, but it was empty, a black hole. Nothing came. Just trying to remember, exhausted her. 'How did I get here?'

'You came in an ambulance. Don't you remember anything?'

'I'm trying,' she said in vain. Then something sparked in the distance. 'Is Suzanne all right?'

'Thank goodness, it's coming back to her,' said Sylvia Golding, turning to her husband. 'Walter? She's coming back.'

Walter cleared his throat. 'When you weren't home by five, we called Suzanne's parents. Suzanne was the one who told us where you were. Seems you and she went out, but Suzanne came home hours earlier. She said that you'd gone to listen to folk music in the park, but that you stayed and she left. Your poor mother called everyone she knew, the police and all the hospital emergency departments, until we eventually tracked you down to here.'

Becky frowned. 'I met her on Eighth Street and Broadway. I remember walking in a crowd, but that's all.'

'You were caught up in a riot and almost trampled by a horse. You can thank your lucky stars that an officer saw you faint and carried you away. Apparently, you hit your head pretty hard on the way down.'

'Am I going to die?'

The nurse swallowed her laugh.

The doctor shook his head. 'Not today—at least, I don't expect you to die from your injuries anytime soon—although you're going to feel pretty bad for a while. You were concussed, that's all.'

Becky's eyes flitted around the room. 'Pop? Please don't be mad.'

'I hope that teaches you a lesson,' Walter continued. 'What in God's name were you thinking? You're not even fourteen years old, you're far too young to be running around the Village, listening to reefer addicts playing bongos.' The vein in his neck was throbbing. 'You're grounded for the rest of your life, young lady. We'll talk more about this when we get home.'

'Pop? Please don't be angry, Pop.'

'Angry? You have no idea how worried your mother was. Darn right I'm angry.'

The doctor whispered something to the nurse and she shooed Walter away from the bed. 'I know how you must feel, Mr Golding, but it won't do any good upsetting Becky right now.'

'She's my child, Nurse.'

'I know she is, and you're all pretty shaken up by this. Why don't you go home? Becky's pretty tired. We can keep an eye on her tonight and make sure she's okay.'

'Walter?' Sylvia picked up her purse and hung it over the crook of her arm.

'Let's go, Sylvia. Becky can think about what she did today and you can see her again in the morning.'

Sylvia kissed Becky on the cheek. 'Goodnight. Your father's worried, that's all. I'll see you tomorrow.' She followed Walter down the hall, her stilettos clicking like castanets as she hurried after him.

'Never mind,' said the nurse. 'It will be fine, you'll see.'

*

Walter Golding always trod the same route to work. With his homburg wedged on his head and dressed impeccably in navy pinstripe, every morning—rain or shine—he waved hello to Mrs Pierpont-Taylor as she swept her stairs. Mrs Pierpont-Taylor (who had once confided in him that she was descended from the Virginian Pierponts) greeted him cheerily in return. He smiled each morning and called out to her that she should come by the store for a bargain, when she was next in the market to upgrade her appliances. Her answer was perennially the same: 'I have a husband, Mr Golding. He's all the appliance I'll ever need,' and they both laughed.

He took the subway from Clark Street to Union Square station and, if he was lucky enough to score a seat, he read the *Wall Street Journal* along the way. Even though it really wasn't on his path, after exiting the station, he walked past S. Klein's department store and gazed up at the façade. He simply had to. At first, he did it for educational purposes. Soon, it became a habit he couldn't shake.

Walter ran a store selling appliances on Fourteenth Street, not far from Union Square, which he'd taken singlehandedly from almost certain bankruptcy to immodest success. Sure, S. Klein sold appliances too, but Walter prided himself in knowing more about his products and providing better service, even if he had to go the extra mile to please his customers. He bettered anyone's price and whenever S. Klein had a sale, he did too.

'Your happiness,' he told every person who came through the door, 'is my delight.'

He had bought the ramshackle business for a song from a struggling Russian immigrant, in November 1945, just after he'd returned home from the war. For a while, he was ashamed about the deal he had done to secure it. The store, with its faded sign and tiny display of dusty radio carcasses whose inner workings had long since been lost, looked more moribund than tired. The old man was desperately out of his depth in a world aiming for the heavens—he was still peddling mechanical solutions when everything was trending to the automatic—and his demise was inevitable.

Walter believed in a future the old man couldn't even imagine. Soon, he was clearing out old-fashioned ice-boxes and wringers to make room for the latest refrigerator freezers and top-loading washing machines. He employed like-minded young men in neat suits and trained them in the psychology of selling. By the time the store reopened for business, he might well have been treading water in a sea of debt, yet all regret had disappeared. He joined the Chamber of Commerce and audaciously and unsuccessfully ran for president. He wasn't hiding his achievements under a bushel anytime soon: he figured he'd earned his space around the corner from S. Klein.

At about the same time, Walter met Sylvia. She had escaped from her sorority to come into the store with her mother, looking to replace an old stand mixer with the latest Sunbeam Mixmaster. She caught his eye even before she and her mother had crossed the threshold. One glance at the leggy college junior with her brunette bangs and her pretty face, and he was love-struck. He always said he could spot a gem in a mountain of rubble.

'So,' she asked coyly, 'if I promise to bake a cake using your machine, and I bring it to you next week, will you give my mother a discount?'

Her business-savvy appealed to him instantly. 'I'll do even better than that,' he replied coolly. 'You bake me a cake and bring it to me next week and, if it's even half as gorgeous as you are, I'll marry you.'

Sylvia's mother's mouth dropped open. She threw him a look that could have petrified a marshmallow. She herded her daughter away but, as she left, Sylvia turned her head and tossed him a sly smile. He was resolute: that was the one thing about him that could never change.

He and Sylvia married one month later to the day. Within two years they had a son and a daughter, and they had just closed in escrow on a brownstone in Brooklyn Heights. The store was such a success that he'd already paid off all of his business loans. Private Golding had elevated himself to Commander-in-Chief, and his life was pretty damned near perfect.

*

The sun, streaming through a gap in the chintz curtains, settled on Sylvia Golding's face. For a while, she ignored the play of light and shadow, but Walter's trilling sinuses coupled with the brilliance of the morning made it simply impossible for her to sleep any longer. She glanced at the clock. It wasn't yet six.

She was exhausted even before she flung back the quilt, and, once she'd orientated her mind, she put it down to the dose of Equanil she took before bed to help her relax. There was numbness in every dawn—a pervading darkness in spite of the sunshine— and if she thought it would help, she would have stayed in bed forever.

She swung her legs out and her toes felt for her slippers. Walter must have sensed the movement, and he groaned but didn't wake. Instead, he rolled onto his back and began to snore. She glanced over and, satisfied that she hadn't roused him, wiggled her toes into her pink, fluffy mules and stood up. Slipping on her matching satin dressing gown, she crossed the room and swung open the door, wincing when it creaked, her ears straining to hear Walter snore.

If he was snoring, he was still asleep. If he was asleep, the world was at peace.

Sylvia wandered into the bathroom and snapped on the light. She revelled in those few, stolen moments when the house was silent, when everyone else was asleep and she was alone, before bustle and disarray and unkind words spread across the day like a rash.

She gazed at her reflection in the bathroom mirror and gasped. In her mind's eye she was still in her early thirties, yet the face that stared back at her was becoming more like her mother's every day. Courtesy of Obetrol, grapefruit and starvation (in continuous rotation), her figure remained teenage trim and she was lithe, but there was no hiding the fact that she was aging. During the day, the tiny creases extending outward from the corners of her eyes she disguised with a tick of black liner, and Max Factor still successfully masked the marionette lines around her mouth, but in the morning's cold light, there was a fatigue about her appearance—a despair almost—that makeup, pills and diet could never hide.

She pushed her precisely curled hair under a plastic cap, slid out of her gown and nightdress, rotated the shower faucets and let the water spill over her outstretched hand until it turned tepid. Then she stepped under the shower head and allowed the water to caress her face. Her makeup melted away under the gentle spray. The tainted stream flowed down the gully between her breasts and fouled the water circling the drain, almost as if she had emptied a vial of Indian ink into it. It was the only time of the day she was laid bare. These days, she wore makeup even when she slept.

She flicked off the hot water and let the shower run cold, because she'd read somewhere (*Ladies' Home Journal*, most likely), that bathing in cold water refreshed the senses and helped women everywhere cope with the demands of the day. Although, beyond keeping a clean house, quite frankly, she didn't really know what those demands were.

She stepped out of the cubicle and rubbed her skin with sweet-smelling towels she'd made fluffy with the addition of Downy to the final rinse. She unscrewed the jar of Pond's Moisture Base and dabbed it on her face, sweeping it upwards with her palms and pressing the pads of her index fingers on the pesky lines above the bridge of her nose. She took out her makeup valise and spread the contents of sticks, jars and tubes over the counter top. Ten minutes later, she scrutinised her image just to reassure herself that her makeup was flawless, and she put the valise away. She fixed her hair and prided herself on the fact that, after the best part of twenty years of marriage, Walter knew just about everything about her except how she looked without makeup and hairspray.

*

Becky was back in school the following Wednesday after a headache that lasted two days. At home, things had changed. There were to be no trips to the drug store after school. She and Suzanne were still friends, but there were no sleepovers or study dates. Walter demanded that she come home directly after class as quickly as she could. He called home every afternoon at four to check. She waited for it to pass, but it seemed that no amount of waiting was going to cure this ailment.

'I'm not a child,' she complained to her mother. 'You never did this to Sam, and he did a lot worse stuff than me.'

'Sam is a boy.'

The distinction was lost on her. 'So? Haven't you heard of President Kennedy's Commission on the Status of Women? We learned about it in civics.'

'Yes, dear, but boys and girls... Well, it's not the same. It's different.'

'Why is it different?'

'It just is,' Sylvia sighed. 'It's a matter of trust. Once it's gone, it's gone.'

It wasn't fair. It wasn't her fault that the New York mayor had chosen April 9 to ban folk singing in Washington Square, or that she just happened to be there. A year dragged by: New York had transformed from playground to prison, all because of an afternoon in the park.

'You know you can't control my life once I go to college,' she said.

Sylvia smiled. 'That's still three years away, Becky.'

Three years. A fifth of the life she'd lived so far. It stretched to the horizon and beyond. 'I can wait.'

She was in her senior year when Sam returned home from Michigan State. He wasn't *summa cum laude* as he'd promised when he'd left for college: he didn't even have a degree. He blew in through the door one autumn evening, along with the leaves.

'Hi, Mom,' he said. 'What's for dinner?'

It was as if he had never left.

He told Walter that he wasn't staying; he was just on his way through, but for the time that he was there, sleeping in his old bed, eating Pop-Tarts and drinking orange juice straight out of the bottle, the dust settled and Sylvia smiled.

On the third night, they ate dinner in the dining room again, at the big table, the one they used for Thanksgiving and birthdays. Sylvia pressed the tablecloth and the napkins until they were as stiff as greeting cards. She brought out her best glasses and made certain that all the flatware matched.

'It's so good to have you back,' she said as they sat down to eat. 'Isn't it good to have Sam back, Walter?'

Walter was helping himself to glazed carrots from a dish. He gazed at Sam. 'Is it?' he said.

'What nonsense,' said Sylvia. 'Of course it is.'

He put down the spoon so that it clattered against the side of the dish. 'I ask myself, what's he been doing these past two years? It's a question for which I have no answer.'

Sam lifted his eyes away from his plate. 'Sociology, Pop. That's what I've been doing.'

'Great,' Walter replied, 'didn't I read somewhere that there weren't enough sociologists in the world?'

Sam swivelled in his chair to face Walter. 'I've been doing exactly what you wanted me to do.'

Walter wiped his mouth. 'I don't remember saying anything to you about sociology. Dammit, I don't even know what a sociologist does.'

'They study humans.'

'Humans, huh? I'm sincerely happy for you. I don't see a career in it.'

'Well then, you should be delighted to know that I quit sociology. In fact,' he continued, 'I quit college. From now on, I am going to do what I was put on the earth to do.'

Becky observed them silently. She placed her hands in her lap and hardly dared to breathe.

'Oh,' Walter said, 'and do you mind sharing with your mother and me what exactly that is?'

Sylvia shifted uncomfortably. Her eyes darted from husband to son and back again. 'Now, now, boys. This discussion's far better suited to another time, don't you think? It's our first dinner together for ages. For the love of Mike, can't we just enjoy it?'

'The world is turning on a different axis and I have to be part of it,' said Sam.

'Seems like the same old world to me. The same dawn. The same dusk.' Walter wiped his palms on his napkin and pushed his plate away. 'So, why don't you explain to me what exactly I fought at Monte Casino for, and what I've been going to work these past twenty years for?'

Sam was scowling. 'What would be the point?' His eyes fixed on his plate.

'The point would be that I'm your father.'

He lifted his eyes. 'That's an accident of biology.'

Becky swallowed hard. She wanted to excuse herself, but then someone might notice she was actually there. She mentally traced the pattern on the dining room drapes from the ceiling down to the floor and back up again, and willed them to be quiet. Neither she nor Sylvia knew what to say or do, so they both kept silent and hung on.

'Okay,' Walter began. 'Then the point would be that I've been paying for you to go to that college of yours and you owe me.'

Sam shook his head. 'That's right, it's always about money with you, isn't it? I never asked to be born, you know. I'll pay you back, every cent, but right now I need to be honest to myself.'

'And what exactly does that mean? When I was your age, I was busy defending the American way of life. And after that, I was providing for you, your mother and your sister. Heck, you don't think I wanted to have a life? You don't think I wanted to go to college? I dragged myself up from nothing so you'd have the chance of a life I never had. And you're about to throw that all away. Without a vocation you're going to make what? Minimum wage? You'll be lucky to even get a job.'

Sam was still shaking his head. 'I don't want this.'

'You don't want a roof over your head or food in your belly?'

'No! I don't want to be like you. I don't want your life.'

Walter pushed his chair away from the table. He reflected for a while, before he spoke again. 'When you were a baby, I watched you like a hawk. When you took your first step, I was there to make sure you didn't fall. Sometimes, at night, I dreamed of all the bad things that might happen to you and how I could prevent them. Of all the things I imagined might happen, this wasn't one of them. What an ungrateful brat you've turned out to be. You want to go, then go. Don't hesitate one more minute. You want to discover the world, there's the door. I'll tell you something for nothing: it costs money to be a bum. A lot of money... Jack Kerouac, you are most certainly not. But go. Go with God. Go without him. Drink. Take drugs. You think for a moment that I give a flying fanny what you do?'

He drew his chair back to the table, settled his napkin on his lap and started to eat. If he was angry, nothing—not his voice, not his face and not even his demeanour—betrayed him. There was no explosion, not even a fire; his was more of a controlled burn.

Sam stood up. He put down his napkin. He bowed to his mother. He kissed Becky on the top of her head.

He went upstairs. He packed. And then he left.

CHAPTER FOUR

Chase's second night in the ringers' quarters had passed almost as quickly as his first. He had always been lean and, having played varsity ice hockey not so many years earlier, still relatively fit. The effort of a day's work under a remorseless sun had taken him to a point beyond exhaustion. Even the caffeine he had drunk before bed, had had no effect. As soon as his head had dented the pillow, he had been dead to the world.

During the night, he had been conscious of someone moving about the hut, and he had struggled to open his eyes, but had been unable to. He remembered it once he woke up. Other than that recollection, he had no sense of the passage of time. If he had been asked, he would have sworn that he had only just gone to bed, and that it was still evening, but the clock showed that it was already past five. He dreaded that soon he would have to face another gruelling day.

The curtain he had forgotten to draw on the first night now formed a barrier to the dawn, and he kept drifting in and out of sleep even after the alarm on his telephone sounded. He slept through it until, from the other end of the hut, he heard someone curse. He recognised the voice as Westie's. He propped himself up onto his elbow, silenced his phone and glanced around. Every bed in the hut was still filled. Westie was snoring again, and Chase had no sense that anyone else was awake.

He threw off the blanket and staggered to his feet. He tried to stretch, but his body was as taut as a rubber band. The efforts of the previous day had made his shoulder muscles tight, and his quadriceps ached as if he had run a marathon. He hoped that a hot shower might ease the discomfort.

As he dragged himself towards the door, he thought about Miss

Golding and bristled. He was too sore and too tired to give a damn about her, or about the station, or about his journey into enlightenment. He wanted to return to the coast and lie under a palm tree on a beach somewhere, and listen to the waves. He might have quit then and there, if he'd had enough money in his pocket to make his way home. The temptation might have been too great to resist. As it was, he had his return air ticket in his backpack, but he would still have to get back to Brisbane in order to fly home. He didn't even have enough to money get himself back to Townsville, let alone Brisbane, so leaving was not an option.

He stripped off, turned on the shower and stood under the thin, warm stream until any thought of leaving the station disappeared. Slowly, hunger replaced fatigue. He was ravenous. He returned to the hut, dressed quickly and went to sit on the back verandah.

The sky had cleared during the night, and the cold morning air bit into his still-damp skin. As he waited eagerly for the clang of Nellie's triangle, he watched the horses jostling playfully around the paddock, a kind of game, blowing steam from their nostrils.

He noticed the kitchen light come on soon after, and not long after that, he heard the sound of Nellie's voice. She was speaking to someone, quietly at first and then a little louder, but no one replied. After a while, he realised that, as early as it was, she must have been talking on the telephone. Although he couldn't make out the words, the conversation was clearly unpleasant. It ended with a squeal. He waited for silence, and then he went into the kitchen.

'Good morning, Nellie,' he said.

She was busy cracking eggs into a large, steel bowl and piling the shells into a second one. 'Morning,' she replied. Her hair was dishevelled. She turned her head, but didn't look at him.

'Can I help you with something?' he continued. 'Anything?'

Nellie frowned. 'Can you cook?'

'A little,' he replied. 'Mom tried to teach me before I left for college.'

'And? Did she succeed?'

'Not really.'

'Then you'd just be in my way.' She pushed the empty egg pallet away from her. 'Since you've decided to come into my kitchen without an invitation, you can just sit over there.' She wiped her hands on her apron and gestured to a chair with her elbow.

Chase moved towards the door instead.

'Where are you off to now?' she asked, picking up a whisk. 'I told you to sit down.'

'Well, you seem pretty agitated. I'll leave if you want me to.'

She softened. 'Well, you're here now, so you might as well stay. Don't go. I could do with some company this morning.' She poured milk and a spoon of salt into the eggs, whisked them briskly and slid them into a deep frying pan of foaming butter. In another pan, bacon sizzled, and a third was crammed with minute steaks. The steaks were grey. 'I've made a mess of these steaks,' she muttered, turning up the flame and prodding them with tongs. 'Not that anyone will notice.' She pursed her lips and grimaced. 'You probably want some coffee, ay?' she said, stirring the eggs with a wooden spoon.

'Would I get in your way if I made some?'

'Probably, but go ahead anyway. The perc's over there, and you'll find the ground coffee in the freezer.' She could hear Chase rummaging through the cupboard, and rolled her eyes. 'Top shelf, right in front of you.'

He filled the percolator with water and ground beans, and set it to boil, while Nellie turned off the burners and ladled clots of scrambled egg into a bowl. She filled platters with the breakfast meats and mushrooms. Instead of fanning them out in neat rows, as she had done the previous day, the pieces of meat remained wherever they fell.

Although he scarcely knew Nellie, he noticed deep folds in the shape of commas around her mouth. Her shoulders were rounded and stooped. 'Are you okay?' he asked.

'I'm always okay,' she replied curtly, 'so don't ask. You may as well take this lot into the dining room, and I'll bring you your coffee when it's done.' In her next breath she added, 'I'm sorry.'

'For what?'

'Your shirt will be ready by tonight. You weren't expecting it this morning, were you?'

'Of course not, Nellie. I'm just sorry that I've given you something else to do.' He left with the platters.

By the time she came into the dining room with his coffee, she seemed brighter. 'I apologise about before; I wasn't really myself. Family trouble, you see,' she whispered, and he understood.

*

During the day, Miss Golding was in the habit of taking her meals whenever she felt hungry, and occasionally not at all. There was no point in anyone telling her that she needed to eat well, since she never listened, and Nellie had given up years ago trying to tempt her with special little tidbits. She ate like a bird: a handful of nuts sometimes served as her lunch, and a slice of cake or a mug of soup as her dinner. Some days, Nellie did not see her at all but, no matter what, she always caught up with Nellie at precisely seven-thirty every evening and, in anticipation of her arrival, Nellie always began brewing her coffee at precisely twenty minutes after seven.

In the morning, Stewart sent Pete off on a horse to ride the boundary alone, while Chase took the ute and a packed lunch to a paddock a half hour's drive away, and mended the fence by himself. The solitude was blissful. He was glad for the trust Stewart had shown him, and determined to do the job well, but it proved a lot harder to tension the fence wire without Pete.

Stewart had shown him two ways, one with a forked tree branch and the other using a wire strainer. In no time, he recognised that the branch would have been more useful to him as firewood, so he tried the strainer. At first, the strainer kept slipping, and the task seemed impossible. His hands were tender and torn where the wire had caught them. He had set the star pickets into the earth easily enough, but if he couldn't replace the wire, the job would have to be left undone. There would be no purpose to employing him. He tried again and again, until he reached the point of frustration and then surpassed it. That was the point at which something clicked.

Chase arrived to collect his shirt that evening, a little past seven. He sat in the kitchen contentedly tired, his best shirt washed, mended and ironed, his belly full, anticipating a good cup of coffee. Seven-thirty arrived and Nellie took the milk out of the refrigerator. She waited for the familiar creak of the door, but it did not come. When Miss Golding still had not appeared by seven-thirty-five, she began to panic.

'It's not like her to miss her coffee. Even when she's sick, she still likes to have her coffee.' Nellie was frowning. 'I want to go check on her, but I… Well, I'm not good with that sort of thing,' she pronounced enigmatically. 'I suppose I could ask Mr Stewart to check on her… But maybe it would be better if I do it myself.' She paused momentarily, her gaze on Chase but her focus much further away. 'I think you'd better come with me, Chase. In case…'

She didn't finish the sentence: she didn't need to.

He followed her through the door which connected the kitchen to the rest of the homestead—a doorway the men were continually told they were forbidden to cross. She paused to snap on the light, and they hurried nearly halfway down the hall and stopped beside a closed door.

Nellie turned and rapped on it. When there was no answer, she called out, 'Are you all right, Miss Becky?' but there was no reply. She knocked again. 'Miss Becky? Are you there?' Still nothing. She clicked her tongue. 'It's me, Nellie, Miss Becky.' She was shrieking now, and thumping her fists against the wood. 'I'm coming in, in three, two…' She had just placed her shoulder to the door, when it opened a crack, and she peered into the darkness.

'Oh, Nellie,' Miss Golding croaked, 'it's you.'

Nellie sighed and lifted her hand to her chest. 'Are you all right, Miss Becky?'

'Why? Shouldn't I be?'

'But you missed your coffee.'

'Oh, did I?' Her voice was hollow and faltering. 'What time is it?' She opened the door wide and blinked, temporarily blinded by the hall light. Her hair stood up like tufts of fairy floss. She was still wearing her nightgown.

'It's about seven-forty now,' said Nellie.

'In the morning?'

'No, not in the morning. It's seven-forty in the evening, Miss Becky. Have you been asleep all day?'

Miss Golding was scratching for a clue to the answer. She couldn't recall being awake or being asleep. It was all the same to her. 'I don't know, perhaps. I've become so forgetful lately.' Her eyes settled on Chase. 'Oh, but I remember you,' she added, 'so I can't have lost all of my marbles, can I?'

'I remember you, too,' he returned. 'How about we go back into the kitchen together and share some coffee and maybe Nellie can rustle you up some supper?' He offered her his arm.

'Yes, that sounds just fine.' She took his arm and he began to lead her back down the hallway. They had only taken a few paces when she stopped abruptly.

'Are you all right, Miss Golding? Am I walking too fast for you?'

She was staring at him, her lips parted and her brows knitted. 'No, I'm simply dandy. I've met you before, haven't I? Who did you say you were again?'

'We met last night. You remember that, don't you? I'm Chase Miller.'

'Oh.' She leaned against Chase. 'But your accent. You're an American.'

'That's right. We talked about that last night. I'm Chase Miller,' he repeated.

'I could have sworn you said your name was something else,' she muttered.

Nellie frowned. She placed her arm lightly around Miss Golding's shoulders. 'You feeling okay, Miss Becky?' she asked. 'No headache? You don't feel sick or dizzy?'

'Really, Nellie, I'm not having a stroke. I must have just been having such a wonderful dream that I forgot to wake up. I'm back now, aren't I?' She smiled, but her eyes never left Chase. 'Now, Chase Miller, let's get going, shall we? I'm starving.'

It took a cup of coffee and a cinnamon bun for Miss Golding to retrieve her memory, and for Nellie's shoulders to settle back into their usual spot.

'So, we never got to the bottom of your sad tale, did we? What sent you scurrying away from that glorious republic to a back-water colony like Australia?'

Chase sniggered. 'Things have changed, both here and there. Isolationism is the new buzz word everywhere these days.'

'You're a liberal, I assume, by the way you're talking.' She replaced her mug on the table and refilled it. 'Not that it's necessarily a bad thing.'

'Well, everything's become rather monochrome lately, and the grayscale has just about disappeared. You're either American or Un-American, with very little room in between. There's no debate, just a lot of polarising statements. I guess I've come here to get away from that, and experience the spectrum. You don't know what it's like. You've been away a long time.'

'I sure have. Came here in sixty-seven and never returned, but I still read the papers. It's not that different here, you know. Sometimes what I read breaks my heart: I had such high hopes for the USA—we all did, back then. Seems to me, from the top down, nobody strives for excellence anymore. There's very little peace, and no love left. Everyone has someone else to blame for their failures. I was part of the flower power generation. Whatever happened to our ideals?'

Chase grinned. 'Consumerism, perhaps? I don't know… So, you think your generation was blameless for what came after you, huh? We are exactly what you made us. These days, most of us are in so much debt that it's hard to think straight. We fall into categories: entitled and outraged, and desperate and defeated. Either way, it's easy to point fingers.'

'Yes it is, isn't it?' She bristled. 'Youngsters are quick to blame everyone else for their own shortcomings, but I hold education—or the lack of it—responsible. Personally, I had nothing to do with what happened after I left.'

Chase blushed. 'No, of course I didn't mean you personally, Miss Golding, but your generation… The baby boomers…'

'It seems to me that there's a pandemic for which there is no cure. Stupid is catching—here too. Dumb is the new black.' She looked away. 'But you sound like a well-educated young man, Miller. Where are you from?'

'A town in New Jersey.'

'Really? But you don't sound like you come from New Jersey. Not Newark?'

Chase shook his head. 'Ringwood. It's small. Pretty. Lots of trees.'

'I've never heard of it.' She took another bun, placed it on her plate and began picking at it. 'You're a college man?'

'Graduated last spring. NYU. Psychology major.'

'Me too. Well, not psychology, but New York University. Such a fine institution. It taught me to question everything.' She nibbled a few crumbs, twisted her face and pushed the plate away. 'And you still haven't answered my first one. I still don't know why you left.'

'I don't know why you did either. You willing to exchange?'

She scoffed. 'My story for yours? I've been alive a good many years more than you have, Miller. I'm not certain that it would be a fair bargain.'

As she spoke, Nellie stepped away from the table. She piled a plate with the gingernuts she had baked that morning, thrust it in front of Miss Golding, and sat down with a cup of tea.

Miss Golding spied them and scowled. 'I see what you did there, Nellie. Dear God, woman, haven't you learned anything after all these years?'

'Well, you may not want one, but I do and Chase might, too,' she returned. 'You want to starve yourself to death, that's perfectly all right with me. Don't let me stop you. I don't know why I care.'

'You care because we're family. Or as close to family as it's possible for two people to be.'

Nellie snorted.

Miss Golding turned to Chase. 'I hate her calling me Miss Becky, you know, but she insists. I believe that she does it precisely because she knows I hate it. One day, she'll call me by my name—Becky, just plain Becky—and I'll fall down dead.'

'And that,' Nellie smirked, 'is exactly why it will never happen, Miss Becky.'

CHAPTER FIVE

Nᴇᴡ Yᴏʀᴋ Uɴɪᴠᴇʀsɪᴛʏ wasn't Becky's first choice—it was her only one. She sat her SAT with a solitary goal in mind, and she did well enough to have gone to pretty much any college of her choosing, but Walter informed her that she wasn't to leave the tri-state area. In fact, she wasn't leaving New York. *Period.*

Everyone else she knew at her high school would be going away for college. Some were headed west, and Suzanne was going as far east as her parents would allow. She was enrolled to study French at the Sorbonne. Becky was happy for her.

That summer, after school had ended, Becky was permitted to go to parties as far away as Southampton, as long as she never left Long Island. The leash had a little give, provided that she telephoned home daily. It was fine. She told herself it was temporary. She was seventeen. In under four years, she would have reached the age of majority. At twenty-one her life was her own.

When her friends spoke about UCLA and Berkeley, she laughed and told them that Sam was in San Francisco. She made it sound as if she would be visiting him there. The truth was she'd only learned that he'd gone to San Francisco last winter, after he sent her a postcard. By the time it arrived it was tattered and frayed around the edges, although she had to concede that perhaps that was the way he had sent it. She took it with her everywhere: it was her passport. In the foreground, a cable car was descending a road, with Sears Fine Food and a red Cadillac in the background. She imagined herself there. She was riding in the Cadillac, her hair tousled by a balmy bay wind, and the driver was a man whose face she could never see.

On the back of the card, Sam wrote:

I'm in Berkeley CA. I'm living with some groovy people. Frisco's a gas. You should come visit sometime. Love Sam.

There was no return address.

As she sat on Coopers Beach watching her friends jump waves, she took it out of the pocket of her playsuit and willed herself to San Francisco—or anywhere far enough away that Walter wouldn't find her. It wasn't as if he was a terrible father, but he was stifling. He and Sylvia both were. Sam wasn't like them and neither was she. For all the traits they shared, they might as well have been adopted and, if it hadn't been for the shape of her nose, she might have believed that she was. It had been a rare act of faith that had led to her holiday by the sea. She was smart. She'd bide her time, while she yearned for the universe.

After five days by the sea, she caught the train back to Nostrand Avenue. Even before it stopped, she saw her mother waiting on the platform. She wore a pillbox hat and gloves, a bit like Jackie Kennedy's. She may have been two years too late, but she looked immaculate.

Becky wiped off the remnants of the ketchup that had oozed from her lunchtime hotdog, straightened her sweater and slipped her feet back into her red ballet flats. She stood at the door of the train until it stopped, with her suitcase in one hand and her purse in the other, and watched her mother scurrying along the platform to catch up to her.

'How brown you are!' Sylvia exclaimed. 'Did you have a good time, dear?' She held Becky in her arms and gave her a hug. The buttons on Sylvia's blouse were as big as saucers, and they dug into Becky's chest.

She smiled. 'It was a gas!' She was thinking of Sam's postcard again.

Sylvia drew away. 'Whatever do you mean by that?'

'Oh, Mom. It just means it was fun.'

Sylvia took Becky's suitcase and click-clacked towards the exit as swiftly as her pencil skirt and heels allowed. Her voice breathy, she said, 'Your father has a meeting at the Chamber of Commerce tonight. What would you say to dinner out? Just the two of us. How about Mama Maria's?'

'Sure.'

They took a cab to Cobble Hill and stopped just outside Mama Maria's restaurant. They sat at a table by the kitchen and ordered sodas, pizza and linguine.

Becky had felt exhausted after almost a week of endless chatter, the summer sun and a slow train ride home, but the meal revived her. 'You know,' she said between bites, 'Suzanne's going to study French at the Sorbonne in Paris, France.'

Nostalgia stole across Sylvia's face. 'Really? Did I ever tell you that I visited Paris once, before the war? I was a girl, a little younger than you are now. What an experience! I suppose you'd say that it was a gas!'

Sylvia smiled and paused for effect, but out of her mother's lips, the phrase just sounded to Becky like a stomach ailment.

She continued, 'If London is the man in a bowler hat, New York is the man in a grey pinstripe and spats, and Paris... Well, Paris is the Grande Dame in a silk dress. Such an elegant city.'

Becky scowled. 'Lucky for you and lucky for her.' She picked an olive off her pizza. 'I never get to go anywhere.'

Sylvia pushed the half-eaten plate of linguine away and placed her handbag on her lap. 'Oh, sweetheart, your life's just beginning. You'll travel one day, I just know you will.' She glanced around, pulled out her lipstick, puckered her lips and hurriedly reapplied it at the table. 'I travelled to Paris with your grandparents. They had some old friends living there and, for a while, we were going to live in Paris, too. But then, my father didn't much like the German Chancellor at the time, so he brought us back to New York. And just as well he did,' she reflected. 'Your father's just looking out for your welfare. He wants to keep you safe. It's not such a bad thing that you'll be close by while you're at college. After that...'

'After that I'll be a hundred years old!'

'You won't be old, I promise. Besides,' said her mother, shutting her bag with a click, 'you really never know what's just around the corner.' She paid the check with a small handful of bills. 'Let's beat it!'

They strolled home along Henry Street arm in arm to the peace of an empty house. Becky climbed the stairs two at a time and threw open the door to her bedroom. After a week away, it smelled comforting and familiar. He mother had placed a vase of pale pink roses by her bed. Their scent was barely perceptible.

She studied her face in the mirror as she brushed the knots out of her hair. She was unremarkable. Pretty but not beautiful. Slender but not emaciated. Wavy but not curly.

She smiled at her reflection, unpacked her case and changed for bed.

*

The leaves of the trees in Brooklyn Bridge Park were already beginning to rust by the time Becky started at NYU. Walter said she should study law or business, but she was going to study humanities without any idea of the end-game. She expected she'd change her major sometime along the way. In the meantime, she waited for an epiphany. Sylvia, on the other hand, expected that Becky would use the opportunity of college to find a nice young man to settle down with. She thought that if Becky really needed a vocation, then teaching sounded compatible with raising a family.

Becky announced she wasn't looking for anyone to settle down with—not yet and, maybe, she told herself, not ever. The man in the red Cadillac was the stuff of her friends' dreams. She had a world to unwrap first.

She met Clark Somers in the spring semester of her sophomore year. She caught his eye one lunchtime, sitting in a café by the park with one of her friends, Carol, from her philosophy class. It was pure happenstance. He looked up from the book he was reading and smiled. She smiled back. She told Carol later that she didn't mean to: it was an autonomic reflex.

Clark sidled over to her table in his best impression of James Dean, hands in his back pockets, and said, 'I have my car parked out front. Want to go for a ride?'

Becky sipped her soda through a straw and glared at him. 'You may have noticed that I'm here with my friend,' she replied. 'Sorry.'

Carol glanced at Becky and then at Clark and shook her head. She picked up her books. 'Don't mind me. I have to go back to class anyway.'

'May I?' said Clark as he pulled out a chair.

Becky shrugged her shoulders. He sat down and introduced himself.

There was something about him that appealed to her. Dark and brooding, he seemed the antithesis of Walter. 'Well, Mr Clark Somers, if you have your car parked out front, then I guess we had better go for a ride in it.'

He grinned.

They walked down the road a few yards, towards a small, Italian sports car sandwiched between a Lincoln Continental and a Dodge. It looked diminutive.

Becky sniggered. 'That's it?'

'That's my car. A 1961 Alfa Romeo Giulietta Sprint. Isn't she beautiful?' He rubbed away a spot of dust with his shirt cuff.

She looked the car up and down. With its curves and its colour—an odd shade somewhere between fawn and yellow—it reminded her of a lemon.

'Is that all? Where's the rest of it hiding?'

After the words came out, she thought she'd probably wounded him. He placed his hands on his hips, flung back his head and laughed.

'She's small but she's feisty. Sounds a lot like you, doesn't she?' he retorted.

'Hey!' she replied. 'You don't know me half well enough to judge me.' She liked the way his eyes sparkled when he looked at her.

'I know trouble when I see it.'

'Is that,' she said, pointing at the car, 'trouble?'

'No end of trouble. I guess it's just as well I know how to fix her when she has one of her many breakdowns.' He unlocked the door and held it open for her.

'And what about me? Are you going to fix me? Am I trouble, too?'

'I expect so. I don't know about fixing you, but I reckon you're nothing but trouble.'

Becky slid into the red leather seat and Clark closed the door. She took a deep breath. The car smelled of leather cleaner and Aqua Velva. He sprinted across to the driver's side and climbed in beside her. He turned the key in the ignition and the Alfa Romeo responded with a throaty roar.

'I'm up for a ride,' he said. 'Are you?'

They inched their way through the lower Manhattan traffic towards Canal Street, and took the Holland tunnel to the New Jersey Turnpike, heading for Woodbridge. Becky, who had taken lessons since her mid-teens but hadn't taken her driving test yet, assessed Clark to be a competent driver, and the car didn't miss a beat. She relaxed for a while. She sank back into the seat and enjoyed the sensation of escape—even if it was fleeting—as she listened to the rhythm of the road and Clark's voice.

He told her he was a senior at NYU, and on his way to an illustrious career in mechanical engineering. He was going to be first of the third generation of mechanical engineers. His younger cousins were certain to follow in the profession, just as his uncles had done. They all hailed from Pennsylvania, and his mother's family had arrived on the *Mayflower*.

So far, so Walter, she thought as he spoke, her eyes glassy, listening to him slide a little further off the pedestal with each word.

His roots were set in concrete—old money and old-fashioned

values. Where Becky was all question marks, Clark had all the answers. They stopped for a while for coffee on Staten Island, in Richmondtown, and then headed across the Verrazano Bridge to Brooklyn.

It was already late afternoon by the time they reached Brooklyn Heights.

'I live there,' said Becky, pointing at the brownstone, two doors down from where Clark had pulled up. For the first time in her life, she looked at the townhouse with a critical eye, and wished her father had painted the windowsills and tended to the plants in pots at the top of the stoop. She bit her lip. 'I don't think...' she began. 'I mean, it's a little soon...'

'I won't come in,' said Clark.

They made plans for a date the following Saturday and Becky let him kiss her cheek.

'Thanks for the drive,' she said as she climbed out of the car. 'It was fun.'

She stood on the pavement and watched Clark leave. He waved goodbye, revved the Giulietta, pulled away from the kerb and disappeared down Henry Street. She felt as if she'd arrived at a crossroads. Suddenly, she had the possibility of a world which didn't just end abruptly at the bottom of the stoop of a Brooklyn Heights brownstone.

*

Clark Somers casually joined the Goldings for a drink three weeks after he and Becky first met. A month after that, she and Clark were pinned. She called Carol first to tell her.

Carol had read Kinsey. She had gleaned from his reports an embarrassment of wisdom. She tossed out words like *orgasm* and *vagina* as if she was reading from a grocery list, and yet, for all that, she remained as wholesome as Donna Reed. Becky listened.

Sex was sex, love was love.

'If you love and want to marry Clark, then let him window-shop, but never give out free samples.' Nice girls, she said, didn't do that. Since all men only married nice girls, the equation was simple.

In turn, Becky made it clear to Clark that she needed a commitment. Free sex was a happening in California, but not in Brooklyn Heights. It was her right to refuse as much as it was his to move on. But he didn't. Apparently, at a time of so many college girls of easy virtue, she was the breath of fresh air.

She penned a letter to Sam at an address in Berkeley that she'd found on one of his few postcards home, and she told him about Clark. *We're getting engaged after graduation*, she wrote. He replied on a postcard of the Bay Bridge, to let her know that he had burned his draft card and might be going underground for a while, perhaps even as far away as Canada. He must have received her letter, but there was no acknowledgement of its contents. She read Sam's card through twice to be sure, tore it up and threw it away.

Now that their relationship was official, Becky brought Clark home for a family dinner. He said he wanted to get to know her parents better, a signal to her that things were progressing nicely.

Sylvia was bursting with happy thoughts she could hardly contain. Clark was perfect: six feet, chiselled, eager, and engineering was a good, solid profession. Becky would be well cared for and Walter could hardly wish for more.

Her life's work had been a success.

She bustled around her kitchen making a Waldorf salad, followed by Chicken Marengo and strawberry shortcake for dessert and Clark wolfed it down as only a starving young college man removed from the comforts of home could.

After dinner, Walter took him aside.

'What do you want to do with your life, son?' he asked.

'Well,' he replied, 'I guess I'll go into the family business, designing and fabricating engines for heavy machinery. That was always the plan.'

Walter tapped out his pipe and refilled it with tobacco. 'Is that something you can do here, in New York?' He tamped the tobacco down and set the pipe between his teeth but didn't light it.

Clark shook his head. 'After graduation, I'll be returning to Pittsburgh. That's where the business, the jobs and the demand are.'

'And Becky? What about Becky?'

'Well, assuming that we're married by then, I guess she'll be going to Pittsburgh with me.'

Walter lit his pipe and sucked on it for a while before blowing out a stream of smoke. 'That's a tall ask for a girl, you know. Women need to be close to their mothers, especially once the children come along. Maybe it's time to break the mould. I'm certain you'll find a good job here. I run a successful store in Manhattan, you know…'

'Well, sir, I think that my mother would be able to help Becky out with the children. My future's in my dad's business and for now, that's in Pittsburgh.'

'Hmm,' said Walter thoughtfully.

On the following day, spring was anticipating an early summer, and Clark swung by again in the morning to collect Becky and drive up Long Island towards Freeport. He mentioned the conversation he'd had with Walter to her—casually, unperturbed, derisive—but she still flew into a rage.

Even an hour later, she couldn't let the thought subside. The image of a future—their future—under Walter's rule was on heavy rotation in her mind.

She muttered, 'How dare he try to control us?'

'He's your father,' he replied. 'That's his job, I guess.'

'I can't believe that he'd suggest you work for him!'

The sky was azure for miles without punctuation, but she struggled to glimpse anything past the Giulietta's hood. She wasn't moving on. They drove to the waterfront and stopped at a crab shack along the Nautical Mile for lunch, Becky picking at the food, her mind still occupied. After that, they watched the boats bobbing in the marina for a while, but her thoughts rose above the clink and jangle of the rigging.

Enough was enough.

They were heading back when she spotted a motel on the opposite side of the road.

'Let's not go home,' she said abruptly. 'Let's stay the night.'

'What?' Clark gulped as the car flew past the motel. 'Where?'

'Back there,' she said nonchalantly with a wave of her hand. 'In the hotel.'

He lifted his foot off the accelerator, but didn't brake. He seemed incredulous. 'Tonight?'

'I can call Mom and Pop later and say we broke down and we're going to have to wait for the repairman till morning.'

He pulled over and swung the Giulietta around. He turned into the carpark and screeched to a stop next to the office. He turned to her. 'Are you sure about this?' he asked.

She looked him straight in the eye. 'I'm sure,' she replied.

*

If New York was the thudding heart of American culture then, in 1965, Berkeley was the buzzing hub of its conscience. Sam hitched across the country with only one objective in mind: to find truth and live an authentic life. He did it with his life savings tucked in the back pocket of his Levi's; by the time he reached California, one hundred and three dollars, two quarters, a nickel and a dime were left. Money was vulgar: it didn't concern him. Besides, even if his father cut him off without another penny, he knew that Sylvia was always there at the other end of the wire.

Walter was wrong: Sam never aspired to becoming Kerouac. He wasn't a writer: he even hated having to write dissertations at college, and the mere thought of facing another blank page made him nauseous. As cool as he was, in reality Jack Kerouac was nearly as old as his father. Route 66 didn't lead to Damascus—Sam wasn't raised Catholic and he wasn't seeking redemption—and there had been no epiphanies on the road for him. He was already well versed in the allure of alcohol and psychotropic substances, and he hadn't the slightest inclination to make an enduring record of his journey. His motivation was simple: there was a scene happening in San Francisco that he needed to be part of.

In Modesto, he picked up a ride with a middle-aged man named Len, who spoke incessantly about his cock-sucking, blood-sucking ex-wife all the way to downtown Berkeley, and who then slipped his business card into Sam's shirt pocket (in case he needed a friend). Sam lifted his duffel bag out of the trunk of Len's car and was instantly flooded with relief. He watched Len wave, honk and pull away. He had no idea where he was going, but after two hours of marital angst, he was grateful for the solitude.

He walked away from the public library and stopped at a modest diner further along on Shattuck Avenue for a coffee and a glazed doughnut. The coffee was good and hot and the doughnut cloyingly sweet, and the combination filled the yawning chasm in his belly. After his second cup he felt sufficiently oriented as to his surroundings to look around.

Outside, the sun had climbed halfway to its zenith and it was still surprisingly temperate for December. He had just hitched all the way through Arizona with its warm days and cold nights, but he wasn't used to heat streaming through the glass at that time of year. Inside, illuminated by the shaft of light, the diner showed signs of neglect that Sam found comforting. Someone had stuck a handwritten flyer on the window next to his table. *Room For Rent—Apply 2410 Telegraph Ave.* He took the flyer, folded it up and stuffed it in his shirt pocket in place of Len's business card, which he tore in half and dropped on the table. As he paid for his meal, he casually asked the waitress for directions.

He found the house on Telegraph Avenue—an old Victorian row house with peeling paint and a large bay window, partly covered by wooden boards—pretty easily. The front door was open, and the inside smelled vaguely of boiled cabbage.

'I'm here about the room to rent,' he called out to a girl sitting on a stool in the hallway, staring at her fingernails. She gazed up at Sam, but she looked straight past him. She was somewhere else. She shrugged her shoulders and returned to her fingernails.

Sam stepped around the girl and walked to the back of the house. In the kitchen, sitting around an old table surrounded by mismatched chairs, were two young men sharing a joint.

'I'm here about a room to rent,' he repeated.

'Yeah? That's great, man.' One of the men handed over the joint.

Sam inhaled and held the smoke in his lungs. As he exhaled, he asked, 'The room. Is it still for rent?'

'Yeah, man.' He stood up and led Sam back down the hallway. He swung open a door. It was empty except for a mattress with old bedding heaped in one corner and a chair in the other. 'Twenty bucks a week.'

At that rate, he'd be broke in a month. 'Ten and I'll cook for you.'

The man shook his head. 'Sorry, man.'

'I can't do twenty,' said Sam.

'Fifteen and you cook and tidy the garden.'

'Deal,' said Sam.

'Deal,' the man replied.

Of the five people sharing the house with Sam, only one, Timothy, actually had a paying job. Of the others, Mick and Paul traded in anything and everything: stolen goods one day, acid of the worst kind the next. The girl in the hallway was Jane, and she was the beneficiary of a trust. Another girl, Meg, only surfaced at night and earned her rent in a way she never discussed. Sam had been looking for nirvana and had stumbled across something else.

The following week, Sam secured a job that paid one dollar fifty an hour washing plates in a Chinese restaurant called Jimmy

Tang's four nights a week. He fed the others by scraping whatever was left on the platters into containers, and taking them home with him. He never took anything off the diners' individual plates: that would have been disgusting, but the platters were meant for sharing and that was precisely what he was doing. The owner either didn't know or didn't care enough to say anything.

Outside the back of the restaurant, Sam found most of the ingredients for the rest of the week's meals in the dumpster. He sought out the vegetables Jimmy Tang's cook had thrown out but weren't yet rotten enough to make anyone sick, carried them home in a paper sack and, with the addition of garbanzo beans, turned them into meals.

The house on Telegraph Avenue was a spitball away from the university. Sam overheard someone say that one of Jane's father's companies owned the house and, as long as she was enrolled at Berkeley, she had the right to live there. Everyone else had come along for the ride.

Mick and Paul had insinuated themselves into the house a couple of years ago and remained there, not because either one of them had any thought of advancement through education, but because it afforded them a steady stream of student customers for whatever they happened to be selling on any given day. They collected the rent for Jane, and they were meant to pay the bills out of it, but they never did. Where the money went was a mystery. Jane cared less about that than she cared about her grades, or about making any progress towards her degree. How she remained at Berkeley, Sam didn't know. All he knew was that Jane was a perennial student, the pot was free and the power was never disconnected.

His life became a pattern cut out of a paper chain: every day was identical to the one that preceded it. He woke late, smoked a joint, did as little as he could get away with, smoked another joint and, most evenings, he went to work at Jimmy Tang's. He knew about a free speech movement happening at the end of the road, but it wasn't of any interest to him. What did he care about political freedom for a bunch of college students? He may have found a happening scene in Berkeley, but he had no intention of joining in. He remained a disinterested bystander until the choices he'd left behind months before and halfway across America finally caught up with him.

It was over a meal of garbanzo bean stew and a joint that he first met Jerry Rubin. While everyone anticipated his arrival like he was the Messiah, Sam had never even heard of him. Somehow, word of his coming had spread. Everyone was home that night, together with at least thirty strangers who had turned up without notice. Even Jane seemed *compos*.

Sam glimpsed Rubin as he bounced through the door and immediately thought he was a short, unkempt man with too much energy and not enough focus. That night, Rubin chatted openly on his plans to face the House Committee on Un-American Activities with all the respect he thought it deserved. He was interesting to a point, and Sam soon understood his allure, but he pegged him as a fantasist. He and Rubin eventually bonded over sociology (which they'd both studied for a while and then dropped) and the legalisation of marijuana, but that was where all commonality ended. If he was being honest about it, Sam never gave the war or pacifism a second thought until it crept into his reality.

Exactly like Clark Somers and just about every other male college student in the States, Sam had deferred military service. He thought he'd fallen off the map when he'd arrived in California but, in 1965, he topped the call-up list. Somehow, somewhere along the line, someone had figured out where he was living and that he now owed service to the US Government.

He watched the news the night he'd found out he was facing the draft, with the sense that the anguished scenes of detonating bombs, weeping women and scorched jungle could soon be his actuality. What did he care about South East Asia? What right did America have to dictate how people half a world away should live or what political regime should govern them? He searched for answers but came up with blanks. He didn't worry about communism infiltrating Vietnam as the gateway to world domination. To fight a war that was not on his doorstep was a wasted effort.

Moreover, Sam had run away from one thing or another for most of his life, and never been held to account. He was irritated that life had found him and now he had to make a choice. The truth was that he held no principles strongly enough to compromise his comfort for, and even fewer to go to war over. This was someone else's argument and he was playing no part in it.

He resented having to leave the routine and relative ease of his life on Telegraph Avenue, but he didn't want to go to jail over a decision of conscience, if that was what it was. He simply had to disappear for a while. He remembered having received a letter from Becky not too long ago, and he probably owed it to her to let her know that he'd be moving away, just in case she had the stupid idea of coming to look for him. He scribbled a note on a postcard, stuck a stamp on it and posted it that day.

Spring was as good a time as any for a young man to walk into the campus of the University of California at Berkeley and stand shoulder to shoulder with other young men and burn his draft card, especially with Jerry Rubin and Abbie Hoffman watching.

By the end of the day, Sam had packed his duffel bag, placed what remained of his savings into the back pocket of his Levi's and accepted a ride with them heading east.

*

In the end, Becky's night at the motel raised more questions than it answered.

College wasn't a challenge for her and social sciences bored her senseless. She faced another two years at NYU unless she dropped out which, as a married woman, she could do without any stigma attached. She understood that the stakes were higher for Clark, so she never grumbled when he missed her call. He was, after all, a principled man and a senior. He would need a degree to support their family. Besides, patience long practised had always been her strong suit.

Clark threw himself into studying for his final exams early and with such vigour that he barely had any free time during the rest of the spring semester to spend with her. She had exams at the end of the semester too, but that was too far away for her to think about. She and Sylvia were so preoccupied with engagement plans that everything else drifted away like flotsam.

He dropped by once or twice more, and then he ceased visiting the brownstone altogether. At first, Sylvia was perplexed. She looked to Becky for answers, but was offered none. Eventually, she stopped asking after him and figured that something must have gone wrong.

When Clark hadn't phoned her in a week, Becky dropped by his dorm and left a message for him to call her urgently. That evening, she waited patiently by the telephone for a call that never came. After checking the line every half hour, she had to acknowledge it wasn't the telephone exchange that had failed her.

It was only when she looked for Clark at the library and couldn't find him that she began to wonder whether their relationship had been something she had imagined. She took his pin from her sweater and jabbed her finger until it drew blood. It stung. If it hadn't been for the pin, she might have believed that he had never existed in the first place. His absence was so abrupt and so complete that she wondered if he'd died. She knew he hadn't when she saw him fly past her in his Giulietta the following day.

She had to ask Carol about it. In the game of life, Becky realised that she knew none of the rules of engagement.

They sat at the same table in the same café where she and Clark had first met, and Carol listened to her talk for a while, heavy lidded and judgemental. Then she asked, 'What did you do to him?'

'What do you mean, what did I do to him? I did nothing,' Becky responded.

'You said that you didn't fight with him, so you must have done something to make him act this way. You and he didn't…'

Becky lowered her eyes. 'No. Well, maybe that's the problem. We spent the whole night together. Nothing happened.' She said that perhaps she'd pushed him too hard, perhaps sex as an act of rebellion had been too much. She rationalised it away. Her impulsiveness had set Clark on edge.

Carol blurted, 'So, you went to a hotel and you didn't have intercourse? I know what's wrong. It's obvious.' She paused for a beat. 'Clark's a homosexual.'

'What? Of course he's not. We were pinned, Carol.'

She sighed. 'That doesn't mean anything. Some homosexuals get married.'

'But we used to, you know, do other things. And he said he loved me. I think he was probably just worried about school. After graduation, we'll get engaged, just as we planned. You'll see.'

'Don't count on it,' she replied. 'If you genuinely didn't have intercourse, then I don't think it had anything to do with the pressure of study. Any man would have jumped at the chance. Wake up, Becky, the tooth fairy's really just your mom, Santa's really just your dad in a cheap red suit, and Clark Somers is gone and he's not coming back.'

Becky groaned. 'But nobody breaks up with someone and forgets to tell them.'

'Yeah, they do. In English regency novels they're called a cad and a bounder.'

'You're wrong, Carol,' she retorted. 'You'll see.'

After receiving a letter from him to say that *their understanding* was at an end, she went to bed and stayed there, while Sylvia, and even Walter, tiptoed around her. A week later, she willed herself upright and back to college. She sat her spring exams and did pretty well. They said nothing when she finally announced that Clark had returned to Pittsburgh for good.

In August, Sylvia asked Becky if she wanted to take a trip over

Christmas. She'd talked it over with Walter and he'd agreed to let her go.

'I suggested to him that you might want to visit your friend Suzanne. The Youngs will be spending winter in France this year.'

'In Paris?' Her eyes widened. 'Honest?'

'Of course. It would do you good to get away, and you don't get much further away than Europe.'

'So when do we go?' she asked.

'Not *we*, darling—you. You're going. I checked with the Youngs already and they'd be happy for you to visit after the fall semester ends. We just have to arrange your passport and your flights.'

Becky embraced Sylvia and held on. 'Mom, you're the coolest mother in the whole world.' She kissed her cheek, wafting away on the scent of Miss Dior. 'Thank you, thank you.'

'Thank your father,' she replied. 'He's paying for it.'

CHAPTER SIX

IN THE END, Becky never took the flight to Paris. Her last-minute, crazy decision to go to Sydney instead wasn't nearly frightening enough to worry a girl from Brooklyn.

Becky arrived on a fresh December morning and moved into a cheap room in The Rocks, with a tiptoe glimpse of the harbour. The boarding house was run out of a terrace, its three storeys listing dangerously, administered by a red-lipsticked woman with a sharp chin and matching tongue. That afternoon, Becky searched the city for work and secured the post of housemaid at the Australia Hotel.

She was cleaning a room when she stumbled across a classified advertisement in the *Sydney Morning Herald*:

> Governess required for Queensland cattle station to teach 12 yo boy.
> Good home. Apply Mrs G. MacGregor.

She wrote to Mrs MacGregor on a whim, telling her she planned to travel to Brisbane within the month, and asking for the reply to be sent there, *poste restante*. She had only a vague idea where Brisbane was, and she had never heard of Townsville or Barkers Hill.

Just before the end of January, Becky arrived at Roma Street station. A suitcase dangling at the end of one arm and a hat and handbag at the end of the other, she passed through the station searching for the main entrance. By the time she found it, her hair was wet with perspiration and an incessant stream of sweat trickling down her neck.

She glanced at the throng bunched around the door, and wondered why they hadn't left the station. Surely they couldn't all be expecting someone to come and collect them? She recognised some of the people as having just alighted the interstate train, and others had joined them from the suburban lines—schoolchildren wearing straw boaters, miniskirted women, businessmen in short-sleeved shirts—the humidity gluing the fabric close to their bodies, the must of their sweat misting the windows and searing her nostrils. They were as disparate as zoo animals, united only by posture.

She followed their eyes past the glass and then upwards. Beyond the station's portico, the grey sky was accented with incandescent purple. Backlit rolling clouds swept across it like a gigantic ermine stole that someone had tossed out, and was trailing behind.

She heard someone mutter that they were caught there; they really ought to wait it out. Murmured agreement drifted past her ear, the rumble of voices low and expectant.

A jagged fork of white light suddenly pierced the mauve clouds down to the horizon, arcing both left and right, the flash illuminating Becky's upturned face. The air filled with ozone. She felt the boom vibrate through the tiled floor and into the soles of her shoes.

Another lightning bolt exploded overhead, followed by another bang, louder this time. It repeated, the delay between light and sound waning slowly until it disappeared, remaining perfectly synchronous for a while, and then waxing again. She was caught up in a Warholian light-play, except this wasn't *The Velvet Underground*, and there weren't any strobe machines.

Like an audience deferring its applause, uncertain whether the show was truly over, the rain held off after the final flash. Beads of water eventually began to rap against the glass, sliding down it, skewing vision of the outside world till the initial cloudburst blew away. The hailstones that followed peppered the road until they had amassed into icy mounds the length of Roma Street, and then they melted: a gurgling stream, drains spewing muck, people sheltering under folded newspapers, cars wallowing, the spray from their tyres drumming the station's walls. Becky expected to feel some relief once the rain subsided, but the warmth returned, not quite as savage as before, although twice as humid.

A few minutes later, the storm moved on, and all that was left of it was a distant growl and the burble of cascading drains.

She glanced down Roma Street one way and then the other, and guessed that the town centre was probably to her left. She chose that way to walk. Below her a riverbank, glimpsed between squat buildings and trees, but no skyscrapers, not a single one.

Brisbane seemed to be a frontier town, the sum of every architectural style over the last hundred years churned together, and not one she liked. There was nothing to rival the audacity of the Flatiron or the deco elegance of the Chrysler building, and the swampy, mangrove-fringed river had none of the glory of the Hudson. It was uninviting, a town but not a city, yet there was something about the scent of the trees after the rain and the unfamiliarity of the raucous birdsong that she found endearing.

And there was a letter waiting for her at the post office.

Dear Miss Golding, Subject to interview, I am willing to consider you for the position of governess, however I will be unable to reimburse your travel expenses, should you decide not to accept the position, or should I deem you unsuitable…

It was an odd offer of employment, if that was what it was. What it seemed to say to her was, take a roll of the dice, come at your own risk. She rented the smallest room at the Bellevue Hotel for one night, and boarded the next train headed north.

In Townsville, she met up with George Lumley, and his piece-of-rubbish Bedford truck.

In the world's most isolated and least welcoming spot, the Bedford truck was as dead as the bamboo grass that surrounded it. After two hours alone, she would have been deliriously happy if she could have just taken the next flight home. To New York. The familiarity of the grime and the slush and the chill made her yearn for it.

After two hours waiting for George to return, the shadow had swung around to the other side of the ironbark and was gradually stretching east-southeast. It had become too hot for Becky to stay with the truck any longer, so she leaned up against the tree and stared towards the horizon in the direction that George Lumley had gone. She was willing the arrival of a vehicle at any moment to rescue her and the Bedford from frying, along with Mrs Mac-Gregor's groceries, under the clear North Queensland sky.

She tried to sip the water slowly since her throat already felt tight and dry, but she didn't want to drain the bottle yet. What if George never made it to the homestead? She propped the gun against the tree and tried to forget his instructions. She had no intention of shooting anything and there seemed to be nothing around to worry her anyway. She heard the distant call of a crow and scanned the sky, but she couldn't spot where it was. If George wasn't back before nightfall, she planned to retreat to the truck and spend the night there. The front bench seat made the perfect bed for a slight young woman. Mrs MacGregor would have to sacrifice a can or two for her dinner.

The effort of continually swatting the flies trying to crawl into her eyes and up her nose had exhausted her. No one had warned her of their dogged persistence, and she hadn't anticipated it. By late afternoon, it had become oppressively hot and every movement sapped her energy. There wasn't even the suggestion of a breeze. Her mind was clouded by the image of Suzanne window-shopping along the Champs-Élysées. She could have been there with her at that moment, instead of sitting by herself, guarding the entrance to Hades, if lunacy hadn't made her trade a ticket to Paris and almost all of her life savings for one to Sydney.

The thought lingered until something moved in a copse of shrubby wattles a couple of hundred yards away. It was all brilliance and shadows ahead of her. She peered at it, but couldn't make out anything. Perhaps it was a mirage. The heat had rattled what was left of her senses. She waited a minute and decided it was nothing. She had just settled back against the tree when the bushes rustled again. Something was out there.

This time, she leapt up and reached for the rifle. She cradled the butt in the crook of her neck and waited. She didn't know what she was waiting for, any more than she knew what she was going to do with the gun. A few seconds later, she saw a streak of grey as something ran from the bushes, directly at her. She took a step back, shut her eyes and pulled the trigger. The blast pushed her off balance, and the rifle slipped out of her hands. Whatever it was had left a trail in the dirt beside her, and had disappeared up the ironbark.

From somewhere, she heard laughter.

'George Lumley? Thank goodness! That had better be you, or so help me...' She kicked the rifle away and stood up. 'You told me there weren't any crocodiles around here...'

'You Miss Golding? I heard gunfire. You said something about a crocodile? Where did you see the croc?'

Becky shielded her eyes from the sun. The voice and the laughter were unfamiliar. George Lumley was nowhere to be seen. A man in a large hat stood in front of her, his shirt sleeves rolled up to the elbow, tanned arms akimbo, trousers the colour of old straw.

'Yes, I'm Becky Golding,' she replied. She was too tired to smile. 'Have you come to fetch me out of this hellhole?' She looked around. 'Where's your truck?'

'Just up the road. I'm Jim. Jim MacGregor.' He offered his hand, but she didn't take it. 'So, where exactly did you say you saw the croc?'

She turned and pointed to the fork of the tree. 'Up there.'

Jim's gaze followed her gesture. His eyes crinkled up and he laughed. He laughed until he snorted. He laughed until he gulped air and wiped away tears. Eventually, he was able to speak again. 'That's not a croc, Miss Golding. It's a goanna.'

'I don't care what it is, it's an ugly, ancient, dinosaur-creature, and it was running straight at me. I tried to shoot it. It's a shame that I missed it.'

'Goannas aren't ugly. They're really quite sweet once you get to know them, although they do have a bad habit of running up your leg when you least expect it. Sharp nails. Not nice.'

'I have no intention of getting to know them,' she replied, glancing up. The goanna had melted into the tree. 'Are they poisonous?'

'Not if you cook them right,' he chortled. He walked over to the Bedford and looked at the engine. 'The radiator's got a leak. Good thing I brought breakfast.'

'I won't need any breakfast. You see, I won't be staying here one minute longer than necessary.'

Jim took the pack from his back, opened it and slung out the contents. 'The clutch on my car's burned out, so you won't be able to drive that, but, if I get this thing going, d'you reckon you can drive it?'

'Why? Where's George Lumley?'

'The walk took it out of poor old George. I imagine he's enjoying a cold drink right about now. So, do you think you can drive it?'

She peered inside the cabin again. 'I doubt it. I learned on a stick shift, but…' Jim was still smiling. It irritated her. 'Of course I can. At least, I could try.'

'Right. Good. These things can be a bit tricky, especially for a girl. What say, I'll get you going, I'll shift you into second gear and once you've got up some momentum, I'll jump out? Then all you have to do is keep the engine revving and follow the road. The homestead's just about four miles. It'll save the groceries and me another trip, if you're up for it.'

Becky scowled. *A girl?* Her gender was hardly likely to be an impediment, if the lack of a licence wasn't. She could drive, but since there wasn't much need for a car in New York she'd never bothered taking the test. All she said to Jim was *fine*.

She finished off what was left in her water bottle while Jim topped the radiator up with water from a canvas bag slung over his shoulder. She watched him crack a couple of eggs and slip them into the radiator, and then she climbed into the cabin.

The hood banged shut.

'Right,' he said, sliding into the passenger seat next to her. 'Foot on the clutch, and start it up. Don't stop the engine unless you see flames coming out of it.'

The Bedford's engine rumbled into life after the second attempt.

She revved it gently, while Jim shifted it into first gear. 'Now, brake off, accelerate and lift your foot slowly.'

'I can drive, you know,' she hissed and stalled the engine.

'Once more. This time, a bit slower, more accelerator and less ego.'

She tutted, flashing him a censorious look, but her anger only amused him. Eventually, they moved off. With a grind, he coaxed the gear into second, opened the door and hopped out. Becky kept the truck moving forward. She passed Jim's Land Rover stopped in a gully by the side of the road, and kept rolling. It took her a good twenty-five minutes before she crossed the cattle grid. Beyond the grid was a gate secured to a post by a thick chain, *Glenstrae* painted across a wooden board which had been strung from its steel frame. Beyond the gate was a pretty garden and, beyond that, a house made of stone and timber and corrugated iron, and surrounded by wide verandahs.

It was an oasis in a wasteland.

She stopped just before the gate. Like a dying animal, the engine shuddered and stalled. Becky moaned. She stretched out her arms and dusted off the filth that clung to them. After eight gruelling hours, she felt the relief of arrival. As she leapt from the cabin, she caught sight of her face in the mirror. She was grimy and tired, and every part of her that wasn't covered by clothing was sun-scorched. She tried to run her hand through her hair, but it was coarse with dust that her fingers couldn't penetrate.

Jim pulled the Land Rover up behind her, jumped out and unhooked the chain. He swung open the gate. 'Go into the house. I'll take it from here.'

She stumbled along the track, through a second low wire gate and down the path that led across the house garden to the front door. A bower of roses draped across the verandah and the scent filled her with thoughts of Sylvia. As she climbed the steps to the door, a woman appeared, silhouetted against the light streaming from somewhere within the house. She wore a brown paisley dress, belted around her thin waist, dowdy and a little old-fashioned. The illumination made her look other-worldly.

'I'm Mrs MacGregor,' she said, wiping her hands on a tea towel. 'You must be Miss Golding,' she continued without a smile. 'You may call me Mrs MacGregor.'

With a sweep of her arm, she invited her in, but there was nothing welcoming in her stance or in her voice. For an awkward moment, they stood silently looking at one another in the large hallway with rooms leading off it. All the doors were closed.

'No point in me asking you how your journey's been, I suppose. It's best you get any idea that life here is going to be easy over and done with right away. That way, if I offer you the job, you're not left with any illusions about what it's like on a cattle station.' She spoke through tight lips. Becky was uncertain if she did it as an affectation, or to stop the flies from entering her mouth. Her voice grated. 'George Lumley said it's been a bit of a trial getting you here. You look dreadful. I suppose you're tired and thirsty.' It was an observation devoid of sympathy.

Becky had no energy to smile. 'I'd really like to freshen up, if you don't mind, Mrs MacGregor. Would you mind showing me to the powder room?'

Mrs MacGregor frowned. 'Powder room?' she began. 'Oh, yes, you must mean the bathroom. Well, there's a sink and bathtub upstairs, but the toilet's outside, by the stockmen's shower. It's septic, you see.'

Becky didn't see. It was too hard to understand her and she was too drained to take anything in. If she had not been as worn out, she might have asked her to enunciate. She muttered, 'I guess I'll head upstairs first.'

'Follow me,' she said. 'I'll show you where your room and the bath are, and I'll get you a towel. Jim'll bring your port up shortly.'

'Excuse me?' said Becky, fumbling for a meaning. 'My port?'

'Pardon?' Mrs MacGregor replied. 'Oh,' she finally continued, 'I had forgotten that you Americans use different words from the rest of us. Your suitcase. He'll bring up your suitcase.'

Becky followed her along the hallway, up a wooden staircase and towards the back of the house. She opened a door and clicked on the light. A single bulb hanging from the centre of the ceiling at the end of a wire lit up. It had no shade. The bathroom was serviceable, but it was an aesthetic desert: there was no charm about it.

She glimpsed her reflection in the mirror hanging on the wall and started.

'Perhaps you'd like to take a bath.' Mrs MacGregor stepped back into the hallway, opened a cupboard and returned with a towel and a washcloth. 'Not too much water, mind; water's scarce around here. I think you'll find anything else you need in that cupboard.'

She closed the door and Becky listened to the click of her footsteps retreating down the stairs.

The towel was stiff and hard and it clattered to the floor when she tried to drape it over the far end of the bath. She ran the tap until the water reached four inches up the side of the tub. It was clear and hot and she would have loved to have filled it to the brim, but Mrs MacGregor's words clung to her ears. She eased herself in.

It was quiet for barely a minute before she heard Mrs MacGregor's voice rising above that of a man. She was yelling about the state of her groceries and who was going to pay to replace them. George Lumley was arguing vainly, but Becky knew that he didn't stand a chance. Seconds later Mrs MacGregor's voice reached a crescendo. Then there came a smash of broken crockery, as if a teacup had been dropped. After that, nothing.

The nickel tap dripped once every eight seconds, and it took a further second for the plop to find the bathwater. Becky stretched out and looked at the line on her thighs, where her shorts reached. Above the line, her legs were milky and below they were ruby. She kept them and her arms raised just above the water. The water stung everywhere the sun had touched. She soaped herself clean, drank in the billowing steam and silenced her mind.

Her tiny suitcase was already sitting on her bed when she returned to her room. She hadn't packed much; just enough for a few changes of clothes, a couple of dresses and two pairs of shoes. She changed into a shift dress decorated with forget-me-nots, put on some lipstick and tied her damp hair into a ponytail. Then she went downstairs to find Mrs MacGregor.

Mrs MacGregor was waiting in the lounge room, just off the downstairs hallway. The door was ajar and Becky peered around the corner. The older woman was perched on the edge of her chair, knees glued together, legs crossed at the ankles, hands folded in her lap. She wore cat's-eye glasses, even though the fashion had passed years earlier. Perhaps the winds of change blew slowly here. Her thin arms were bare and she wore no jewellery, except for her wedding band. Her lips were shaded scarlet and her eyebrows drawn in pencil. She was probably forty, perhaps a year or two older, but she seemed to be wearing away, even as she sat still.

She looked up. 'Don't just stand there like a shag on a rock; come in!'

Becky tugged at her dress and wished it wasn't quite as short. She sat on a chair opposite Mrs MacGregor, conscious of wanting to appear modest. Until now, she had felt ambivalent about whether she wanted the job, but having made the long trip north, she hoped to stay longer than a single night.

'So why do you want to work here as a governess?'

It was a fair question. Why indeed? *I'm running away from home, can't you tell, and this is about as far as I could go without having to learn a foreign language.* 'Well,' she replied, 'I've been studying education at college. I've always wanted to visit Australia. It seemed an opportunity too good to miss.'

Mrs MacGregor appeared satisfied with her response. 'You would be expected to teach a twelve-year-old all the basic subjects. Do you think you can do that?'

'I'm certain I can, as long as I have a curriculum to follow and the textbooks.'

She sighed. 'What say we give you a three-month trial? If you prove to be satisfactory, we can make it an ongoing arrangement.'

'That sounds fine to me.' She waited for a signal as to what she should do next. 'Shall I…'

Mrs MacGregor sat stony-faced. 'Dinner's in the room down the hall in ten minutes. We all eat dinner together. You can meet Teddy then. He's a lovely boy. You'll like him; everyone does.'

'Yes, Mrs MacGregor,' she replied and stood up. 'Please thank your husband for bringing up my…port.'

She peered at Becky over her glasses. 'My husband?'

'Jim. Mr MacGregor.'

Her laughter was as effusive as anyone else's snigger. 'Why, James isn't my husband, Miss Golding. What on earth gave you that idea? James is the head stockman. He's my husband's nephew.' She shook her head. 'Imagine that!'

If Becky could have blushed she probably would have, but it wasn't in her physiology. 'Yes, ma'am,' she said and left the room. She hadn't warmed to the woman at all, and she was fairly certain that the feeling was reciprocated.

Mrs MacGregor was definitely all cauliflower without any cheese sauce.

*

There wasn't much to like about Edward MacGregor either. He arrived for dinner just after Becky and before anyone else. Teddy had a permanent sneer and more limbs than he knew what to do with. It was as if the proverbial wind change had caught him poking fun at someone, and fixed him like that for the rest of his life. He seemed incapable of smiling, a trait she supposed he'd probably inherited from his mother.

He looked Becky up and down. 'Mum says you're my new teacher,' he muttered, pebble eyes resting on her. 'I didn't like Helen much. I suppose I've never liked any of them, so…'

'So? So, you think you won't like me either?' The words hadn't left her lips when Jim MacGregor strode in and clipped Teddy behind the ear.

'Manners, Edward,' he said, sitting opposite Becky.

He had bathed since she'd last seen him, and changed into a starched shirt and clean navy trousers. He looked much younger without the dirt resting in the tiny creases around his eyes. He wasn't thirty. She understood how ridiculous she must have sounded to Mrs MacGregor.

'Don't mind him,' he continued. 'Ted can be a right little bugger sometimes. Helen was the name of his last governess.'

'Oh,' she replied. 'I'm Becky.' She stuck out her hand. 'I'm pleased to meet you, Teddy.'

'I hate that name.'

She withdrew her hand and smiled nervously. 'And which one is that? Becky or Teddy?'

'Teddy. It makes me sound like a bear.'

She looked at the boy. The comparison was unfortunate. He was lumbering: a bear struggling with a dining chair too small for his bulk. 'Well, what name do you like?'

He didn't answer. He was still fitting himself under the table.

'Let's see. Your mom calls you Teddy. I think Teddy's sweet, but rather young for an almost-teenager, wouldn't you agree?' she remarked. 'I have an idea. How about I call you Mac?'

He pulled his chair in and brightened monetarily. 'I like Mac.' Then the light went out again.

'Then it's a deal. Mac it is.' She glanced towards the doorway and noticed Mrs MacGregor hovering like an apparition, and wondered how long she'd been there and what she'd heard.

'I see you're old friends already,' she spat out, her mouth rigid. She walked around the table to the far end and settled herself there. 'Mr MacGregor had a meeting in town. He rang earlier to say he was running late and we shouldn't wait for him.' She placed a napkin on her lap. 'James usually eats with the men in the other room, but since it's your first night here, he agreed to have dinner with us. It's a special treat.'

Becky wasn't certain whose treat it was, but she had the feeling it wasn't hers. 'That's nice.' She was non-committal, until the silence became unbearable. 'So there's another dining room here?'

'Attached to the kitchen, yes. For the ringers.'

'The ringers?'

'The stockmen, the men who work here. I suppose that you'd probably call them cowboys. You'll learn the language soon enough.'

Becky wondered if she would. She already felt like a spawning salmon which, having taken a leap of faith, had beached itself on a dry riverbed. Footsteps echoed along the hallway and stopped at the door. She looked up, hoping for salvation. She saw a young woman there instead, her face soft, skin burnished, body shapely, with pleasantly rounded hips that promised to fill out further as she aged. She carried gilded platters in each hand, a whisper of a smile stealing across her lips. The warmth of the gold, the excess of food, the gentle light: it was a scene painted by a Dutch master. She placed the food on the table, and then disappeared again.

'That's the cook,' Mrs MacGregor remarked sharply. 'You can meet her tomorrow.'

The platters were stacked with steaks and potatoes, peas and carrots snuggled next to them in a shallow dish separated by a small gap, a no-man's land between the vegetables. On another plate stood a tower of buttered white bread sliced thinly, each slice bisected into triangles.

Mrs MacGregor waited until the cook left. 'Would you say grace, James?' she asked. 'I always think it sounds better coming from a man.'

Becky burned to comment that God didn't listen to the prattle of people, no matter their sex, but she decided that her discourse on theology could come later. She had arrived safely. She was refreshed. There was something to feel grateful for.

Jim took the fork out of Teddy's hand and placed it back on the table. 'Thank you, Lord,' he said, 'for your generous bounty.' He picked up one of the bottles of beer from the table, snapped off the top and poured out a glass. Eyes closed and head tilted, he drank right to the bottom, and paused to refill his glass.

Mrs MacGregor served Teddy first, and then herself. After she had finished, Jim nodded at Becky, passing the platters across the table to her. She picked up a pair of tongs and teased the pieces of meat apart as she searched for the smallest piece. The steaks were uniformly enormous. She placed one onto her plate, and crowded it with vegetables.

Mrs MacGregor's knife scraped against her plate as she cut her meat, and the squeal it made caused Becky to wince. Mrs MacGregor lifted her gaze momentarily, eyes flinty. Unperturbed, she continued sectioning out her meal, as if she was cutting it up to feed an invalid. Once it was all perfectly uniform, she began loading it onto the back of her fork, pressing it down with her knife, gluing it together with a dab of gravy, and posting it into her mouth: minute pieces of meat, pea, carrot, potato, repeated endlessly, in that order.

She paused just long enough to remark, 'You won't believe that Miss Golding mistook you for Donald,' her mouth describing busy circles as she chewed. She continued, 'She asked me to thank my husband for bringing up her port.' She was as close to laughter as a person could be, yet it still came out as a sneer.

Becky stared at her plate. 'It was the heat and the dirt and I was so tired,' she explained. 'I'm sorry, I really didn't mean to insult anyone...'

Jim waved away her apology. 'Don't be. Aside from a couple of decades difference, we probably look enough alike to be uncle and nephew.'

'Well, I suppose I couldn't say, seeing as I haven't met your uncle yet.' She prodded the steak with her fork, slicing off a piece. It was tender, but the prospect of eating an entire steak seemed daunting, and it was too large to bury under the vegetables.

'So, Becky,' said Jim, sensing her discomfort and steering her away from it, 'where are you from exactly?'

'I'm from Brooklyn Heights, exactly,' she replied, severing another morsel. 'Do you know where that is?'

'New York, isn't it?'

She nodded. 'Brooklyn's one of New York City's five boroughs.'

'I can't imagine what it'd be like living there,' he replied. 'I lived in Melbourne for a little while, but the biggest city I've ever visited was Sydney. I'm a bush boy: Sydney made my head spin.'

'Aside from me, there are around seven million people living in New York City and yes, sometimes it can feel like we're all riding the subway at the exact same time. You get used to it pretty quickly. I guess I like the feeling of having people around me most of the time.'

'Well then,' Mrs MacGregor began, 'you better start getting used to your own company.' Her tone was supercilious. 'You'll see very few people around here. If you thought it was going to be a party...'

Becky frowned. 'It'll make a welcome change.' She drenched her steak in a mixture of gravy and tomato sauce and resumed eating.

Mrs MacGregor watched her, her fork loaded and poised. 'There's nothing wrong with your steak, I hope.'

'Oh no, it's fine, it's just so much bigger than I'm used to. Back home, we have steakhouses but most people aren't lucky or rich enough to enjoy quite so much steak in a single meal.'

Mrs MacGregor sniffed. 'The men work hard here and they need good food to keep going, so we eat a lot of meat here. You're a slip of a girl; it might put some flesh on those bones. It might do you some good.'

Becky tried to smile good-naturedly, but her heart wasn't in it. From that point on, she ate as much as she could, said as little as she could get away with, and waited patiently for her ordeal to end.

After dinner, she negotiated the outhouse, and discovered that it was just like any other toilet, except that it was located in a tiny fibro-cement shed in the middle of the yard, with gaps between the panels wide enough to admit a stiff breeze as well as insects. The bedroom was another triumph of function over form. Except for a tiny rug, the floor was bare boards, waxed indifferently a long time ago, so that some of the boards projected a dark, satiny gleam, while others were still bare timber. There was a single set of wooden drawers in one corner, and a chair tucked under a tiny desk. The bed frame was made of painted iron, and the paint was flaking, giving the illusion that it was constantly shedding pale blue dandruff.

She turned down the sheet. The linen was immaculate and smelled vaguely of lavender water. Even though she weighed not much more than a hundred pounds, the wire springs creaked under her as she lay down. She drew the mosquito net around herself, closed her eyes and sank into the mattress, and hardly moved until shards of light passing through the space between the curtains woke her up. She had slept so soundly that the night had passed without her hearing a sound. She picked up her watch from the nightstand. It was a bit after five.

She shut her eyes and tried to steal a little peace, but she couldn't return to the place she was before. A bird was screeching outside to a deafening cackle of butcher birds and miners, and a flock of cockatoos quarrelling in the apex of the flowering gum. The hum of men's voices travelled through the open window into her room and lingered about her ears. From a distance, the whinny of horses floated in the breeze. Someone was frying bacon.

She remembered hearing Jim say that once he'd fixed the Bedford, he would be mending fences with his uncle in the morning, and with someone called Jock. After that, Mrs MacGregor had said something about Becky's first work day, that she should remember that lessons started promptly at nine, and she should take best advantage of the chill of the morning, while Teddy was still fresh. She reflected that if Teddy's freshness disappeared with the rising mercury, it was understandable that by the time dinner rolled around he was moribund.

She felt no urgency about the school day. It was still nearly four hours away. Teddy wasn't an enigma. There was no panic for the day ahead. She stretched, her toes seeking out the cool corners of the bed. The sounds and the scents of dawn hung long in the air, ebbing gently, and only disappearing entirely once they were replaced by something else.

She drifted in and out of sleep for a while, conscious of dogs barking, the clatter of metal outside and the rumble of George Lumley's incessant whine. When even the cool corners of the bed had warmed up, she willed herself awake and peeled back the mosquito net. She sat up and yawned. It seemed a good time to start the day.

CHAPTER SEVEN

Miss Golding hadn't thought about the time she had spent with the MacGregors at Glenstrae station in decades. There had simply been no need for her to.

With the advent of the strange young American, the seduction of a forgotten accent and his seeming interest in her life, memories percolated to the surface, frightening, strange, unsettling, unwelcome. The more she tried to suppress them, the more vividly they returned, scents and sounds, her senses engulfed, until her present and her past became intertwined.

The memories had become a tango, swaying to a pulsating rhythm, their limbs entangled, no longer able to tease themselves apart; her passion to join them was overwhelming. For a while, she could stand back and watch the dance, conscious that they represented a mere shadow of a spent reality, but not reality itself, until they beckoned to her, seducing her with the romance of life observed from a distance, and she lost herself utterly in the dance. She was caught up in a place where time meant nothing, her past and her present nudging each other until the boundary between them was blurred.

She was falling without a parachute. It was glorious and it was terrifying. It was liberating and it was confining.

Had the young man asked her to explain, she couldn't have.

The doctor said that he knew what it was, when no one else did. He told her it was dementia.

Dementia.

It was such an ugly word. The doctor knew nothing. It was simply that she preferred to forget.

There were periods of lucidity, of certainty, when she knew precisely who she was and understood perfectly her circumstances relative to her age, but the more she clutched at it lately, the more it slipped from her grip. She was seventy-something. She was old and her bones ached. She was that white-haired ghost, glimpsed floating in front of the mirror, that sad, ancient facsimile of the woman she used to be. But once that clarity passed, she might have been twenty once more, and beautiful, vibrant and energetic. Or thirty-five and authoritative. Or fifty and wise.

But she was never twenty-two.

She tried to remember why she had bypassed it, perhaps she simply didn't like the alliteration. The chasm between twenty-one and twenty-three had become insurmountable. She had to ask Nellie about it one day.

If she remembered to.

*

Once breakfast was over, Mrs MacGregor stacked the materials for Teddy's lessons on top of a large pine table on the verandah, towards the rear of the house. That done, she disappeared.

There were two chairs positioned on either side of the table, overlooking the bath house and the men's quarters, and beyond that, one of several cattle house yards. It was an uninspiring view. All of the house yards were empty and, since the men had left to mend the fences, apart for the baritone call of a solitary crow from time to time, the rustle of the wind catching the flowering frangipani and wafting the scent across the breadth of the yard, it was quiet.

The cook was a woman called Nellie with a complexion the colour of taffy. She had already begun baking, and the fragrance of her pies drifted past in fits and bursts. It made Becky unexpectedly hungry.

Mrs MacGregor had explained that the radio didn't always work, so Teddy couldn't attend the school of the air. He had to learn his lessons by correspondence. She was too busy to teach him

herself, although Becky suspected the truth was Mrs MacGregor
had neither the inclination nor the ability.

The last governess, she said, had proved to be entirely unsuitable and she'd been shipped back to Melbourne.

Becky wondered whether she'd also prove to be entirely unsuitable. She was surrounded by a heap of lesson outlines, and worksheets printed on a roneo machine in vibrant blue ink and stapled in
the corners. The books stood in piles according to subject: English,
Mathematics, Geography, History and Science. The basics. She
questioned if any of it would be of use to Teddy at all. He was
expected to take over the station, and she suspected that he would
have been far better served by learning skills that he might actually
need.

To distract herself from her groaning stomach, she glanced at
the books and waited for Teddy's arrival. They were almost invari-
ably heavy, hard and brown. She picked one up. *The Jacaranda
Atlas.* She put it down again and breathed out.

A few minutes later, the wire door creaked open and slapped
shut. She listened to the sound of feet dragging along the floorboards, the approach slow and desultory. It had to be Teddy. He
eventually arrived and stood beside the chair opposite her, without
any apparent intention to sit down.

'Good morning, Mac,' she began. 'Did you sleep well?'

Teddy was tousled from head to foot. She imagined the conversation between him and his mother that had wrenched him from
his bed. He was crumpled, shoeless and angry. He grumbled.

'A grunt is not a reply. I will be polite to you and I expect you to
be polite to me in return. Let's try again.'

'Good morning.' The words were poison. He didn't look at her.

It wasn't the most auspicious start. 'Better, but not perfect.
We don't need to be friends,' she said, 'but I want you to do well
in class. If you don't, there will be consequences for both of us.
Understood?'

His head still hung. 'I suppose so.'

'Good. Just so we're clear, I'd like you to call me Becky.' She opened her notebook. 'Take a seat, Mac, and we'll begin.'

After five minutes, it became apparent to Becky that Teddy showed absolutely no aptitude for anything and no interest in acquiring knowledge. He wasn't engaging. Extracting a single word became a struggle. She began to wonder if he was just purposely difficult, or if his problems had some other, darker origin. She put down her pen and snapped shut her notebook.

She moved her chair around next to his. 'What do you like to do?' she ventured.

'I dunno,' he replied. He was using the tip of his finger to trace the outline of a knot in the wood around and around. 'Nothing?' He said it as if he wanted her to challenge him, to pull something unexpected out of her pocket, and prove to him that existence wasn't wasted on him after all.

'I like to listen to music,' she said. 'What about you?'

He shrugged his shoulders. 'I don't know… I think the Beatles are sissies.'

'Have you heard of the Rolling Stones? Now, they're not sissies.'

Teddy finally lifted his head. 'You like the Rolling Stones? I've heard them on the radio.'

Yeah,' she continued. 'They're groovy. Do you have any of their records?'

Teddy shook his head. 'Mum thinks they're a bad influence, so she won't buy me any. She likes Perry Como.'

'Perry Como, huh?' said Becky. 'I have an idea. Provided you're a good student, you do what I say, as long as you're punctual and studious, I'll let you listen to *December's Children*. I picked it up when I was in Brisbane.'

It was true. Although she hadn't had a turntable at the time, she had an expectation that there would be one where she was headed. Besides, the front cover—the insolence of their expressions, Mick's pout as he peered around the corner, Keith's hand-in-pocket leer— they had all spoken to her anarchic soul.

He brightened. 'Can we do it when Mum goes out? She goes for long walks by herself sometimes.'

'Not before you prove yourself worthy of it. It's a reward. And if you're a really quick study, well, who knows?' She glanced around. 'We better get learning before your mom thinks we're up to no good.' She picked up a worksheet on English grammar. 'Let's talk about subjects and predicates for a while, huh?'

For the rest of the morning, they rotated lessons in one hour blocks, with a twenty-minute break halfway. They stopped at twelve-thirty for lunch, and the afternoon lessons ended at three. Becky's head spun by the end of the day and Teddy flopped like a sponge well past saturation. He slumped in the chair and waited for the last lesson to end. She asked herself if it was really possible to do this every day.

At three, the temperature peaked. The breeze that had swept along the verandah for most of the day disappeared and hot air swayed over them like hops in a barn. There was no escape. At two minutes past three, Teddy scooted away with unexplained vigour. Becky straightened the books and moved them into a cupboard leaning against the house. She was confident that something must have seeped into his brain. The truce they'd brokered had held. If he stayed as attentive for the rest of the week, the Rolling Stones would be on the agenda.

Becky remained at the table until she'd corrected Teddy's worksheets and then she returned to her room. Someone had turned on the fan. It was making sluggish sweeps of the ceiling and some of the warm air flowed down to her. It wasn't much, but the gentle draught it created was welcome. She picked up her case, placed it on top of the drawers and opened it. She had been too tired to unpack last night. She divided her clothes into small stacks and put them away in the drawers. She wished she'd brought more with her; she'd have to find the laundry before it was too late to wash her clothes and hang them out to dry.

She looked out of her window—it shared the same aspect as the school table on the verandah—and she watched the men returning to their quarters. One of them was Jim. Even from a distance, she could tell that he was exhausted. She expected that he'd have a room in the house, but she observed him entering the ringers' quarters and coming out again a few minutes later, naked to the waist, a towel tied around his hips, clean clothes draped over his arm. She noticed the breadth of his shoulders and how the muscles under his brown skin rippled as he moved. He stepped over the gravel in bare feet without discomfort, towards the hut which housed the men's shower, and then disappeared inside for a while.

She watched him emerge again, this time in shorts and flip-flops, still bare-chested, his wet hair slicked back. To her surprise he stopped halfway, looked up with a smile and waved at her. She hadn't counted on being seen. She gasped and turned away. The heat was stifling. She needed ice, or water, or something—anything—to cool her down.

She picked up her dirty clothes and galloped down the stairs and out the back door towards the toilet, and eventually found the laundry tucked away behind it. Inside the shed stood a huge concrete trough, a copper, a mangle and a washing machine lined up like a progressive display of laundering through the ages. She didn't have enough to justify using the machine, so she selected the trough. She filled a plastic basin with warm water and put it in the trough, picked up the bar of carbolic soap and made a lather. Satisfied that her clothes were now relatively clean, even if they smelled like tar, she rinsed them off and hung them outside, on the T-post clothesline.

Jim stepped out of the ringers' quarters just as she was returning to the house. She saw him from the corner of her eye but she pretended that she hadn't noticed him and kept walking.

'Hello there!' he called out.

She feigned surprise. 'Oh, hello, Jim. I didn't see you there. I was just…doing my…'

'Washing?' He was smiling.

'Yes. Were you able to fix George Lumley's truck?'

'We got him going all right. He's long gone.'

'And the fences?'

'Yep, yep. Can't fix the lot in a day, but fixed the worst of them.'

'Well,' she said, 'seems like you're a real Mr Fix-It.'

He looked confused.

She bit her lip. 'I mean, you're the guy who saves the maiden stuck in the bush and then gets the truck going again. A knight in shining armour.' It wasn't getting any better. She wished she'd just said a breezy hello and left it at that.

'I'm no hero, if that's what you're saying.'

'What?' she stammered. 'No...yes...of course. Well, you're a hero to me.' Her brain was telling her to stop talking, but the message simply wasn't getting through to her mouth. She heard herself say, 'I could have died out there, except for you.'

He was shaking his head. 'I don't know about that.'

'No, of course not. No, not died, exactly. But seriously dehydrated.' She glanced at her watch. 'My, it is getting late. I'd better go inside. Nice catching up with you, Jim. Goodbye.' She felt his eyes follow her as she walked back into the house. Awkward wasn't the word for their exchange. She'd embarrassed herself twice in under thirty minutes. What was wrong with her?

She sat on her bed and obsessed over the conversation she'd just had for the next hour, running it over and over in her mind until she forced herself to stop. She worked out why it mattered that she felt a fool: there weren't many people around her age at the station and she'd simply hoped they might be friends. That was all. She just wanted someone she could talk to. As it turned out, she couldn't talk to him, because all she could do was blabber.

She changed into a different dress, this time a mini with a white pique collar and swirls in psychedelic colours. She teased the crown of her hair so that it added another four inches to her height, and painted her nails and her lips coral. She looked a tiny bit like Lulu. Except for the nose.

*

Becky was first down to dinner again. Even though the pendant light was on, it took a while for her eyes to adapt to the gloom. She wasn't early, but it seemed to her that by dinnertime, the punctuality that had been so evident in the morning had pretty much disappeared.

Alone in the dining room, she took the time to look around. This was clearly a room for guests. Unlike the bathroom and her bedroom, it was styled for show as much as for usefulness. The table was made of a timber she didn't recognise. It was beautifully figured, and inlaid with a thin banding made of cherrywood. She ran her finger along the banding. It was silken-smooth.

Stacked against the long wall were three additional table leaves, and a sideboard made to match. Ten chairs surrounded the table and another ten stood in pairs along two of the walls. Paintings in ornate, gilt frames hung from the picture rail that encircled the room. The window opposite the door was dressed with drapes of heavy brocade.

Just below the window stood a gilt brass drinks trolley with a marble top, full of bottles of various spirits, and wine decanters that glowed like jewels. Becky lifted up one of the bottles and was reading the label when she heard a man say, 'What's your poison? Can I pour you a drink?'

The voice sounded like Jim's. She spun around, expecting it to be him. Although the man standing in the doorway shared some of his features, he was much older and weather-worn.

She tried to recover her composure. 'You must be Mr MacGregor. I'm the new governess. I'm Becky.' Her expression must have betrayed her surprise. She thrust out her hand.

Mr MacGregor looked at the tiny hand being proffered and clasped it in his own enormous, rough palms. His nails were split. They were worker's hands.

'Sorry I startled you,' he began. 'I'm very pleased to meet you.'

He picked up a bottle of Glenfiddich. 'Would you care to join me?'

'Oh, no, thank you,' she stammered. 'I'm not old enough to drink.'

He grinned. 'What nonsense, girl. If you can swallow, you can drink.'

He picked up two crystal tumblers, placed them on top of the trolley, uncorked the bottle and poured two generous measures in each glass. He handed one to Becky.

Of course, she'd drunk a few times before—she'd even been falling-down drunk once—but it occurred to her that this might be a test of her character. 'But I'm not twenty-one yet,' she protested.

He chortled. 'That's only in pubs, not here. Besides, you sound like a bona fide traveller to me. Liquor laws don't apply to bona fide travellers.' The skin around his eyes wrinkled when he smiled.

She took a sip. The amber liquor was smooth and warm in her mouth, but she didn't much like the taste. She crinkled up her nose as she swallowed.

'Not a fan?'

'No, not really. I'm sorry, Mr MacGregor.' She put down her glass.

'Don't apologise. All the more for me.' He took her glass and tipped the contents into his own, until it was almost full. He took a deep draught of the liquid and sighed. 'Better already.'

The words had barely left his lips when Mrs MacGregor strode into the room with Teddy in her wake. Her face looked like a storm that had set in for the evening. 'I see you've met Miss Golding.'

'Yes. Becky and I were all set to become drinking chums, except that she doesn't like to drink.'

Mrs MacGregor glared at Becky. 'I'm glad to hear it.' Her face conveyed nothing remotely connected to gladness. Her gaze flitted across to the bare table and remained there. 'It's ten past six and the table's not set yet. What's the silly girl doing?'

Teddy drew out one of the chairs and eased himself down at the table expectantly.

'She's probably making sure the men are fed,' replied Mr MacGregor, downing the rest of the whisky, as his wife frowned.

The storm was gathering momentum.

'We,' she said, emphasising the pronoun, 'are always served first. Surely, after two years she's got that through her thick skull.'

'That's a little harsh, isn't it?'

Teddy sniggered.

Mr MacGregor had downed at least four—possibly five—tots of whisky, yet he wasn't slurring. Becky figured that he was well-seasoned. The cataclysm had reached the horizon and she didn't want to be caught in the tumult.

'May I help?' she asked. 'If you tell me where everything's kept, I can lay the table.'

'It's not your job to lay the table,' Mrs MacGregor spat out as she sat down next to Teddy. She took a slender, gold cigarette case from her pocket and a matching vesta box and placed them on the table. 'It's the cook's.'

'Yes, of course. But I really don't mind…' she continued. She bit her lip.

'Fine,' blustered Mrs MacGregor, 'since we pay you to work, you may as well set it.' She waved her hand at the sideboard. 'The crockery and cutlery are in there.'

Becky opened one of the doors, took out five plates and began to lay the table.

'Four of us tonight,' said Mrs MacGregor, crossing her legs and lighting up a cigarette. 'You can put one back.'

'Jim won't be joining us, then?' said Becky, returning the plate and sliding open the cutlery drawer.

'That's right, he won't. Why should he?'

Why should he indeed? Becky had no answer. She positioned the knives and forks on either side of the plates, while Mr MacGregor poured himself another large whisky, calmly crossed the room, slipped the cigarette from his wife's lips and butted it out.

'Not before dinner,' he said. He sat down at the head of the table and took a further swig.

She took out another cigarette and lit up, her eyes trained on Mr MacGregor. 'It calms me down and keeps me in shape,' she said. She inhaled deeply, held in the smoke and then exhaled in his direction.

In turn, he put down his glass, stood up, sauntered towards her, took her cigarette and twisted it between his fingers. He let the tobacco tumble onto her plate. 'Not at the table, I said. This isn't a public bar.'

Nellie bustled through the door at that moment, balancing two large bowls, one on each hip. She glanced at Mrs MacGregor's plate, scurried to the sideboard, put down her load and swapped the dirty plate for a clean one.

Mrs MacGregor glared at Nellie, until she lowered her eyes. Becky understood how she must have felt, and if she could have disappeared with Nellie into the kitchen, or eaten her dinner with the ringers, she would have.

'Dinner is served promptly at six, Nellie. If you value your job, you'd do well to remember that.'

Becky glanced away from Mrs MacGregor and settled on Nellie. She had a round, sweet face and deep-set, dark eyes, which, at that moment, were filling with tears. She glimpsed a line of red welts on Nellie's arms and wondered if they were burns.

'Yes, Mrs MacGregor. Sorry, Mrs MacGregor, it won't happen again.' Nellie hurried away blindly, just before the first tear ran down her cheek.

The rest of dinner was silent and solemn, and interspersed with Mr MacGregor pouring himself endless glasses of whisky until his eyes glazed over. Meanwhile, Mrs MacGregor ate her dinner through clenched lips like a postman delivering letters through a slit in the door. Teddy gobbled his dinner as his mother observed, her gaze atypically soft, his chicken curry vanishing, picking out the raisins and leaving them in an untidy pile by the side of his plate, oblivious to the tension that surrounded him. Becky mused that was probably only because it was so familiar to him.

Mrs MacGregor finished off her meal with a wineglass full of sherry. She rose from the table and teetered away without a word. Becky took it as her cue to leave. She wished Teddy and Mr MacGregor good night and disappeared upstairs.

Twilight melded with the ambient darkness too rapidly, and she found herself missing the lingering sunsets of a New York summer. She switched on the fan to disperse the sodden, stagnant air and opened the window. It was a moonless night and the lamps in the men's quarters glowed below, shimmering halos in the darkness, since no one had bothered to draw the curtains yet.

She watched figures come and go for a while, but the view was unchanging. The house lights reflected white off the post-and-rail which sectioned off the nearest paddock, but beyond that was a black chasm. Past the fence, there was nothing but an endless expanse of gloom with no illumination to punctuate the horizon, no Brooklyn Bridge, no Manhattan skyline twinkling across the river, nothing at all to make the eye stop and linger. The wilderness might have been beautiful in the daylight, but at night, cities came into their own. She craned her neck to stare at the sky. It was sprinkled with stars, some as bright and bold as diamonds, some so fine that it seemed that an iridescent dust had been strewn across the heavens. Without the moon, she had to admit, they shone as radiantly as anything along Broadway and Seventh.

She pulled the curtain, snapped on the light and lay on the bed with a sheet of paper and a pen, trying to compose a letter home which she knew she wasn't ready to send. For a while, she blamed the television blaring from the living room below for not having gone past the solitary phrase: *Dear Mom and Pop*. She played around with *you've probably found the note I left you by now, so you know that I'm not in France* in her mind, but it never made the page.

She stowed the letter away in a drawer and sighed, and lay prone on the bed with her chin cradled in her palms. A few minutes passed before someone turned the television off and a few minutes after that, she heard a glass smash. She turned her head.

Directly below Becky's bedroom was one of the rooms she had not yet been in. She could hear a loud conversation reverberating through the floorboards, but she couldn't quite make out the words. The voices were those of a man and a woman and she was fairly certain that they belonged to the MacGregors. She was tempted to press her ear to the floor and listen in, but to do that seemed churlish, so she tried to ignore them for a while. Moments later, she thought that they might be arguing and, when the smashed glass was joined by another and then yet another, she was in no doubt.

Someone must have opened the window in the room below, or possibly the glass hit and shattered it, but suddenly the voices were crystal clear and there was nothing Becky could do but listen. Mr MacGregor was clearly drunk. In his rage, he was shouting something about a betrayal of trust, and how could she do what she'd done after almost twenty years of marriage. She, in turn, was screeching about how he was never sober enough to be a real husband to her.

'Haven't I always provided for you? I've worked bloody hard to give you everything you asked me for. You have a beautiful house, a child, money to burn—everything a woman could wish for. It's never enough, is it? What more could you possibly want?' Becky heard him say.

'I want to be happy. You're nothing but a drunk and a liar. You,' she cried, 'don't make me happy.'

'Happy?' For a moment there was silence, then a scuffle and a scream. 'Are you happy now?' he shrieked. 'You ungrateful bitch. My only mistake was marrying you and bringing you here. Dad was right: I should have left you in the pub where I found you, serving beers to the scum of Townsville and doing God-knows-what-else to pay the rent. My mistake.'

Becky heard a door slam and Mrs MacGregor wail, 'I hate you,

I hate you, I hate you…' Her voice eventually faded away, drowned out by the chirping of insects.

Their fight had stirred up the cicadas.

CHAPTER EIGHT

IAN STEWART caught up with Chase the following Monday morning after breakfast, and let him know that there would be a final muster before the rainy season. There were stray cattle on the far boundary of the station unaccounted for, and they needed to ride out, check them and brand them. Stewart told him that he was expected to accompany the ringers. On horseback. And that meant that he would have to learn to ride.

'You have a problem with that, son?'

'No sir, Mr Stewart,' Chase replied. Horses held neither mystery nor power. He had been shown how to fence and he fenced. He would be taught how to ride and he'd ride. It was just another part of his job.

'Right, then,' said Stewart, trying in vain to read him. 'I'll meet you in a quarter of an hour. The horse yard next to the shed.'

From where she stood at the kitchen sink, Nellie had a view of the outhouses and, if she rose onto the balls of her feet at the far left and peered, she had a glimpse of the horse yard in the distance. Over breakfast, she overheard Stewart tell Thommo that he would be teaching *the American* how to ride.

Thommo sniggered, 'Americans can't ride. Even the ones that do ride, can't really ride. Not like us, at least. They have those big, ugly, bloody saddles. What's wrong with a stock saddle, anyway? Maybe it's because their arses are so big, they'd probably just swallow a stock saddle up and you'd never get it out again. I reckon a western saddle would be like sitting in a frigging armchair. The only good thing about them is that you couldn't fall off it if you tried.'

'Well,' Stewart replied, 'you and Westie'll be out at Ten-Mile Paddock all day. By the time you get back, I reckon I'll have broken him in. He'll ride out with you to Stillwater Paddock on Thursday, and help you muster. Some fresh green pick out there, but we need to move the stock off it and let it grow a bit. I expect they'll be all fat and sleek and quiet. It'll be an opportunity for the lad to learn.' He watched Thommo for a moment, and his mouth tightened. 'I want him to learn from you, right, but I don't want any of your bullshit. I hear that you're giving him the run-around and you're gone for good: you'll never work for me again. Now, you will be nice to him, won't you, boys?'

Thommo scowled. New ringers were worse than useless. 'Yeah, all right. But he better be ready by Thursday, or he gets left behind.'

'Don't you bloody dare,' Stewart returned.

Nellie decided that she wanted to watch the riding lesson, but even on her tiptoes, her view through the kitchen window was limited. She had a better idea. The kitchen garden was a lot closer to the horse paddock, and, except for the boy who tended the house yard and did odd jobs around the station, nobody would be likely to notice her there.

She finished off the washing up as quickly as she could, picked up a basket and scuttled towards the raised beds. She peered out from behind the row of immature tomato vines, just as Stewart held a chestnut gelding still for Chase to mount.

Chase's left foot nosed instinctively for the stirrup iron and, with a dancer's grace, he launched himself up and swung onto the saddle. Nellie had only ridden a handful of times and she hadn't liked it much, but Alf had been an outstanding horseman. Alf had been one of the best ringers she'd ever seen. Out of her seventy--five-years-long life, she'd spent nearly twenty years married to him, and she owed him everything she had learned about horses and riding.

Chase settled himself into the saddle and circled the yard twice slowly, his hands soft, balanced and unperturbed. As she watched him nudge the gelding effortlessly from a walk into a canter and then into a gallop—all in a matter of minutes—she found it impossible to believe that he wasn't a seasoned rider. She hadn't sensed subterfuge in him, and there was nothing remotely equestrian in what she was observing. He was simply in his element. He had what they called a natural seat.

She saw Chase glide his hand along the gelding's mane, easing him back to a walk, whispering reassurance in his ear, and she caught her breath. Something had shaken her, but for a moment she couldn't pick what it was.

Stewart wasn't immune either. He placed his hands on his hips as he watched Chase ride and shook his head, his mouth ajar, trapping flies.

Nellie was breathless. She scrambled to the kitchen, jittery, her mind racing. She put the kettle onto the stove to boil and spooned leaves into a little, battered silver teapot. As she waited for the tea to brew, she recalled things she had pushed out of her mind. She sat down, steaming cup in hand, and tried to make sense of what she had seen.

To give it context, she needed to remember. In order to remember, she would have to expose a past secured in a cupboard long ago, along with the rest of the skeletons. There were words to be said, but she had no idea how to say them. However uncomfortable, she would simply have to seek him out and talk to him.

Still, she couldn't help but wonder how much Chase Miller already knew.

CHAPTER NINE

Tʜᴇ ʙᴀʙʏ sitting astride Nellie's pelvis had fallen asleep, rocked by the rhythm of her hips as she sidled between the clotheslines, pegging out clothes. She had perfected the art of hanging washing singlehandedly on the lengths of cable strung between the two T-posts: with four children and barely a year between each one, she'd had a lot of time to practise. And she had yet to turn twenty-five.

Home was the tiny wooden cottage tucked behind the Mac-Gregors' kitchen garden. It was invisible from the track that led to the homestead, and it was only past the fruit trees that it became apparent. A while ago, someone had painted the weatherboards pale blue—hard to miss in a landscape which, fruit trees aside, was dominated by shades of taupe and grey.

Mr MacGregor's grandfather had built the cottage at the end of the century, and it passed down from housekeeper to housekeeper, along with the job. It had a cheerful indigo door and white windows dressed with gingham curtains. With its three rooms, power and running water, it was by far the best home Nellie had ever enjoyed.

When she wasn't working at the homestead, she was busy at home, tending to her children, or scrubbing floors, or reading. She only ever rested at night and she was always up before dawn. She read the bible by lamplight in the morning, before Mr MacGregor started up the generator, and she tried to improve herself every evening, one book at a time. Even when she didn't understand what she was reading, she still read, a tattered Collins Dictionary her companion.

Knowledge, she told her children, was everything.

Education, along with the paleness of her complexion, distinguished Nellie from *the others*, the Aboriginal ringers and their wives, who arrived for a while and then disappeared. She wasn't like them; they hung onto a way of life she didn't fully comprehend. *Full-blood, half-caste, quadroon*: the words appalled her, even though she'd occasionally uttered them herself. These were the words the superintendent applied to Aborigines, as if they were stock to be classified.

She wondered, which of these was she?

She was Aboriginal and then again she wasn't: she slipped simultaneously into both cultures and into neither.

As pale as she was, she scrubbed herself daily from head to toe in an attempt to take away what was left of her colour. Since the superintendent at the mission had said that all people of her race were stupid and lazy by nature, she had to prove herself clever and industrious. It was a thankless task. No matter how hard she tried, the superintendent then, and Mrs MacGregor now, still found fault with everything she did.

Her husband, like her mother, considered themselves pure, both Murri, although they weren't from the same clan. He was *Ngaro*. Except that they had both been at the Palm Island mission, they would never have met.

She encountered Alf Turner at the Palm Island State School, but since they each lived in separate children's dormitories, they rarely saw each other. Whenever she did see him, he'd grin and slip a trinket into her hand as she passed. His talent lay in making something beautiful out of nothing. He showered her with gifts—necklaces and bracelets fashioned out of shells and string, extraordinary sculptures carved out of flotsam—but her mother knocked them out of her hands. A single, purposeful step and they shattered underfoot, ground back into dust beneath her toe.

She said, 'You trust your family, and no one else. This fella is not your skin.'

So it seemed to Nellie to be the right thing to do to marry Alf the moment she was old enough.

Blood ties and loyalty were only important to those who held with tradition. Tribes and kin, Nellie eschewed them. She moved without a mob. Her clan had a membership of two. Family could never be to her what it was to her mother.

One day, Nellie spoke up. She pointed out the irony that her mother placed such emphasis on kinship, when she herself had had a white man's child. Her mother's eyes were as dark and as unfathomable as the open sea at night. She let them settle on Nellie's face for a while, heavy-lidded, unblinking, emotionless. Her calmness was unsettling. Then, as a cat might pounce on a mouse, she struck Nellie with an open hand. She had never laid a finger on her before.

The slap stung more than just Nellie's cheek. Her eyes watered, although not from the pain.

'Don't you ever say that to me again, Nellie. You're a stupid girl. You don't know nothing.' She turned her broad back and trudged away.

Nellie's tears slipped out silently; she was too overwhelmed to sob.

Years later, after her mother fell ill, one of the women from her clan visited them. There was an unspoken antipathy between mother and daughter, even with her mother barely lucid. The woman sensed it.

'You know why your mum went to Palm Island, don't you?'

'No, Aunty. But she must have done something very bad to be sent there.'

'She done nothing bad, Nellie. Your mum, she was always a good girl; respectful of the ways of the white man and the laws of the black man, your mum was. But back in them days, she was a pretty child.' She snorted. 'We was all pretty and young back then,' she reminisced, absent of nostalgia, as if it were nothing more than a fact to be shared.

'Your grandparents, they had to move away with your mum to find themselves work in town. They left the young ones with us, and they walked off with everything they owned on their backs.

I remember waving at them when they left.' She sniffed loudly, drew the phlegm into the back of her throat and swallowed. Unhurried, she continued, 'When they got there, they built themselves a humpy out of wood and bark and tin, just outside of town, by the bend in the river. They thought they was safe there, and that nobody would see them.

'One day a whitefella—' she faltered. 'Malone, that's what his name was, well, he seen your mum in town and he followed her all the way back to the humpy. Your grandparents were at work, and your mum was there all by herself. Well, that Malone fella, he was real bad. He come up on your mum from behind and he grabbed her. She screamed and screamed, but there was no one there to hear her. More she screamed, she reckoned the more he laughed at her, and then he spit in her face. He hit her with his fists until she couldn't see. She couldn't run away, so she just cried and waited for him to kill her. Except that he never killed her. He pushed her down on the floor and he done things to her, you know? She didn't know about them things, coz she was a girl and she never had a man. After he done his business and he left, she cleaned herself up in the river, but she reckoned his smell stayed with her for days. She didn't want to tell nobody coz she was ashamed, but everyone knew. Her face got all swollen up.

'When your grandmother seen her, she cursed that Malone fella, you know, and I reckon it worked, coz we heard that he burned to death in his bed smoking a cigarette not too long after. Stupid bugger. Didn't do anyone much good, but, coz it was already too late. She already got you inside her. Back in them days, a girl couldn't have a baby and bring it up. Back in them days, a girl had to go to the mission to bring up her baby.'

Nellie hung onto her words. Her heart ached until it sucked the breath from her lungs and left her mind reeling. It was too late to tell her mother that she understood, that she was sorry, that she regretted the rage she'd inflicted upon her. She comprehended the reason for the perpetual sadness in her mother's eyes, and the laughter she never heard. She didn't know how to feel about herself. Except for Malone, she would never have been born. Because of Malone, she and her mother had to endure the worst conditions, the hardest work and the random punishments of a cruel superintendent.

Eventually, she and Alf left Palm Island to work on the stations, and a little later a baby arrived, but marriage was a concept that neither of them had ever seen in practice. Alf understood nothing about commitment. He came and went as he pleased. It wasn't his fault. Even though he'd been raised in a white-dominated community, he was a blackfella, and they were nomadic in nature. Nellie understood. She had read all about it in a book. Nellie didn't know how to be a wife any more than Alf knew how to be a husband. The babies came too soon and too often.

During the muster, Alf usually picked up work, and sometimes he was gone for weeks, even months. When he wasn't around, Nellie had Ernie, the station hand, to help her around the homestead and to keep an eye on her babies. It all worked out fine. She was content to work sixteen hours a day, as long as she could hope for a better life for them.

She knew the graziers were meant to send all of the wages for their Aboriginal workers to the government, but the Mac-Gregors never did. Nellie always received her wages in full, just like everyone else on the station: the MacGregors were fair about that. Mr MacGregor told her once when he was drunk that that he had never forgotten his roots. The MacGregors had been the children of the mist, despised and persecuted, but they left that injustice behind them when they sailed from Scotland. They squabbled between themselves, they were intemperate and volatile, hard-living and demanding, but they were always good to work for.

Every day, Nellie thanked God in her prayers. She sat in her parlour surrounded by her books and her babies and revelled in the love when Alf was home, and the peace when he wasn't. She had everything she needed.

Truthfully, she would have done just about anything to keep the cottage and, had Mrs MacGregor asked her to, Nellie probably would have worked for food and board alone. The best thing about her job was that she was central to everything that went on at the station, and she knew most things before everyone else. The best thing about her colour was that it made her invisible to everyone. As far as Mrs MacGregor was concerned, Nellie wasn't really a person: things she might have hidden from anyone else, she didn't bother to conceal from her.

Becky aside, no one realised that Nellie had eyes to see and ears to hear.

*

The next morning dawned much like the previous one, except that by the time Becky woke up, the men had already left the homestead. She wondered how the day was going to greet the night before. It was quiet except for the cockatoos.

Instead of lying in bed for a while, she rose immediately, bathed and dressed. She descended the stairs two at a time and peered down the empty hallway. She could hear a woman humming outside. There was no sign that anything was amiss.

At the back of the house stood the kitchen: a large, square, lime-washed room tacked onto the end of the house. Once again, it was purely functional. A long oak table with turned legs stood in the centre of the room, shelves lined one wall, a refrigerator and two dressers were pushed hard against the other wall, and every piece a mismatch. At the end of a windowless wall was a door leading to an enormous pantry and, beyond that, another door led to the ringers' dining room with its own separate entrance from the outside.

Becky took a loaf out of the bread bin and hacked off two pieces for toast. She located the toaster—an old-fashioned flopper— squeezed in the slices and plugged it into the socket. She placed the kettle on the stove to boil while she looked for the coffee. She was still combing the pantry when Nellie came in.

'What are you looking for? I'll find it for you; you're messing up my shelves.'

'Is there any coffee?' she asked. She'd drunk tea the day before, but only because it was the only beverage she'd been offered. She needed coffee.

'There's instant,' Nellie replied. She pulled out a jar of Pablo instant coffee from behind some large jars of preserves.

'Oh,' she replied, staring glumly at the sombrero on the label. 'I guess that will have to do. I don't suppose you have a percolator?'

Nellie chuckled. 'I'm not sure I've ever seen one and I wouldn't know what to do with it if I did.'

Becky smiled. 'I'll ask Mrs MacGregor if she'll buy one. Once you've tasted real coffee, you'll never go back to the stuff in the jar.'

'I don't expect she'll buy one for you. No one ever drinks coffee here.' She took out the tea caddy and the pot and bustled over to the refrigerator. 'Milk?'

Becky turned off the toaster and flipped open the sides to check her toast. Both slices were scorched on one side but she couldn't be bothered turning them around and waiting for the other side to brown. 'Please. And would you pass me the butter and the jelly?' She eased the slices away from the grille and placed them on her plate.

Nellie frowned. 'Jelly? What...'

'Jam. I mean jam. Jelly's what we call jam in the States.'

'Huh,' Nellie grunted. 'So what do you call jelly, then?'

'Jell-o.'

'Huh. So, why don't you just call jelly jam, like everybody else? It'd save the confusion.'

'We do sometimes.'

'Huh. So what do you call marmalade?'

'Marmalade.'

'Huh.'

They sat at the table opposite each other and sipped their drinks. Becky nibbled her toast and thought that she'd probably better get used to drinking the tea. The coffee was stale and unpalatable.

'Is Mrs MacGregor up yet?' she ventured.

'She went out for a walk an hour ago. Probably won't be back this side of lunchtime. Why?' As Nellie spoke, a man came into the kitchen and poured himself a cup from the teapot. He stirred in spoonful after spoonful of sugar and sat down to drink it, without uttering a word. He was tall and as thin as a reed. He wore moleskin trousers and a checked shirt, sleeves rolled up to the elbows. Although his clothes were superficially grubby, his boots were polished and there was a neat patch on one leg of his moleskins.

Becky wiped her hand on her handkerchief and stretched out her hand. 'I'm Becky. I'm the new governess,' she said.

The man looked up but not at her. He glanced at Nellie.

'That's just Ernie,' she said. 'He does odd jobs around here. He's Aboriginal.'

Ernie extended his arm reluctantly and shook hands.

'Pleased to meet you, Ernie,' she said. 'You're the first Aborigine I've ever met. I'd love to ask you about your people one day.'

Nellie was shaking her head. 'Nup,' she said. 'You're wrong. You met me first.'

Becky swivelled around. She'd noticed the dark eyes, the soft face, the full lips, but she'd never put the features together. Nellie had freckles and her skin wasn't much browner than her own. 'But you don't look...' she began. 'I thought you were Italian.'

'Italian, huh?' she giggled. 'That's because I'm half-caste. My father was Irish. My mum was from the Murri people, just like Ernie.'

'Are there many Aboriginal people working here?'

'Here? On the station, you mean? Besides me and Ernie, there's my husband Alf, but he's away right now. There are some contract ringers. They come and go, so I guess there are two, but that's not counting the other homesteads,' she replied.

'There are other homesteads?'

'For a teacher, you don't know a lot, do you?' said Nellie with a laugh. 'Five MacGregor brothers, five homesteads: Glenstrae, Glen Orchy, Glengyle, Glenlochy and—let me think—Glen Eira. Funny names, hey? Four of them are married and then there's Mr Edward, but we never see him. He lives somewhere down south. He's the eldest. They named Teddy after him.' As Ernie stood up to leave, she took his empty cup to the sink and washed it.

'It was nice meeting you,' Becky called out after him. She watched him retreat from the kitchen silently, and wondered why he looked so uncomfortable.

'Don't mind him,' said Nellie. 'He's not used to strangers.'

She turned her attention back to Nellie. 'I met Mr MacGregor last night. He seemed nice enough.'

'He has his faults but he's a fair man,' she replied. 'He treats everyone like they're the same as him, even the Aboriginal ringers.'

'Well, why shouldn't he? Back home, I supported the civil rights movement. Aside from the superficial, we're all the same.'

Nellie shook her head. 'Not here. Not in this country. Aboriginal people still aren't counted as part of the population. And every state can make its separate laws about us. It's like Aborigines aren't really human.'

'I don't understand...' she muttered.

'Yeah, it's true. You ask me about it one day. There's going to be a whatsaname...a referendum...this year to change all of that. If enough people agree, Aborigines are going to be the same as everyone else. But until then...'

Becky shifted uneasily in her seat. She was about to fill the silence with platitudes, but all she said was, 'People are just people. That's the way I was raised, I guess. For all his faults, seems to me Mr MacGregor feels the same way.'

Nellie guffawed. 'You got an earful of his faults last night.'

'And what about Mrs MacGregor? I don't know what to make of her.'

Nellie paused for a while before she answered. 'She doesn't like me much.' She went into the pantry and returned with a box of flour, after which she took a packet of butter from the refrigerator. She weighed the flour, tipped it into a bowl and began to cut in the butter for shortcrust pastry.

'I don't think she likes anyone much, herself included. You're right about one thing, Nellie: they sure can argue.'

'Oh, Mrs MacGregor likes some better than others. As for them fighting, you'll hear a bit of that from time to time. Once, I heard Mr MacGregor threaten to kill her.'

'Kill her? Why?'

Nellie grimaced. She whipped around and lowered her voice. 'Word was going around that she was seeing one of the ringers. She was having, you know, an affair.'

'What!' Becky sat open-mouthed. 'And do you think it's true?' She couldn't imagine Mrs MacGregor sharing a piece of cake, let alone someone's bed.

'Well, she often goes off on her own without a word to anyone, and comes back before Mr MacGregor. The thing is, she never goes out alone when they're mustering. She's always at home during the muster and she's as cross as two sticks.'

'Do you know who she's having an affair with?'

'I have my suspicions, but I'll keep them to myself for now.'

Becky dusted the last of the toast crumbs from her hands onto her plate and stood up. There was probably another explanation. 'School in an hour. I'd better get ready.'

'Remember,' said Nellie, rubbing the butter into the flour with her fingertips, 'you didn't hear it from me.'

'That secret's safe with me. Besides, I don't know anyone except you and her, and I'm sure not going to tell Mr MacGregor about it.'

'If I were you I'd keep my wits about me, Becky,' she added. 'Don't go being too friendly. You're a pretty young girl in a station full of hungry men. Some of them blokes are no good. They'll be sniffing around you like you were a bitch in heat in no time.'

Becky was aghast. 'Thanks,' she replied apprehensively. 'I will.'

*

School went exactly according to the lesson outline: together they studied percentages in mathematics and medieval Europe in history. Teddy was struggling. Becky could see that he was mostly making an honest effort to learn, but she suspected that she was trying to build a brick house on a straw foundation. Every so often, his concentration waned and his eyes turned glassy, until she snapped him with a sheet of paper she'd concertinaed into a fan. From time to time, she had the sensation that she was being observed, but she couldn't see anyone when she glanced around.

Just before three, Mrs MacGregor approached from the far end of the verandah and waited for the day's final lesson to end. Becky realised that she could barely look at her. She was ashamed that the tale of Mrs MacGregor's dalliance weighed so heavily on her mind. When she did finally gaze at her, she found herself scrutinising Mrs MacGregor for a hair out of place, a twisted stocking or a mismatched earring. She tried to let the thought go, but it returned in waves.

'I want to speak to you in the lounge room in five minutes,' said Mrs MacGregor. Her lips were ever so slightly misshapen, as if there was an unpleasant taste in her mouth.

Becky felt unwell. Mrs MacGregor had had that effect on her since they'd met. 'May I ask what it is about?'

'No, you may not.' She turned on her heel and left.

There was nothing warm about the woman. Becky sighed, and packed up the books. She nipped upstairs to her room for a moment to change, before descending to the lounge for the meeting. Through the window, she glimpsed Jim outside the ringers' quarters, rolling a cigarette. As she watched, Mrs MacGregor approached him, took something out of the pocket of her dress and handed it to him. Her hand brushed his forearm and remained there for a moment.

If there was any conversation, she couldn't hear it. Becky strained her eyes to see what it was that she had given him. Whatever it was, it fit comfortably into his palm. He glanced at it and slid it into his pocket. He slipped the cigarette between his lips, lit it and blew a smoke ring as Mrs MacGregor retreated into the house. Her mind racing, Becky changed into shorts and a sleeveless blouse and rushed back downstairs.

Mrs MacGregor was already seated in her favourite chair when she entered the room. Becky scrutinised her face for a clue but, as ever, the older woman gave away nothing.

'Sit down,' she ordered, her lips barely moving.

As Becky perched on the sofa, Mrs MacGregor remarked, 'I heard that you had breakfast with the cook this morning.'

Becky wondered what else she'd heard. 'I ate breakfast in the kitchen and Nellie was there, that's true. Was that wrong of me?'

'No, of course not, but you American girls think differently from us. I just wanted you to know that we keep our place in the household, here. I am the mistress of the house and you are the governess. We both belong upstairs but we are not equal, you and me, you understand? It doesn't do anyone any good if you go social-ising with the workers. The governess should not mingle with the cook.'

Becky pursed her lips. When everything was telling her to quit and hightail it upstairs, she shifted back into her chair and unclasped her hands.

'Back home,' she began, 'I worked in a deli while I was in college.' She shifted her weight, pausing for dramatic effect. 'Mr Cohen's deli on Hanover Street. It was very busy and it was hard work. Now, Mr Cohen was a very nice man, but he was old-fashioned. At work, we had to call the customers ma'am and sir, and that was the right thing to do. Sometimes we saw those same customers outside of work but I never called them ma'am and sir, and if Mr Cohen had asked me to, I would have told him that it was none of his business what I did on my own time.' She took a deep breath. 'You pay me to teach Teddy, and I work for you from nine till five every day, but I eat breakfast on my own time. I chose to eat breakfast with Nellie this morning. Respectfully, Mrs MacGregor, I don't understand why that's any concern of yours.'

Life returned to Mrs MacGregor's face. She was as pale and drawn as ever, but her mouth was contorted with anger. 'You're wrong, Miss Golding. Everything that happens in this house is my concern.' She spat out the words. 'You may have your breakfast in the kitchen—we all do that—but I forbid you to chat with the cook. The cook has two children and a good-for-nothing husband. She needs her job, even if you don't.'

'Is that all?' she asked, syrupy-superior in her knowledge that Mrs MacGregor really knew nothing about Nellie, not even the number of children she had.

'And one more thing. If I ever see you hit Teddy again, I'll have you charged with assault.'

Becky was aghast. 'Hit Teddy? When did I ever hit Teddy?'

'I saw you hit him with that thing in your hand.'

'The piece of paper? He was daydreaming and I tapped him with a folded-up piece of paper.'

'I don't know what it was, but whatever it was it must stop. Even a piece of paper can take out an eye.'

Becky drew in a sharp breath. 'I understand perfectly, Mrs MacGregor,' she said after a few seconds, 'and it's fine and dandy. No chatting to the staff, no pieces of paper, no loud noises, nothing. And if Teddy wants to sleep through every class, I shan't stop him. Thank you for pointing out the error of my ways. Since it's still during my work hours and I have lessons to prepare, I'll go up to my room.'

Mrs MacGregor's eyes followed her as she stood up and strode towards the door. 'Don't you think for a minute that your inso-lence,' she said, 'has gone unnoticed.'

Becky ran upstairs and was tempted to slam her bedroom door, but this wasn't her house and Mrs MacGregor was certainly not her mother. She sat on her bed, reconsidering her options while her stomach performed somersaults. She told herself that Mrs MacGregor was just a mean, angry woman, and anyone who'd take up with her had to be crazy. Did she want to go home? She had spent almost every penny she had just getting there and, besides, she wasn't a quitter. She knew she hadn't done anything wrong.

It was too soon to admit defeat.

CHAPTER TEN

Becky skipped breakfast altogether the next few mornings, and her first week at the station finally ended with a whimper. At last, it was Saturday. After a quick wash, she put on a shirt, a pair of trousers and boots that had just arrived from town, courtesy of George Lumley and his truck.

Mr MacGregor had warned her that she really needed to invest in a good pair of boots, if she intended to wander much beyond the house garden. He'd taken it upon himself to ring the order through to Beck's Shoe Emporium in Barkers Hill a couple of days before, on the understanding that he'd gradually deduct the cost from her wages over the next month. Had Mrs MacGregor done such a thing, she would have called it interfering and she'd have been furious, but Mr MacGregor was different. He seemed to do it out of genuine concern for her welfare and she responded well to the gentle resignation in his eyes.

The boots arrived in a box wrapped in brown paper and secured with string. She left the package under the bed where she'd stowed it the night before, until the morning. Then she slipped off the string, tore open the paper, and opened the box. The boots nestled together snugly in the tissue paper like a pair of brown puppies. She lifted them out and turned them over in her hands. The leather was smooth as butter, supple across the vamp and stiff across the toes. Someone had taken the time to tag the leather: *R.M. Williams*. From the tapering toe to the heel made of stacked leather, they were beautiful. They were meant to be functional.

She lifted one to her nose and sniffed the warm, smoky-sweet perfume of the leather. She didn't know why the scent made her think immediately of Jim. She slid her foot into the shaft, wriggled her toes along the insole and stood up. She glanced down and smiled. They supported her feet perfectly.

She glanced at the clock: it wasn't quite five-thirty. The generator was silent although the birds were already chirping and squawking. Back home, she'd still be fast asleep, oblivious to the wailing sirens and the noise of a city waking up to another late winter's day but then, back home, there were so many things to do in the city that, despite her father's filthy looks, she rarely came home before midnight. In contrast, there wasn't much activity at the station once the sun set. There was a single black-and-white television in the house, and the very thought of having to share it with Teddy and his parents made her nervous. Once she'd prepared the following day's class, she was usually in bed by eight-thirty and she was up around five.

She crept out of her room, avoiding as many of the creaking floorboards as she could recall. Her new boots clattered as she descended the stairs, but by then she'd passed the bedrooms and she didn't care. The morning sun filtered through the panes set into the front door and partially down the hallway, but the rest of the house was still dark.

She swung open the back door, squinting until her eyes adjusted to the light. She scurried along the verandah, bounded down the stairs and past the ringers' quarters. She had never gone any further than the cattle yard behind the sheds, but a wilderness extended far beyond it, unfolding slowly as she progressed, stretching to the horizon.

A dirt track easily wide enough for a truck led away from the house and wound its way through the low scrub. She opened the gate that isolated the homestead and the outbuildings from the rest of the station, passed through it, and closed it again. She followed the track until the house entirely disappeared from view, obscured by a line of sandalwood, and then another twenty minutes further. She was utterly alone, surrounded by spindly brigalow trees and spiny bluestem grasses. Above her was a cloudless sky and the dusty track rolled beneath her feet. She closed her eyes and drank in the elation of utter isolation until it flooded her soul. Impulsively, she threw her arms up and gulped in the air. It was tepid and sticky, but a little of the misery of the preceding week drained from her with each breath.

After a while, she took up again until the track broadened to a clearing beyond the trees. It split there and disappeared in opposite directions, each track worn by the constant scrape of tyres. Narrow pathways barely as wide as her hips snaked between the sharp grasses to the left and right, but she couldn't decide which track to follow. She sat on a rock and listened to the breeze, until she heard the grind of footsteps. Her seclusion shattered, she shot up and began scampering back, aware that whoever was approaching had longer legs than she did. There was nothing timid about the gait; she was certain it belonged to a man.

'Hello there!' he called out.

She didn't recognise the voice, so she kept moving forward.

'Hello, I said,' he repeated.

'Can't stop,' she replied, her voice wobbling, 'I'm in a hurry.' She felt a hand on her shoulder and spun around.

'Nobody's ever in a hurry out here. Who are you?' he asked.

She didn't like the way his lip curled or the snigger in his voice. He wore a canvas hat with a broad rim, sweat-stained, a faecal shade between brown and grey. He was filthy all the way down to the fraying hem of his trousers.

'I'm the governess at Glenstrae station. Who are you?'

He eyed her from head to toe. 'You're that new American girl I heard about, aren't you? What are you doing all alone out here?'

She figured she was probably only about a mile away from the homestead, although the isolation made it feel ten. She tried to shrug his hand off her shoulder. 'Who said I was alone?'

The man's eyes flitted around. 'Well, I don't see anyone else here with you.'

'Maybe I am and maybe I'm not. Pardon me, but how is that any of your concern?'

He shifted weight but didn't move. He parted his lips, a glint of yellowed teeth revealed. His hand weighed heavily on her shoulder.

'You don't know these parts. Just looking out for you, that's all.'

'Thank you, I appreciate it. If you'd be so kind as to remove your hand from my shoulder, I'll keep going, Mr....'

He took his hand away. 'The name's Reilly. I work for the MacGregors. You ever feel lonely and need a friend, you can look me up. Reilly. Bet I see you around.' He sauntered off, turning his head once before disappearing, just to gawp.

Nellie's words thundered in her ears. She crouched down and waited for a while, listening for the crunch of Reilly's boots to fade away. She took a deep breath, stood up and continued along the track back to the homestead.

The generator was pounding, but there was no sign of anyone in the yard and even the kitchen was empty. A little after eight, the kettle rumbled on the stove and, although Becky was still craving coffee, she made herself some tea instead. Now that she'd received her first pay, she'd put some of it aside and call in an order for some real coffee and a real pot to brew it in.

A few sips later, she'd shrugged off Reilly and was scanning the previous edition of the *Australian Women's Weekly*, wondering why almost every recipe she read featured prunes, and whether there something collectively wrong with the country's digestive system. She flicked through the articles until she reached the story of the week—something about an old woman doing her grocery shopping along Main Street—*blah, blah, blah*. She let it slip from her fingers.

It wasn't *The New Yorker*.

She was pouring herself a second cup when the wire door opened. She caught her breath as Teddy walked in. She had a growing list of people she didn't want to see, but he wasn't on it.

'I saw you come in,' he mumbled. His hands fiddled while he scratched around for words. Finally, he said, 'You know how you said that we were going to listen to your record?'

Becky smiled. 'I promised you, didn't I? When do you think would be the best time?'

'The record player's in the lounge but Mum hates pop music. Dad's gone out somewhere and Mum's getting dressed up, so maybe we could listen to it after she leaves the house?'

She was already nodding. 'Let me know when that is,' she returned, watching Teddy leave the kitchen. She didn't mind listening to the Rolling Stones on a Saturday morning when she had nothing else to do.

She was still stirring sugar into her tea when she heard the wire door slap against the frame again. She called out, 'Did you forget something?' without turning to see who it was. She heard a voice reply, 'Not that I can remember,' and immediately placed it as Jim MacGregor's. She turned to check if she was right.

Jim stood in the doorway, neat as a pin, hair smoothed back, arms akimbo. 'I'd kill for a cup of tea. D'you reckon you could squeeze another cup out of that pot?'

She took a cup from the dresser and drained the pot into it. 'It's very strong, I'm afraid. I'd let you have mine, except that I already drank from the cup. I'm more coffee than tea, but you take what you can get, I suppose.'

'No worries,' he replied, 'I like strong tea.' He glanced at the syrupy brown liquid which filled just over half of the cup. He topped it up with boiled water from the kettle, stirred in three teaspoons of sugar and pulled out a chair. 'Mind if I sit here?'

'Why,' she replied coolly, 'should I mind?' He smelled like freshly mown grass, slick in a rustic way. She looked him up and down. 'Going somewhere?'

He sipped his tea before he answered. 'Going into town with Glad.'

'Glad?' said Becky. 'Who or what is Glad?'

'Glad is my uncle's wife: the fair lady, Gladys MacGregor, the Eliza Doolittle of Glenstrae station. You've met her.'

'Mrs MacGregor?' she responded. 'Gladys? I had no idea that

that was her name.' She was in the hunt for information. 'So, you'll be away with your Aunt Gladys all day?'

'She'd hate to hear anyone call her my Aunt Gladys; it would make her feel so old. But yes, we'll be away for the rest of the day and some of the night, I'm hoping.'

His reply made Becky splutter. She added up two and two. There was nothing wrong with her grasp of simple arithmetic: it was little wonder that Nellie hadn't told her that the stockman Mrs MacGregor was seeing was Jim MacGregor. How could she? It was obviously something that everyone knew but no one openly talked about, rather like the raging argument between the MacGregors that had kept Becky awake half the night. She wondered what type of man had an affair with his uncle's wife. She glanced at Jim as he drank his tea; she understood what Mrs MacGregor saw in him, but what on earth did he see in her?

She finished up her tea and washed out her cup, leaving it upended on the drain board. She wiped her hands dry on her shorts. She was intending to leave the kitchen, but there was something she was aching to say first. She turned around. 'Everyone knows, you know.'

Jim looked up at her, his brows knitted. 'Everyone knows what?' he asked.

'About your aunt. And may I say that it's not very polite talking about her as you do. It's one thing to run around behind your uncle's back and something else altogether to flaunt it publicly.'

Jim's face fell. He put down his cup. 'So you've heard about that already.'

'Yes. Since I'm Teddy's governess and his welfare is my business, I hope you don't mind me saying that I think it's disgraceful and it must stop.'

'It's not that easy, you see...' he began.

'But I don't see. People make choices. They choose to marry. They may not choose who they fall in love with, but, once they have, they sure as heck have a choice about what they do about it.'

Jim chuckled. 'Haven't you ever done something you never thought you'd do and, by the time you've had the time to think about it, it's already too late?'

'Well, no,' she replied. 'As I see things, you could do something about it now before it gets out of hand and hurts Teddy.'

'Me? Why me?'

'Excuse me? So, you don't want to take any responsibility for this sorry mess? You should be ashamed. There's an innocent child in the middle of this; think about that, if you dare. Now,' she blustered, turning on her heel, 'you be sure to have yourself a nice day!'

She utterly missed the confusion on his face. As she left, she told herself she'd handled that well, and her wisdom shared would surely make him see Gladys MacGregor through different eyes.

*

Of all the songs on *December's Children (And Everybody's)*, Teddy liked *Route 66* best. He and Becky listened to the album twice all the way through, and that song once again. She didn't want to tell him that the song was older than she was. For the first time since she'd arrived, Becky watched Teddy break into a grin and act as a child should.

'I get my kicks...' He danced to fractured lyrics, jiggling and whipping his legs around until he fell exhausted on the couch.

It may have been Saturday, but on Monday Becky would have to resume her role as Teddy's educator, so she kept her distance, tapping vaguely along to the song and holding him back when he tried to dance with her. Somewhere, she'd read that students and teachers could be friendly, but they could never be friends. It made perfect sense, and she was going to stick to that rule, even if Teddy seemed intent on breaking it. When he brushed against her once too often, she lifted the record off the turntable and slipped it into its cover.

That's enough,' she said. She dismissed his protests with a hush.

'That's enough for now,' she repeated. 'If you behave, I'll see if I can buy *Aftermath* somewhere.' She lowered her voice. 'And by the way, Mac, just so you know, it's not polite to touch girls on the chest.'

He stopped in his tracks: her remark turned him into stone. He glared at the floor for a while, but when his hands closed into fists, she wondered if he was going to hit her. He turned away abruptly and stomped out of the room. Becky sighed and followed him out, but she had no intention of tempering her message. He'd have to sort that out for himself.

She climbed the stairs back to her room and took out the letter she had started writing earlier that week. It still read: *Dear Mom and Pop.* Except for the garlands of roses around the border, the rest of the page was blank. She picked up the pen and added, *I am well and I'm writing you this letter from Australia. I suppose you're shocked and maybe a little disappointed that I didn't go to Paris like I said I would...* She'd put off writing to them for almost two months. The rest of the words trickled out like bore water filling a horse trough. An hour later, she'd finished. She reread the letter. It was perfect: one page full of apology, one of justification and the third of hopeful ambition. She tore the pages away from the pad, folded them carefully in half, slipped them into a matching pink envelope and addressed it. She put it on her desk to give to Mr MacGregor to post on Monday.

The rest of the day crept along. There wasn't much happening around the homestead either. *It's as slow as molasses on a January day in Yonkers,* she thought. She napped, watched the ringers smoking outside their quarters, two horses cavorting in the paddock and then she rearranged her clothes. At three, she rummaged through the bookshelves that lined one wall of Mr MacGregor's office and selected a book. She returned to her room with a first edition copy of *Casino Royale* which, from the look of it, nobody had ever opened.

She woke up an hour later with a fly buzzing on the windowsill and the book on her face, having barely read ten pages. It was always the same. The moment she lay down to read anything—textbook or novel—she fell asleep, no matter how racy the contents. She pushed James Bond to one side, stretched out and sat up. It was unbearably hot in the bedroom and she had to find something more productive to do with her time.

Downstairs, the house was still empty and dark and sealed up against the sun, but, despite everything, the sting of the afternoon had begun to fill the rooms. Becky longed for a breeze through the open door, but there was none. She stepped out onto the verandah but it was just as still. The birds had disappeared and the horses were too tired to whinny.

Nellie's singing soared out of the kitchen, her voice cutting through the airless afternoon like a scythe. Becky felt immediately and irresistibly drawn to it, not because she loved Gershwin— which she did, like any New Yorker—but because of the purity of her pitch and the pathos in her intonation.

Nellie stopped singing the moment she walked into the kitchen.

'Oh no,' Becky protested, 'don't stop on account of me. Please keep going. It sounded so beautiful.'

She lowered her eyes. 'I can't sing in front of people.' She seemed more circumspect than the last time they'd spoken. Becky turned to leave. 'I'm not chasing you out of the kitchen, or nothing,' she added, peeling an onion. 'You don't have to leave, Miss Golding.'

'Well, I don't want to disturb you. And please, please call me Becky.'

'I can't. Mrs MacGregor says I have to call you Miss Golding and not to be too familiar or else…' her voice trailed off.

'Or else?'

'Never mind.'

Becky was angry, but she didn't want it to show. 'Or else? You can tell me. What did she say?'

'Or else I'll lose my job and I can't afford to lose my job. I've got four mouths to feed.' She waved the knife in the air as she spoke. 'You think we're alone and who'll hear us talking? Let me tell you, around here, even the snakes have got big, waggling ears.'

'That's okay. I had nothing much to do and I just thought I'd like to help out, but I don't want you to be punished for talking to me, so I'll go,' Becky stammered.

'Wait,' said Nellie as she sliced the onion in half before chopping it. 'There is something you could do for me. I sent that good-for-nothing Ernie out a half an hour ago to pick me some tomatoes and he hasn't come back yet. I'm starting to think he's gone walkabout. Do you think you could go to the veggie patch and bring me back three ripe tomatoes, Miss Golding? Big ones, please.'

'Sure, I can do that. But you'll have to point me in the right direction.'

Nellie gestured towards the far wall. 'It's on the other side of this,' she said. 'And if you see Ernie you can tell him that Nellie's still waiting, and she says thanks for nothing.'

Behind the far side of the kitchen were a series of garden beds each about one and a half yards wide and three long. Beyond that was a copse of fruit trees set out in neat rows. The beds were filled with vines and shrubs, few of which Becky recognised. That wasn't because they were unusual (although some of them were), but because she'd rarely seen fruit or vegetables before they arrived at the store. Since she almost never shopped for food, she'd rarely seen them there either.

Although she didn't know what tomato vines looked like, she recognised the fruit hanging off them. Glistening in the daylight, they looked like Christmas baubles. She eliminated some of the fruit for being too small, and then she eliminated others for being imperfect. Finally she plucked three large, sound orbs. The tomatoes were warm and the scent of the vine where the fruit had come away was heady, sweet and green. She cradled the fruit in her shirt and headed back to the kitchen.

As she turned the corner, she spotted Teddy walking towards the horse paddock. Whether it was the way he walked or mere imagination, it somehow felt wrong. He clutched something under his arm, but she couldn't tell exactly what it was. From afar, it appeared to be a stick. She carried the tomatoes towards the kitchen, turning back to take a second look, but Teddy had already disappeared.

*

Donald MacGregor had returned early from visiting Glen Orchy station and was sitting in the kitchen waiting for the kettle to boil, when Becky came in with the tomatoes. He hadn't gone for a social visit: there was sweat and dust in his hair and in every pore of his face. She nodded at him as she swept past and laid the fruit out on the table next to Nellie. Then she sat down, glad for some company at last.

Nellie glanced at the tomatoes and grinned. 'You really did pick three of the best ones. Thank you, Miss Golding.' She wiped her hands on her apron and turned one of them over in her hand. 'They're so full of the sun,' she said, 'they shine.'

Mr MacGregor tipped the water out of the kettle and into the pot, stirred it, and set it aside. 'Shall I get you a cup?' he asked.

'No, thank you,' Becky replied, swatting a fly. The door and all the windows were open, yet it was even more oppressive inside the kitchen than it was outside. The idea of drinking hot tea seemed absurd. She poured herself a glass of water instead and took a sip. She had barely swallowed it when one of the horses squealed.

Mr MacGregor sprang from his chair. 'What the... If some-one's caused that, I'll flog the living daylights...' The rest of the sentence was lost, as he darted through the door.

Becky followed him out and watched him running in the same direction as Teddy had walked. She heard a crack, and watched one of the horses spring straight up into the air. The other horse was still bucking and rearing.

On the far side of the paddock, Teddy glimpsed his father, leapt off the fence rail, dropped his air rifle and ran.

Mr MacGregor followed him, yelling and cursing. 'Stop! Come back here, you little bastard!'

Teddy weaved and dodged as he ran, but he was at a disadvantage. His legs were shorter than his father's, he carried far too much weight and he clearly wasn't used to exercise. Within seconds, his father had caught up to him. He dived forward, wrapped his arms around the boy and felled him onto his back. Then he flipped him over, held him down with one hand and began slapping the top of his thighs with his other, open hand, over and over. When Teddy thrashed about, he sat on his legs and forced him down.

'You never, ever hurt a horse, you hear me? Never ever!' he yelled, slapping Teddy in time with each word. 'Shooting them with an air rifle? You bloody little bastard.'

'I didn't do it! Get off me!' Teddy sobbed.

'Get off you?' he echoed. 'Get off you? You're a spoiled little shit and I'm ashamed to call you my son.'

'Get off me!' Teddy repeated. 'I didn't do it!'

'Right!'

The two ringers were watching from the side of their quarters, puffing on their cigarettes, nothing on their faces. Still keeping Teddy pinned, he called out to one of them to bring him the air rifle and some rope. Becky watched as Mr MacGregor took the rope in one hand and trussed Teddy up like a Thanksgiving turkey.

'I don't know what's worse,' he muttered, 'that you shot the horses or that you tried to lie to me about it.' He stood up, walked away from him, climbed back over the fence, and aimed the air rifle towards Teddy's buttocks. 'This is going to hurt you a lot more than it hurts me.'

Teddy lay face down in the dirt and whimpered. Mr MacGregor looked down the sight for a while, but he didn't fire. He lowered the rifle and shook his head. Just as Becky was admiring his use of fear and anticipation as punishment, he suddenly took aim again. Then, without warning, he fired once. When Teddy screamed, Mr MacGregor said calmly, 'If this hurts you, it hurts them ten times more.' He bit his lip and watched Teddy gulping for air. 'If you ever, ever shoot anything again without me telling you to,

I'll flog you so hard you'll think back on today and think it was a cuddle.'

He walked back to the boy, bent down and, with a flick of the wrist, the rope fell away.

Teddy leapt up and ran past Becky, tears flooding down his face. He ran into the house, as she watched openmouthed. She heard his feet thudding up the stairs and the door of his bedroom slam shut.

Mr MacGregor walked back, his usually square shoulders rounded, the air rifle dangling from his hand. His face betrayed his weariness. He hadn't enjoyed the punishment, and she swallowed all the words of indignation that had formed on her tongue as she'd watched him aim at the boy. She admitted to herself that Teddy needed to learn a lesson and that this was one she never could have taught him.

She followed Mr MacGregor into the kitchen and pulled out a second cup for herself. As they shared the pot he'd already brewed, she prattled away. She didn't really know or care what she was saying, as long as it filled the silence. At one point, she heard herself tell them that iced tea was a far more refreshing beverage, and she promised to teach Nellie how to make it. It was clear neither he nor Nellie had heard a word she'd said.

Once Mr MacGregor had drained his cup, Becky asked quietly after Teddy. 'Will he be all right?' she ventured.

'He'll be fine; the pellet never even touched him. It's the horses I'm more worried about. You can ruin a good horse doing something like that.' He shook his head. 'He's crying because he copped a hiding and that'll serve as a reminder of what he did wrong for the next few days. Hopefully, the fear I just put into him will last the rest of his life.'

Once he'd finished his second cup of tea, he went out to check the horses, and Becky followed. The only horses she'd ever seen were either in a fair, or trotting along the bridle path in Central Park. She stood well back while Mr MacGregor sat on the fence, lit up a cigarette and studied them for a while.

One of the horses, a large bay stallion, was still skittish. He watched Mr MacGregor nervously from the corner of his eye, ears flicking back and forth. The other, a black gelding, tried to ignore him, but from the twitch of his shoulder muscle, even she could tell that the horse was sore and unhappy.

After he finished his cigarette, Mr MacGregor slid off the fence and ambled across the paddock, his hands in his pockets. Each step was slow and deliberate. The stallion's eyes followed his path, still guarded, but calmer now. The gelding, however, turned away and began to tremble.

Mr MacGregor stopped dead, retreated and climbed back over the fence, shaking his head. 'I paid good money for them,' he muttered. 'If he's ruined them…'

'Can't you mend them?' asked Becky.

'I'll bloody well try. My old dad used to say that with time and patience, you can heal just about any animal.'

'Well, that's good, isn't it?' She meant it as encouragement. 'I mean, you won't have to get rid of them, will you?'

He raised his brows and looked at her. 'There's an awful lot of work to do running a cattle station, without having to fix things that weren't broken to begin with. I'm still pretty damned angry. Teddy's got to learn that he can't hurt animals. Not ever.' He glanced down at his shoe. 'He's done his dash, that boy. You're the third governess in nearly as many months. I bet Mrs MacGregor didn't mention that, eh?'

She shook her head. 'She didn't, but I heard something…'

'If it had been up to me,' he continued, 'he'd have already been in a boarding school. After today, that's exactly where he'll be heading as soon as I can get him in. I'm truly sorry.'

'Oh,' she replied. She began to think. If Teddy was at school, she would be superfluous to requirements. 'I guess you won't be needing me much longer, then?'

'It could take a term before they accept him, so I'd like you to stay for a little while if you don't mind. The question is, would you stay here after what happened today?'

'Well,' she said, 'I'm a very long way from home and I don't have anywhere else to be right now.'

He raised his head. 'Thank you, Miss Golding.' As they walked back towards the house, he added, 'I need a drink after this. Will you join me?' He paused for a moment and smiled faintly. 'That's right, you're not old enough to drink. Well, Mr Walker and I have a meeting scheduled in five minutes in the dining room. If you need me, you know where I'll be.'

'I'll keep that in mind,' she replied.

CHAPTER ELEVEN

B y ten o'clock Mr MacGregor had sunk into an alcoholic stupor, courtesy of his earlier meeting with Johnnie Walker. Becky knew that, not because she'd joined him for that drink he'd promised, but because she'd glanced at the clock and that was the time that he'd stopped talking to himself.

From her room, even with the door shut, she'd caught bits and pieces of his monologue, always loud, mostly slurred, and largely about his unending unhappiness. The greater proportion of his misery emanated from his marriage, and the rest by virtue of being a grazier. He had yelled at God, and when he had finished with that, he had yelled at his long-dead father.

She had forgone dinner for a long bath, and at ten her stomach began to rumble. She'd tried sleeping, but after a day spent napping, she simply wasn't tired. The generator was still whirring below, although the lights in the ringers' quarters were out. With Teddy probably asleep, Mrs MacGregor still absent and Mr MacGregor passed out, Becky decided to go down to the kitchen and find something to eat.

She made herself a roast beef sandwich and, balancing that and a glass of milk on a large plate, she stepped out of the house and into the darkness. There was a crescent moon in the northwestern sky and a scattering of stars around it and everywhere else. The stars were as breathtaking as anything she'd seen in a showcase in Tiffany's. As far as she remembered, they never shone as brightly in the night sky over Brooklyn.

She sat on the bottom step of the verandah and nibbled her sandwich, listening to the noises and basking in the warmth of the night air. She'd imagined that, without the incessant rumble of traffic, the country had to be quieter than the city. She was wrong. The minute Mr MacGregor had fallen asleep, the cicadas had begun chirping. They were louder than crickets by far; they filled her ears with a high-pitched, constant, unmelodious screech. It was maddening. They were deafening. There was no escaping it.

There was nothing to do and nowhere to go. She missed the limitless diversion of life in a city that simply didn't have an off-switch, the familiarity of neighbours on the doorstep and, for the briefest moment, she even missed her family. The distances here were too vast to comprehend, the animals unapologetic killers, and the people strange and self-absorbed. Having finally wriggled free of the river bank, she was now a solitary fish struggling to swim upstream.

She sipped the sweet, creamy milk that had come from one of the cows that morning, and tried to drive the homesickness away. She told herself that she wasn't sentimental, that wasn't her style. It was only at times like these that her thoughts floated back home. Very occasionally, she thought about Clark Somers, although not with any affection. It was her own fault that it had ended. After she'd thought it over, she'd concluded that Carol knew as little about men as she did.

She put the plate and the glass down by her side and exhaled. She missed the intimacy of a relationship, even if she didn't miss Clark. She stood up, wiped the crumbs off her shorts and took the glass and the plate back to the kitchen. She didn't feel inclined to return to an airless room, so she settled on one of the squatters' chairs on the verandah. She extended the wooden stretchers on either side of the canvas seat, sat back and placed one leg on each stretcher. It was as inelegant as a birthing chair, yet comfortable enough, and there was a gentle breeze coming off the river. Moments later, she drifted off to sleep.

She was startled awake by an other-worldly scream. She thought she'd dreamt it, somewhere between consciousness and oblivion. She was too tired to open her eyes. It wasn't real. Moments later, she heard it again. She tried to go back to sleep, but this time, the screams persisted. She struggled to lift her eyelids. Another shriek sent her springing to her feet.

Someone laughed. 'Relax, it's just the curlews,' she heard him say.

'What?' she replied. Her heart was thumping through her chest.

'Bush curlews. They're birds.'

'But I heard someone scream,' she replied. 'I'm sure I did.'

'No. Just curlews.'

The screams repeated and then faded away and Becky sat down as her heartbeat settled. She opened her eyes as wide as she could but it was dark and she only barely detected someone stretched out in the chair next to hers. She had a hunch who.

'Is that you, Jim?' she asked.

'Yep, it's me,' he replied.

She tried to look at her wristwatch, but there wasn't enough light. 'You don't happen to know the time?' she asked.

'Half past two, maybe a little after.'

'But I thought you were in town,' she said, 'with your aunt.'

'I was. Next time, you should come with me,' he replied. 'We could have a lovely night out together,' he replied. 'Some dinner, perhaps.'

'What?' She frowned. She shook the sleep out of her head. 'Are you asking me out on a date?'

He hesitated. 'I suppose I am.'

'And what about Aunt Gladys? What will she think of that?'

'I wouldn't worry about her, if I were you. She doesn't need to know.'

'What? You think I'm just someone you take out to dinner when you have nothing better to do?'

'What are you talking about? Are you still asleep?'

'Maybe.' Her head spun. 'I'm flattered, really I am, but no, I am not interested in having dinner with you in town.'

As she headed back into the house, she heard him say something she couldn't make out. She climbed the stairs to her room and shut the door. She wasn't the kind of girl who would take up with a man capable of having an affair with a married woman. She spent from three o'clock until dawn, tossing in her bed and thinking about exactly that.

*

She must have fallen asleep at some time because, when she woke up next, it was already past nine. Her head throbbed from the heat and having slept too little—or possibly too much—and the awkward position she found herself in.

She stood up and stretched. Through the open window she saw the two ringers leaning against the post smoking outside their quarters and doing nothing. They weren't talking. They weren't even looking at anything. The thing to do on a Sunday morning apparently was nothing at all. Becky watched them resentfully. They were unperturbed by the temperature and the flies. If she had gone down there, she would have felt compelled to fill the void with chatter, swatting every fly within two feet of her. She simply didn't know how to do nothing. She needed to learn it or find something to do on weekends, or she'd drive herself crazy.

She found Nellie in the kitchen baking pumpkin scones for morning tea. Becky sat down without a word, watched her cutting out fat discs of dough and positioning them on the oven tray so that they brushed each other. After tucking the last one into a corner, Nellie placed the tray in the oven, wiped her hands on her apron and turned to Becky.

'You ever eaten scones before?' she asked.

'Scones? Yes, I've had them before only, back home, we call them biscuits,' she replied.

'Huh. So what do you call biscuits, then?'

'We call them cookies.'

'Huh. So, have you ever eaten pumpkin scones before?'

'Mom makes cornmeal biscuits—I mean scones—but I've never had them made out of pumpkin before. We make pumpkins into pie.'

'Huh. Is it savoury, this pumpkin pie?'

'No. It's sweet.'

'Sweet, huh? I don't want to insult you, but you Americans are very strange,' she said. 'You had any breakfast yet, Miss Golding?'

'No, not yet,' Becky replied.

'Good. If you wait fifteen minutes, you can have one of my scones, then. Oh, and there's something in the pantry you might be interested in.'

Becky opened the pantry door and looked around. 'What am I looking for, Nellie?' she called out.

'On the left, middle shelf, near the tea.'

Even before she spotted the box, the aroma of ground coffee drew her to the spot. Adjacent to the old jar of instant coffee was a paper sack, and next to that a Pyrex percolator still in its box. She lifted them up carefully and returned to the table.

'Where did these come from?' she asked.

'I dunno. I got up today and they were there. I suppose Mr MacGregor must have bought them. He's the only one with any money around here.'

Becky smiled. 'Would you like a cup of coffee?'

'Nah. I don't drink the stuff. I tried some once but I didn't like it. It tastes a bit too much like mud for me.'

'Well, I'm brewing up a pot, so in case you change your mind, you only have to ask.'

'Thanks, Miss Golding.'

Fresh out of the oven, Nellie's scones looked like pillows of burnished copper. The coffee had brewed and Becky poured out a cup. The scent made her head spin. She took a draught and sighed. After weeks of stale instant coffee and days of no coffee at all, this was the best start to a day she could imagine.

That afternoon, according to Nellie, everyone was going swimming. 'You can swim, can't you?' she asked.

'Of course I can swim. There are beaches back home, too, you know,' Becky replied. She nibbled the velvety, still warm scone and took a sip of coffee, enjoying the sensation.

'Oh, we're not going to a beach,' she explained, 'we're going to the river. That's where we swim.'

'We have rivers back home, too, only we don't usually swim in them.' She swallowed another mouthful of coffee. 'Pardon me for asking, but don't crocodiles inhabit the rivers around here?'

'Yeah, they do, but Mr MacGregor checks the river all the time. He shoots any croc he sees, so there shouldn't be anything to worry about.'

'So, you're not afraid?'

'Of crocs? Everyone's a little afraid of crocs; you have to be. It's just that crocs don't trouble us much.'

'Us? You mean the Aborigines?'

'Uh huh. You see, crocs don't like the taste.'

Becky couldn't tell if Nellie was serious, so she said nothing.

'Oh, they eat us from time to time if they're desperate, but they'd sooner eat a whitefella any old day. Whitefellas aren't used to a hard life, they're soft. My mum said that the trick is, if you're a blackfella, you always swim with a whitefella,' she chortled. 'That way you're safe. There's enough blackfella in me, I suppose, that I won't be one of the first taken. By the time the croc gets to me, he'll have filled up on whitefella and he won't be hungry anymore.'

Becky glanced at Nellie and assumed that she was joking. She giggled nervously. 'I don't think there's any difference between white people and black people and I'm sure we don't taste any different to a crocodile.'

'Hmm.' Nellie's face hardened. 'You can say that because you're not from here. Blackfellas and whitefellas aren't the same. You know that blackfellas couldn't even vote here till a couple of years ago, right? If we're all the same, how does that happen?'

'It's wrong. They used to do that back home, too. The law was changed there and it'll change here too,' said Becky.

'I dunno. I guess we just have to wait for that referendum. We'll see,' she replied. She studied Becky for a while and eventually smiled. 'I guess, if we really are all the same like you say, then you won't have to be afraid of the crocs.'

'I accept that Mr MacGregor's a crack shot but, somehow, that doesn't make me feel any better,' she replied. 'I'll come along, but I'm not promising you that I'll swim.'

Nellie took Becky's plate away and wiped the table. 'Oh, you'll swim all right. It's too hot just to sit and watch everyone else having fun. You just make sure to be ready and waiting outside at one.'

*

At ten minutes to one, Becky tied her hair in a ponytail, slipped her swimsuit on under her shorts, and packed a towel in a canvas bag. She wasn't certain if Teddy was coming too, but since they hadn't spoken in a day, she thought it was probably best to leave him alone. Instead of going past his room, she skipped down the stairs two at a time.

Outside, Mr MacGregor's Land Rover was idling. She sidled up to it, pressed against the chalky green paint and peered inside. There wasn't enough space for everyone to ride up front in the cab. She peeked at the back of the vehicle. It was already crowded with a tartan metal drinks cooler, towels and baskets, but there was still a little room to spare. It would be tight, but fortunately the ride would be short.

Moments later, Mrs MacGregor materialised, a dismal apparition in a dressing gown, sunglasses and a large hat. She glimpsed Becky, and asked after Mr MacGregor to no one in particular. Donald MacGregor had disappeared. Becky thought about walking away, pretending she hadn't noticed her, but she lingered too long and the opportunity was lost.

Mrs MacGregor made a bee-line for her.

'Since there's no one else within cooee, I guess you'll have to do, Miss Golding,' she muttered. 'When you see Mr MacGregor, tell him that I won't be going swimming. I have a headache and I will be staying behind.'

'And Teddy?' Becky began. 'Teddy's all right?'

She watched Mrs MacGregor's face contort.

'Why shouldn't he be?'

It occurred to her that, having returned so late last night and feeling so poorly today, perhaps Mrs MacGregor hadn't yet heard about yesterday's fracas.

'No reason,' said Becky. 'I was wondering if Teddy was coming with us, that's all.' She bit her lip.

Mrs MacGregor frowned. 'He most certainly is. He has no business staying here. I'm sick and I need all the peace and quiet I can get, today. So, you'll let Mr MacGregor know?'

'Of course, ma'am.'

Mrs MacGregor turned away so abruptly that her gown swirled and wrapped itself around her legs, and the air filled with the scent of gardenias. With a scowl, she tugged it free and left without uttering another word.

Becky knew better than to excuse her rudeness as a symptom of her illness, but she passed the message on to Mr MacGregor as soon as she saw him.

'And thank you for the coffee and the percolator,' she added.

Mr MacGregor blinked at her. 'I'm not sure I understand,' he said.

'The coffee pot you bought? I just wanted to thank you for it.'

'That's nice, but I'm afraid you're thanking the wrong person, Miss Golding,' he replied, handing her a plastic water jug.

Without Mrs MacGregor to occupy the front seat, the plan was that Becky would ride alongside him, with Teddy and Nellie in the back, and everyone else would be walking the thousand yards to the river.

Teddy appeared, silent and morose, precisely at one. He clambered into the back of the Land Rover next to Nellie and sat side-saddle, as she watched and stifled a giggle.

'How are you, Mac?' Becky asked, but he didn't reply.

'You answer when you're asked a question, Edward,' Mr Mac-Gregor snarled. He raised his hand and, if Teddy hadn't been well beyond his reach, Becky thought he probably would have cuffed him behind the ear.

Teddy mumbled that he was okay and fell silent again. Mr MacGregor glanced in the mirror, shook his head, shifted into gear and moved off.

For a few minutes, they followed the same dirt track that Becky had walked along, lurching and dipping with every corrugation. Once or twice, she thought she heard Teddy yelp. She turned to see Nellie hiding a grin behind her hand.

After almost half a mile, they veered left along a secondary track that she hadn't noticed before. The track continued for a while between the brigalows and acacias, and then descended sharply towards a ford in the river. Instead of heading for it, Mr MacGregor turned a quick left. With a clunk of the handbrake, he pulled up just short of the bank.

At the ford, the track led down to the river and out again on the far bank. To the right of the ford, the bank sloped gradually towards the water, creating a beach where Mr MacGregor spread out an old Black Watch blanket. Teddy leapt out of the back of the Land Rover and ran towards the river, stripping off his t-shirt and shorts as he went.

'Oi!' Mr MacGregor yelled gruffly. 'You get straight back here, boy, and help me unload.' When Teddy was beyond earshot, he muttered, 'When will the boy ever learn? How will he ever take care of this place when I'm gone?'

Becky didn't answer. It wasn't necessary. It was clear to her that Teddy had taken twelve years to make and nothing—short of a disaster—was going to break him. She took the water jug, a basket and her canvas bag and plodded down the bank.

Ernie, a few of the ringers and one of the ringer's wives arrived not long after, and within minutes everyone, except Becky, was in the river. She sat on the rug hugging her knees and watching them splashing and diving under the surface like ducks. The men took turns swinging from a tyre tied to the bough of an overhanging willow, and dropping into the murky water. The afternoon sizzle and Nellie's pleas weren't nearly enough to lure her in.

As she sat and watched them play, she felt something brush against the nape of her neck, once, and then once again. She waved whatever it was away with a sweep of her hand. From a distance, she heard the crunch of twigs and, to her right, a shadow grew alongside her. She looked up. It was Jim.

'Hello,' she said awkwardly, shielding her eyes from the sun and adjusting the strap of her swimsuit. 'I didn't know you were coming.'

'Neither did I. So, what are you doing watching from the touch line? Why don't you go in and cool off?'

She glanced at him again and smiled. 'Oh, you know, crocodiles…'

'Crocodiles? You really worry about them, huh? Well, there aren't any around here. And no goannas either.' He pulled off his shirt and undid his belt buckle as he spoke. 'Come on in with me. I promise you'll be safe.' He held out his hand.

'I doubt that,' she said, standing up and peeling off her shorts. She didn't take his hand. Instead, she scurried into the river as his eyes followed her.

It was brown with tannins and as warm as stale tea in the shallows by the bank.

'It's just dandy,' she shouted as Jim bounded past her. 'But just so you know, if I get eaten, I'm holding you responsible.'

He chuckled. 'Crocs don't much like the taste of Americans, you know,' he yelled back at her. 'You can just ask Nellie.'

She laughed. In less than a minute, she had forgotten about the crocodiles and was swimming the breadth of the river breaststroke. The water grew colder and denser as she swam towards the middle of the river, warming up again as she approached the far bank. Beside her, Jim floated on his back, barely moving his wrists, his legs obscured by the murkiness. Even when she lengthened her stroke and kicked away, it took no effort for him to remain next to her. He never even broke the surface. She swam over to the ford and lay with the water barely lapping over her, basking, her arm shielding her eyes.

Jim stretched out beside her, tanned and lean. 'You seemed out of sorts last night. Have you had a better day today?' he asked.

'Tolerably, thank you. At least I had a cup of real coffee for breakfast.'

'And was it good?'

'It was very good…' She suddenly sat upright, as if jolted by a cattle prod. 'Did you—?' She hadn't finished the sentence when he began to smile. 'Was it you?'

'Well, I know how you Americans love your coffee, and you looked like you could do with some, so while I was in town…'

'You thought of me?' She was touched until the vision of Mrs MacGregor in her dressing gown flashed into her thoughts. 'Thank you. You're too kind,' she said too quickly.

He glanced down at his hands. 'It was nothing. I hope you enjoyed it.'

'It was a complete surprise. I hardly expected you to buy me a coffee pot while you're busy enjoying the delights of town.'

He caught the roll of her eyes and it was his turn to sit upright. 'Are you kidding?' He glared at her as if he was trying to work out her meaning. 'The delights…' he stopped abruptly. 'Is that what you think…'

'Well, everyone knows what's going on here.'

'Really? And what do you think is going on here? Exactly.'

'You can't expect me to say it out loud.'

'If you can think it, you can say it. Go right ahead. Let's clear the air, because I can't figure you out. I do you a favour and you accuse me of visiting what? A brothel?'

'No! Did I say that?' Becky's mouth dropped open. 'I meant Mrs MacGregor. You went with her. In fact, you made a point of telling me.' She looked at her toes, sensing Jim's outrage but unable to raise her eyes to counter it.

'Yes, that's right. And so what?' he began. 'You think…' He was absorbed in thought. 'You know what, I don't care what you think.' He swam to the riverbank, climbed out and walked away.

Becky didn't feel like swimming after that. She didn't want to stay there watching Teddy dive bomb from the swinging tyre, and wondering whether he would ever surface again. She waded along the river crossing and back to the other bank, sliding on pebbles worn smooth by the constant flow of water and catching herself when she stumbled. She chided herself for saying too much. He was just looking for friendship. Jim was right; his life was none of her concern. She dried herself with her towel and sat down glumly to wait for the others.

Just as she had settled in, Donald MacGregor approached her. 'You all right?' he asked.

'Yes, thank you,' she replied. 'Would it be okay with you if I walked back now?'

'You want to go back to the homestead? You and Jim had words, hey?'

'Oh no, we barely know each other. It was just a misunderstanding, that's all.' She threw her towel back in her bag and stood up. 'Well, I just thought I'd better let you know I was leaving.'

Mr MacGregor chewed his lip. He checked the diver's watch on his wrist. 'Wait a bit and I'll give you a lift.'

'No need to drive me, honestly. I can walk.'

He was already putting on his trousers. 'Don't be silly, it's too hot for you to walk.'

She was still protesting when he strode away to ask one of the ringers to keep an eye on Teddy.

He started up the Land Rover and swung open the passenger door. 'Come on, Miss Golding, I'll drive you back.'

She turned to look at the others splashing in the river. 'Only if it's not too much trouble.'

'No trouble at all.'

She climbed in beside Mr MacGregor and they sped off. Without a load in the back, the car was nimbler than before, and Becky had to cling on tightly as they swayed and jerked along the track.

He drove like a man possessed. In a matter of minutes, the homestead came into view and not long after, he pulled up quietly behind the ringers' quarters.

'I wouldn't want to wake Her Ladyship,' he said, but there was something peculiar in his delivery that Becky couldn't grasp.

As soon as she stepped out of the car, she heard music blaring from the house: *Love in the afternoon…* Listening to records at full volume seemed an odd thing for a sick woman to do. She glanced across at Mr MacGregor. His face was crimson. He was already marching purposefully towards the house, as she struggled to keep up. She hoped that, if Jim had rushed back from the river, he was listening to the music alone.

CHAPTER TWELVE

Donald MacGregor deviated as he passed the ringers' quarters, and Becky gasped, relieved that she was wrong. The sight of him returning moments later with an axe in his hand, however, made her squeal.

'Please, Mr MacGregor,' she implored. 'Please, Mr MacGregor, don't.'

He didn't seem to hear her. He stomped past her, his left hand clenched, the axe dangling from his right hand, and his eyes fixed on the house. She doubted that he'd even noticed her.

'Think of your family!'

She didn't know why she followed him into the house. Perhaps, she was hoping that her presence would moderate his reaction. Perhaps, she just wanted to catch Jim and Aunt Gladys in the act, so she could justify her cynicism. Either way, she trailed him up the steps, along the verandah, down the hallway and into the living room.

As her eyes adjusted to the dimness of the weak, yellow light, she made out the outline of a man and a woman in an embrace, swaying to the tempo of the song. At first, the couple was oblivious to their presence, caught up in a private moment. It was only when Donald MacGregor raised the axe above his head that they turned and parted.

Becky's gaze fell immediately on Gladys MacGregor, still in her dressing gown. She swung around, lips drawn tight, ready for an argument, shrieking when she sighted the axe. It was then that Becky glimpsed the man. He wasn't Jim. For a while, he was a complete stranger.

The man gawped at Donald MacGregor and darted away, but MacGregor followed him across the room, the axe still raised.

Becky wanted to turn away, but she simply couldn't. Although her heart was pounding in her ears, her feet were glued to the spot.

'I knew it! You bloody bastard, Jock Reilly!' MacGregor shouted, still charging forward. 'You good-for-nothing, two-faced, snake of a man!'

'For mercy's sake, Donald,' screeched Gladys MacGregor, propelling herself forward, 'you can't kill him! Not with me like this… Stop it! Stop it!'

Her words made him wince. He paused momentarily. 'What are you saying? You're not…' he stammered. 'His?'

She lay her hand across her belly, protective, silent.

'You're a whore,' he returned quietly and with sudden restraint, 'and I should have left you in the gutter where I found you.'

Becky recognised the oily man, dressed in his Sunday best and cowering in the living room, as the same man she'd encountered on her walk. It was obvious to her that he and Gladys MacGregor had been drinking, even before she noticed the upended bottles of beer on the side table. Meanwhile, Mr MacGregor had resumed his advance.

She watched as Reilly tried to lunge at him in a feeble attempt to disarm him, but MacGregor had the advantage. His reach was far greater and he was tolerably sober, so he simply shoved him away with his left hand, the axe still poised in his right. Reilly darted left and right, but Donald MacGregor had cornered him as deftly as a cattle dog. Soon, Reilly had exhausted his options. He raised his hands to his face. He was now waiting for the blow.

Donald MacGregor turned slightly, raised the axe high over his head, and thrust it down. It whizzed past Reilly's ear and landed in the centre of the record player barely two inches away from his right hip, as Frank Sinatra sang how the right night had turned out, and then abruptly fell silent. The record player split in half and the blade stuck fast in the cabinet beneath it, while shards of vinyl and plastic rattled to the floor.

He caught Reilly up by the shirt collar and dragged him past

Becky and out of the room, as Gladys MacGregor fell onto the sofa weeping. There was little point in consoling her.

Becky glided past the door and down the hallway, unaware of her arms and legs, as if in a trance. It was only when she found herself on the back verandah, blinded by the sun, that she began to take in what had just happened. She perched on the edge of the squatter's chair and watched Mr MacGregor toss Reilly over the fence and chase him around the paddock with his utility knife poised. It was a French farce.

'I'm going to castrate you, Reilly!' he yelled as Reilly lurched around him in ever decreasing circles. 'I'm going to cut off your balls and you can watch me feed them to the dogs!'

Eventually, Reilly was simply too drunk and too puckered to run. He rocked back and forth on the spot while Mr MacGregor hacked off his pants with the knife. Even from where she sat, Becky could tell that he had wet himself.

Once Reilly's pants were lying around his ankles in a sodden heap, Mr MacGregor calmly returned his knife to the sheath hanging from his belt. With one hand, he held him upright, and then, with the other hand Mr MacGregor made a fist, wound up his arm like a baseball pitcher about to deliver a fastball, and landed a punch on Jock Reilly's jaw. The force of it lifted him off his feet, and flat onto his back.

As she watched Mr MacGregor climb back over the fence, stride across to the Land Rover and drive off towards the river, a parade of fears and thoughts flashed through her mind. She had no idea what any of this meant for her short and eventful career as governess at Glenstrae station, but she wasn't particularly optimistic that there was going to be much of a future there for her.

Whatever happened, of one thing she was certain. She owed Jim MacGregor a huge apology.

*

Things moved pretty quickly for everyone after the events of Sunday afternoon. Jock Reilly had disappeared and no one knew where he'd gone. By Monday, Mr MacGregor was already making enquiries to send Teddy to one of the boarding schools in Townsville. Or Charters Towers, perhaps. Lessons had been suspended for the moment, and Teddy was temperamental and demanding. There was no longer a turntable on which to play the Rolling Stones, and any leverage Becky had enjoyed was lost.

Since term had already started, none of the schools seemed particularly keen to place Teddy. Had Teddy had a gift—academic or athletic—they might have found him a spot, but he had none and his reputation as a difficult child was already well-known. Governesses, it seemed, were connected. For the MacGregors, being Jacobites and therefore Catholic, the two protestant schools were never really in the race. It was to be Abergowrie or Mount Carmel, or if that was impossible, then he'd be shipped down to Melbourne for the remainder of his education. Becky, meanwhile, read *Casino Royale* in her room and waited patiently for someone to tell her what was going on. It seemed to her that she had been forgotten altogether, and left to swim or drown in the maelstrom.

Becky didn't meet Gladys MacGregor again after Sunday, although she did overhear her say, *I'm not going to have the baby taken, no matter what. That would be a mortal sin.*

She also heard Mr MacGregor respond to her curtly, 'Do you think that's a greater or lesser sin than adultery?'

'Oh, so much greater, no question of that! The baby is a living being, Donald. That would be murder.'

'Well, I don't much care what the Pope thinks about it, but I won't be raising another man's bastard.'

Becky heard her moving about the house for the rest of the week, but, from Tuesday on, all discussion about her predicament was muted. Nellie stayed in the kitchen and barely uttered a word, and even Mr MacGregor crept about the house. The ringers were subdued and Ernie went walkabout. It was as if someone had thrown an enormous felt blanket over everything.

On Wednesday morning, Teddy knocked on Becky's door to say goodbye. He shrugged when she asked him where he was going.

'I dunno yet,' he replied. 'Dad and I, we're going to Charters Towers and then Townsville to see the schools I might be going to.'

'Well, goodbye, then,' she replied. On an impulse, she turned away, took the album out of her drawer and handed it to Teddy. 'For when you have a record player again.'

He mumbled, *thank you*, and left. From her room, Becky watched Donald MacGregor place a navy suitcase in the back of the Land Rover. A few minutes later, Teddy climbed in the passenger seat, and they drove away.

She heard Mr MacGregor return late that night, but decided to wait until the next morning to ask what was intended for her. She was in a familiar spot. At home, her father called all the shots, then Clark did, and now Mr MacGregor. Aside from the decision to travel to Australia—and she was questioning the sanity of that—she'd spent a lifetime waiting for a man to dictate the events in her life.

The moment she heard Mr MacGregor stirring, she scurried downstairs. The last few days, she'd skipped breakfast and made herself a sandwich after everyone else was busy doing something else, but today she had awoken with purpose. She needed to have clarity about the future, no matter what. Embarrassed didn't begin to describe how she felt; she would also seek Jim out and put things right before she left.

The sun hadn't quite begun to rise, and the sky over the shadowless yard was nacreous. After the intense heat of the day, there was a pleasant bite to the dawn. She crossed her arms as she hurried outside, the gravel scrunching noisily under her feet, the doors on the outhouses still shut tight, nobody yet afoot, serenity in the isolation. She hadn't become accustomed to an outside toilet, and now it seemed unlikely she'd ever need to. She might have felt nostalgic about it if she hadn't disliked it so intensely.

She scampered back to the kitchen. The scrape of the door as it opened ascended through the thin, morning air and stirred up the birds. She stepped inside and drew it closed as quietly as she could. Nellie hadn't arrived yet and she was alone. The generator wasn't on, so she lit the gas stove and began to brew some coffee by the halo of the flickering flame.

She heard Mr MacGregor start the generator, and he came in soon after. It was clear from his face that he hadn't expected to find her in the kitchen making coffee in the dark.

'Good morning,' he murmured, clicking on the light.

'Good morning,' she replied. 'Coffee?'

He glanced at the teacup he had just pulled out of the dresser, and held it out to be filled.

Becky gave him a startled glance and poured the coffee. 'Say when.'

He didn't, but she stopped pouring before it reached the lip. He retrieved the cup and sweetened it. 'During the war, we had nothing but chicory and coffee essence, you know, and hardly any sugar to sweeten it.' He drew in a slurp. 'It's not tea but it's pleasant all the same.'

'Thank you,' she said, pouring herself a cup. She sat down and drew breath.

He glanced at her. Before she could say anything, he added, 'You're probably wondering about your future here.' He hesitated for a moment. 'With Teddy at school, we won't be needing a governess, Miss Golding.'

'Yes,' she replied, 'that's exactly what I was thinking. I'll leave whenever you say. I'm really sorry, but I'm afraid that I won't be able to pay off my boots, Mr MacGregor.'

'Take them as a gift from me. It's the least I can do.' He lowered his cup. 'I spoke to my brother out at Glen Orchy station. Not quite as big as Glenstrae, but pretty big all the same. He and his wife have a little boy, you see; Bill, his name is. He's barely nine.

They've had a hell of a time finding a teacher for young Bill. I hope you don't mind, but I suggested you for the post. Only if you're interested.'

Her heart leapt. 'Sure, of course I'm interested,' she replied, trying to sound nonchalant.

Mr MacGregor relaxed. 'They'll be very happy to hear that. As soon as you're ready to go, they'll come and get you.'

The swirling waters were finally beginning to calm, and there was even a glimpse of sunshine. 'How about this weekend? Is that too soon?'

'Not at all. I'll let them know.'

He drained his coffee and left just as Nellie arrived. Becky had begun wrestling with the toaster and was prising chunks of carbon off the wire elements when she walked in.

'That was Teddy's doing,' said Nellie, glancing at the toaster. 'Personally, I think it's broken.'

'I'll clean it up and give it a try,' she replied.

'Just as long as you don't electrocute yourself or burn the house down.'

She checked that the wires were still intact, positioned the slices of bread in the toaster and plugged it in. As the wires glowed, the room filled with the smell of burning cheese. She said, 'There, it's fixed.'

'Hmm,' Nellie retorted. 'We'll see.' While Becky took the butter and jam from the refrigerator, she continued, 'You hear about Mrs MacGregor?'

Becky didn't know what to say. 'I heard something,' she began diplomatically. 'Why, what did you hear?'

'I heard Mr MacGregor walked in on her and her boyfriend canoodling. What did I tell you? I knew she was having an affair with Jock Reilly.'

'I wish you'd told me his name. All this time I thought it was Jim MacGregor she was having an affair with.' She opened the toaster and checked the slices.

'Why on earth would you think that? He's her nephew! That's disgusting.'

'Well, you'd mentioned her lover was a ringer, so I figured... And they seemed pretty close...'

'So that's why you've been acting funny around him? I thought he was sweet on you for a while, although I noticed he looked pretty pissed off with you at the river.'

Becky frowned. 'I don't know about that. Anyhow, we were talking about Mrs MacGregor... You were saying?'

'Oh, that's right. I heard she's pregnant. Three months gone. I thought she'd be too old for that, but there you go.' She glanced around the kitchen. 'I think you better check that toast of yours.'

Becky flipped open the sides of the toaster and fanned the smoke away with a tea towel. The bread was russet from smoke. It was warm but it hadn't toasted. She closed the toaster up and switched it back on. 'And?'

'And she's going away to Brisbane to have the baby. I heard she's going to give it up to be adopted. They're trying to keep it all hush-hush, but I reckon everybody knows. When she comes back in a few months, we'll all have to pretend that she went away on holidays, or some such.'

'She's coming back here? After the baby, I mean?'

'Uh huh. The MacGregors don't believe in divorce, no matter what.'

'But what about Reilly?'

'Oh, he's taken off. Don't know where.'

Becky switched off the toaster and took out the bread. It wasn't toasted, but she spread it with butter and jam and ate it anyway. 'You're right, it's broken. You think Mr MacGregor can fix it?'

'Knowing him, he'll try.'

Becky exchanged glances with Nellie and was left pondering whether they were both talking about the same thing.

*

On Friday, Gladys MacGregor—pristine in black high heels, hat and gloves and steel grey suit—placed her suitcase in the back of the Land Rover. Becky watched her slide into the passenger seat alongside Mr MacGregor, and drive away. She was glad that there had been no awkward goodbyes.

The moment the Land Rover disappeared from view, she felt blissful. The pall that had hung about since her arrival had lifted.

*

Donald MacGregor had driven back through the night from taking his wife to the railway station in Townsville, yet he was still up at dawn. By ten o'clock Saturday, Becky had packed everything she owned into her suitcase. She ached to speak to Jim before she left, to clear the air with him and leave things as neatly stowed as she had found them.

Since she had no chance of finding him by sitting alone in her room, she went downstairs and sat on the front verandah, watching the horizon. She brushed her face with the back of her hand. Sweat caught in the fine hairs of her forearm and glistened in the sun like droplets of mercury. The trade-off for the previous day's heat was rising humidity. The air had become damp and heavy, and that made the wait uncomfortable. She had the appearance of someone waiting for a train that was running late.

At eleven, Mr MacGregor came out to tell her that his brother had phoned to say that he was leaving Glen Orchy homestead, and would probably arrive around lunchtime. He remarked, 'You know it's cooler inside the house.'

'I'd prefer to wait here, all the same,' she returned.

As he strode back inside she heard him snort, and shake his head.

The other ringers had ridden out at dawn to bring down some cleanskins on the far side of the river, but Nellie had told her over breakfast that Jim hadn't gone with them. Becky had concluded that he might have been avoiding her, so she took her letter pad out of her suitcase, scribbled a note and sealed it in an envelope.

At eleven-thirty she decided that waiting for Jim to pass by was becoming a fool's errand. She needed to stretch her legs, so she strolled down to the paddock where the horses had been the week before. The stallion and gelding were gone, and in their place stood a mare nuzzling her foal. She hadn't heard anything about the other horses' fate. Perhaps they'd been sold. There was no occasion at Glenstrae for sentimentality: birth and death, grief and joy were faces of the same coin.

She held her breath and listened to the harrumphing birds and the exhaling breeze, all played to the constant thump-thump-thump bass of a Southern Cross generator. As she ambled back to the homestead, she glimpsed a second Land Rover parked next to Mr MacGregor's. This one was battle-scarred, older and world-weary. She glanced up at the house. There were two men seated on the verandah drinking beer.

Mr MacGregor waved the moment he saw her. 'Come and meet your new employer,' he called out.

She trotted up the stairs, doing her best to seem agreeable. The man sitting next to Mr MacGregor was taller and younger, and unmistakably his brother.

'Hello,' the man said, standing up and stretching out his hand. 'Callum MacGregor.'

She put out her hand. 'Pleased to meet you, Mr MacGregor.'

He squeezed her hand so tightly that she thought he'd crushed it. 'Cal, Callum or—if you must—Mr Mac, but never Mr MacGregor. That used to be our father's name and now it belongs wholly to my brother.'

She shifted feet, her hand throbbing. 'Mr MacGregor said that you're the laird of Glen Orchy station.'

'Did you tell the poor lass that, Donald?' He tittered. 'Laird's a bit strong, don't you think?'

'Well,' she remarked. 'I suppose your family owns all of this.'

'Well, we do and we don't. The government sold us the right to graze the land on a very long lease. The family company owns the leasehold for all of the stations except for Glen Eira, and I run one of them. Glen Orchy's not as big as this—a hundred and fifty square mile all up—though we're running about one and a half thousand head on it. Angus Shorthorns, that's what we run.'

Donald MacGregor spotted the furrow across Becky's forehead and chuckled. 'The girl's still learning the language. Cal's station's the size of the boroughs of Queens and Brooklyn combined, and he's got fifteen hundred cross-breed British cattle grazing on it. All together, the family owns the rights to land the size of a small European country. Not bad, when you consider that our grandfather arrived in Australia without a shilling to his name.'

'But don't think it was delivered to us on a silver tray. You stay here long enough, and you'll get to know the land and learn what it takes to do what we do,' said Cal, rubbing a callus on his thumb. 'What I want to know is what brings a lass like you to a place like this? A bit out of your neighbourhood aren't you?'

'I answered an advertisement, I guess,' she replied. 'My parents offered me a vacation, and, without getting into the details, here I am.'

'A bit remote for a vacation, isn't it? I mean, it's not exactly your usual holiday destination. I have to take my hat off to you and your parents.'

'I suppose I'm rather like your grandfather, in a way.'

'What? Running away from his family in Scotland?'

She smiled. 'Something like that.'

The men swigged their beers, legs crossed, leaning back into their chairs, mirror images of one another. A day had been enough to change Donald MacGregor. Perhaps it was the midday beer dulling his sharp edges, or the arrival of his brother, or the absence of his wife and son, or everything in combination. Cal had an open, easy way about him. She couldn't imagine him married to a woman like Gladys, or raising a child like Teddy.

Although she was itching to leave straight away, they stayed for lunch on Donald MacGregor's insistence. Nellie put out a cold collation of meats and salad. After they had cleared lunch, Cal dozed in one of the squatter's chairs. Becky was too anxious to nap. She watched the hands on her wristwatch rotate, her chin in her hands.

He woke up precisely at three, stretched, put on his hat and announced, 'Right, then, we'll be off.'

Becky shook hands with Donald MacGregor, casually passing him the note for Jim, as if it was an afterthought. She wanted to appear cool. 'Would you please see that Jim gets this?'

'Of course,' he replied with a playfulness that made her smart. He peeked at the envelope and hid his smile by clearing his throat. 'I've put your port in the Land Rover already, but there's one more thing,' he said handing her a package. 'Here, take this with you.'

In a cardboard box, cushioned by crumpled newspaper, he had packed the percolator and the coffee.

'Oh no,' she protested. 'I can't accept this.'

'Well, you're the only one who drinks coffee around here. Besides, I get the feeling it was bought for you.'

'If you're sure,' she murmured. 'Thanks for everything, Mr MacGregor.'

He looked sheepish. 'I'm sorry it didn't turn out better for you. No need for goodbyes: I'll see you out at Glen Orchy, anyway.'

Cal was already in the Land Rover, warming up the engine. Becky stowed the box in the back, braced it against her case and climbed into the cabin. She felt nothing but relief as they moved away. A few minutes later they'd passed the gate, crossed the cattle grid and Glenstrae homestead disappeared behind a wall of dust.

CHAPTER THIRTEEN

GLEN ORCHY station was about forty miles away from Glenstrae. It wasn't just distance which isolated one homestead from the other: they were remote in style and substance. Where the homestead at Glenstrae was made of brick and stone and embedded in the landscape, Glen Orchy sat proud of the earth around it, like a shed.

Becky first glimpsed the gable end of the homestead when she opened the gate for Cal MacGregor to drive through. As the Land Rover climbed the last three hundred yards of dirt road curving to the right, the homestead revealed itself foot by foot. It was raised slightly off the bare earth on stumps, with caps of tin on top of each that looked like coolie hats. It had a brief, central wooden staircase, but beyond that it was single storey and modest. Topped by an unusually steep tin roof and surrounded by broad verandahs, the house looked like it was wearing a fedora. It had more than a little humour: she imagined it might pick itself up at any moment and run away. The thought made her smile.

As they drew up in front of the house, a woman appeared at the top of the stairs wearing a striped lemon dress and an apron, frantically tucking her curls back into her ponytail and shielding her eyes from the late afternoon sun. Becky might have mistaken her for the housekeeper if Cal hadn't shouted out to her and called her *love*.

The woman was taller than her, and whippet-slender, but that was where all comparison with Glady MacGregor ended. Her face was tanned and worn.

'Hello,' she yelled as Becky climbed the stairs. 'I'm Sandra.' Her tiny, repetitive movements reminded Becky of a bird. 'We'll have something to drink and then I'll show you the house.'

On a small round table encircled by cane chairs stood a tray with glasses and a jug. Sandra poured out three glasses, plopped a few ice cubes into each glass and handed one of them to Becky.

'Lime cordial,' she said busily. 'I have a tree out back. I make it myself.'

Becky took a sip. She felt saliva pooling. 'It's very refreshing.'

Sandra frowned. 'Not too sour, I hope?'

'Oh no. It's perfect.'

She smiled. 'You think so? I'm glad. I didn't know what Americans drink. I remember reading something about mint juleps in a book by F. Scott Fitzgerald and I've always wanted to try one. Or was that Long Island iced tea?'

'Well, I can't say I've tried either one. The lime cordial tastes just fine.'

Cal had reached the top of the stairs with Becky's suitcase in one hand and the box tucked under his arm. He put them down, took off his hat and wiped the sweat from his face with the back of his hand. He picked up one of the glasses and downed the contents in one go. He refilled the glass and repeated.

'Tired, darl?' asked Sandra.

'Done in. Off for a shower. I'll catch you both later,' he said, kicking off his boots at the door and striding into the house.

Inside, shutters kept the house dark against the sun but offered no barrier from the clamminess. Becky's room was at the far end of a narrow hall that ran down the centre of the house with rooms on either side. Sandra brushed her hand against each door as they went by, calling out the rooms and letting Becky peek inside each one, except the bathroom.

'And,' she said, flinging open the last door, 'this is your bedroom.'

Becky gazed around her room. It was clean and pretty, a thoughtful welcome for a homesick girl. There was a large, bright rug made out of scraps of cord underfoot, a mirrored wardrobe as well as a chest of drawers at one end and a wooden bed, desk and chair standing sentry along the opposite wall. Nothing jarred.

Above her head, the obligatory fan beat furiously. She crossed to the window. This time she had a view of the house paddock.

'It's perfectly lovely,' she said. 'Thank you. And the bathroom?'

'Is down the hall.'

'I'm sorry, I meant to say the lavatory...'

'Outside I'm afraid. Out the back door and first on your left.'

'Oh.'

Sandra scrutinised Becky's face and smiled. 'I remember that look. You'll get used to it pretty quickly.' She paused momentarily. 'I'll let you unpack. Come and find us whenever you're ready. We'll be around.' She left quietly, easing the door shut behind her. Her footsteps were barely discernible, as if she flew over the floorboards rather than walking on them.

She was ethereal and as calm as her house: an unpretentious piety pervaded them both. Unlike Glenstrae, with its unadorned private spaces and its grand reception rooms filled with expensive, antique furniture, here there was no startling incongruity between what strangers saw and the owners' private lives.

For the first time since she'd left America, Becky felt completely at peace.

Half an hour later, she was sitting in one of the cane chairs on the verandah, enjoying the caress of a gentle wind that had risen up, and eating a supper of pastry-encased ground pork, that Sandra called sausage rolls and Sylvia would have called pigs in a blanket. Next to her sat Cal and Sandra's son, a shy, skinny, blond ferret who looked much younger than his years. As Billy chewed, he watched her with his enormous cornflower eyes.

'What's your favourite subject?' she asked him.

He put down his sausage roll. 'History.' After a while he ventured, 'And geography.'

'So,' probed Becky, 'why history, exactly?'

He paused for a while. 'Because I like to learn about the world and how people used to live in the past.'

'And why geography?'

'Because I like to learn about the world and how other people are living now.'

Cal beamed, while Sandra fidgeted, her attention elsewhere. She turned away. 'I didn't want to ask you this before, Becky,' she faltered, 'but sometimes I might need you to lend a hand with things around the station. Do you think you could do that from time to time? When you're not teaching, that is? It's just that sometimes I need a hand cooking for the men. Although, if you prefer, you could help out with the horses or the cattle. Or anything, really. Cal would be happy to teach you whatever you don't already know.'

'Don't you have a cook like Nellie, here?'

She tittered. 'Oh no, we don't need one.'

'Then, you're the cook?'

'I'm it. You might say, I'm the station hand, cook and house-keeper. I do a bit of everything around here.'

'Well,' Becky added, 'I should warn you I can't exactly cook. I watched Mom plenty, but she never taught me and I never learned.'

'Of course,' Sandra resumed, 'you're here as a governess and that's how the company employed you. It's just that I sometimes need help. You can always say when you've had enough.'

For a while, Becky was silent. 'You know, I was loneliest at Glenstrae when there was nothing for me to do.' She stood up, catching the crumbs in her palm before they scattered and sweeping them into her plate. 'I think I'll have an early night,' she said. 'Good night, all.'

The next morning, nobody woke her and she slept in. It was almost nine by the time she dressed and rushed into the kitchen clutching her coffee grounds and her percolator. The kitchen was integrated into the house but, like Glenstrae, it had a second entrance from the yard, so that the ringers would never need to pass through the homestead in order to access it. She glanced around. Scrupulously neat and clean, the kitchen's cupboards and benches were old and idiosyncratic, a million miles from her mother's homogenous, fitted kitchen with its gleaming electric hotplates and state-of-the-art gadgets. This was basic, unambitious, tired.

She brewed the coffee and settled down for her first cup.

Sandra entered a few minutes later. 'That smells nice. I usually make a big spread for the family on Sunday, but I missed the alarm and slept in this morning for the first time since I don't know when. Thank goodness, the ringers are away, or...'

Becky knew how the sentence ended. A smile flitted across her face. 'Would you like me to pour you a cup?'

'That's very kind of you, dear, but I don't think so.' She brewed herself a pot of tea and settled down to a cup, leafing through an old cookbook while Becky nibbled some cereal. Then she stood up, tied her apron around her waist and rubbed her hands together. 'The men will all be back by dinnertime,' she announced. 'Would you care to help me get started?'

As they worked, she told Becky how the MacGregor family ruled this part of North Queensland, but that there was a disconnection between the youngest member of the family, and the eldest.

Becky didn't mind the work, and there was a peculiar satisfaction in watching a bejewelled mountain grow and then cascade out of its enormous enamel bowl. She pushed the vegetables aside. 'You do this every single day?' she asked, stretching out her fingers.

'Not exactly this, but, yes, when the men are here I prepare three meals and two tea breaks every day.'

She flung out, 'Well, I hope they pay you a lot of money to do it,' without a thought.

Sandra put down her knife. 'Oh, no. I can't be paid just for being a housewife. I have to cook for my family anyway, so what are a few extra mouths?' She dragged the enamel dish across the bench and spread the contents out in large trays, ready for the oven. Then she pulled a large ceramic bowl and an egg beater out of a cupboard.

Becky's mind flew elsewhere. It puzzled her that in all the time she was at Glenstrae, she never saw Gladys MacGregor do any work at all. She leaned her back against the sink. 'So, what do you think would happen if you decided you weren't going to cook for the men any longer?'

Sandra crossed to the refrigerator and returned with eggs and milk. 'Oh, but I could never do that.'

There was a placid fatalism to Sandra that Becky yearned to shake out of her. 'Okay, but what if you had to go away, or you couldn't work? The company would have to pay someone to do what you do, wouldn't it, so why shouldn't they pay you? The way I figure it, at the moment, the whole family is getting the benefit of your hard work, when you and Cal should be getting all the benefit.'

Sandra blushed. 'Do you always say what you think?' she asked. 'You know, I really don't feel comfortable talking about this with you.' Eventually, she resumed, 'I have to tell you, you're very forth-right.'

Becky blanched. 'You're right, it isn't my place, I'm sorry.'

She watched the changes in Sandra's expression, and how her eyes latched onto the far wall in an effort to avoid her gaze. She had to learn to pull her punches. She bit her lip, and hoped that she hadn't wrecked any boundaries she couldn't mend. Again.

They measured out the ingredients for the lemon surprise pudding into a row of bowls, ready to mix up and bake once the roast was done. Becky did as she was instructed, and they both remained quiet. Her words had cut a swathe. She didn't know what to say to make amends: she'd said enough—too much—and so she said nothing.

*

When Sandra sat down to drink another cup of tea in a quiet corner, she tried to push Becky's words away, but they persisted.

Edward MacGregor was the laird and sole proprietor of Glen Eira, the only station that wasn't leased. He never dirtied his hands, but he made all the important decisions from his triple-storey townhouse in Toorak fifteen hundred miles south, as far removed from the cattle station as it was possible to be. He was the absentee landlord, directing the company remotely, contributing nothing, and yet keeping a share of its profits for himself. Edward had always been self-indulgent, his decisions questionable, yet the family company remained omnipotent and indivisible. Sandra had never reflected much on it. Now, it made her seethe.

A long time ago, a rumour had swirled that Malcolm Mac-Gregor's wife, Margaret, out at Glenlochy station, received a regular housekeeper's wage for doing nothing more than what Sandra did for free. She'd always assumed that feeding the men was her obligation as a grazier's wife, and she was content enough. Nobody needed to hear her troubles, so she didn't broadcast them: she was raised to do her duty without grumbling. All it had taken was a casual conversation to rob her of her happy complacency. She knew that she could never return to her bliss. Now that she'd questioned why the family hadn't just paid her for her work from the outset, emotion rose in her throat and threatened to choke her. She determined to talk to Cal about it that evening.

But that decision didn't sit comfortably with her for the rest of the day. It wasn't as if he was a difficult man, but he was obstinate and he was proud. Cal loved her—she was confident of that—but the family's welfare was paramount. He was loyal to the point of self-sacrifice. Quietly, she knew it wasn't reciprocated. What she'd always previously thought of as a quality, she now considered a frailty.

After dinner, once everyone else had left the dining room, Sandra and Cal wandered into the living room. She took a decanter out of the Tantalus cabinet, filled his glass and sat on the couch next to him. He was partial to a port or two after dinner and, unlike whisky, it left him pleasantly agreeable. She was banking on that.

'How are we doing, Cal?' she ventured, tucking her feet under her and snuggling into the cushion. 'You never tell me and I never ask.'

'What?' His eyes glided away from her face and settled on the painting of an English landscape on the opposite wall.

She felt like waving her arm at him. 'Moneywise. How are we doing?'

He glanced back at her and smiled. 'You know you never need to worry your tiny head about things like that, Sandra. Don't I always provide for you?'

'Of course you do. I know I don't have to worry, but something's been playing on my mind all the same,' she began.

He reached into his pocket, feeling for his wallet. 'Whatever it is, within reason, of course you can have it.'

Sandra frowned. She was already shaking her head. 'I probably should have raised this with you years ago, but I've been thinking about Margaret getting a housekeeper's wage and me not. Why's that, do you suppose?'

'She asked for it, I guess.' He sipped his port and settled back into his seat. 'What's brought up this nonsense?'

'Nothing,' she sniffled. 'What I do around here is as valuable as what Margaret and Nellie do, isn't it?'

'You keep a clean house and you can cook rings around both of them, love, you know that.'

'Then,' she said, drawing a deep breath. 'I want to be paid for it. I deserve it.'

'Right.' He put down his glass. 'That's enough of that, Sandra. I don't know who's been in your ear, but we're not like Malcolm and Margaret. We don't go begging for money. Besides, we don't need it that much. If you want a new dress...'

'Nonsense, it's not about silly dresses. I was thinking that we could use it to buy a few cattle, instead of the family keeping it.'

The muscle in his jaw pulsated as he clenched his teeth. 'I won't discuss it any further. I'm bloody tired and I want some peace.'

'Yes, of course you do. I'll say one more thing and then I'll let it drop, I promise, dear. Maybe if the family valued me enough to pay me what I deserve, then you could use that money to get yourself the help you need so you wouldn't have to be so tired all the time. It's not like the company couldn't afford to pay me, and Billy and I would love to spend more time with you.' She stood up. 'Now, I've said my piece and I'll say no more.'

She strode out of the room and back into the kitchen. She glanced at the plates piled high by the sink and sighed. There weren't any more of them than usual, yet the effort required to wash them seemed to have increased exponentially.

From the cupboard below the sink she took out a cake of yellow soap in a wire cage and placed it in the bowl. Then she slipped on a pair of pink rubber gloves, plugged the bowl and turned on the taps.

CHAPTER FOURTEEN

Becky settled into a routine at Glen Orchy far quicker than she had at Glenstrae. Billy was nothing at all like his cousin; he was quietly studious and painfully shy. He was diligent and systematic, but easily overwhelmed. If she asked him one question, he responded quickly and confidently. If she asked two or three in quick succession, he was flummoxed. Whenever he was overcome, he retreated into himself and set his eyes on her like a frightened pup. Quite rarely, he'd chatter to her freely about history, drifting from the emperors of Rome, to the Britons and across the rampaging Scots. Then, in his next breath he retold his uncle's war stories.

At night, she'd heard that he read the World Book Encyclopedia voraciously. He hung on her every word all day, eager to gain knowledge. Once he had learned to trust her, and she had learned to stagger the lessons, he was a sponge. In return, she rewarded him with her New York tales and by coaxing him a little bit further than the syllabus required. She trusted that he might be destined for great things, that education might liberate him from the hundred and fifty square miles that made up his world. But even if he never left the station, she was certain that his curiosity would set him free.

After lessons finished for the day, Becky sought out things to do. Work broke the tedium of isolation, and she mostly wound up in the kitchen, although not necessarily from choice. She'd begun to learn to cook, recording recipes in her notebook. She was relieved beyond words that her relationship with Sandra had remained effortless and cordial.

Seven weeks flew past before she received the response to her letter home. It came as an aerogram, the red and blue banding a bit tattered, her name printed carefully on the front: she recognised the writing immediately. She slit the flimsy, gummed paper and opened it flat.

Dear Rebecca, it began, *I hope you never have to suffer the anguish your disappearance has caused your father and me. I wonder what we could have possibly done to you and your brother to make you both so inconsiderate?*

The rest of the letter was filled with guilt and regret in equal measures and Becky see-sawed between sympathy and indignation as she read. She learned that Sam was now an entrenched draft-dodger, while Clark Somers quietly accepted his duty. Sylvia wrote that Clark visited the Goldings shortly after Becky left. He particularly wanted to see her to let her know he'd soon be undergoing basic training before being shipped out to Vietnam. He told Sylvia he was sorry the way things had ended and he hoped that Becky would be gracious enough to forgive him and write to him when she had the time and inclination.

Perhaps you might do the right thing for once, and write the poor boy. Clark is such a lovely young man, after all...

Sylvia wrote that she left him with the impression that Becky was still in Paris.

I think of you out there in the Australian wilderness and I despair. Never forget that all that heat and sun is so aging. It will ruin your skin. You don't want to have wrinkles on your face before you're thirty. Or married, at least. Do they sell Pond's out there or should I post you some? She finished off, *If you have any kindness left, you'll write me again soon.*

She folded up the letter and slid it in the drawer, under her sweaters. Of course, Sylvia had struck a chord: she always did. Obviously, Sylvia had already mapped out a future with Clark that Becky was determined to have no part of. She was like that: no matter how mean someone was to her, she forgave and forgot everything the moment they apologised. Unlike Becky, she never held a grudge. Still, Becky decided that she would write to Clark, not because her mother wanted her to, but rather in a display of magnanimous indifference. It was, after all, her patriotic duty.'

The next morning, she awoke to the sound of raised voices. After listening for a while, she realised that they weren't raised in anger; it was simply a robust discussion and the sound of men preparing for a day's work.

She opened her eyes and glanced around. Even though there was enough light to navigate through the room, it wasn't quite dawn yet. She shook lethargy out of her head and listened to the voices and the clink of metal. In the cacophony, she detected Cal saying something about being let down.

'Talk in town is that a lot of the Aboriginal ringers have been put off, now that the graziers have to pay them real money.'

'Hmm,' Cal replied. 'I'd have them all come work for me, if I could afford it. I bet they never thought for a minute that winning the referendum was going to cost them their jobs, poor buggers.' He snorted loudly. 'I expected to have the help of two ringers this morning, and all I have is you. No offence, mate, but I desperately need another pair of hands.'

Becky leapt up. She pulled on a t-shirt and jeans, slipped on her boots and bounded through the door before she'd even brushed her hair. Cal still had his hands on his hips when she threw open the back door.

'Today is a correction day,' she spluttered, 'and there's nothing for me to do. Maybe I can help you today?'

Both men turned to look at her, and the ringer sniggered into his palm.

She shuffled nervously. 'Only, I overheard you saying that you were a pair of hands short and I thought that maybe I could lend you mine.'

Cal lowered his head and raised a hand to his face to disguise a smile. 'That's very kind of you, Becky, but what we're doing is hard work, even for a man, and you're—well—you're just a little girl.'

'I'm not particularly tall, I know that, but I'm pretty strong.'

'It's tough work building a yard. It's not the right kind of work for a girl.'

She felt the blood rushing in her ears. 'Oh,' she snapped, 'and what is the right kind of work for a girl?'

He looked sheepish. 'You have to realise that there's work for men and different work for women…'

The words flew out of her mouth like bullets from a Gatling gun. 'Like cooking and keeping house, huh? Sandra works like a Trojan in the kitchen and around the house—you've said so yourself. It may not be heavy work by your standards, but it's hard and it's constant and I keep up with her. I overheard you say that you're a man short and I'm not a man of course, but I have two strong arms and a good back. If I stink at it, you can fire me and I'll go back into the classroom and the kitchen and never say another word about it, but please, please don't underestimate me and please don't judge me before I've at least had a chance to try.'

There was something about her face that made Cal crumble. 'Okay, fine, I'll give you a go,' he replied as the ringer glanced at him in disbelief. 'Just don't go crying to my missus the moment you break a fingernail, right?'

She glanced at her nails trimmed close to the bed and lifted her splayed fingers in the air. 'You don't have to worry about that, Cal, I don't have any. See?' she said with a smirk.

'Right.' He rubbed his hands together. 'Harry, I don't think you've met our governess, Becky. Best not to cross her: she has a kick in her like a mule.'

*

The one thing that Cal hadn't underplayed was how hard it was to build the yard for the horses. He had already pegged out the fence and dug the post holes, but righting and setting the posts and shifting the timber for the rails made the muscles in Becky's arms and legs burn. When Sandra came out with a jug of home-made lemonade, she could barely lift the glass to her lips. She glanced at her trembling hand, gulped the lemonade, chewed the ice and never said a word.

To be equal to the men, she knew she had to be better.

It was nearing lunchtime when the whine of gears shifting down signalled the approach of a vehicle. Becky was too busy and too worn out to look. She was holding up one end of a post as Harry positioned and secured it, trying to stop her arms from shaking and conscious of the perspiration dribbling down the back of her neck. An old, borrowed hat on her head, her hair was soaked with sweat and grimy with dust. Suddenly, she heard Cal chuckle and call out, 'It's about bloody time!'

Even if she'd wanted to turn around to see who was wearing the boots that were crunching up the track towards them, she simply couldn't. There was something about the footsteps that seemed vaguely familiar— agile, deliberate, even—although for the briefest time she couldn't quite place them. The laughter that followed, however, banished all doubt.

'Well, well,' Cal shouted, 'if it isn't my wayward nephew! Glad to see you finally found your way here.'

'Engine trouble, Uncle,' Jim replied. 'You started without me. I've been replaced, I see.'

'Of course you have. Work waits for no man. What do you think this is? Bush week?'

Becky's face was beetroot from heat and sunburn. She hadn't seen or heard from Jim for nearly two months and had no idea if he'd received her note. She listened to his footfall, felt him brush past her arm and the shock that the casual connection sent through her. The weight of the post suddenly disappeared. She looked up.

'I'll take over here,' he said.

She peeked at Cal, uncertain of what she should do next, and then she stepped away. There was no greeting from Jim, no smile, nothing at all to suggest that they'd ever met. His demeanour didn't reveal his thoughts. It was disconcerting.

Her eyes settled on the ripple of the muscles in his forearms as he rammed in the post and then moved along to the next one. In a matter of seconds, he had broken a sweat.

'Thanks, Becky,' Cal said, 'you're done for the day. You might want to have a bit of a soak in the tub.' He hooked his thumb through the belt loop on his trousers and followed her gaze, glancing from her to Jim and back again. 'You two have met before,' he ventured, pushing back his Akubra, his brow furrowed. 'You have, haven't you?'

'Yes,' they answered simultaneously. Jim was looking past her, occupied with the next post.

'We met once or twice when I was out at Glenstrae,' she explained, pulling off her hat and fanning her face with it. Her aching hands leapt to her hair. It was tacked to her head and felt as stiff as a board. She grasped the stray tress snaking down the centre of her back and twisted it into a chignon. 'I could still help out here, if you want me to. I'm not really tired.'

'No, it's fine,' Cal replied. 'If you're not totally exhausted, I'm certain Sandra could do with some help.'

'Well,' she responded, 'if you're sure I'm not needed here.'

'We'll be right. And if could you remind Sandra that Jim'll be staying for the week at least.'

'Of course.'

She walked away from the yard in the direction of the house, undecided how she felt about seeing Jim again. Her mind raced as she climbed the steps onto the verandah. Was she forgiven? She had a compulsive need to square things away, a need to make everything all right. Unspoken words and misunderstandings always stole her peace.

After soaking in a bath of barely three inches of tepid water, she pushed everything out of her consciousness, changed into fresh clothes and went down to the kitchen.

'Don't you smell nice,' said Sandra as Becky came through the doorway.

'Lemon verbena body lotion,' she replied. 'It was a gift from my mom.'

A clouded smile flickered across Sandy's face. 'You must miss her.'

Becky thought that her first response, *I hardly even think about her*, sounded too insensitive. 'Sure, I do,' she replied, instead.

'I miss my mum all the time,' said Sandra. Her eyes were ringed with shadows and her face was drawn 'She died when I was very young. I have a stepmother in town; she's nice, but it's not really the same.'

'I'm sorry,' she replied. 'Is there anything I can do?'

'It's just about all done. Meat pies for lunch and jam drops for afternoon tea.' She brightened. 'Would you let the boys know that lunch'll be ready in ten minutes, please? And then if you could shell the peas for me? I saw Jim drive in. Tell Cal not to worry, there's plenty for everyone.'

The yard was still far from complete by late afternoon when the men finished up. There were dozens of posts to cement in, and all the rails for the perimeter still lay uncut in neat piles. Cal had salvaged a world war two Nissen hut that he was going to modify for use as a shelter for the horses. It remained a mound of rubble topped with corrugated iron at the far end of the yard. Now that she understood the enormity of it, Becky couldn't see how three men could possibly finish the project in a week. That thought cheered her.

In the evening, Harry and Jim ate with the family. There was only one dining room at Glen Orchy, and the heavy mahogany table was the only piece of any consequence in the room. It was already long enough to seat eight. Two more leaves to add to its length stood propped against the wall.

Becky carried in the chicken stew they had prepared that afternoon and placed it near the centre of the table. She pulled out the chair in the middle of its length, and sat down. On one side of her, Billy already had his head buried in a book, but the other chair was unoccupied. When Jim came in he glanced at it, and sat opposite Billy.

'It's good to see you again, Jim,' Becky remarked, straining to sound indifferent.

'So, how are you settling in here?' he asked her as he flicked the cap off a bottle of beer and poured out two glasses.

'Oh, fine, thank you. Cal and Sandra have been very welcoming.'

'I suppose you've found things a bit different from Glenstrae.' He placed one of the glasses at the head of the table and took a sip from the other.

She wasn't certain how to reply. 'Oh, you know, I'm sure Mr and Mrs MacGregor tried to make me feel welcome there too, but I guess I was fresh off the boat. I wonder how they're all doing back there.'

'Well,' Jim began, watching Cal snap Billy's book shut, sit down at the head of the table and pick up the glass, 'Glad's still away visiting relatives down south. I haven't heard anything about Teddy since he went to boarding school, but they'll soon straighten him out, no doubt. It's a lot quieter there now without them. Donald's much the same as usual.'

'I hope that it all works out for them.'

Sandra sat down at the other end of the table. She flashed Jim a look that spoke volumes.

He swiftly changed subject. 'I brought a letter for you. I hope it wasn't anything too important; it's been sitting around Glenstrae for a while.'

She frowned. She hoped he wasn't meaning to return the one she'd written him. 'I can't imagine who might write...'

He put down the dish of potatoes that he was passing around and wiped his fingers on his napkin. He leaned forward, reached into his trouser pocket and pulled out a crumpled envelope.

She didn't recognise the stationery.

'Sorry, it's a bit creased.' He turned the envelope over. 'It's from a C. Somers, Pittsburgh, and it looks like someone else has re-directed it here.' He leaned across the table and handed it to her.

'Thank you,' she replied, tucking it into the pocket of her dress.

'Anyone you know?' he asked.

She bit back the words on her tongue, *why, do you know many people who'd write to a complete stranger? Of course it's someone I know.* Instead, she simply responded, 'An old college friend.'

Sandra remarked, 'It must be nice to hear from home.'

'Sometimes, it feels as if the rest of the world has ceased to exist,' she returned. 'I guess it's good to be reminded that home is still out there somewhere.'

'This friend of yours must think a lot of you to write,' said Jim as he dissected a piece of chicken with his knife and fork.

Sandra glanced at Jim and Becky, and smothered a giggle.

'I don't know about that,' Becky began. 'He's just a friend. Mom mentioned that he'd been drafted into the army. I guess he just wanted to write to say "so long".'

Cal cut in. 'I assume he'll soon be deployed in South East Asia, same as our boys. We're all the way with LBJ, you know, although I'm hoping that this time no one in our family has to ship out to Vietnam. It's hard enough to find good workers as it is, and I can't afford to let anyone go right now.'

'I'm hoping no one ever has to serve in any war ever again, period,' Becky rejoined. 'I can't imagine having to kill an animal, let alone another person.'

'Animals are one thing and humans are another entirely. You eat meat,' Cal remarked.

'Yes, but I don't have to kill anything to get it.'

'Yes, well something has to die in order for that meal to end up on the table. Everything and everyone dies eventually,' said Cal. 'Animals die, we eat them and we live. We're all born, we labour and we die. It's just what happens.' He took a swig of his beer. 'We don't always get a choice whether we go to war or not.'

'I know, but I'd hate to go to war, especially to one we have no business being part of. I guess, if I was drafted, I would have to be a conscientious objector. Sometimes I'm glad I'm a girl.' She searched their faces. 'They don't draft girls into the army here, do they?'

'No. No girls or Aborigines,' Sandra replied. 'Oh, Aborigines can volunteer, but they don't have to register for military service,' she continued. 'I'm hoping most of them don't, because if they do, we might lose some of our best stockmen.'

Cal glanced over at Becky and frowned. 'I don't get why kids like you are so against the war,' he said. 'They're all out there, protesting and making nuisances of themselves. We have the right—no, we have the obligation—to protect our way of life. When the communists are on the doorstep, you might think very differently about it then.'

Becky put down her cutlery. 'That's what lots of people say, but I guess I just don't believe that. I don't believe for a minute that Mr Ho's gonna be knocking on my door anytime soon.'

'Mr Ho's a puppet. It's what's behind him that I'm worried about. If Vietnam falls, what's left to stop them? You mark my words, if we lose this war, the rest of 'em'll fall like dominos and then where will we be? Wearing funny grey suits, standing in line and speaking Chinese, that's where.'

'Well, I'm against all war, not just this one. War is futile.'

'War isn't futile, Becky, it is necessary. You take what you have for granted, but only a couple of years before you were born, there was a maniac on the warpath on the other side of the world. Lots of people underestimated him, too.'

'Yes, but that war was in our backyard and we had no choice. Vietnam isn't our war.'

'You're still young and idealistic, I suppose,' he responded. 'Life toughens you up. I hope that either we win this war or I'm wrong, like you think I am. For Billy's sake.' He leaned across and ruffled Billy's hair. 'I hear Chinese is a very hard language to learn.'

Becky winced, but said nothing. After dinner, she helped wash the dishes and tidy the dining room, while the men sat on the verandah drinking beer and smoking American cigarettes. When everything was squared away, Sandra joined them.

Becky stayed behind. She made herself a cup of coffee, sat down at the table and took Clark's letter out of her pocket. She split the envelope with a knife, pulled the fine, lined paper out and smoothed the leaves flat. Clark was usually neat and methodical, but his writing was uncharacteristically irregular. She glanced at the top of the sheet: the letter was dated before her mother's.

Without a hint of apology for anything that had happened between them, he wrote of his sadness that things had ended as they had, as if he'd had nothing to do with it. Might they still remain friends, and could she write to him, please? He would find it very comforting, if she'd write regularly while he was in Vietnam.

She scanned the rest of the letter. It was all the same. She tore the letter into strips and the strips in half, and threw it way. Then she went outside and sat downwind of Cal and Jim.

'It hasn't rained for four months,' she heard Cal say, 'not a drop.' The soil beneath his boot was bone-dry and as friable as talcum powder. He lit up a cigarette, and the sulphur of the struck match wafted on the breeze.

'And even then not much,' Jim replied. 'And nearly six months before that, hardly anything. How are you bearing up?'

'Well, you know the main dam's spring-fed, so it's still holding up pretty well, considering. But I'd like to check on the cattle up on Blindman's Ridge, as soon as the yard's finished. Do you reckon Donald can spare you that long?'

'I think so. I'll phone him tomorrow and make sure.'

'You do that.'

*

The following day was Saturday, but Cal was still working on the yard with Jim, although Harry was absent. The sky was streaked with clouds and Becky thought there was a hint of dampness in the air but, over breakfast, Sandra dismissed it out of hand.

'It's not going to rain,' she said. 'Why the sudden interest in the weather?'

'I overheard Cal talking last night and then I realised, it hasn't rained once in all the time I've been here. It doesn't seem normal. Is that normal?'

Sandra tittered. 'You're a teacher, so you must have heard of Dorothea Mackellar, right?'

Becky shook her head. 'Can't say that I have, although...' She paused for a moment. 'Mackellar... Is she on the curriculum? A poet?'

'Yes, that's her. You'll soon learn, that it's all drought and flooding rains around here. That's our kind of normal.'

'But how can you live like that? What if we run out of water? Don't you worry about running out of water?'

'I try not to think about it. You seem to lose sleep over every little thing, Becky. You have to stop. It'll make you sick.'

'Pardon me for saying so, but that's rather like the pot and the pan calling each other black. I see you taking everything to heart but saying nothing.'

Sandra smiled. 'Really? Then let's do a deal. Let me worry about the weather and the water, and you can worry about Billy's education.'

Once she had finished breakfast, Becky wandered outside and over to the new yard, where Billy sat on a rock cradling his chin and watching Jim and his father working. There was a sweet, sappy scent of new timber in the air. It was comforting.

Jim tossed her a glance. 'We have an audience,' he said to Cal. 'What about putting them to work?'

Cal righted himself, stretched out his back and placed his knuckles on his hips. Then he wiped his brow with the back of his hand. He gestured towards an open toolbox, and gave Billy the task of bringing them the tools when they were needed, while Becky began sawing lengths of timber to size. After a while, she graduated to measuring and marking the cuts herself.

'You know,' Cal remarked to her, 'once we finish building the yard, Jim and me, we're riding out to check on the cattle. You could come along too, if you're free.'

'That's very kind of you,' she replied, 'but I can't ride. Where I come from, there's not much call for it outside of the Upper East Side girls trotting their ponies through Central Park.'

Cal grinned. 'Jim's a crack rider. I'm pretty sure he could teach you. You can't work on a cattle station and not know how to ride.'

'You sure can when you're the governess,' she returned. 'I can't see that it's a necessity.'

'Maybe not, but it's a great opportunity.'

Jim glimpsed her face. 'I don't know, Cal.' He rubbed a blister on the palm of his hand with his finger and thought for a while. 'If she doesn't want to, she doesn't want to. Prancing horses and girly stuff aren't my thing.'

She began gingerly, 'It's not that I'm scared, it's just that I can't see what use horseback riding will be to me. Like buying a car when you live in Manhattan—what's the use of that when everyone rides the subway?'

'I guess that depends on where you're going in life,' Cal interjected. 'There are places that even the New York subway can't reach. The world doesn't begin and end with Manhattan, you know.'

She sniffed. 'Maybe. Depends on how you look at it, I suppose. The world doesn't begin and end here, either.' She looked away. 'I don't know about horseback riding.'

When Becky asked her opinion, Sandra said she could ride, and she thought Becky should learn. Then she went off to tend to her garden, while Becky prepared corned beef for lunch.

By the time the men had washed up and changed into clean clothes for lunch, she had made up her mind. Her reluctance to try something new smacked of the very narrow-mindedness she loathed. She couldn't dismiss something without trying it first.

She uncovered the platters at the table, the clove-studded onions like sea mines, the slabs of meat like submarines beneath, and listened to murmured words of approval. Cal sawed off a dozen flabby slices and doled them out.

She ladled carrots and peas onto her plate, and sectioned off some of the fat from her meat. Then she quietly announced that she had decided to take the riding lessons after all.

Jim put down his cutlery. 'What did you say?'

She glared. 'I know you heard me. I'll try it, but if I don't like it, I walk.'

'Right,' he responded. 'Great. I'll meet you by the saddle room at three-thirty.'

She swallowed hard. 'You don't mean today? This afternoon?'

He picked up his fork again and stabbed a chunk of carrot. 'This afternoon.'

It was too soon. She needed to ease herself into the notion of riding first, not scald herself by sudden immersion. The only animals she had known growing up were squirrels and rats. She wasn't used to animals; she didn't know how to relate to them.

'Three-thirty,' he repeated. 'Wear boots and don't be late. The more practice you get in, the better.'

By three, the haze that Becky had earlier mistaken for rain-clouds had moved away, replaced by a lumpy sky. In New York, such a sky would have brought freezing temperatures and a flurry of snow with it. In the tropics, it only brought stifling humidity.

Her clothes were already damp, as much from sweat as from dankness. Her jeans clung to her thighs and tugged at the downy hairs that covered her legs. Horseback riding had never even made the bottom of her long list of things to do in life. Now that it had writhed its way to the top, she was as moody and sullen as the weather.

She ambled across to the outbuilding where the tack was kept and where Jim was leaning and smoking a cigarette. He glanced at her and stubbed the cigarette out on the gnarled newel post that supported a weathered lean-to. The whole building was five minutes from derelict.

'You're early,' he observed.

'So are you.'

He looked as if he was about to move, but had thought better of it and simply shifted weight. Thoughts scrolled through Becky's mind like reels on a slot machine. Should she mention the letter she'd written him? Should she apologise? Had she already said too much? She glimpsed at the sky. 'It looks like it might rain.'

'Doubt it.'

He seemed put out. She couldn't quite work out why.

'Well, if we're going to do this, then maybe we should begin,' she ventured.

'All right,' he replied.

In the old yard were two horses, saddled and hitched to the rail. One was an enormous black gelding with a blaze on its forehead and rolling eyes. The other was much smaller, gentler but not nearly as handsome. She followed Jim around the boundary of the yard to the horses. He pulled a carrot from his pocket, snapped it into two pieces and handed them to Becky.

'Ever met a horse before?'

'No. You ever met a grey squirrel before? No? Then I guess we're even.'

'This is Cochise,' he said, running his hand along the gelding's mane, 'and the other horse is Tony.'

'You know that Cochise was…' she began.

'An Apache chief? I know. My dad named him. He loves American history and all that stuff. You can feed them some of that,' he said, nodding at the carrot.

'Sure. How do I do that exactly?'

'Stretch out your palm.' He took back the carrot pieces and positioned one on Becky's outstretched hand. 'Keep your fingers well out of the way.'

She offered the fragment to Tony. His eye fixed on Becky, he lowered his nose, sniffed her palm and, with a curl of his lips, the carrot vanished. Cochise watched as Tony crunched the treat, and then he moved forward expectantly. Becky offered him the second fragment and watched it disappear. 'Before I went to Glenstrae, I had never realised just how big horses are. Their heads are just enormous.'

Jim smiled. 'They're big. You just can't let them know it.' He climbed over the fence and dropped into the yard. 'Come on!'

He untied Tony and led him to the centre of the yard, as Becky ducked between the fence rails. Cochise wheeled around and sniffed her.

'Be patient, Cochise,' he said. 'I'll get to you. Tony's very old and very quiet. Let's get you up on his back and I'll lead you around. Now, hold the strap on the saddle and stick your foot in the stirrup.'

The stirrup was a long way up. She held it still in one hand, and lifted up her foot.

Jim snorted. 'The other foot, Becky, unless you're really aiming to sit on him backwards, that is.'

She felt the blood rush to her face and concluded that she was capable of blushing after all. 'Not all of us were born to ride,' she remarked. 'Just wait till you're in Manhattan and then we'll see how you do.'

'Cities aren't for me: I'd sooner face a wild boar. Now, try again. Stand alongside his shoulder and grab hold of a tuft of mane and the near rein. Your left foot goes in the stirrup iron, knee into his left shoulder and swing up. It's like anything, I suppose, so much easier if you have someone to show you how.'

She smirked. 'And point out your mistakes.'

Jim was shaken by her last remark.

'Oh, I'm sorry, I didn't mean to say it the way it came out,' she mumbled, stepping back. 'I do that a lot, don't I? I don't know what's wrong with me.'

'There's nothing wrong with you. You're feisty. You say what you mean.'

'So people tell me. I say things without thinking it through sometimes, and I hate doing it, but I just can't seem to help myself. I'm sorry for what I said about you and your aunt. I feel so stupid.'

'It's forgotten. Now that I think about it again, it was pretty funny. Me and Old Glad? I hope I have better taste than that.'

'I know. It was really stupid of me.' She searched for absolution.

He glanced away. 'How about you forget about that and concentrate on this, hey?'

Without waiting for her to mount, he lifted her up and into the saddle as if she weighed almost nothing. Tony was a small horse, but from the saddle the ground was far enough away that it worried her. Jim led her around the paddock, urging her to break into a trot.

Eventually, he took away the lead rope. 'You're on your own, now,' he said.

*

The next day he suggested that they ride out to Little Creek for a picnic, and Becky agreed. Sundays, as far as she was concerned, were days without purpose. She wasn't raised in any faith and so she wasn't particularly religious. As far as she could tell, neither was Jim.

Cal and Sandra listened to mass over the radio every week. The only time they didn't was when they were in town, and consequently in church. Jim slipped away while the rest of the family was occupied with spiritual matters. By the time Becky reached the yard, the horses were already saddled and hitched to the rail.

Cochise was young, and his belly was full of spring hay trucked in from somewhere that had seen rain. He was tossing his head and snorting. Tony, on the other hand, simply stood quietly with his head hanging, half asleep. He glimpsed Becky and assumed a look of silent resignation. He swung his head around and his focus shifted towards her hands, but there was no carrot, so he turned his back on her and resumed his previous posture.

She turned the moment she heard the sound of Jim's footsteps. He had a saddle bag and a water bottle slung over his shoulder, and a billy can in one hand. His free hand was full of small apples. He fired them off at her, laughing as she fanned out her hands and wriggled about, so that they wouldn't hit her.

'Hey!' she protested. The apples had fallen into the dust around her feet. 'But they're all bruised now,' she continued, stooping to gather them up.

'No worries,' he shouted. 'They're not for you anyhow.'

She stuffed her pockets with the fruit and ducked between the rails. Tony raised his head again and brightened, as she approached him with an apple sitting on her palm. He pressed his lips against her outstretched hand and sneezed the fruit off it. Before she could pick it up, it had vanished, and she noticed that Cochise was snorting and milling about smugly.

She wiped her hand on her pants and tried again. This time, Tony gripped the apple between his teeth, bit down and munched it. Her hand caressed his mane and she rested her cheek lightly against his for a moment, and listened to him chew. The crunch resonated as he ground the fruit between his teeth: it was as if his head was a sound box.

Jim unhitched the horses and watched Tony nuzzle her, sniffing out another apple, and the pleasure in his eyes when he finally found one. As she offered Tony the fruit, Jim brushed past, reached into her bulging pocket and took out the remaining apples, and gave them to Cochise.

She slapped his arm and spun around.

'Fair's fair,' he muttered, opening the gate and mounting Cochise.

This time, after a couple of misplaced hops, Becky swung herself onto the saddle unaided, and walked Tony once around the paddock, exactly as Jim had taught her. She followed him through the gate and along the track leading to the river. He rode next to her for a while, urging her to try a canter, but when she refused, he pushed slightly ahead.

They arrived at a junction and turned right, and followed that track up a gentle incline and then back down again. About an hour further along, they reached a dry creek bed. Jim dismounted and led Cochise a few yards further along.

'Oh,' said Becky, sliding off Tony's back, and toeing the silt.

'Is this Little Creek?' In her imagination, creeks held water that tripped over rocks and gurgled down ravines. Here, there was nothing. Except for a stand of coolabahs on either side of the bed, it was desolate.

Jim nodded.

'But there's no water.'

He smiled. 'You want to make a bet?' He picked up a broad piece of bark, crouched down and scraped back the dirt. Once he'd hollowed out a few inches, the depression he'd made filled up with water as rapidly as he could dig. 'Gallons of fresh water, just below the surface.' He scooped some of the water into enamel mugs and let the dirt settle before pouring the clean water into the billy.

He watered the horses and tied them up a little further away, under a blue gum, and then disappeared behind the trees to gather kindling. When he returned, he built a fire by the creek. When the water in the billy began to rumble, he unpacked the saddle bag and took out a small packet of tea. He threw in some leaves and pushed the billy aside.

'You hungry?' he asked.

Becky hadn't thought about food—she had been far too preoccupied. 'I guess I could eat,' she replied.

'Good.' He took out a plaid tablecloth and spread it out on the flattest area he could find, flicking away any rocks with the toe of his boot. Out of the saddle bag he produced plates and cutlery, scotch eggs, bread rolls and salads, all stored in plastic boxes. Becky tittered at his domesticity. He poured out the tea and placed both cups alongside the containers of food.

She sat down next to him. 'So,' she asked, 'what did you do before you were a head stockman? Is there such a thing as stockman's college? Or maybe you were a deputy head for a while?'

He chuckled. 'I was at boarding school, down south. You ever heard of CBC, St Kilda?'

She had no idea what he had just said. 'Uh, no. It's not a penitentiary, is it? You're not about to confess that you're an ex-con, are you?'

Jim roared with laughter. 'Well, that's open for debate. It's a school down in Melbourne. Run by the Christian Brothers. I went there because that was where my father went.'

'That sounds like a long way to go for an education. So, what did you do next?'

'Next, I tried university. I stayed down in Melbourne with my uncle Edward, and I studied medicine.'

'What?' she spluttered. 'So, you're a doctor?'

'Hardly. But what if I were? Not everyone who runs a cattle station is poorly educated.'

'I didn't mean that. It's just that medicine seems a million miles away from raising cattle. So,' she continued, 'I guess you never graduated?'

'I was halfway through my fourth year when I realised it wasn't for me.'

'Hmm, that sounds familiar. My college career went much the same, I suppose.'

'I was doing okay, but I just couldn't settle down. Medicine satisfied my intellect, but my soul could never get away from this place. I wasn't born to be a doctor, and I guess I didn't have a choice in the end.' Jim picked up a leaf and turned it over with his fingers, end over end, again and again. 'So, how did you end up here?'

'Well, I had the chance to leave home and I took it. I was supposed to go to France, but I wound up here, instead.'

'That's one hell of a wrong turn.'

He brushed the leaf softly against her cheek, and she smiled. Without saying anything, he leaned across and kissed her. They clutched each other for a while, silent, content just to feel the warmth and comfort of a caress, until he pulled away. He kissed her again, lingering this time. The picnic was forgotten. Eventually, the fire burned out, and the tea grew cold.

Jim glanced at the sky and then at his watch.

'Is it late?' Becky asked, her head nestled in the crook of his arm. 'It's late, isn't it.'

'No, it's not late. Relax. It won't get dark for a while yet.'

'Oh, that's good.' She closed her eyes and tried to doze, but her mind kept racing. 'It won't be dark before we get back, will it? You know Tony and me, we're really, really slow.'

'I know. Don't worry. It's not late.' He shifted his arm and rested his head against hers.

'Maybe, we should get going soon all the same,' she said as she wriggled free.

Jim was silent. He packed up the uneaten food and strapped the bag back onto his saddle, while Becky leaned against Tony and waited. He turned towards her, wrapped her in his arms and pulled her towards him. 'Are you okay?' he murmured, his mouth resting on her forehead.

'Of course.' She raised herself onto her tiptoes and pecked him on the lips. 'Why shouldn't I be?'

'No reason.'

'Are you okay?' she asked as she untied Tony and led him away from the tree.

He didn't reply. He pulled her back by her shirt tail, cradled her face in his hands and kissed her once more.

CHAPTER FIFTEEN

I F LIFE had taught Becky anything, it was that fortunes often turned along with the seasons. While some seasons consisted of days of endless sunshine, others were blanketed with a blinding fog that never seemed to lift. Two world wars had scarred the MacGregor family, but not defeated it. This new season was different: she felt it in the rain that refused to fall, in Jim's frequent, unapologetic absences, and in the increasing pallor of Sandra's cheeks.

One morning as she showered, Sandra's soapy fingers glided over something unfamiliar. Where her breasts had always been light and smooth, there was an unaccustomed hardness. She caught her breath and felt again. She pushed into the fleshy part, pressing down, almost to the bone. There it was again. It was a lump. It was large. It was unmistakable.

Her fingers flew to the same spot on her other breast, but there was nothing there. She felt around her nipples, systematically, radiating outwards, and her fingers found another. There were lumps in both breasts. She was aghast. How long had they been there and she had never felt them?

The GP in Barkers Hill reeled when she palpated them. 'I can't say what they are for certain, but I want you to see a specialist as quickly as you can.'

'Can't it wait until after the muster?' she asked.

Her doctor's expression told her it could not, far more eloquently than words could have ever done. She arranged for Sandra to see the oncologist in Townsville before the end of the week. She and Cal returned to the station for a few days, preoccupied and saddened, but silent about the cause.

All they said was that Becky was to take charge of Billy while they went away, with Jim in charge of the station. At the last moment they decided that Billy would go with them. Although glad to be relieved of the responsibility, a single thought persisted even when Becky willed it away: could they be looking to place him in a school in town?

Sandra entreated Becky to take care of the men, and she said she would. They hugged each other, but Sandra pulled away.

'Is everything all right?'

'Ask me that when we get back.'

The following day Jim and Harry rode out to check on some cattle halfway through the morning without telling her, and didn't return until dinner. Becky spent the day cooking, and waiting for them to reappear.

She wanted to be angry with Jim, to admonish him when he left without explanation, but unlike her relationship with Clark, there were no promises to break, no expectations of family, no awkward sentimentality. He was free to do as he wanted, as much as she. It was a new age: she was liberated. She didn't feel it. She gazed out over the empty yard and willed him back. The isolation was maddening. She was peeved that she had been left behind.

'Two reasons,' he said, when she brought it up over dinner. 'Firstly, it would have been too hard and too far for you and Tony. Secondly, I thought you'd be pretty sick of horses by now.'

Harry returned to the ringers' quarters after dinner, nursing a large bottle of Abbot's lager, while Jim stayed behind and helped her with the washing up. When it was done, he wrapped his arms around her and buried his face in her nape.

'You smell sweet, like a lavender bush crossed with a barbecued steak.'

She pulled away and flicked him with the tea towel. 'You know, that's exactly what I was hoping for.'

'Well, I like it anyway.'

He took the tea towel away from her, folded it, and draped it over the back of the chair. Then he took her hand and led her away from the kitchen, and outside. It was past dusk, but they didn't bother with the lights: the glow from the kitchen was enough. The thick night air made the perfume from the jasmine bush adjacent to the back door heavy. As they stepped a little further down the verandah, the jasmine ceded its sweetness to the citrus of a lemon myrtle. That was where Jim stopped.

He sat on a cane chair in the shadows, and pulled her onto his lap. 'It's been a long day, but some things are worth the wait,' he whispered, brushing his lips against the length of her neck.

The sensation of his mouth on her skin burned away her response. She tilted her head, swivelled about and kissed him, her palm resting on his breastbone.

'Let's go,' she murmured.

When they reached her room, he turned to her and asked, 'Should I come in?'

She opened the door and drew him through.

He was still there when she woke up the next dawn. For a while she watched him sleep, the sheet crumpled and abandoned, half on and half off, her fingertip tracing his oblique muscle down to his bare hip. She quivered as his breath caressed her face, as stale as the sweat on his body, but welcome nevertheless. She lifted her hand, but didn't dare move further for fear of disturbing him. He awoke anyway and stretched out, hooking her entire body in the crook of one arm and flipping her onto her back.

She cooked breakfast in the morning. Harry must have been up for ages; he had already helped himself to tea, toast and eggs, and that made her smile. He had left a trail of crumbs behind, and his plate and cup in the sink, but she didn't mind.

Jim propped himself against the table while she made herself coffee and brewed him a pot of tea. Something was weighing on his mind: she could see it in his stance. She served up breakfast and sat down next to him to eat. He was reticent, even more than usual.

She was reluctant to ask him why: she didn't want him to think that she was monitoring him and, if he confirmed that something was wrong, she wasn't certain that she wanted to know. As far as relationships went, she still had no gauge by which to measure soundness.

After breakfast, he went in and out of the pantry, stacking tins, packets of pasta and vegetables until a neat pile of food had accumulated in the middle of the kitchen table.

'Harry and I will be away for the next couple of days,' he said, 'and I'm not sure when Cal and Sandra are coming back. I'll show you how to get the generator going. Will you be all right here on your own, do you think?'

She stopped abrading the clumps of egg that had fused to the saucepan, and turned away from the sink. 'Oh,' she mumbled. 'Where are you going?'

'We're going to check on those cattle—the ones Cal spoke about before he left for town—and we'll be back as soon as we can. It's too far to ride there and back the same day. Depending on what we find, we might be away an extra day or two.'

'Can't I come too?' She hated that she'd said it.

He softened a little. 'I wish you could, but it'd be a tough trip for an experienced man, let alone a novice. I mean, you haven't even fallen off a horse yet. That's bound to happen, and I'd sooner it didn't happen in the middle of nowhere. Maybe once you've graduated to a proper stock horse and you're confident that you know what you're doing.'

'So, what do I do while you're gone?' She willed him to say *miss me.*

'I don't know,' he began, glancing around the kitchen. 'I suppose you could clean up? Bake? Freeze a few meals? I don't know, use your imagination.'

Each of his suggestions stung like a slap in the face. She glanced around. Apart from the mess Harry had left, everything seemed tidy to her. 'Well,' she sniffed, 'I guess my standards aren't as high as yours. I never realised that I'd answered an advertisement for a maid.'

He recoiled. 'Are you angry at me for something?' The softness had disappeared again. He searched her face. 'You are! Look, I have work to do and I really don't have the time for this. I know you're young, Becky, I get that, but you can't keep examining every single word I say, searching for the insult. You're not Cinderella and life isn't a fairytale, you know. Toughen up.'

Her lips parted, but no words emerged.

He darted out of the kitchen and returned moments later with some worn bags made out of canvas. He began packing the food into them, while she sat glumly.

He caught a glimpse of her expression. 'I don't know what's going on here: maybe you need to explain it to me. You asked me what you could do, and I made some suggestions, that's all. If what I said upset you, then I'm sorry. I have a lot on my mind right now.'

She could have hurled his words back at him. 'Perhaps you're right. I guess the universe probably doesn't care much about me, or anybody for that matter. I'm reading too much into things,' she returned. 'I understand.'

'Good. Okay, then.' He laid the bags on the floor and placed one hand on his hip. 'You can be hard work, Becky. You drive me crazy, you know.'

'You, too,' she mumbled, shuffling forward and burrowing into his embrace. 'So, I guess we're even.'

He kissed her on her forehead and then lightly on the lips. She followed him outside to the shed that housed the Southern Cross generator, a stinking, clunking, ugly beast made mostly out of cast iron, as far as she could tell. He stopped it, and for a moment there was bliss. Then he showed her how to start it again.

On her first attempt, the flying hand-crank hit her on the forearm, and left its mark. After two more failures, Jim began to wonder if she had the strength to start it up. If she didn't, he couldn't leave her there alone. She read the doubt in his expression, clenched her teeth and tried again. When he began to intervene, she waved him away. On her fifth attempt, she managed to crank the flywheel fast enough to get it going.

Jim gasped. She thought momentarily that she'd glimpsed pride, but he had already locked it away.

He said, 'We'll be out past the river flats, and then we'll be moving up the ridge. If you need anything, get on the phone and call one of the stations, okay? You've got the radio, too, and the instructions are stuck to the wall. I'll be back tomorrow, or a day or two after, at the most.'

She watched him stride out to the paddock and load up the packhorse. In a matter of seconds, he rode out ahead of Harry and the packhorse, along the track and out of sight. After he had gone, the silence became maddening. In the distance, a solitary crow called out, but received no reply. It called again. The din it made was anguished and unrequited. She understood how it must have felt.

She wandered back inside, but the more she looked for things to occupy her time, the less she found, and the heavier the solitude weighed about her shoulders.

The following day, Cal telephoned the station, asking for Jim. He voice was thin and indistinct, muffled by the clatter of activity surrounding him.

'We'll be away for bit longer than we thought, and I've spoken with Donald. He's agreed to let Jim help out until we return. Could you let him know?'

Becky felt her heart jump. 'Is everything all right, Cal? I mean, there's nothing wrong with Billy, is there?'

Cal paused, choosing his words. 'Billy's fine. He's staying with Sandra's dad and stepmother in town for a while.' He paused again. 'You should know this, I guess. It looks like Sandra's going to be having an operation.'

She wondered if Jim already knew that. 'Is she all right?'

'I'm not sure. I hope so. If you're that way minded, would you say a little prayer for her recovery?'

'Of course I will,' she replied. 'And you? Is there anything I can do?'

'You're doing it,' he replied. There was despair in his voice.

She didn't want to press him further. She often made pacts with a higher force, although she never prayed: she wasn't sure she knew how. A priest visited all the homesteads occasionally, but she had little to do with that and nobody seemed to mind.

Without the shackles of a religious education, she could afford herself the luxury of cynicism, in the complete absence of guilt. She had noticed two things: the visiting priest always brought with him a box to secure the offerings, along with his travelling Eucharist case, and the MacGregors always filled it with money before they took communion. She might have known a little theology, but she knew a lot more history, and the words *indulgences* and *Martin Luther* sprang into her head. The MacGregors were influential, and if they'd asked for it, they could have had the might of the entire Catholic Church behind them. Donations and genuflection weren't really going to help Sandra.

She hung up the telephone. Her own cares were selfish and paltry. She doubted that a solitary agnostic could possibly make any difference, but she still crouched down and muttered something aloud. Past her uncertainty, she didn't find faith, although she did discover sentiment. For a while, she thought of something other than herself.

*

Sandra's surgeon was celebrated in his field. He travelled up from Sydney every fortnight for a surgical list at the Townsville General Hospital. He was revered: called *mister* but never *doctor*, he had an alphabet of letters after his name, said little and charged a fortune. His eyes scanned the oncologist's report, after which he examined her briefly. Could she please go home now, she asked.

He shook his head, remained stony-faced, and added her to the top of his surgical list for the following day. It had to be done straight away. It was at that point that Cal and Sandra's harmony with the rest of the world ceased.

In the morning, while Cal wrung his hands in the waiting room, the surgeon methodically excised lumps from each of Sandra's breasts and gave them to the pathologist behind him. Oblivious to the hubbub of the theatre, she lay on the table unconscious, her life supported by a bored anaesthetist and a phalanx of machines that huffed and whirred. The pathologist fixed the samples, analysed and classified them. It was unmistakably cancer. Still operable, but only just.

The surgeon lifted his scalpel and, with light, deft sweeps, he cut away both of her breasts first, and then the muscles that supported them, the nodes under her arms and anything else the cancer might have touched. He was confident with his incisions: he removed just enough, but not too much, convinced that pathology would confirm that the margins were clear. Then his assistant stitched her up. From neck to waist, she was a patchwork doll swaddled in bandages.

The surgeon handed her over to be wheeled into recovery, left the theatre, stripped off his gloves and mask, and drank tea in the doctor's lounge. He never reflected too long on any patient— sentimentality was an indulgence he could not afford. There was a hierarchy, of which he stood at the pinnacle, and boundaries that could never be crossed. He always sent the surgical registrar to speak to the family, while he and his assistant prepared themselves for the next name on his list.

Sandra was taken to her room in the afternoon, after the nurse had sent Cal home. The nurse told him she needed to heal. He caught a glimpse of her as they pushed her trolley along the passageway, but she was asleep and there was no point to him remaining there.

He called again to speak to Jim the following morning, and again Becky had to tell him that he was away.

'How's Sandra?' she asked hesitantly.

'She's had her operation and they've got her on some pretty strong stuff for the pain.'

She hardly dared ask the next question. 'Do they know what's wrong with her? I mean, if you don't mind me asking, that is.'

'No, no, that's fine; I'll tell you.' She heard a sob catch in Cal's throat and the hum of the telephone line. Eventually he said, 'She has cancer.'

It wasn't entirely unexpected, although Cal's confirmation struck hard. In her parents' circles, cancer was the death sentence spoken of in whispers, and only ever by insinuation.

Have you heard? It's bad news. It's the Big C.

'I'm so sorry,' she replied, but it wasn't enough. She wiped her eyes on the hem of her blouse. 'How is she getting along?'

'I don't know if she knows what's happened yet. The doctor said that once she recovers from the operation, she's got to have drugs to kill off any of the cancer that's left, and to stop it from coming back. He says it's going to take a while before we know anything more.'

'You asked me to pray for her. Is there anything else that I can do?'

'Just take care of Glen Orchy for us. And will you ask Jim to do the same?'

By the time Jim returned later that week, the house was as neat as pins, not because he had suggested it, but because she had needed the diversion. She had frozen a week's worth of meals in Tupperware containers, made some scones that had toppled over as they baked, and a cake like a volcano.

She told him about Sandra after Harry had gone out to put on a load of washing.

He shook his head. 'Cal'll be taking it pretty hard. They're a pigeon-pair. Glad and Donald can't bear to spend an evening together and Cal and Sandra can't bear to spend one apart.' He sat silently for a while, his lips drawn tight over his mouth but not smiling. 'I reckon that if it had happened to Glad instead of

Sandra, you'd have heard Donald whooping from here, and there wouldn't have been too many people standing in line to scold him. There's no logic and no justice to it.'

'Life is arbitrary. I'm praying for her every day, although I'm not sure that there's anyone up there listening.'

'I don't know what I believe anymore,' he muttered.

Cal called again the following day, and said he'd be returning in a few days. He said that the station was his responsibility, not Jim's, and he suspected Donald's patience was wearing thin. There had been an uncomfortable telephone call; he didn't want to go into the details of it. Donald was never a jovial drunk under the best of circumstances. There was always too much work to be done and not enough pairs of hands to handle it. Donald had made it clear that Jim was needed back at Glenstrae immediately. In the end, he agreed to let Jim stay on for another week.

Jim returned to the ringers' quarters the moment Cal arrived at the homestead.

Harry watched him and scoffed. 'Good to have you back, mate,' he spluttered.

'Is it?'

Besides being head stockman, as family Jim always had the right to sleep in the homestead if he wanted to. He usually bunked with the ringers because he thought it lent a feeling of brotherhood among the men. He had to trust his men as much as lead them; lives depended on it. Harry's reaction irked him. It was no one's business where he decided to spend the night.

Harry fell asleep the minute he stopped sniggering, and began to snore. Soon, he was as noisy as a double-cut bandsaw.

Jim stretched out, but his bed was unyielding and empty. He glanced over at Harry and groaned. The contrast from the night before was simply too stark. His nights in the ringers' quarters were over. He picked up his bedding, folded it up under his arm and decided to sleep on the verandah instead.

CHAPTER SIXTEEN

THE WEATHER was particularly savage the summer that began at the end of 1967. Throughout December, there was the expectation of rain every day, yet Glen Orchy station never seemed to see a drop of it.

The hospital at Townsville wasn't equipped to deal with ailments like Sandra's, so, as soon as she was well enough to travel, she had to go south. She stayed in an old Queenslander in Woolloongabba with her sister, barely a full toss away from the cricket ground. From her front door she could just about see the Mater Hospital, where doctors regularly administered a chemical cocktail that left her too ill to speak. Cal telephoned her every night, even when it meant delivering a monologue, punctuated only by the sounds of her dry-retching.

On the days that she felt well enough to talk to him, she asked about the station and he steered the conversation elsewhere. When she queried whether it had rained yet, he felt compelled to lie. The effort of sounding cheerful left him drawn and sullen. After each call, he retreated to the comfort of whisky—*uisce beatha*, the water of life. He couldn't worry her with the truth. Even when the spring dried up and the water in the dam had turned syrupy and fetid, in the living room, the water of life still flowed. It had been a constant since the MacGregors roamed the Scottish highlands: it sustained them when they were persecuted then, and it still did.

Billy stayed with his grandparents in Townsville and it was planned that he'd go to school there after the summer. Cal broadcast that he was coping well without his family, but what he meant was that he was doing what he had to, and no more. He missed them, and he hated relying on Becky. He made deals with God all day, pledging every drop of whisky for the rest of his life in exchange for his family's swift return. Until then, he told Becky that she had to assume the role of housekeeper, because that was what was needed. It was the cattle station, rather than the people who ran it, that dictated what had to be done and when. The effort left Becky depleted.

The luxury of sentimentality ended the minute Cal returned to Glen Orchy. From that day on, she was plunged into a vigorous cycle of cooking and cleaning, unrelenting and unrewarding, until she began to wonder if Sandra had willed herself ill, just so that she could have a break from it. Counting the contract ringers, there were suddenly five ravenous men to feed five times a day, as well as a house to run. The skin on Becky's hands had become sandpaper rough, and she imagined herself as a hamster on a wheel she was incapable of stopping.

After Jim left, she barely existed from their last call until their next, willing the telephone to ring every time she walked by it. He called her once and sometimes twice a week, but their conversation didn't flow as easily as it had before. She put it down to her own fatigue and the strain of being apart. Face to face, there was always an understanding, an ease to the dialogue, even when they argued. The chemistry that made her yearn for him all but disappeared over the telephone. There weren't many days left in 1967. With Christmas approaching, she told herself that at least she would see him once before the New Year.

Cal left Glen Orchy a few days before Christmas, to collect Billy and travel south to spend time with Sandra in Brisbane. During his absence, Harry stayed with Becky at Glen Orchy, and they were invited to spend Christmas Day with everyone else at Glenstrae homestead. It was tradition; family and workers were always welcomed at the homestead at Christmas and Easter.

Becky bought Jim a compass as a Christmas present and it arrived a week before, together with a dress she had ordered out of a catalogue. She intended to wear it on Christmas Day, and imagined herself dazzling him over dinner, but when she tried it on, the dress was too wide and too long. She spent the precious hours between the end of her long workday and her bedtime using Sandra's sewing machine to alter it. When she finished, the gold silk sheath skimmed her body and stopped mid thigh. She embellished it with some sequins and a huge bow at the nape that she had sewn out of the remnants. When she put it on, she looked like an expensive bonbon, the luxury gift for the man who had everything.

She wrapped Jim's compass in paper with bunches of holly on it, and she and Harry left Glen Orchy on Christmas morning. They drove to Glenstrae without stopping, in order to reach it ahead of lunchtime. Christmas dinner always began early there, with tots of rum and the exchange of presents. Harry was keen not to miss out.

The homestead's gate was strewn with tinsel, and paper chains cut out of newspaper linked the rosebushes to each other. As Harry pulled up, she imagined the glittering garlands along Fifth Avenue, Central Park carpeted in snow, Sylvia's eggnog and the decorated spruce tree in the entrance hallway of their brownstone: it was pure nostalgia for which she had no time.

She climbed out of the car and teetered on her high heels along the path leading to the house. Calmness had settled over the homestead; the tension that Gladys MacGregor carried with her everywhere had finally dissipated. The living-room door was wide open and Becky glimpsed inside. The curtains were drawn back and, for once, the room was bathed in natural light. The furniture had been moved around, and the old record player replaced with a modern, Danish-style Kreisler lowboy in teak. A tall, forked limb from a gum tree stood in a deep bucket of sand in the corner, decorated with glitter, foil and glass ornaments, its leaves drooping, limp from the heat. It wasn't Christmas. To Becky, it was as ridiculous as dressing a decomposing corpse in evening attire, in order to pass it off as a living being.

Donald MacGregor was already drunk by the time they arrived, but not yet belligerent. Teddy was home on holidays, just as sullen and as surly as she remembered. School had done nothing at all to temper him. Becky checked the room. Mrs MacGregor was still away, *visiting family* and she didn't spot Jim. With a few exceptions, the faces were mostly unfamiliar.

A woman she had never met was sitting at the piano, tinkling but not playing, sipping a sherry from a stemmed crystal glass. She hammered out an unsteady version of 'Jingle Bells', but no one sang. In the middle of the room, bottles of lager lay in a zinc tub filled with ice. Joy was spreading among the guests in line with the beer. When Mr MacGregor saw Becky, he waved and shouted out something she couldn't understand. He tottered towards her, the neck of a quarter-full bottle of Dewar's in one fist and a glass of ice in the other. It was her cue to slip away.

She found Nellie in the kitchen elbow deep in potato peelings, saturated in sweat.

Nellie turned when she walked in, but kept frowning. 'Thank God,' she muttered. 'It's a hundred and ten degrees in here and with Mrs MacGregor away, I've been left on my own. Honestly, if I had a half-decent husband, I'd be walking out right now and they'd never see me again. It's only a merry Christmas around here for some.'

Becky pulled a clean apron out of a drawer and wrapped the ties twice around her waist and knotted them. She pushed Nellie away from the sink with her hip.

Nellie's expression softened and her shoulders dropped. 'Thank you.'

By two, they had finished cooking the feast that Nellie had begun preparing at dawn, and it was ready to serve. Becky smoothed out her dress and sat down at the dining table next to a ringer she hadn't met before. Having prepared the meal, she had little appetite for eating it. A turkey roast on a scorching day seemed utterly ridiculous, and she never liked ceremonial occasions anyway—everyone tried too hard to be pleasant. It bored her. She did her best to hide her indifference, but the chatter that swirled along the table was tedious and irrelevant. She tuned in and out of it, only nodding when she had to.

It was late afternoon before Jim walked in.

He glanced at Becky briefly, but he was ushered to a chair at the other end of the table and swamped with offers of drink and food, and wishes of good fortune. She heard someone ask him about one of the neighbouring properties, and if he had enjoyed Christmas so far, but she didn't catch his reply. Someone turned up the record player in the lounge room. 'In the Mood' was playing and a few of the guests drifted out of the dining room to dance, while others sat outside on the verandah in a stupor.

Eventually Becky and Jim found themselves alone in the dining room. Jim stood up and walked over to her. 'Merry Christmas,' he said. 'Have you been well?'

It was awkward, as if they were abruptly strangers again. She had expected him to smile, to engage with her, to recount what had been happening, but he said none of it. It was uncharacteristic for him not to compliment her, and she suddenly felt overdressed and self-conscious.

'So,' he asked again, a little too mannered, 'you've been well?'

'Yes, thank you,' she replied, her brow furrowed, foraging for answers. 'And you?'

'Yes, well,' he muttered, preoccupied. 'Come for a walk?'

Uncertain, she picked up her bag and followed him outside.

His arm brushed hers as they walked along the track that led to the river, but he seemed distracted and she was certain he hadn't sensed a thing. Still, she felt the hardness of his biceps through his shirt and she yearned for him to pause there for a while. She longed to listen to his relaxed chatter, to lose herself in his company, but he kept pushing forward until they had walked so far that the generator was barely audible over the music wafting past them, ebbing and flowing, caught up in a capricious wind.

They couldn't be overheard there. He stopped and crossed his arms. The intimacy she had been anticipating had been replaced by an iciness she had never known before.

'We need to talk,' he said tersely.

Becky felt her throat constrict.

He rotated his torso a little towards her, but he still didn't face her. 'Something has happened since the last time I saw you,' he began. 'I thought it was best if you heard it from me.'

It wasn't an auspicious start. He turned his eyes away from hers, his face lowered slightly, so that she desperately wanted to sandwich it between her palms and force him to look at her.

'There's a property next to my dad's,' he resumed, uncharacteristically staccato. 'It's huge. The Kavanagh family owns it: three girls and a son, all about my age. I've known them forever. We all used to play together when we were little. I have to tell you, that's where I was earlier today.' He inclined his face towards hers, intimate, close enough to steal a kiss, but he still didn't meet her gaze.

'How does this concern me?' she asked. She tried to read his demeanour, but all she understood from it was confusion.

He shifted his weight from one foot to the other, chewing the inside of his lip and drawing away again. 'Well, one of the girls, Lyn Kavanagh and I... After I left Glen Orchy... Well, we met up again. I guess it was always understood... Between the families, that...'

Becky's world somersaulted while he stammered.

She frowned. 'I—I don't understand, Jim... What are you trying to say?'

'Well, people always joked we'd end up together... I never thought...'

She swallowed the bile rising in her gullet. 'Are you trying to tell me that you and she... That you and she are...'

He hung his head. 'We're engaged. I'm not sure how it happened.' He hesitated. 'I never meant to hurt you, Becky. You have to believe me, I wouldn't deliberately hurt you for anything in the world.'

She felt her eyes fill with tears and the flush of her face. 'You and this, this Lyn Kavanagh?'

He lifted his eyes momentarily.

She glimpsed his grief, but it hardly held a candle to her own. 'Getting married?'

Sheepishly, he mumbled, 'I guess so.'

Her tears threatened to spill over, held back only by her dignity. 'So, what was I? To you, I mean. What was I?'

She glared at him, as if by glaring she might expose to him the idiocy of this pact of his with Lyn Kavanagh, and that he might resile from it. She glared at him until his features no longer made sense. He had eyes, a nose, a mouth, but they were mere parts now, parts but not a whole. Jim—*her* Jim—had ceased to exist. The man that stood next to her, smelling of freshly mown grass— vital, strong, pathetic—this man was utterly alien. Her world had turned into a facsimile of what she understood it to be, a reflection through a camera obscura.

She took a step backwards. He had never told her he loved her, although she thought it was implied in the honesty of his every look and in the softness of his caress. He had pursued her, even after she had repelled him, even after she had humiliated him. As heartbroken as she felt at that moment, it was true that they had never spoken of a future together. To her, he had made no promise. To her, he had broken no promise.

Sullen and defeated, she muttered, 'Was I just another conquest for you? A fling?'

He hastened to say, 'No, of course not. I care about you, Becky, a lot. But it was always expected I guess... The Kavanaghs are big landowners around here. And they're Catholic...'

'So, it was your duty?' She didn't want it to sound pleading. 'But I thought you didn't care about things like that.'

'I should have told you.'

The sting of her tears resorbed, she retorted. 'Yes, you should have. That would have been the honourable thing to do. You know what hurts me more than anything? I thought you were decent. When you told me that you left medical school to follow your heart, I thought, man, that's really something. I thought you cared about things that really mattered, but you know what? That decent, honourable person was never you, it was me. All along, it was me who was dignifying your actions, putting you on a pedestal, turning you into a noble person in my tiny, sad, deluded mind. And you knew, and you let me. Shame on you. And shame on me.'

'I never...'

'Meant to hurt me?' she caught his gaze and held it until he looked away. She opened up her bag, pulled out the gift and tossed it at his feet. Then she floundered along the track, blinded by tears she had finally set free. He had the good sense not to follow her. What more could he have said?

She returned to the homestead alone. Nellie glimpsed her passing by as she stood at the sink, washing up.

Becky went straight into the bathroom and splashed water into her eyes, but her mascara ran. It simply made things worse. With a red nose and her eyes ringed black, it had to be obvious to all that she had been weeping.

She went back inside, poured herself a large brandy and sat down. Nobody noticed a thing—not her eyes, not her sadness, not Jim's absence. Eventually, the carol singing, opening of presents and supply of food petered out. She sat in silence, sipping her brandy and willing the day to end.

With the dozy remnants of Christmas cheer still twirling around her like a carousel, she wondered why it was that people who said that they would never hurt others for anything in the world, always did.

*

Becky was glad when Harry decided that they would drive back to Glen Orchy that evening, rather than staying overnight at Glenstrae, like just about everyone else. She knew he was drunk and that he probably shouldn't drive but she didn't care. Apart from Cal's reliance on her to keep the station running, her life suddenly made no sense. She couldn't have cared less if they had wound up wrapped around a tree. As it was, Harry kept mostly to the road, and stayed mostly awake. They arrived back at Glen Orchy, unscathed, well after midnight, and she went straight to bed.

The morning brought with it the sickening realisation of what had transpired the night before and, no matter what she did, it stung. Although they were never really a couple, Becky had grown accustomed to the telephone calls that she knew she would never receive again, and to the illusion that she mattered to someone other than her parents. On Christmas Eve she had been full of hope for the year ahead. Suddenly, she had lost all possibility of a future with Jim. His future lay with Lyn Kavanagh.

She longed to shut out the world for a while, but she knew that Sandra and Cal needed her. She wanted to cry out, to run away, to rage against someone, but her seclusion was already absolute, and there was no shoulder at Glen Orchy for her to cry on, and nowhere else for her to go. She told herself that she could make herself an island so that loss and grief wouldn't find her, but when that failed, she returned to her room and re-read a letter that Clark Somers had sent her after she hadn't replied to his last one.

Please don't stay mad at me. When I come home from my tour, I want to marry you and take care of you for the rest of your life. I dream about it. The thought of you keeps me going. I want us to raise a family together...

It unsettled her.

On Boxing Day, she wrote to Clark Somers, implying a change of heart and agreeing to consider his proposal. After that, she penned a meandering letter to her mother, barely disguising her confusion and pain, and apologising for the suffering she had put her parents through. She sealed that envelope with her tears.

Cal returned from Brisbane two days later, and the stopped clock began to run again, but without Sandra, a malaise settled once more over the homestead. He told Becky that Sandra seemed to be doing much better, and that she would probably be back in a month or two. His brother had agreed that, with Gladys MacGregor due to return to Glenstrae from visiting her relatives at about the same time, Nellie might be spared to help him out for a while. Becky could then resume her life as Billy's governess. The thought cheered her up a bit.

New Year came and went, although neither she nor Cal stayed up to see it in. He had no reason to celebrate Hogmanay that year; the wet season had failed to arrive.

She watched him as he studied the sky every day and consulted the weather station hourly, tapping the barometer, hopeful of detecting the first signs that the weather was about to change. The only thing she wanted the New Year to bring with it was good health and rain. Sometimes, late at night, when she watched the shadows, she even prayed for it. By late January, it seemed that the protracted dry was never going to end.

She had never had to think about drought before, and although she had a vague understanding of what the word meant at a distance, she had never seen it up close. Her education commenced with the abrupt cessation of bathing in water that could be used for a higher purpose. Bore water looked like stale ginger ale and smelled like a fart. It was impossible to lather, no matter how much shampoo she poured onto her hair, and if she drank it, it was guaranteed to cleanse her system within an hour.

Cal knew all about drought: he had lived it before. It was impossible to have run a station in the dry tropics for longer than a few years, and to have never encountered it. His father and grandfather had gathered wisdom through painful experience, and they had passed it along. They made modifications where they could, sinking bores and digging dams, and they taught their children the value of forbearance, where they could not. Cal knew that Glen Orchy station could comfortably survive a short drought, but a prolonged one would almost certainly ruin him. He didn't have endless resources like Glen Eira, or the advantage of a ceaseless river flow like Glenstrae. He prepared himself for a fight. The thing was, he could only discover the true measure of his opponent once he had defeated it. Until the rain came, he would be battling blind.

They moved the stock down from the distant paddocks closer to the homestead, not just so they could deliver feed and water to them more efficiently, but so that they could shoot and dispose of them if it came to that, without having to go off and search for them first. Cal sent five hundred head off to auction in one lot. Their condition wasn't prime and he wasn't expecting to be paid much, but he reasoned that it was better to be paid something rather than nothing. He kept the remaining thousand just in case, and prayed that the drought would not endure.

Over the next month, he watched his paddocks turn to dust, and fissures appeared so deep that he expected at any moment to see the earth's mantle split and its core to bubble up and leak out. He brought in feed, but it was expensive, and no matter how much he bought, there was never quite enough of it.

By the end of the month, he decided to sell off most of the stock that remained, giving the ones destined for market the best of the feed, while the cattle he intended to keep were getting barely enough to keep them alive. They all lost condition in spite of it, and he took a huge loss with every head he sold. He hated letting them go: they were the blood that kept the heart beating. Without its stock, his station had no purpose. Without a station, Cal struggled to make sense of the world.

Even in the dead of night, the lowing of starving cattle shattered the silence. Cal drowned out the noise by drinking himself into unconsciousness, but the plaintive wails that swept into Becky's room sometimes nearly drove her mad. In the early hours of the morning, exhausted from work and unable to sleep, she begged tearfully for it to abate. Eventually, the cattle grew so thin that their ribs showed from beneath their skins like the bars of a xylophone, and they lost the energy to cry out. Cal hated shooting his cattle, but their anguish corresponded with his own, and he couldn't bear to watch them suffer. Ultimately, he would run out of options.

Summer was more than halfway over by the time the rain finally arrived. With the first drips, Cal ran out of the house, his hands outstretched, praying that this wasn't going to be yet another sprinkle that was over before it began. Even in the moonlight he could tell that the ropey sky was deeply mauve, but it had been like that before, reached this point, and then flitted away. He was too afraid to walk back inside the homestead, superstitious, in case he drove away the drizzle. As he stared into the sky, the swollen clouds abruptly burst, and drops began thudding on the roof, thick and heavy, a few at first, then a few more, growing in frequency until soon there was a thunderous drumming.

He stood in the yard, the rain soaking his hair and streaming down his cheeks, conscious of the lightning crackle around him, sniffing the ozone mixed with the glorious scent of wet dust. He heard the cattle, invigorated by the downpour, calling out quietly. And he laughed. He tore off his shirt and then his trousers, and danced around the yard in his underpants—a man possessed—chortling and catching the soft water in his mouth.

It kept raining through the night and it was still raining the next morning. Without any grass to cling onto, the water rolled off the soil like mercury: the ground was simply too dry to absorb any of it. The run-off swept topsoil along with the rain into the empty dams. The cracks in the earth eventually filled up, but the torrent had cut rivulets and ruts into the landscape. Having taken forever to arrive, the rain persisted like a leaking tap. Now, he prayed for moderation.

He was suddenly Noah without an ark.

Now, he drove out to the river at least twice a day to check on the level, shaking his head when he returned. 'The river's up another two feet.'

'Is that bad?'

'Well, it's not a problem yet. And it won't be if it would just stop bloody raining.'

By late February, Cal MacGregor was preparing for a flood.

The cattle that had survived the drought were already crowded into the house paddocks, the highest ground on the station. While the road was still passable, Cal and Becky drove into Barkers Hill and stocked up on water and tinned food. They hurried back to Glen Orchy, and Becky began to fill hessian sacks with dirt, and stack them around the perimeter of the homestead. Meanwhile, Cal and Harry worked from first light until dusk in the driving rain, moving rocks with a tractor, and lining the lowest parts of the river with them, until they had built themselves a small dyke. It was meant to repel the river and gain them a little more time. Cal knew it was probably futile, but he needed the activity.

The evening bought no respite. After dinner, they lifted anything that wasn't impervious to water on top of packing cases. Cal's rifles and ammunition were stowed safely above the wardrobes. Once they had done everything they could think of, inertia descended. They watched the river level rise, listened to the drumming torrent, kept an eye on the weather, and waited.

The river burst its banks at twenty-three feet. The lower parts of the road had already flooded from the rainfall, and the rising river water only added to the deluge. Slowly, the murky, stinking, swirling water began creeping towards them.

'Stay out of it as much as you can,' he told Becky. 'There'll be snakes and corpses and shit from the septic in that water.'

By the time Cal had to use his tin rowboat to get about, he knew that the homestead wouldn't be spared. How high the river would rise, he couldn't tell. He found himself in the embrace of the unknown, a puppet dancing to the whim of a mysterious force, but he convinced himself that the force wasn't God. *God* was too close to *Good* for this. This was something entirely different.

With nothing else he could do, he prayed. His faith was strong. His faith would save them. Where before he had looked to the skies for rain, he now looked to them for a rainbow.

The following day, the tepid downpour stopped intermittently, but it was never for long enough. Soon, the cattle were standing up to their hocks in water, and the sandbags had done nothing to stop it from lapping the bottom of the front door.

In the afternoon, Becky also prayed that the rain would end. That evening it did.

Even without the rain, the river continued to rise for another day and a half. Cal loaded up his rifles, expecting to have to put down his cattle before they drowned. By the time the river finally reached its peak, the water in the homestead was almost as high as the dining table.

He contemplated his cattle, bunched together in a pen that was too small for them to stand comfortably, and he groaned. The water was up to their shoulders and they were crying out, necks extended, soft tongues lolling, fear in their wide eyes. He watched them like that for an hour. Then, just when he had accepted that he would lose the rest of his stock, the water began to recede.

He watched the discolouration left from the filthy water revealing itself with the retreating tide, swept-up possessions and dead wildlife dangling from tree branches like strange fruit. He knew there was more suffering to come, even if it didn't rain again. He expected footrot to savage what little was left of the herd, and yet he hung onto a solitary thought—Sandra needed a home now more than ever, and he had to make certain she still had one.

Once the water had drained away, he glimpsed his cattle—mud-mottled, skinny and only barely alive—and he yearned to stand in their midst, a general among his soldiers, euphoric in the silence that followed war, toasting their good health with the finest scotch, appreciative of the battle hard-fought and won. He leaned over the top rail and counted them. He might yet have enough head left from which to breed a new herd. It could have been much worse.

The next morning, as she prepared breakfast, Becky heard Cal sobbing by the cattle yard, and it broke her heart.

The other homesteads hadn't been inundated. The land that surrounded them wasn't nearly as flat and the homesteads were elevated on tall stumps, so that even if the land surrounding them did flood, the houses probably would not. Cal swallowed his pride just long enough to call out for help. The moment the road cleared, Nellie and her children arrived at the homestead with Donald MacGregor.

Cal looked done in, and Harry and Becky weren't much better. Becky had never understood what indomitable meant until then. As soon as Nellie had settled her children into a room set aside for her to stay in, she nudged Becky aside, pulled on a pair of rubber gloves and began to sweep out the water. After that, she scrubbed the floors and the walls.

When they were alone, Nellie mentioned in passing that she had seen Becky crying at Christmas. She had wondered what had happened, but hadn't dared to ask.

Becky was surprised that she had noticed anything that day. Nobody else had. She said, 'I suppose Jim didn't feel the same way about me as I did about him.'

'I don't know about that,' she replied. 'I think his getting engaged was all about money and duty. Since his brother died, I reckon Jim's felt like he's had to stand up and keep the family going.'

Becky was startled. 'I didn't know he had a brother. When did he die?'

'Oh, four or five years back. Jim was away at university. His older brother, Bruce… Well, they reckon he had an accident with a gun. Sometimes things like fire and drought and flood can be an awful lot for a man to bear. Jim came up from Melbourne for the funeral and he never left again. These days, he probably feels like he's an only child and everything depends on him. I reckon he genuinely liked you, Becky. These big families marry off their kids a bit like they breed their cattle. I don't reckon he had a choice.'

Becky was uncertain whether knowing that made her feel better or worse. More than two months had passed since Christmas, yet Jim's words still reverberated. Nellie had provided a context for his decision, but it excused nothing.

'Everyone has a choice,' she muttered.

It took the best part of a week to scrape off the mud and to reinstate most things in their usual places, while the house slowly dried out. Donald MacGregor thought that the walls on the whole seemed pretty sound and probably wouldn't need replacing, although the place reeked of damp and Dettol and faintly of sewage. Fortunately, the wiring had been put high enough that the water hadn't penetrated it. Donald MacGregor said that they were lucky. Cal knew that luck had played no role in the foresight which had made him shift power points halfway up the wall, to Sandra's frustration and the mystification of everyone who visited.

Having finished the course of chemotherapy, Sandra moved back up to Townsville in March. She called Cal and told him that she wanted to drive back to Glen Orchy immediately, but he insisted that she remain there to wait for things to settle. The house was still dank and musty. He told her that he would fetch her as soon as he could.

A fortnight later, Becky finally unfurled the last of the rugs that they had stored on top of the furniture, and returned it to the lounge-room floor. That signalled the time for Cal to drive out to Townsville and return his family to Glen Orchy.

*

Becky's life had been in turmoil for long enough and she craved routine, so the appearance of Cal's old Land Rover just beyond the gate lifted her spirits. She watched it kick up the dust as it approached, three heads in the cabin outlined in shadow, swaying and bouncing with each rib in the road.

She waited for them on the front verandah. Nellie's children had decorated the posts with balloons, and Becky had scrawled her welcome on a banner, which Harry had draped across the top of the front door. Back home, she would have arranged a ticker-tape parade. Back home, she would have had a marching band to greet them.

Billy bounded out of the car the moment they pulled up, like a pup that had been confined too long. He barely acknowledged Becky as he sprinted past her and into the house. Sandra slipped out of the car and carefully mounted the front steps. Her dress had swallowed up her thin frame, and sunglasses hid the dark circles that surrounded her eyes. She wore a scarf, but it had slid past her ears, and did little to mask her baldness.

Becky tried to stifle her gasp. 'Welcome back,' she whispered.

'Thank you for taking care of my home,' she replied.

In honour of their homecoming, Nellie had baked a cake with six layers and covered it in chocolate buttercream, but Sandra looked at it with sunken eyes and pushed her plate aside. She sipped her tea. She said she needed to lie down. She had no desire for food. Nellie nodded and said that she understood, and then she returned to the kitchen with a stack of Sandra's cookbooks.

In the afternoon, she baked appetisers made of pastry flavoured with cheese, chives and mustard, and tiny egg and bacon tarts.

'I've got to fatten her up before I leave,' she said. 'She won't get better if she doesn't eat.'

On one occasion, Becky remarked to Nellie that she had become the groundhog, anticipating the advent of spring, waiting for the hollows in Sandra's hips to fill out and to signal the time for her to go home. Once she discovered that she could pique Sandra's appetite with little morsels, Nellie spent hours devising recipes, while her youngest child played around her feet on the kitchen floor. She made certain there was always something for Sandra to pick at, sitting on covered plates, positioned high above the children, hidden away from the sugar ants and the flies.

At the end of each evening, Nellie gathered up the empty plates and smiled.

During the day, Nellie's children sat in the improvised schoolroom with Billy. They were reserved and inscrutable, and Billy had changed as well. Becky tried to teach them, but she couldn't tell if anything she said resonated with Maggie and Sonny Turner.

Although they sat quietly and attentively while she taught, she couldn't coax a syllable out of them. She tried to connect with them in play, but it was as if they didn't know what to do. She read them funny books and showed them the pictures, but they never laughed. All in all, she needed a better strategy. She would have to ask Nellie about it.

Billy, too, had been soured by the unfamiliarity of a routine and the jibes of the other children who knew all about school as an institution, but nothing about education. He watched her silently with his enormous eyes again, mistrustful and frightened. She wanted to lure him out, but he'd shut down, and whenever she engaged him in chatter, he remained guarded.

Eventually, she threw away the book, took her lessons out to the house paddock, and they all sat cross-legged under a grey gum. Healing arrived in the caress of an autumn wind. Soon, her stroke of genius began to pay off. A couple of weeks later, she broke through.

Just before Easter, Cal received a call that his brother Edward had suffered a heart attack in Melbourne, and had been taken to the St Francis Xavier Cabrini Hospital. Not to worry, he said, Edward was doing fine there, and expected to recover. About an hour later, Donald MacGregor called again to let him know matter-of-factly that Edward had died.

'He never wanted to be buried down there, so we're bringing him back here,' he said. 'I've arranged the transport already.'

Cal couldn't speak. He was despondent. Edward was the eldest, and the first of their generation to die. Although his nephew's, Bruce's, death had hit him hard, he reasoned that Bruce's death hadn't been random: the unspoken truth was that he had chosen to die. Edward had remained vital, handsome and energetic, the *bon vivant*, the driving force of the MacGregor Pastoral Company. He wouldn't have wanted to die and, at sixty and childless, no one had really expected him to.

His body arrived in Townsville later that week, and a funeral was arranged at the church.

Aside from a fleeting introduction to him last Christmas, Becky had never met Edward, and they had never exchanged a single word. She had two reasons not to go to his funeral: she needed to stay at Glen Orchy with Sandra and, most importantly, she didn't want to see Lyn Kavanagh on Jim's arm or hear of their pending nuptials. Nellie stayed behind as well, and the three women sat together in the kitchen, relieved of all responsibility, and toasted Edward's memory with cups of tea, whisky shots, and scones with jam and cream.

'Now, the next bit will be interesting,' Sandra remarked brightly, sipping scotch out of a glass not much bigger than a thimble. 'You girls think that the MacGregors are one happy family united by their common blood, hey? Just you watch what happens next.'

Becky frowned. 'I don't get it. I thought they always acted as one.'

Sandra continued, 'Well, they won't now that Edward's gone. You know Teddy, of course, Donald and Gladys's little brat? You know he was named after his uncle Edward, don't you? Why do you imagine that was?'

'Mr MacGregor wanted to honour his eldest brother?' she ventured.

Sandra put down her glass with a clink. 'You don't actually believe that. No, of course not.' She pinched off a morsel of scone, wiped off a little of the cream, and popped it into her mouth. 'They did it because they thought that, by naming their kid after him, Edward would be sure to leave Glen Eira to Teddy after he died.'

'But he hasn't?'

'Well, I don't know anything for sure, but Cal's one of Edward's executors. He and Malcolm, he's the second youngest, are the co-executors of his will. Donald was left out, and so was Jim's dad, Angus. So, I overheard Cal talking to the solicitor over the phone the other day, and I heard Jim's name come up. Teddy's name didn't come up once.

'Putting two and two together, I think that maybe Jim is Edward's beneficiary. That man was worth a small fortune. Now, I know that Angus has been having a tough time lately, but I tell you what, if Jim is the beneficiary, he won't need to go to the bank for any more loans. He'll only have to go and ask his son for the money.' She picked up her shot glass again and took a large mouthful. She settled back into the chair with a smirk on her face.

Nellie threw Becky a look, but she didn't notice. Becky felt uncomfortable listening to the conversation, as if she had been caught peeking through someone's window at night-time, when they had forgotten to close the curtains. She wriggled in her seat. 'Lucky for him, I guess.'

'Very lucky for him. I suppose that Edward must have taken a shine to Jim while he was boarding with him. He's a likeable young man.'

Becky tried not to reflect on Sandra's last remark. 'And Cal? How does he feel?'

'It's been really hard for us lately—what with me being sick, and the drought and then the flood—you both know that. Cal's not motivated by money, I don't think he'd care. Neither is Malcolm, for that matter. They're both simple men. As long as they can pay the bills, Cal and Malcolm are happy. I guess Edward knew his brothers pretty well.'

'Do you think anything will really change? I mean, if it turns out to be as bad as you imagine?'

'If I'm right, I think that by doing this, Edward's just locked up the cat and the pigeons in the same cage.'

'It would be a pity if the family ripped itself apart over money. Perhaps it won't be as drastic as you think, Sandra.'

'Perhaps.'

Nellie thought about her little cottage with its pretty, gingham curtains, and worried she might never return there. If there was trouble to come, she knew that anything might happen. She sat back and picked up the whisky shot she had been nursing, and hoped that Sandra was wrong.

*

Before another month had passed, it became obvious to everyone that Sandra hadn't been wrong, but she hadn't been completely right either. When Cal and Malcolm flew down to Melbourne to sign the probate documents, they left behind a simmering pot. Having discovered that Jim stood to inherit ninety percent of Edward's wealth, suddenly the family was embroiled in a battle royal, and lines were drawn.

Cal aligned himself with Jim, while Malcolm relinquished his role and threw his lot in along with his brothers. They weren't united, except in their mission to topple Jim's inheritance. Except for Cal, they each argued that Jim had unduly influenced their brother, that Edward had signed his will when his mind was unsound and that, even if that were found not to be the case, they were nevertheless entitled to a greater share of such an enormous estate.

Becky watched the family indivisible shatter into a thousand jagged pieces.

Edward had been a little cannier than anyone had given him credit for: he didn't simply leave all of his fortune to Jim. He mentioned each of his relatives in turn, leaving bequests of varying sums of money to his brothers and to their children, in the expectation that it might be enough to avert a war he clearly anticipated. He even took the time to write them all letters, explaining his reasoning for the sums, and leaving duplicates with his solicitor. It was soon evident that his strategy had failed utterly.

Amidst the turmoil, Jim postponed his June wedding, and Lyn Kavanagh announced that she was delighted to wait, no matter how long it took to sort the mess out. He followed his uncle down to Melbourne and quickly reached a settlement with Malcolm, but Donald and Angus dug in. Where money was involved, Donald felt no shame in holding out against his head stockman, and Angus against his only remaining son. Jim and Cal braced for a fight.

Donald and Angus joined forces just long enough to commence proceedings in the Probate Division of the Victorian Supreme

Court, but Cal knew that their pockets weren't as deep as their aspirations. He had the reserve of Edward's entire estate behind him, and he could afford to starve them out, if he needed to. He knew that, after Malcolm, Angus would be next to waver. Race-horses and other poor investments had savaged him, and he'd taken out an enormous loan just to keep Glengyle station afloat. Jim never knew what his mother thought of his father's financial decisions; he never asked her. All his parents would have had to do to secure their future, was to telephone him. They had survived unspeakable tragedy: he would have shared whatever he had with them. He waited patiently for a call that never came.

Evidently, the problem was that they had no intention of sharing it with him. He stood his ground and they theirs. In Jim's mind, his mother's silence was testimony of her acquiescence. She became as estranged to him as his father already was.

The following spring, Cal negotiated a settlement with Angus, more generous than he thought Angus deserved. With it, Angus retreated to Glengyle with enough money to cover the mortgage for the next decade at least. The only person who now stood between Jim and his inheritance was Donald.

While they were still in Melbourne, Cal and Jim decided to visit Edward's townhouse in Toorak, to ascertain whether Jim wanted to take anything back to Queensland with him. Together, they checked the inventory that Edward's solicitor—a drawn, humourless man named Culpepper—had compiled, and made a list of what Jim wanted sold, and what he wanted to keep. Since probate hadn't yet been granted, their visit wasn't really authorised, but neither Cal nor Jim cared about that.

As he scanned the inventory, Jim detected that something was missing from the list. It was tiny, and more precious to him than the immense suite of family silver, which had been Edward's, and which would probably soon be his. Its value was negligible, yet he had no intention of letting Donald have it, if he managed to break the will. He needed to find it.

A diminutive antique secretaire, with a hinged writing slope as its lid, stood in the far corner of Edward's bedroom. It had belonged to Jim's grandmother, and it was where she kept her meticulous books of account. It was carved out of Australian cedar, made rich honey by the patina of countless hands over many years. With its gently curved legs, it was unmistakably feminine, but Edward had always loved it and so did Jim.

He swept his hand across the slope—it felt as supple and as satiny under his touch as the finest kid leather—and then he lifted the lid. The belly of the desk contained rows of small drawers with round, ebony, button-like pulls, and a central drawer that was longer than the others. He pulled the drawer out, and laid it on the chair adjacent to the desk. His fingers felt around the void in which it had sat. He found a lever and pushed it gently. With a click, a small hidden door popped open, and from that, Jim withdrew another drawer. He glanced at its contents and smiled.

Among Edward's gold cufflinks, diamond tie bar and his collection of sovereigns, Jim found what he was looking for. He picked it out of the drawer while Cal was out of the room. He turned it over in his hand and pocketed it, and then he carefully replaced the drawer in the space where he had found it.

CHAPTER SEVENTEEN

Normality only resumed at Glen Orchy station once Sandra had recovered. The frenetic rhythm of life on the station returned, along with the arbitrariness of the nature that surrounded it. Every day, she grew more robust. The colour returned to her cheeks and the down that had covered her head when she arrived was beginning to develop into a curly mane, thicker and darker than it had been before her illness. Once she had filled out enough to finally fit into her clothes, Nellie realised that she had to leave.

For Becky, who had grown used to the sisterhood of three, the notion of losing Nellie was almost as difficult as it had been losing Jim. On Friday, Malcolm arrived as the peacemaker, to drive Nellie back to Glenstrae. He and Cal had reached an understanding since the dispute over the will—a détente cordiale. It was a negotiated harmony that Cal could never have reached with Donald. Donald had refused to even consider an offer of settlement. He was still holding fast on breaking the will entirely. As a result, Cal had become as entrenched as Donald, and vowed never to set foot on Glenstrae again.

They all sat down together to drink tea out of Sandra's best china while the children played tiggy around the yard. When they had finished, Becky walked to the car with her left hand in Nellie's and her right in Sonny's. Billy was going to miss their company and so would she. It was hard to be the only child within forty miles. Though he was still very young, he understood the way stations operated—people were both necessary and disposable: they came and went with the seasons.

Becky heard nothing further about the dispute over Edward's estate until the eve of her birthday. She knew that Sandra had already baked her a cake: she had glimpsed it in the back of the refrigerator when she had helped her prepare lunch for the ringers. She and Sandra were sitting on the verandah sipping lime cordials and watching the shadow from a box gum creep across the yard, when Cal unexpectedly began whooping. Sandra leapt to her feet, knocking the tray off the table and sending the jug toppling to the floor.

'What's happened?' she shouted, as he ran over to her, lifted her up by the waist and twirled her about. 'Are you all right?'

'It's done!' he sputtered. 'It's over! Donald's had to withdraw his case!'

'What?'

'Yes, it's true. The solicitor just rang me. He said that Donald's withdrawn his case and probate's been granted. I called Jim and he's coming straight over.'

Fortunately no one had eyes for Becky at that moment. She had blanched. She hadn't asked after Jim, and, apart from Nellie and the occasional, unsolicited comment, nobody had spoken openly to her about him recently. She didn't know where he was living, whether he was married or not, or what had become of him. She had only assumed that the wedding was still delayed, since she hadn't heard anything about it from Sandra. She presumed that, if he had married, Sandra and Cal would have been invited, and she would have at least seen them dress up and leave. Given the issue that had caused the delay of their marriage had been resolved, she imagined that he and Lyn Kavanagh were now free to marry.

Sandra picked up the jug and replaced it on the tray and bustled towards the kitchen. If Jim was coming, there would be more mouths to feed. Becky sat on the verandah alone with her head in her hands, anticipating the scene that was going to unfold over dinner. How should she avoid it? Could she avoid it? Could she feign illness and stay upstairs while Jim and Lyn Kavanagh held court and chattered about their upcoming nuptials? She decided that it would be impolite, so she would face the happy couple, let them know that she too was engaged to be married (sort of), and talk of plans for her own wedding with Clark.

Becky helped Sandra prepare dinner by gutting and plucking two chickens from the yard that Cal had killed. She could only imagine what Sylvia would have made of the sight of her daughter pulling out gizzards and plunging the birds into boiling water so that the feathers came away.

Sandra flung Becky a sideways glance. 'Are you all right? It's just that you seem a bit peaky. I can take over the chickens, if they're making you sick.'

'Oh no, I'm fine.'

'Is it Jim?' she asked. 'I don't mean to pry, but Cal mentioned that he thought something was going on between you two last year.'

Becky grimaced. 'I'm not sure what happened. I guess it was just a summer fling. It's over. I'm fine. I'm engaged to be married anyway, to a boy I met back home in college. He's doing a tour of duty in Vietnam, and after that...'

'You'll leave us, go home, marry him and live the American dream?'

'Exactly.'

Sandra paused. She wiped her hands on her apron. 'You know that you don't have to do that, don't you?'

'I know, but my mom would be thrilled to see me and Clark settling down and starting a family in Pittsburgh.'

Sandra sighed. 'When I was young, that was all we expected. You left school, found yourself a fella, hooked your claws into him, got married and he took care of you while you had babies and kept house. Either that, or you became a nun. They were the choices; it was the same then as it's been forever. We never had the freedom back then, that you girls have today. Look at you, things have changed so much, you can make your life whatever you want it to be. You don't have to marry just to keep your mother happy; you're free to have a life all of your own.'

Becky placed the chicken on a tray, washed her hands in the sink and wiped them on a towel. 'I'd like to believe that, but I don't know if it's true. I feel as if all of my life, I've waited for someone else to give me permission to be who I am. It takes a lot to break a habit. The first decision I ever really made alone, was to come here. I suppose I don't have to settle for marriage, but if I do, then surely that's my prerogative too.'

'All I'm saying is that, with everything that's happened to me lately, I've had a chance to think about things.' She chuckled. 'Besides, I'd sooner that you never marry. That way, you could just stay here, with us, instead.'

Becky laughed. 'Well, Billy will grow up one day, and then you won't need me any longer.' She paused for a moment. 'Yeah, you have changed, Sandra. And maybe, so have I. I promise that whoever I marry—if I marry—it won't be just because I've run out of options.' She kissed her on the cheek. 'Every so often, something happens—good or bad—just to shake things up. I'm guessing that life's more about the journey, rather than the destination. Seems to me, we've both come a long way.'

*

Becky was upstairs deciding which dress to wear, when she heard the rumble of an approaching car. She drew in a breath and held it. It was true that women always dressed for other women, and tonight she was dressing exclusively for Lyn Kavanagh. She wanted to look gorgeous, to shine that little bit brighter, not *for* Jim but to spite Jim. She had to look perfect.

In the end, she picked out a minidress, embossed with tiny white hearts.

Twenty years of Sylvia had taught her a lot. She twisted lengths of white ribbon through her hair and fixed them in place with Gossamer spray, lined her eyes black, and her lids lilac. She'd heard that, being on the opposite side of the spectrum, lilac made green eyes pop. She daubed her lips pale pink. A splash of L'Interdit and she was done. She stepped into a pair of white patent leather heels and checked herself in the mirror. She had become Jean Shrimpton at the Victoria Derby.

When she walked into the living room, Sandra gasped. 'Wow! My goodness! You look beautiful! Doesn't she look beautiful, Cal?'

Becky laughed. 'Yeah. If I were only five inches taller, I'd be a fashion model, huh?'

'Stop it,' said Cal, on his way out. 'You look really lovely, Becky. Dressed to impress.'

Sandra grimaced. 'Don't mind him. I know what you're thinking. Last time I saw her, Lyn Kavanagh had a face like a cheese grater and the personality to match. No contest as far as I can tell.'

Becky didn't reply. She followed Sandra out and helped her set the table.

It took a while for anyone to come into the homestead, and when they finally did, she discerned only two voices: Cal's and Jim's. Becky leapt up, picked up a plate and positioned herself next to the table, her best angle, replicating a pose she had seen once in a magazine, pretending that she was still setting the table. Sandra caught a glimpse of her as she passed by, shook her head and chuckled.

Jim strode into the dining room and stopped abruptly. His eyes scanned Becky and settled on her face. His mouth dropped open.

She put down the plate, turned towards him and straightened out her dress. 'Oh, hi. It's so nice to see you again.' She strained forward, peering down the hallway. 'Your fiancée—what did you say her name was—she isn't with you?'

He couldn't reply for a while. 'Eh, you mean Lyn? Eh, no, no, she isn't. I mean, she didn't. And she isn't. My fiancée, that is.' He huffed. 'No, no, Lyn isn't here.'

She had never heard him as rattled before. She swallowed hard and she wondered if she had understood him correctly. 'Excuse me?' she gasped. 'What did you say?'

He looked sheepish. 'Lyn got sick of waiting. She gave me an ultimatum a couple of months ago, get married now or get going. I couldn't do it, so she broke off the engagement, which is good, because if I'd done that instead of her, then she'd have got me for breach of promise. I've had enough of lawsuits to last two lifetimes.' He paused, his eyes resting on Becky's. 'Although I think the real reason it was never going to happen was that there was someone else hanging around.'

'Oh, I'm sorry to hear that,' she gulped. 'So you're a free man, again.'

'Yes,' he replied. 'Yes, I suppose I am.'

In the hallway, Cal cleared his throat and walked in. 'I'm starving,' he announced. 'It's nearly Billy's bedtime. You two done saying hello? Can we eat now?'

Jim pulled out a chair for Becky, and then he took the chair next to her and sat down, cautious and over-attentive. He offered every dish to her first, before he took anything for himself, as if a humble act of kindness might somehow redress the pain he knew he'd caused.

While the others were distracted, he leaned in and murmured, 'I am so sorry.'

She wanted to forget that she had previously seen the same earnestness in his eyes, the same grief, the same affection. He'd been all that before—loving, gentle, thoughtful—and yet he had still gone and hurt her.

He was sorry: words so easily spoken, flung out a million times a day by people around the world and gathered up again, as if they were of no real consequence. She searched her soul. Should she forgive him? Could she expose herself to him in the same way again? She felt the smart of her own tears. She glanced away. She didn't know what to make of it.

'I know,' was her only reply.

After dinner, Jim offered to wash up and Sandra let him, while she and Cal sat in the living room watching *Till Death Us Do Part*.

Becky stood next to him, drying up, contented and at peace for the first time in almost a year.

His shirt sleeves folded up, hands deep in the suds, he ventured quietly, 'I don't think I'll ever be able to apologise to you enough for what I did.'

Becky tossed him a glance, but he kept his eyes on the swirling dishwater.

'Well, we all do hurtful things,' she replied, pausing for a moment before adding, 'sometimes even to people we love.'

He took his hands out of the water and leaned on the sink. 'Yes, that's it,' he returned. 'That's it exactly. And you deserve an explanation.'

'It doesn't matter. You and I, we'd made no promises to each other. We weren't anything…'

'But we were, you know? I agreed to marry Lyn Kavanagh because I believed I had to help out my family, and I didn't know any other way to do it. The thing is, when you own a cattle station, and it's been in your family for generations, you feel as if you have an obligation not to be the one who loses it. Dad had the bank breathing down his neck, and I thought it was my duty to help him out. Her family's as rich as Croesus. I was prepared to marry Lyn just to pay out his debts. And now, I wouldn't care if I never spoke to my father again. Ironic, isn't it?'

She nodded. 'I heard something about it. I'm so sorry, Jim.'

'The truth was I didn't love Lyn. Never did, never could. The marriage would have been a disaster. We both knew it, I guess.' He put down the dishcloth. 'It was only after Edward died, that I worked out what my family was really made of. Parents are meant to sacrifice themselves for their children. But not my parents. The only good that came out of Edward's death—if there could be such a thing—was that it got me off the hook with Lyn. Not that I ever wanted him, or anyone, to die.

'I never wanted any of it—not hurting you, not Edward dying, not losing my family—but it happened and I can't change that.

It was just as well that Lyn gave me that ultimatum, you know, because it set me thinking, is it what I want? Is it what I really want? That's when everything changed. If I'd gone ahead...' He stopped and shook his head, as if he was trying to clear out an unpleasant thought. He left the sentence hanging.

'My biggest regret is that you were the sacrificial lamb in all of this.' He gazed at his hands. 'That night, at Christmas, when I told you about Lyn... Well, I had to bury a brother that I loved, and I can honestly say that it still hurt me less than that night.' He finally turned his head towards her. 'You were so bloody miserable, I desperately wanted to run after you, and say sorry, and take it all back. I wanted to tell you how bloody awful I felt, but I couldn't. I'd already proposed to Lyn.'

'You don't owe me an explanation. Obligation is a hard affliction to shake off. Besides, it's all water under the bridge now,' she replied.

He paused for a while, giving order to his thoughts. Quietly, he began, 'I knew at Christmas I'd proposed to the wrong girl. Shit, I knew the moment I proposed to Lyn that I really wished it was you. I love you, Becky. I think I've always loved you, ever since that day I watched you trying to shoot that bloody goanna. You make me mad and I love it; sometimes you make me bloody miserable and I still love it. I even love that you drive me crazy. I knew that if I'd married Lyn, I could have never kept you out of my mind. I had to admit to myself that you were it, and if I thought that I could marry anyone else, I was deluding myself.'

She comprehended his words but she'd already built a wall against the sentiment. While doubt raced through her mind, his gaze remained unflinching, eyes of indigo, indomitable, steadfast.

'I can't... I don't...' She wrung the tea towel and turned away. 'I...' Eventually, she said, 'Do you really feel that way about me? Honestly? I mean, I want to believe you, of course...'

'Honestly. Truly,' he said. 'I swear on everything I hold dear.'

'I just don't want to wake up one day to find that you were...'

She watched him slip his hand, still wet from the dishwater, into his pocket and rummage about. She offered him part of her tea towel, but he shook his head. Eventually, he pulled his hand out, although she couldn't see anything in it.

'Here. If you ever doubt me, all you'll have to do is look at this.' He gave her his grandmother's ring. 'It's yours.'

The ring was tiny: three diamonds in a platinum setting. Snug over the joint, he slid it on her finger.

'After everything that's happened, would you marry me?'

She spluttered, unable to find a reply. She read his demeanour, still searching for the artifice in it, but found none. Tears trailed down her cheeks, and she buried them in the towel. He tugged it away, cupped her face in his hands, drew her in and kissed her.

'So, will you?'

She drank in his touch, the freshness of his skin, and the comfort of his embrace. It was a homecoming. 'I love you, Jim. I've tried really hard not to, but I guess I just couldn't help myself either. You know that I would have walked through hell if you'd asked me to. All I know is that I want this to be forever.'

The anguish had been dreadful. He sensed it as well. 'I'll never leave you again, Becky. Not ever. From this day onwards, I promise on my life, we'll always be together. No matter what, and forever more.'

She lifted her hand and placed it lightly on his chest, as if she needed proof that he was real. She felt his heart thudding, reassuring, strong, regular. Patience long practised had proven to be her strong suit.

'I know,' she replied.

*

As a child, Becky had been taught that men were stoic and unconnected to their emotions. Walter told her that women were feeble because that was what he'd been taught, and he might have evolved from there except that he never questioned it. He spent a lifetime quashing sentimentality with not much more than an acerbic tongue and his character. Clark Somers was much the same. He had done nothing to overturn Becky's understanding that all men were ruled by reason, and women by passion. He and Walter reinforced the rule that, in emotional hierarchy, passion was always inferior.

Jim wasn't like that. It surprised her that he was barely keeping himself together. As she took his hands, she felt them trembling. She held them close. He had thrown away the shackles; they shook because there was no longer anything left to bind them. They returned to the living room, still holding hands.

The black-and-white images of the British working class projected from the television, jarring, the laughter of the audience too brash. Cal stood up, turned the volume up a little, and sat again. Without uttering a word, Becky slid her hand between Sandra's face and the screen, and watched her adjust her gaze. A moment to grasp what she was seeing and Sandra leapt up.

'Is it what I think? Are you two—?'

Cal turned his head lazily, uncomprehending. He watched Sandra wipe her eyes and scurry out of the living room, bewildered until Jim explained. Then he said, 'I put some bottles on ice after I rang you, to toast the end of the lawsuit, mind, but I never thought we'd have a second reason to celebrate. Here you go, Jim. Crack this open for luck.' He gathered up his Zeiss camera in its fitted leather case, and slung it around his neck.

Sandra hurried back with Becky's birthday cake. She pulled out plates and champagne coupes, and strew them the length of the table. 'This was going to be for your birthday. I was going to save it for tomorrow.'

Becky laughed. 'I couldn't care less about tomorrow. Tonight is enough of a celebration to last a thousand birthdays.'

Cal snapped photos as Jim eased the cork out of the bottle, as the mousse surged up the neck and spilled down the side, as Sandra dashed forward with a coupe to catch it in. Their laughter echoed down the hallway, the television still blared, and Alf Garnett yelled. Cal posed Jim and Becky together in a clichéd pose, arms intertwined, sipping out of their coupes, faces flushed and beaming.

Her parents ought to have been there.

The last time she had tasted champagne she had still been a child: sips stolen from Sylvia's glass when she had been distracted by something else. Back then, the champagne had chafed her tongue and left her mouth furry. Champagne was a drink for adults. In the shadow of the stockyards, with the peaceful, distant bellow of cattle growing sleek with the fresh grass after the rains, Becky sheltered in the company of people who conjured triumph out of the worst possible adversity. Perhaps she didn't need Sylvia and Walter there after all.

They toasted the couple and drained the bottle and then Cal brought out another one, and they drained that as well.

Becky slumped into an armchair, her head spinning as much from the emotion of the occasion as from the alcohol. There was so much to be grateful for. Jim stood behind her, his hand sitting lightly on her shoulder. She belonged—not to him—but to this. Their relationship had travelled away from the tenuous half-light, it was brilliant now, and there was now an accepted term for the role that they played in each other's lives. Abruptly, there was legitimacy in their pact. She sipped another glassful, and let her head flop back. The champagne had taken away her reserve. It didn't matter. She was secure in a way she had never been before.

After her third glass, she declared aloud that she loved everyone and wanted to marry them too, and they called it a night.

Out of respect, Jim took her as far as her bedroom door and no further.

In the morning, Becky woke up with a headache that seared her eyes. She felt as if someone had scoured her irises and lined the sockets with lead weights.

'Oh Lord,' she muttered as her stomach lurched.

She tided herself up and stumbled towards the kitchen, unsure if she was hungry or ill, and wondering if it was possible to be both simultaneously. She could hear Billy playing in the yard and willed him to be quiet. There wasn't any chance that she could teach him anything.

She glimpsed past the door and groaned. They had been waiting for her to arrive.

'Happy birthday!'

Wool had replaced her brain. She clasped her hands to her forehead to stop it splitting apart.

'There she is. There's the beautiful bride,' chirped Cal, as irritating and bright-eyed as she wasn't.

Sandra was partially obscured by a teacup, but her eyes followed Becky as she sat down. They were red and humourless, and Jim's weren't much better. He rose, gave her a peck on the cheek and sat down again.

The percolator was keeping warm on the stove. Becky couldn't have cared less if the coffee had been stewing there for days. She poured herself a mugful, sat down and sipped it neat.

Sandra thrust the toast rack over to her. 'I'm not even going to ask you. I feel the same.'

'Never, ever again,' Becky muttered.

'Don't say that. You all need to get into training,' quipped Cal. 'Seasoned drinkers don't get hangovers. Although, I have to admit, champagne always pushes me right to the edge.'

Sandra snorted. 'And you're proud of that?'

Becky took a slice of toast and buttered it. She nibbled at the crust briefly and put it down.

'Vegemite,' Jim mumbled, pushing the jar closer. 'On your toast. Good for hangovers.'

She had placed it on a list of things never to be eaten. Not ever. She lifted the lid, glimpsed its tarry black glossiness, and sniffed it. It was an unusual smell—suggestive of the sediment that adhered to the pan after frying steak but not half as appetising. She scooped out a blob.

He darted forward and took the knife out of her hand. 'A little of this stuff goes a very long way.' He barely smeared her toast with it, and handed it back. 'Here, try that.'

She touched the toast with the tip of her finger and licked it. It was intensely salty. For some reason, she had anticipated some sweetness, but there was none. She took a bite and chewed. She felt the flow of saliva over her tongue. She swallowed, and bit off another piece. The savouriness began to chase away the nausea.

'See? She's a convert,' he said with pride. 'This is the first day of the rest of your life.'

She scowled, and pushed it aside. After a second mug of coffee, she was finally awake.

Jim announced that he was impatient to take over Glen Eira station as soon as he could, now that it was indisputably his, and he left the kitchen briefly to call the manager. While he was gone, Becky said that she wasn't inclined to repeat the anguish of separation.

'Well, it'll be your home once you're married, of course,' Sandra remarked.

Married or not, her place was with Jim. She declared, 'Oh, I won't be waiting till then. From this minute on, I'm going wherever Jim goes.'

Sandra flashed Cal a look. 'No! You can't mean living together! People talk, Becky,' she continued. 'I can't imagine where you got such a thought! If you move in with Jim without being married, well…' She was flustered. 'It's simply not done. Not by nice girls, anyway. Are you sure you want to have that reputation, you know, of…'

Becky frowned. 'Of what? Is it really that bad to live with the man you're planning to marry?'

'It is around here. Everyone knows everyone else's business, and they all have an opinion about it. Even if all you're doing is sharing a house and not a bedroom, it will get around. You can't imagine what they'll call your children. Maybe in a big city it's different.'

'So, they're all small-minded hypocrites. You know what the last few months have taught me? I can't waste any more of my life waiting to live my life. I can't imagine that either of us is planning to have any children before we get married, but, if we do, then they'll have to be tough enough to cope with what people say. These people you're talking about, who are they, anyway? I know it means a lot to you, and I respect your opinion—you know that—but I can't live my life according to what other people think.'

Sandra looked as if she'd been struck. 'But it's a sin. Don't you see that?' she whimpered. She turned to Cal for reassurance, but he was already at the sink, washing out his cup.

'I guess we don't all look at religion in quite the same way. You and Cal have been wonderful to me, and I hope I've made a difference for you, too. I love you both, and I know you'll worry about my immortal soul, but as I see things, Jim and I have to make up for lost time.' Becky reached out and placed her hand on Sandra's. 'I'll leave here when he leaves.'

She shook her head. 'Oh Becky, you don't always have to be in such a hurry. I know that nothing I say will make any difference, but I wish you would reconsider what you're about to do.' She could tell her words weren't sinking in. 'I know Jim's a decent man and I'm sure he won't let you down, whatever you decide.'

Jim strode back in, a fresh energy to his step. He glimpsed their faces, puzzled by the soberness that suddenly confronted him. 'I've set up a meeting at Glen Eira tomorrow,' he said. 'I want you to come with me, Becky, so you might as well start packing now. We're about to start a new life.'

*

It was an uncomfortable meeting with the manager of Glen Eira. Since Edward almost never visited, Dennis Curtis had elected to move himself out of the manager's residence, and into the homestead. He took the meeting with Jim there, in a bedroom that he had turned into his office.

Everyone had assumed that Edward personally controlled his own, as well as the MacGregor family's, interests, and that he was meticulous in doing so; however, the reality didn't match the expectation. Once Edward had installed Dennis Curtis to run Glen Eira and advise him on the company's holdings, he seldom checked anything beyond the superficial. It seemed that he trusted Curtis's judgement in all things, and took his advice without question. Without constant scrutiny, Curtis's record-keeping had, like the man himself, become flabby and self-satisfied.

Now that Jim had shown up, demanding to see the books of account and the stock books for the previous five years, and asking about the company minutes, Curtis baulked. He sat on the studded leather chair behind the wide oak desk that Edward's money had paid for, eyes hooded, leaning back, his arms crossed.

Jim was the stranger in his own home.

At first, Curtis was surly and uncooperative. Then, he became loquacious and tried to dazzle Jim with detail. He deflected every demand with sleight of hand and responded to every question with a labyrinthine answer, never reaching a conclusion. He pushed piles of papers around, as if they were significant.

'You want documents?' he snarled. 'Then, here.'

Jim was patient. Probing but respectful. Unyielding. And then he caught Curtis grinning under his moustache. Jim bristled, but Curtis was too dim to notice: he thought he'd already won.

As Becky listened, she understood that Jim could be taciturn when he needed to be, and authoritative when the situation demanded. He returned everything Curtis threw at him squarely. He told him he had a week to turn over the books in good order, or face the scrutiny of an auditor, and certain legal action. Curtis dug his heels in, informing Jim that in the absence of a vote of the shareholders (of which he had appointed himself one), he didn't recognise Jim's right to remove him from the position of manager, and he wasn't going anywhere.

When Jim took her hand and walked out of the homestead, Becky was aghast. She hadn't figured him for being a quitter. Instead of climbing into the car, he told her to wait for him there, and, if anything went wrong, she was to get in and drive away as quickly as she could.

'What do you mean?' she asked. 'What could possibly go wrong?'

'You'll soon know if it does.'

His jaw clenched, Jim strode off towards the cattle yards. He returned a few minutes later with two men, and they marched back into the homestead together. One of the men, an Aborigine, carried a length of rope in his right hand. After they had passed by, Becky left the car, scrambled up the stairs and stole along the verandah to the office window. She stood to the right of the window, peered in and listened.

She saw Curtis still sitting at his desk, pulling sheets of paper out of drawers and tearing them into strips. There was a box of matches positioned by his left hand, one drawn out and wedged at an angle, ready to strike. He had already half-filled a wire basket, and was ripping the papers up so feverishly that his face had turned plum. She heard the men's boots clatter up the hallway. Curtis swung about in his chair, the moment he noticed them enter the room.

'Put that down, Curtis,' Jim shouted, 'and stand up.'

'What in God's name?' He remained seated and swivelled away from the desk and towards the basket again. 'Haven't you left, yet? Fuck off, MacGregor.'

Jim walked up to Curtis, his arm outstretched, until his fingers nearly touched Curtis's temple, his voice snarling, 'Get up, I said.'

Curtis glimpsed Jim's .45 FN Nationale pistol out of the corner of his eye, and flinched. He put down the papers and turned himself about. 'B-boys,' he stammered. 'You going to just stand there and let him shoot me? The man's mad.' He searched their faces. 'Hey? Patterson? Maurie?'

'Do what, boss?' the man with the rope replied. 'I dunno what you mean.'

'I dunno, either,' said the other ringer. 'He looks pretty angry. Wouldn't want to cross him. Maybe, you better get up then, ay?'

Curtis rose gingerly, his arms extended as if he was ready to embrace Jim, his face flushed. Jim stepped back calmly and adjusted him aim to Curtis's torso. 'Uncle Edward taught me to always aim at the biggest part of any target. That way, when you shoot, you're certain to hit it. A bullet in the gut can make an awful mess, and it's almost always fatal—four years' study of medicine taught me that.' He tutted. 'Shame you never got to know the real Edward MacGregor. He was no pushover. And neither am I.'

Curtis was flustered, his eyes darting from man to man and back to Jim, but Jim never wavered.

Patterson sidled forward, grabbed Curtis's wrists in his gigantic hands, and shoved them behind his back. Curtis lashed out with his feet, but Patterson moved away without letting go, holding himself clear with his superior reach. Then Curtis tried to push against him, but Patterson was unmovable. He was seasoned. He could take down a scrub bull singlehandedly, and a portly man with palms like two goosedown pillows was no match.

Maurie secured Curtis's hands with twine he took out of his pocket, looping it over and over again, until there was no give in it.

'This is for every time you never paid me,' he mumbled. 'And for what you done to my missus.'

Jim replaced his pistol in his belt and led Curtis outside. He took the length of rope from Maurie and lashed Curtis to the brick verandah pier. Once he was certain that he was secure, the men walked away.

'How long are you going to leave me here?' he shouted.

'Dunno,' Jim replied. 'It all depends.'

'What if I need to do a piss?'

'What do you reckon?'

Becky returned to the car. Jim stood for a while with Maurie and Patterson leaning against the post-and-rail fence next to the old press, but the cattle were milling about and she couldn't hear any of their conversation. Eventually, he patted each of the men on the shoulder, and moved away.

'What are you going to do with him?' she asked. 'I mean, you're not going to shoot him, or anything?'

'I've got plans.' He grinned. 'I saw you at the window. Bet you weren't expecting that, ay?'

Jim unlatched the tailgate and unloaded the Land Rover, and he and Becky carried their luggage into the homestead. Curtis watched them with half-closed eyes, his face scarlet.

'Watch that you don't blow a fufu valve, Curtis,' Jim remarked with a chuckle.

They stripped Curtis's bed and bundled his belongings into a sheet, tied it up and lobbed it outside. When his swearing became intolerable, Jim took off his boot and stuffed a sweaty sock in his mouth, and watched him gag. He replaced it every time he spat it out, until Curtis eventually fell silent.

George Lumley drove up in his mail truck in the afternoon. Glen Eira was the last stop on his run; after unloading the delivery, the back of his truck was empty. He and Jim sat on the verandah sharing a pot of tea, the breeze blowing off the river, while Curtis looked at them and scowled.

When they had finished, George stretched his legs.

'Got a special delivery for you to take back into town,' said Jim.

George glanced over at Curtis and chortled. 'No worries, Jim. I'll be very glad to take the rubbish out for you.'

Patterson untied Curtis from the pier and led him towards George Lumley's truck.

'You'd better give him a drink and let him have a piss. I wouldn't want him to mess up the truck along the way,' said Jim. He turned to Curtis. 'And don't you even think of coming back here. If I ever see you anywhere near this place again, I won't hesitate to shoot you and feed you to the crocs. Understood?'

He thought he heard Curtis whimper.

Patterson did exactly as he'd been asked. He hobbled Curtis by the ankles, let him gulp down a bottle of water, watched him urinate, and then he tied him up again. After that, he opened up the back of the Bedford and dropped in Curtis's bundle. Despite Curtis's bulk, Patterson lifted him up almost as easily as he had his belongings, and he tossed him in the back of the truck too, and then he closed the doors and secured the latch.

George climbed into the cabin and fired up the engine.

'Thanks,' said Jim. 'I appreciate it a lot, George.'

'Your family's always been pretty good to me,' George Lumley replied. 'I never, ever liked Curtis here, or that Mrs Gladys for that matter. Hewn out of the same rock, them two, I reckon. So, good luck with this place, young Jim, I'll catch you up in a few days, ay? And don't you worry about him,' he laughed, gesturing with his thumb towards the back of the truck, 'I'll be sure to take the scenic route back into town.'

*

It took Jim several weeks to unravel the mess that Dennis Curtis had left behind. Aside from his involvement in cattle duffing with a nefarious, rat-faced, small-time criminal named Jennings, Curtis had misappropriated a considerable sum of money, and he had short-paid almost all of the ringers. It seemed that he had cheated everyone, but he had treated the Aboriginal stockmen especially badly.

Curtis had continued to withhold their wages, despite the system being outlawed. In practice, he only ever paid the Aboriginal workers at Glen Eira a pittance. The men never complained, believing Curtis when he had said that he was remitting the money to the government, and that their families would be able to go to the police station at any time, and draw on the funds. They were used to that: in their experience, it was the way the state of Queensland had always dealt with the Aborigines.

But of course, Curtis hadn't paid a cent.

Jim assumed that Curtis simply kept the money for himself. Edward would have been distressed if he'd known about it. Like all the MacGregors, he believed in paying a fair wage for a fair day's work, but since it was his disinterest that had allowed this dishonesty to flourish in the first place, he wasn't entirely blameless. Jim was repulsed by what he'd uncovered. Curtis had feathered his nest on the back of modern-day, state-sanctioned slavery.

So Jim sold the townhouse in Toorak. It was an asset without purpose. Although he'd lived there for a while, he felt no nostalgia for it, no need to keep it as a token of his family's success. He paid off the debts with much of the proceeds, and then he put the rest aside. Having seen how financial uncertainty had embittered his father, he was determined to do everything he could to avoid it.

Once he'd sorted out the finances and made amends with the ringers, he set about straightening out the station itself.

While the ringers had done whatever they could to keep the station operating efficiently, they came and went, and Curtis never employed a head stockman. He kept his workers ignorant and itinerant. A head stockman worth his salt would have asked more questions than Curtis could have answered and, without a firm hand to drive it, the station had been directionless. Curtis was a bookkeeper: he taught himself only as much as he needed to know, to keep himself comfortably entrenched, and to avoid detection.

The rest, as far as Jim could tell, had been left to rot.

The first thing he did was to give the ringers job security. The next thing he did was to offer Nellie the position of housekeeper at Glen Eira, with the inducement of the use of the manager's residence. Since Gladys MacGregor had returned, Donald had reduced Nellie's hours and cut her wages, not to save money or to disadvantage her, but he reasoned that Gladys would be less inclined to stray, as long as she was kept fully occupied.

What sealed it for Nellie wasn't the anticipation of a better home: she was happy enough with the one she had. The money wasn't an issue for Nellie either: she cared very little for it beyond what she needed in order to live. It was Jim's promise to pay for her children's private education, which proved an enticement she could hardly refuse. She never dared hope that one of her children might attend a university, but Jim's offer allowed her that dream. She packed up her children, gave Alf the option of coming or staying, and then she left Glenstrae as soon she could.

Becky anticipated her arrival more keenly than anyone else. Curtis hadn't maintained the homestead either, so her priority—beyond cooking for the men—was to sort out what needed doing and to get it done. The roof leaked when it rained, the kitchen cupboards were falling apart and the pipes were so rusted that it spoiled the spring water and turned it tan. In a matter of weeks, she had composed a very long list.

Although she and Jim had set the date for their wedding in the spring, she wasn't preoccupied with it. Now that their relationship was universally acknowledged, she felt secure enough: she would have happily postponed it indefinitely, if he'd asked her to. That they were together meant more to her than anything else.

What she couldn't hear were the whispers that had spread between the ringers and their wives. Behind her back, they called her Jim's common law wife—his *de facto*—a phrase which, as far as they were concerned, took away her credibility and her right to their respect. Without a wedding certificate, she was a fallen woman, no better than a black gin.

Sandra had warned her. Jim was a man, and men had appetites, and it was a woman's obligation not to yield. A *decent* woman, that was. Sandra didn't want to judge, so she took her worries to bed every night, and every night she prayed for them both.

For Sandra, their wedding couldn't arrive soon enough.

As far as the rest of Jim's family was concerned, he was a young man doing what young men did. He was bringing shame onto the family name by sowing his wild oats so openly, but there was certainly no need for him to marry her. They thought of it as an unfortunate interlude, and blamed Becky for the family rift. Except for her, he'd never have treated his family in that way. She must have worded him up to cut them off as he had. He'd be free to toss her out and move on, once he was sick of her uppity, foreign ways.

Nellie heard the gossip, but she never repeated it to anyone. Becky exasperated her; she simply hadn't grasped the importance of appearances. Cattle stations were claustrophobic, censorious, close-minded societies. In order to be respected by the men, Becky needed to demand respect from them. She drew her authority from Jim, so if he didn't value her enough to legitimise their relationship, then neither would the men. If they thought of her as a whore, they would treat her as such, and Jim would have the devil's work to change their opinion. Becky and Jim simply had to marry straight away.

Jim understood that, by leaving the wedding until the spring, he might draw criticism. He wasn't ignorant of the implications of not having sorted out the fine details before moving in with Becky, but he didn't consider it vital. He would have happily removed any of the men at gunpoint if he'd heard them disrespecting her, but they never did. They had the good sense to keep their opinions beyond earshot.

While they waited for the spring, he and Becky spent as much time as they could together. She had to understand the business of running a cattle station, and it was up to him to teach her. He had to be certain that, if anything ever happened to him, she could at least keep the station functioning until he recovered. He needed a partner as much as he needed a wife, and she had a lot to learn.

While Nellie took over the house and the cooking, he showed Becky the books, explained the dynamics of the family company and the basics of running the station. He made a list of who they bought from, who was trustworthy, and he took her to a stock auction. He taught her to shoot, and encouraged her as she learned stock riding.

Once she was competent enough, they rode the boundary together. The scrub cattle had pushed over a long section of fencing, and mixed in with a mob past the river. The scrubbers were huge, unruly beasts, and he needed to clear them out, before they bred with his cattle and tainted the bloodline. He shot two of them off his horse at a gallop—a cow and a bull with long, curved horns—but the others scattered. It was too great a job for Becky and him to tackle alone. He would have to come back in a day or two with the dogs and a couple of ringers, and sort them out. Then he'd have to repair the fences.

On the way back to the homestead, they came across a stray bullock near the river. It was a vast animal, perhaps a thousand pounds; its head was bowed and it was bellowing strangely, obviously in pain. Jim signalled for Becky to stay behind, and he approached it alone.

As he inched Cochise forward, he checked the bullock over and his jaw dropped. He shook his head and frowned. There were claw marks running down the length of both of the beast's flanks, deep and jagged, like seismic fissures. Although he had never seen anything like that before, he knew exactly what it meant. There were crocodiles in the river, and at least one of them was big enough to have tried to tackle the bullock. Enough salties like that, and they could decimate a herd. If they could take down cattle, then they could easily take a man. He had to get rid of them.

He would have to hunt them down.

CHAPTER EIGHTEEN

J IM RETURNED to the river the following day on foot, carrying his Mauser 9.3 bolt action rifle. Becky desperately wanted to come with him, as if her presence would act as a talisman and keep him safe, but he told her that crocodiles were sensitive to movement and smell, and he needed to do this alone. When he returned, he promised to make her a pair of shoes with the fine belly skin.

She stayed at home with Nellie reluctantly, her heart in her mouth, knowing that she wouldn't settle until he returned.

It was a still morning when he left, with barely a whisper of a breeze. He needed to stay downwind of any salties, or they would sense him, and his efforts would have been wasted. He strode to the river briskly, only creeping stealthily the last two hundred yards. He stood about fifty yards from the bank and watched the tips of the leaves at the apex of a nearby sandalwood tree, but they divulged nothing to him beyond a gentle quiver. Which direction the breeze came from, he couldn't tell. He held up his hand, but detected no wind at all. He opened his mouth and felt the lightest draught graze the end of his tongue. It was coming from the west-southwest, and he was fine.

The river crept along at the point that Jim had chosen to begin the hunt, meandering slowly between the flats. It was muddy and brown and infinite, a gentle sweep with wide banks and sheltering trees at its fringes. The tangled mess of roots made a perfect place for the salties to nest, and for their hatchlings to hide. There was no movement, no shallow rocks for the river to tumble over, nothing to break the tension of the surface. Despite the apparent tranquillity, he was certain that there would be crocodiles there. They were certain to choose the mud flats to bask in. The Mauser was loaded and ready to fire. He just had to wait for them to appear.

At about nine, the sun was high enough to reach the near bank and to warm the shallows. Jim's legs were sore from inactivity, but he simply couldn't afford to move them. He tried to keep the blood flowing by tensing and releasing his quadriceps from time to time, but it wasn't enough. If nothing happened soon, he would be compelled to stretch out, to shake the blood back into his feet, move further along the river and try again.

As he watched, he detected something gliding the width of the river. At first it looked like a broad log, only barely beneath the surface, drifting along with the flow, nothing unexpected, too placid to be anything sinister. It wasn't until the surface broke and a pair of eyes emerged—somewhere between the colour of olives and raw meat—that Jim was certain he had located his prey.

He watched the crocodile emerge from the shallows and drag itself lazily onto the bank, but he still did nothing. It was about thirteen feet long and three wide, and probably a male, not quite large enough to have been the one that had savaged the bullock. After a while, the young croc was joined by two others. They were sunbathers on a sandbank, blissfully unaware of his presence.

Jim raised the sight and shot all three in rapid succession, the bolt handle flying in his hand between each shot. He caught two in the head, but he only injured the third, a juvenile, and in the matter of a second or two, it had slipped back into the water and disappeared.

He replaced the spent bullets, secured the rifle, shouldered it and walked on. He might have rid himself of two of the salties, but he hadn't yet located the one he was looking for.

He stopped again about five hundred yards downstream, at a sandbank not that unlike the one he had left, but he must have made too much noise, and by the time he'd lifted his rifle, all that was visible of the crocodile was its tail. A swish, and that had disappeared as well. He sighed and moved along once more.

From there, the river turned sharply to the north and then it doubled back on itself again, and he knew there was a swampy area in between, the size of about three or four football grounds, a perfect habitat for salties. When it rained and the swamp flooded, it turned into a large billabong, and the crocodiles picked off any birds that were silly enough to land on it, or any livestock guileless enough to stop there to take a drink. It was a dangerous spot to hunt crocodiles. There was only one way in and one way out, and if he wasn't cautious, he could easily find his only exit cut off.

The moment he stepped onto the marsh, he realised his mistake. His feet stuck to the ground and began to sink in. He had stepped into quicksand.

It wasn't that he was worried about being swallowed up by it—that only ever happened in B-grade horror movies—rather, that he had just made a quick retreat impossible. As he lay down and stretched out, slowly working his way back to solid ground, he had the sense of being watched. In front of him and to his left was a saltie, an enormous adult, at least eighteen feet long. It had already spotted Jim and was slithering towards him, eyes locked, claws pawing the mud, tail gliding slowly from side to side.

Jim's heart rate soared. He needed to stay calm if he was to survive.

He heard something move, closer and to his right. A second saltie had lifted itself out of the river—much slighter, but still big enough to kill a man—and was creeping towards him across the swamp, its maw slightly open, tasting the air. He was too low: it was an impossible angle to shoot from, but his life depended on the steadiness of his hand and the precision of his Mauser. He had seconds to make up his mind.

He decided to take the shots: the closer one first, and then the one farther away. Two cracks, quick but not quite clean. The smaller crocodile stopped, although he couldn't be sure that he'd killed it outright, but his second shot merely glanced the larger crocodile, and he heard it strike a tree on the far side of the swamp. Stung by the bullet, it sped up, scampering, aloft on its powerful legs, soul-less eyes intent on him and nothing else. Time was running out.

Jim held his breath, took aim and fired once more.

Barely fifteen yards away, the crocodile halted abruptly and didn't move again. Jim sucked in a lungful of air and lay down the rifle, his hands shaking. He had shot it square between the eyes.

*

Becky leapt to her feet when she heard the gun fire. She counted the shots off, shivering until Nellie reassured her that it was a good sign, and all it meant was that Jim was fine, and doing exactly what he'd set out to do.

'I can't just wait here,' she said. 'I don't care what he says, from now on, I'll always go with him wherever he goes.'

'Well, that's just about the stupidest thing I ever heard,' Nellie replied. 'He's got a job to do, and if you're there, he'll spend so much time just making sure you're all right, that all you'll be doing is making it harder for him.'

She fell back into the chair, and watched Nellie for a while with half-shut eyes. Eventually, she picked up the silk that she had cut into strips, coiled a length of wire around it, and coaxed it into a rosebud. Once she made enough of them, she intended to twist them into a crown for her wedding. For the moment, they were just a distraction.

At about one-thirty, she gave up making silk flowers and decided to have some lunch, just to pass the time. She fixed herself a sandwich, but was unable to eat it. She looked at it for a while, but it churned her stomach, and she pushed it aside and tried to concentrate elsewhere. Beyond the window, something caught her attention. She looked out. On the horizon, she glimpsed Jim stag-gering up the road, caked up to his neck in filth.

'Thank God,' she breathed. She darted through the door and scampered up the road.

Jim saw her, but he was too tired to smile.

'Are you all right?' Her eyes flew down his body. Every pore and every hair was cloaked with mud, but he appeared to be intact.

'Yep.' He placed the rifle down, and stood with his hands on his hips. 'That's four gone. There's enough croc skin down by the river to make you a set of ports, along with those shoes.'

She tried to laugh, because it seemed to her that that was what he wanted, but after a morning of dread, there was no humour in it. All she felt was relief. She tossed back her head and gazed at the sky. The tears streamed down her face, and she was unable to curb them. 'I love you more than my life, Jim. Whatever happens to you, happens to me, too.'

He exhaled loudly and gripped her tightly to his chest. She smelled the foul sourness of the swamp.

'Nothing will ever happen to me,' he said, 'you have to know that. I was born into this life and I know what I'm doing. You just have to trust me.'

'I trust you,' she replied.

They walked back to the homestead together, his arm heavy on her shoulders. It was as if he didn't even have enough strength left to bear his own weight.

CHAPTER NINETEEN

ELLIE SNIFFED and wiped her nose with a fresh hand-kerchief. It was a man's, monogrammed with the letters *A.T.* in blue silk, and beautifully pressed, creases like the blades of knives. It had been Alf's, a birthday gift from her. He had never once used it, and it remained behind the last time he had left.

Her head was buried in a book when Chase came into the kitchen, as he so often did these days.

'It's beautiful,' she huffed, placing it flat open on the table. 'All the experts say that sugar is bad for your body, and that we've all got to eat kale, but sometimes you just feel like having a slice of good, old-fashioned chocolate cake. A little sugar's got to be food for your soul, doesn't it? This,' she said, gesturing at the book, 'is my devil's food cake.'

He glanced at the title. *Mistress of the Glen*, it read, and the picture that graced the cover was of a damsel, her bodice ripped just enough to reveal the roundness of her bosom, swooning into the embrace of a half-naked Highlander in a kilt, with pectorals almost as bulging as hers.

'That's great,' he muttered, pulling out a chair and sitting down. His hand slid along the silky oak armrest and settled on his thigh. A spectre drifted across his mind, and his face suddenly clouded. 'You were telling me about the crocodiles?'

'Oh yes, that's right. I was telling you about your...' She stopped and glanced away.

Chase glared at her. 'Pardon?' he muttered. 'Who did you say, Nellie? My...'

'Sorry,' she began. 'I get myself so confused sometimes. I was talking about Jim, wasn't I? Pity he's not here for you to meet him. Jim was the sort of man you'd want to go into battle with, that's what Alf used to say. Straight as an arrow, hard as nails, heart as big and as generous as a whale's. Isn't that how the saying goes?'

'Hmm.' It was dismissive, inattentive.

She fastened him with her eyes like deep wells, unblinking. Her lips puckered as if she had been considering an admonition, but then second-guessed herself. 'Well, by the time Jim finished with them, there weren't any crocs left in the river. There's a photo of him somewhere... He was in the paper... With a croc he shot back when he worked for his uncle out at Glenstrae. All strung up, hanging from a tree, a big bastard, maybe four, five metres. They came down from town to talk to Jim, and he was all coy about it, but inside I reckon he was pretty happy with himself. If I find the clipping, I'll show it to you.'

'But I thought that crocodiles are protected around here. Don't you need a licence to hunt them?'

Nellie was shaking her head. 'Not back then you didn't. If you'd have told the MacGregors back then that there would come a day when they'd have to ask permission to shoot the crocs, especially on their own land, they'd have called you crazy. Last I heard there's a hundred thousand of them salties out there in the wild. What for, I ask you? What's wrong with culling the bastards? In the olden days, we could go swimming in the river anytime we wanted to and we'd be safe as houses, but you wouldn't do that now, no fear, not unless you wanted to turn yourself into croc tucker.' She stood up with a groan, sauntered across the room and filled the kettle up from the tap. She flung a handful of leaves into a teapot, placed the kettle on the stove, and sat down again.

Chase softened. 'Anything I can do for you, Nellie?'

'I'm slowing down,' she grumbled. 'Can you find me a new body?' She stretched out her fingers on the table, still fine and straight between the joints, but the joints between the phalanges were thick and as knobby as pecan shells. She gazed at them and exhaled loudly, rubbing her swollen knuckles. 'I only hope that I've got enough left inside me to outlast her.'

'If you ask me to, I'll always help you.'

She studied his face and a whisper of a smile passed her lips, and was gone in a flash. 'Yep, I reckon that you would.'

Chase turned his attention back to the topic of discussion. 'So, did he ever get rid of all of them?'

'He and the boys shot as many as they could find. I wouldn't know if they got them all, but he never complained of losing any stock down by the river again. So I'd say he was pretty successful.'

Chase leapt up when the kettle began its asthmatic wheeze. By the time he reached the stove and turned it off, its cry was as shrill and as maddening as a whip-poor-will. He poured the water out of the kettle and into the teapot.

'I like talking to you, Nellie,' he remarked sharply.

She grinned. 'Me too. You come here anytime you got some spare time and you want a chit-chat. There'll be a cuppa and a biscuit waiting. I reckon that you and me, Chase, we've got a lot to say.'

CHAPTER TWENTY

Early one Sunday afternoon, Jim said that he wanted to take Becky swimming.

It was winter, and while the nights were just about cold enough to keep milk fresh, the morning sky stretched cerulean as far as the line of ironbarks. Winter had the advantage of most of the heat, but none of the oppressive humidity, of summer. In winter, the days were clear and warm.

Becky was apprehensive. 'What about the crocs?' she asked.

Jim smiled. His frequently tensed shoulders relaxed under his work shirt, sleeves folded back on themselves, revealing strong, capable arms. Since they'd come to Glen Eira, he always spoke with authority that didn't invite question, but there was playfulness in his eyes, which he only ever revealed to her.

He said, 'There aren't any crocs where we're going,' and nothing more.

He caught and saddled the horses and they rode along the wide, dirt road to a ford in the river, which the cars and trucks used to cross it. While the road continued on the opposite side, he and Becky stayed on the near bank, turned off onto an old track and followed the river upstream. For a mile, it ran at the same level as the river, parallel to a second, newer track, wide enough to drive on.

They crossed the river at a broad, rocky concourse, carefully, Becky refusing to ride, leading her mare across as Jim rode on, both of them subdued by the dappled sunlight and the tranquillity of the scrub. The flinty strike of the horses' shoes against the polished river stones cut through the hum of the trickling water and the trill of the black butcherbird overhead. He warbled twice, paused for an answer, and then twice again, repeating the pattern, on and on, as if persistence would ultimately reward him with an answer. Eventually, they had moved too far away to hear whether the answer ever came.

A few hundred yards further on, they departed the river and followed a stream. As they ascended, the track turned stony and overgrown, and the horses picked their way through patches of barbed-wire grass and spinifex tussocks. As the track rose, it meandered past a series of small cascades, barely dribbling at first, the lower ponds fed by an underground flow which rose to the surface intermittently and disappeared again. They stopped in a secluded glade, high above the river plain.

Jim watered the horses at the stream just below the highest cascade, and then he tethered them to a fallen gum. They were surrounded by a copse of rivergums. Above the stream was a waterhole, fed by a noisy cataract which flowed through a deep crevice in the granite. Becky gazed at the pool and sighed. It was mostly in shade, and any sunlight that did manage to reach the water was gentle and stippled. It was a sheltering paradise, a sanctuary, beyond which the light was white, and harsh and hot.

Becky gazed at the water uncertainly. Jim traced the frown on her forehead with the pads of his fingers, and said, 'Don't worry, Becky, it's safe. No one ever comes here. It's ours and nobody else's.'

He stripped off first and jumped in, without waiting for her. She examined the smooth, tanned firmness of his body as he broke through the surface, and the ripple of the waves he had made, moving rhythmically outwards, concentrically, towards the rocks. She slipped off her clothes and slid naked into the rock pool. She duck-dived into water so translucent, that she could see Jim's form suspended, hanging invisibly, as clearly as if there had been nothing between them other than glass. She turned corkscrews as he breasted the water; she rose up and then descended like a water ballerina, arms outstretched, unashamed, intoxicated by the freedom.

Under the cascade, the water was unexpectedly cool. It pummelled her shoulders with its force, not unpleasantly, but vigorously, like a therapeutic massage. He swam across to her, lifted her up and pressed her against a rocky ledge where the water was only inches deep, and kissed her repeatedly. He felt the strength of her thighs around his body, and the nectar of her breath on his face. He caressed her gently, until he couldn't wait any longer. In that moment, there was no one and nothing else.

Eventually, they fell apart, basking lazily in the tepid water lapping over the boulder, dozing and waking up again. Where so much of their lives up till then had been discordant, at that moment everything was perfect.

All the elements were in flawless synchronicity.

*

Nellie read the signs long before everyone else.

Two months before the wedding, arrangements were in place, the dress made, the rings bought and the church booked. It was going to be a tiny wedding: Becky and Jim had invited barely enough people to fill a few tables at a restaurant, let alone trouble a community hall.

With Jim's old school friends fifteen hundred miles south, it was pointless inviting any of them. Cal had agreed to stand up as his best man, and Sandra was to be Becky's matron of honour. A few months ago, once they'd fixed the date, Becky had written her mother another long letter. Sylvia replied matter-of-factly that, since Walter hadn't forgiven Becky for wandering off to the other side of the world, he was barring Sylvia from going to her daughter's wedding. Becky had written to Sam, too, at the last place she'd heard from him, but received no response. That hadn't surprised her. As far as her family went, none of it had, really.

The rest of Jim's family was unwelcome. His father had written to him, to let him know that he had heard of his engagement *to the American*. She was little better than a streetwalker, and couldn't Jim tell she was only after his money? He had broken his mother's heart twofold: once when he left Lyn Kavanagh at the altar, and again over this nonsense. The wedding, his father wrote, must not happen. He'd underlined the sentence twice, for emphasis. If Jim chose to go through with the damned wedding, then he and his issue were dead to them forever. Angus MacGregor apparently hadn't noticed that Jim had consigned his parents to the same fate some time ago, and so he didn't care tuppence what they thought.

Three weeks before the wedding, Becky began to feel unwell. It took a colossal effort for her to rise in the morning, and by mid-afternoon she was spent. She put the nausea climbing up her throat down to pre-wedding jitters. When she had an appetite, she constantly felt like she needed to eat fresh buttered bread and jam. Her habitual cup of coffee had suddenly become so unpalatable that she asked Nellie what she'd put in it.

Nellie made her a cup of sweet tea instead.

'I know exactly what's wrong with you,' she said, handing her the cup and decanting the contents of the coffee pot down the sink. 'I knew it over two months ago, just by looking at you.'

'Oh, really?' Becky stirred the cup with a tiny silver spoon, tapped it on the lip, and placed it on the saucer. 'And what's that?'

'Simple. You're pregnant. Nine weeks gone. I know. I have a gift.' She poured herself a cup and sweetened it with honey. 'I always knew with my own, right down to the very day, and all of my cousins, too. You think back, and you'll work out that I'm right.'

Becky's cycles had never been regular. Sylvia had taken her to see a doctor about it once, when she was sixteen. The doctor had examined her, and told her bluntly that, chances were, she would never be able to bear a child. It was something she never thought about (and didn't completely believe), so she never discussed it with Jim. Yet she didn't take precautions, either. She counted back. Nine weeks placed them at the waterhole. She had noticed her clothes had become a little tighter around the waist lately. Jim had only recently remarked that her nipples had darkened, and she'd wondered if it might have been from exposure to the sun.

Becky was flustered. Her face was crimson.

'You are!' Nellie sipped her tea. 'You don't have to feel ashamed with me. It's all right, you know. It's not as if you and Jim aren't about to get married. All you have to do is keep quiet and pretend that the baby's come early. It's been done before, you know.'

'Yes, but by the time we get married I'll be twelve weeks gone. You can't pretend a baby's that early.'

'Yeah, you can. By then, you'll be Mrs James MacGregor, and who cares anyway? Tell Jim, by all means. But don't you tell another soul, Becky. People around here are mean old gossips.'

Becky thought for a moment, then asked, 'So, what happened when you knew I was pregnant? I mean, how could you tell?'

'Oh, I just get this feeling. It's as if I see you, and I see right past you. It's there—a flash—and then it's gone. I guess you'd call it a vision, but that sounds odd, like I can see things that other people can't. My aunty was like that.' She sniffed as if she was holding back a sneeze. 'But it's never the same vision for every person. For you, it was this: I saw you coming out of the sea, like some kind of goddess, and you were holding a baby in your arms.'

'Really? That's odd.' She shivered. 'See, you've given me goose-bumps.' She displayed her forearm, with her fine hairs standing on end. 'We'll be in town for a couple of days before the wedding. I'll go to the doctor then.' It made perfect sense, and she might have suspected it sooner herself, if it hadn't been for that earlier doctor. Her hand flew to her stomach. It felt pleasingly full. Regardless of what anyone else thought, she knew Jim would be happy. She rose, and kissed Nellie on the cheek.

'It's a girl,' Nellie blurted out, without a second thought. 'I just saw it, now, when you kissed me.'

'Oh!' Becky gasped.

Nellie saw more besides, but she kept it to herself.

*

Jim woke up just before the first light. The room was still bathed in ghostly shadows, except where a moonbeam had pierced an opening between the curtains and drawn a jagged silver stripe along the floor, up and over the footboard and diagonally across the bed. He checked the clock. It was eight minutes to five. As if to affirm that it wasn't yet day, a mopoke called outside.

He flipped back the blanket and shivered in the early chill. Becky was fast asleep. As he dressed, he listened for her breath. It was imperceptible; her face was buried in the bedclothes, hair tousled. In the absence of light, all detail of her was lost in the variegated shadows. He might have believed she was dead, except for the lazy rise and fall of the blanket. He considered waking her for the briefest moment, but she tired so easily lately, that it would have been unkind. He kissed her sleeping form, picked his watch up from the top of the drawer, and tiptoed out.

He stepped past the ports crammed with the things they were taking with them into town later that week, clothes and toilet bags, gifts for Cal and Sandra. From largest to smallest, they were stacked in a neat pyramid, adjacent to the front door. Next to the luggage was an old cedar coat stand. He lifted his hat off the hook by the pinch in its crown, and worked it onto his head. He glanced at a chit on the key box, but it was illegible in the darkness. He knew what was written on it anyway. The doctor's appointment was booked for Friday—wedding eve—although they didn't need a doctor to confirm what they both accepted to be true. Nellie was infallible. He grinned with the joy of anticipation. Since neither he nor Becky had a family anymore, they would grow one of their own. They would raise their children right: they would be adored, but never indulged.

He and Maurie were riding out to muster the scrubbers, the wild cattle that had evaded him before. They were mean old buggers, but Maurie was a gun ringer, and he had a way with cattle, even the feral ones. Jim would have sooner had nothing to do with them, but that option wasn't available. He couldn't let them be, without sacrificing his herd. No matter how quiet the breed that was put over them, the progeny was inevitably just as wild as the parent. Even if he could get them to market, he couldn't sell them. Scrub cattle were untamable. Behind them, they left a wake of wrecked fences and empty feed troughs. They were poor eating. The only useful thing to do with them was to shoot them and feed the meat to the dogs.

Outside, the horses were milling around, snorting, the haze of their breath hanging in the air, amid the clatter of stirrup irons as Maurie emerged laden from the saddle shed. The dogs were quietly eager, eyes darting from side to side, paws outstretched, ready to spring up and get going at a single word. The dogs were Maurie's: Jim hadn't had a cattle dog since old Gypsy died, three years ago. She had been intelligent and well-mannered, but he had managed without her just the same.

Nellie was already up; Jim could tell from the smoke chugging out of the chimney from the old Metters stove. Jim's grandfather had bought it in Sydney, and had paid to have it hauled up by horse and cart. It had been replaced long ago. Nobody had bothered to use it in decades, and bits of it had gone missing, but Nellie discovered the flat cups corroding in the yard and put them back on the stove plate. She scraped off the rust and polished it until the enamel glistened like a cloudless sky. Then she fired it up. She said that nothing could match the taste of her roast beef cooked in a proper, wood-fired oven.

Jim and Maurie ate eggs and steak, and drank a cup of tea with Nellie, Maurie standing in front of the stove, warming his buttocks.

'You gonna get piles doing that,' she muttered.

Maurie grunted and kept eating.

She packed their food for the day in tinfoil parcels, the joins running along the top of each parcel pleated neatly, and then she stowed them in their billies.

Maurie lit up a cigarette. 'If you was ten years younger or I was ten years older, I'd marry you.'

Nellie harrumphed. 'Never mind that I'm not nearly as old as you suppose, Maurie Crowbar, but if I was ten years younger, I'd still be too married and too smart for you, and if you were ten years older, you'd be way too old to be of any use to me. It's best that some things stay just as they are.'

Maurie chuckled.

She raised her eyes. 'You boys be careful now, hey?'

'You know we will,' said Jim as he drew himself up. 'Tell Becky she was sleeping so soundly when I left, that I didn't want to wake her up.'

Nellie grinned. 'I'll tell her that you said that you love her.'

'Yep. That too.'

Outside, the sun had just begun to rise, and stained the eastern horizon pink. The birds had stirred, honeyeaters and scrubwrens, perched in the tallest of the narrowleaf red ironbarks now luminous in spidery full bloom, while they caught up on their gossip. Their chatter was ear-splitting. To the west, the livid sky persisted where the glow hadn't yet penetrated, the gunmetal buildings outlined darkly in the half-light of dawn. The men swung onto their saddles, Maurie whistled for the dogs and they rode away.

It was mid afternoon when Becky heard the clatter of hooves thundering down the road at full tilt. Even as a novice horsewoman, she picked up on the rider's urgency. The horse was stretched out, its gait long and quick, struggling to breathe, lips foaming, grunting as it gasped for air. It had been pushed to its limit and then a little beyond.

She ran outside to meet them.

The rider was solitary. She knew from afar that it wasn't Jim. Maurie gathered the reins and drew the horse up hard, right next to the back verandah and leapt off.

'Quick,' he cried, 'get the ute!'

Becky ran at him, her stomach heaving. 'Where's Jim?' she yelled, glancing past him. 'Is he with you?'

Maurie didn't answer.

She repeated, 'Where's Jim?'

He paused, but didn't look at her. 'There's been an accident, Boss Lady.'

'Is he all right?'

Her shriek echoed. Her voice was as sharp and hollow as a curlew's, yet no one seemed to hear her.

'Maurie, is he all right? Is he all right?' She screeched it over and over again, willing him to say yes and relieve her of the dread that he had awakened inside her and which was threatening to eclipse the sunlight, her eyes darting nowhere and everywhere.

Nellie bustled up beside her and grasped her around the waist. 'Maurie!'

Maurie's honey-brown face was bloodless, and his eyes rimmed red. He gazed at his boots when he answered her, toeing channels into the dirt. 'No,' he mumbled, his voice strangulated, haunted by a vision he had no words to explain. 'No, Boss Lady,' he repeated.

Becky teetered backwards, supported by Nellie's right arm, strong and muscled, holding her steady so that she wouldn't fall. All her dreams and hopes and desires were spinning out of control and colliding into each other, then breaking apart, like atoms in a reactor. Random images. The ports sitting by the doorway, suddenly rendered superfluous. The flash of his smile. The broadness and comfort of his chest. She was reaching out, trying to grip onto something which had already crumbled into dust and blown away.

'He can't be dead… Is he dead?' she heard herself ask.

For a long time, Maurie couldn't answer.

'Yes,' he said at last, his voice an echo, sucking the breath out of Becky's body.

The best of days and the worst of days had a lot in common. For one, they both began with a sunrise.

CHAPTER TWENTY-ONE

Nearly fifty years later, the mention of that day still bathed Nellie's eyes in her tears. She searched for her handkerchief, but it wasn't in her pocket, so she wiped them on her apron. Chase's mouth remained partly open, as if he wanted to say something, but the words wouldn't come out.

'Enough,' Nellie began, chiding herself for crying. 'That was by far the worst day of my life up till then, although I've had plenty to match it since.' She straightened her apron, silently smoothing out nonexistent creases, her mouth pouty, looking but not seeing. On the stove, she was making jam from a crop of early strawberries and for a while the plop-plop-plop as it boiled filled the silence.

'Maurie drove the ute out and stayed with him until the police came out. Then he brought him home on the back of the flatbed. Maurie said that one of the scrubber bulls had reared suddenly and spooked Cochise, who had leapt straight up in the air like a jack-in-the-box, just as Jim was getting off. Jim's foot was caught in the stirrup. He was hung up and dragged under, and the horse fell on top of him. Maurie said he heard Jim's neck snap like a twig. The only mercy was that he was dead before he had time to see it coming.'

Chase nodded. He didn't trust himself to speak.

'After that, I helped Miss Becky back inside but she refused to go upstairs to her room—to their room—because she said it would have torn her apart. You can imagine the scene that followed: Miss Becky weeping, and then insisting it wasn't true. She wailed and screamed until the police let Maurie tidy him up a bit and cover him up with a blanket, and then we walked her out to the ringers' quarters where Jim was laid out. It was awful. She covered his face in her tears, placed her hand right over his heart, and then she

kissed him that one last time. Then they took his body away into
town.

'We took her back inside the house; she had one of us holding
her up on either side, light as a ghost, and the howls that came out
of her tore out my heart. Five days ahead of their wedding. If only
he hadn't gone out that day… If only the horse hadn't bucked… If
only he'd stopped to wake her and say goodbye… It's all the little
things that make the difference between living and dying, and you
never know which one will lead to what. Come or go? Leave or
stay? Wait one minute or five? Which of these things kills you and
which saves you?

'I've seen plenty of tragedy in my life and none of it makes any
sense. Maybe there's no rhyme or reason to any of it. We think that
what we do makes a difference in our lives, but maybe it's not true.
He was just twenty-eight when he died, with his whole life ahead,
the best of men in so many ways, and with everything to live for.
If we choose our destiny, who would choose to die like that? I have
lived fifty years since and there isn't one day I haven't thought of all
of the no-good, layabout, waste-of-timers out there, and wondered
why they're alive and he's dead. It makes no sense to me.'

Nellie paused for a moment, the pain of that memory echoed in
the slack folds of her skin, as if she'd been sapped of any desire to
hold her jowls taut.

After a while, she resumed. 'Jim was always organised in life
and that never changed when he died. For such a young man, he
must have understood the risks he took, because he made sure all of
his affairs were in order. After he inherited Mr Edward's estate, he
made a will and he made sure it was watertight. I reckon he didn't
want anyone to go through what he went through with his father
and uncles. He wanted to be buried here at Glen Eira. He wanted
his family to respect Miss Becky. He didn't want any fighting over
his will. Mr Cal got left something out of it, or at least that's what
I heard, and everything else went to Miss Becky. Through his will,
Jim spoke to his family from the grave, but he didn't have much

to say about them that was nice. He wrote about them one by one, and why he hadn't left them a thing.

'There was talk about them contesting the will for a bit, but it all settled down pretty quickly. I reckon they had no money to pay the lawyers, and the way Jim wrote his will, it would have been a lost cause anyway. Funny, how some people grieve the loss of someone close until their heart bursts and they're broken by it forever, while others just see it as a business opportunity.' She braced her hand on her hip, turned towards the stove and stirred the jam, the fragrance that filled the room scalding and intense.

'My mother's people have their view of death, and I have mine. Blackfellas can choose when they die, and after they're dead, the living aren't supposed to say their name again. I say their names, no worries, because I know that their souls aren't gonna get trapped here, no matter what. It took me a long time to work out that only the living and the damned are here on earth, and they're exactly the same thing. The living *are* damned, and just the dead are free. That thought keeps me going. When I cry for Jim, I cry for me and Miss Becky and everyone else who knew him and lost him, and I even cry for those who never knew him but should have. I don't cry for him anymore. I know he's good where he is.'

Chase interrupted. 'And the baby?'

She snorted, turned off the stove and shook her head. 'The baby. Now, there's a sorry story. I thought that by the way that Miss Becky was crying and grieving and wouldn't swallow a single mouthful for days, the baby in her belly was sure to die. I thought I got it wrong this time: there was going to be no baby, not born to her at least, and not then. Maybe the woman with the baby in her arms that I had seen, wasn't Miss Becky at all.

'I took her to my cottage, put her into my bed and let her rest for a while. I started her with thin soup, like she was an invalid, me sitting on the bed with a bowl and a spoon, and feeding her like she was a sick child, while my own babies peeped at us through the door. I made her lamb shank and barley, and gruel out of the

Country Women's Association cookbook. I told her she couldn't die, she had a baby inside her, but she said that she wanted the baby gone, and would I please tell her how to get rid of it.

'I saw red. I put down the bowl and the spoon. That was the first and only time I ever slapped her. I slapped her hard. I slapped her so hard that her cheek was red in the shape of my hand. I slapped her and then I said to her, "You've been given a blessing and you don't even care. That baby is Jim's as much as it's yours. He's not here to say anything to you, so I have to say it for him: you kill that baby and you're killing Jim a second time, except this time it'll be your fault. He wanted that baby of yours more than anything else in the world. He loved you both the same. He hears that you killed his child, and he won't want anything to do with you, living or dead, so you better not go looking for him in the next life."

'I told her that and I reckon that some of it got through. "But I can't have this baby, Nellie," she said to me. I said, "You have it and you let Nellie help you raise it. We're doing okay with mine, we'll do okay with yours, too." She said to me, "If this baby's born, I don't think I could look at it without thinking of Jim every day, and you might as well bury me now." I told her we'd see, then I went into her old room and got one of her letters out of the drawer, and I wrote to Mrs S. Golding in Henry Street, Brooklyn Heights, myself.'

*

Sylvia Golding was surprised to find a letter from Australia in her letterbox, written in handwriting she didn't recognise. When she turned it over and checked the return address, unease rose from her stomach. She kept her composure long enough for the neighbours to sense nothing in her cheery hello, or in her smile, or in her brisk climb up the front steps, past the wide entrance of her brownstone and back inside. Her hands shook. She cut the envelope with a paper knife she took off Walter's desk, and slipped out the letter.

She tripped over the lines at first, scrambling to understand the gist of their contents without worrying about the detail, solving word by word the mystery of why someone she had never heard of had written to her.

Then she slowed down and reread the letter.

It wasn't that she couldn't make out Nellie's writing—it was perfect copperplate—and her meaning was clear enough, but Sylvia was torn. She knew what she wanted to do: the anguish in her soul was enough to tell her that Becky needed her. The instinct to smooth the way for her children had never deserted her; since Sam and Becky had gone, she had learned how to repress it. It was the only way she could maintain harmony. Her choices were crystal clear. Sylvia's problem was Walter.

Everything in his world was either right or wrong, day or night. He was glad that he wasn't burdened with Sylvia's ridiculous, feminine sensibilities. As far as he was concerned, his children were ingrates. Women had frailties and men—real men, of which he counted himself one—had none. He had no time for either of his children, no money to bail out Sam and no emotion to waste on Becky.

Even before the children had left home, his reign had been autocratic. He had worked hard and he told himself that that was enough to deserve all of their adoration. When each of the children departed, he was wounded. He believed that he had ruled his dominion as a benign despot, his only motive to protect a way of life. They had eschewed it, and so he slammed the door shut after them. He built battlements and ramparts against them, but Sylvia could have blown them away with a single word. She was the only one who had always lived within his rules, which was what wives did. She never thought to question her husband's despotic right any more than she might have questioned her father's. Or the President's.

To realise she had lived forty-four years and never felt doubt and discord before, was more unsettling for her than the feelings themselves. They had always been there, a lava lake bubbling under a thin crust, but she had numbed them away with pills and lotions for long enough. He was intractable; she knew that. Until that moment, she hadn't really grasped why her children had chosen to flee Walter, rather than face him. It increasingly occurred to her that in order to save Becky, she might have to do the same.

Sylvia had a passport and access to all of their savings, and she could have bought herself a ticket without telling Walter. After a day wasted in furious self-debate, she decided not to run away without explanation. She wanted him to understand.

The women's movement meant nothing to her; apparently she was liberated, yet his approval meant everything to her. She vaguely recalled a time when she had been indomitable, a sassy teenager, fiercely Democratic, decades before anyone burned a single bra. That girl had lost her way, lured into Walter's Republican ideal with the promise of financial and emotional security, compromise and compliance attained by degrees, in the same way that a frog boiled. Cooperation had certainly resulted in comfort and harmony in the home, but she was done with all of that. It was time to reacquaint herself with the indomitable, sassy girl who had walked into Walter's store that day with her mother, and had offered to bake him a cake.

Sylvia talked to Walter after dinner.

He was sitting at the far end of the dining table, draining the last drops of beer from his glass, his empty plate pushed away.

She leaned across the table, her hand reaching forward but not touching him, and steadily, quietly told him of her plans.

He put down the glass and frowned, the muscles in his brow contracting into a dozen creases, sad-eyed, his mouth taut. 'You want to do what? Are you crazy?' he barked.

Sylvia used her smile as a weapon. She had scarcely touched her meal. She folded her napkin deliberately, and placed it on the table. 'She needs me, Walter. Can you imagine our poor girl, out there in the wilderness, expecting a baby and her husband dead?'

'But I need you,' he replied, his mouth crooked. He suddenly looked far older than his years. It was Walter exposed, the first acknowledgement of his vulnerability.

Sylvia sighed. She classified his words as belonging to the category which she labelled manipulation. He didn't need her. At best, she was merely the buffer against his own discomfort. 'Yes, I know you do, dear, but don't you see that Rebecca needs me rather more than you do right now? Surely, you could make do without me? Even just for a little while?'

It was becoming a game of wills; he had picked up the other end of the rope and was tugging back. Walter hardened. 'What I see, is that Rebecca made her bed the day she left here, and now she's lying in it.' He sat, stony-faced, waiting for the remnants of their dinner to be taken away. The lingering smell of the steak, the stale beer foam stuck to the lip of his glass, the channels his fork had created when he had scraped up the gravy on his plate, it irritated him and he wanted it all gone. His lip twitched. 'Well, I forbid it!'

'What?' Her voice was a semitone higher than before, shrill with disbelief. 'You what?'

'I am your husband and I forbid you to go, Sylvia. No more to be said about it. There, that's it.'

'You what?' she repeated. Instinct had become her imperative: her child needed her. Lionesses killed for less. 'I have been your wife for twenty-four years. In all that time, I've been loyal. I've cooked, cleaned, raised our children as best as I could, and I've never asked you for a single, damned thing.' She was finally ready to draw a line under it. 'I'm not asking you for permission to go, Walter, I'm telling you that I'm going.'

He sat unblinking, as stunned as if she had stood up, walked over and struck him.

'Now, you don't have to do a thing,' she continued. 'I'll fill the freezer full of meals for you. Mrs Rossetti will do your laundry and clean the house. You won't even notice that I'm gone.'

'You can't do this to me, Sylvia.' His voice was breathy and hollow, piped though a flute. Perhaps he had sensed her determination, or he had been worn down by loss that he had never understood, but he looked uncharacteristically broken.

'I'm not doing anything to you, Walter, I just really need to go. It doesn't mean that I love you any less. I could have gone without telling you, but your support is important to me, it would prove to me how much you love and respect me.' She added gently, 'I'm not running away from you, I could never do that. They're our children, you know, and no matter what's happened in the past, we have to do everything we can to protect them. It's our duty. How would you feel if we didn't help Becky, and something bad happened? That's when you'd lose me, because I couldn't live with myself.' She walked over to him and took his hand in hers. He still bore his battle scars on the dorsal side, but the palm had become softer and fleshier with age. She pressed his hand to her lips. 'I love you as well as our babies, and I always will.'

Sylvia left New York in the autumn—her favourite season—just as the beeches in Central Park were turning the colour of overripe grapes and their leaves beginning to drop. Walter drove her to JFK airport, where she boarded an American Airlines flight to San Francisco, and he waved her goodbye. She arrived at Glen Eira just under a week later, glued to the seat, alongside George Lumley in his stinking truck.

She had begun the mail run in Barkers Hill with her hair in curls stacked high above her bangs, wearing false eyelashes and a safari-inspired linen pantsuit, a geometric silk scarf that she had bought at Saks knotted around her neck. Ten miles later, she began shedding layers. She took off the jacket and the scarf, tied the scarf around her head, and packed the jacket away in her suitcase. By the time she arrived at her destination, she had stripped down to a sleeveless satin waistcoat and trousers. Her hair was flattened by sweat, her makeup had slipped by half an inch, and the once-cream trousers were tainted with all the bull dust that had kicked up as they sped along.

She gazed at the homestead, at the garden wilting under a tire-
less sun, deep verandahs mucky with dirt caught up in a sudden
shower, dumped there and left to dry. It looked as exhausted as she
felt. George Lumley carried her bag inside and down a long, dim
hallway, as she followed in his bandy-legged wake. He passed a
door to the left and Sylvia glimpsed Becky curled up on a sofa, her
body hardly making an impression on the cushions, eyes closed,
breathing lightly. She crept into the darkened room, close with the
humidity of the approaching wet season, brushed the loose strands
of hair away from Becky's sleeping face with her fingertips, and felt
the urge to weep.

CHAPTER TWENTY-TWO

CHASE WAITED for Nellie to open the door of the manager's residence; she had asked him to drop past in the evening around eight. She had said that, since he seemed interested in the history of the MacGregors and the Goldings, she had a few things to show him. He arrived at eight sharp, clutching a tin of salted caramels he had bought on a whim when he was last in town.

He'd passed by the residence often, but he had never really looked at it. It stood behind the homestead, dominated by it, tucked under its long shadow.

Although the residence didn't resemble the homestead at all, the incongruity of the buildings jarred in a way that reflected worse on the homestead. The homestead was heavy and ostentatious, a water buffalo in a lake of lily pads. The residence was fundamentally a cottage: older and simpler, without pretence or aspiration, built to house the family until the homestead supplanted it, and then handed down for the manager's use. Since she'd taken it over, Nellie had planted the garden with snapdragons, hyacinths, marguerites and roses: it would have looked perfectly appropriate in a village in Dorset.

He knocked again and heard the distant scour of slippers against floorboards growing louder as she approached.

The door creaked open. Nellie had taken off her apron and changed into a fresh cotton dress in a china blue print almost as joyous as she was, with cut-outs at the shoulders. Her skin peeked through the gaps like bronzed crepe paper.

'Ah,' she breathed, 'it's you.' Her voice was nuanced, as if she had been expecting someone else to arrive, but was pleased enough to see him on the other side of the door nonetheless.

He took off his boots and left them on the threshold, and padded along behind her.

The cottage was light and fresh, five rooms in rapid succession, all neat as pins, a short hallway leading to a modest kitchen and then two steps down to a chlorine-infused bathroom that had been added much later, and which served as the home's full stop.

They paused at the kitchen.

'How about we sit down here?' She motioned towards a small, round table covered with a lace cloth.

He pulled out one of the four matching chairs, popped the caramels to one side, and sat down. 'These are for you.'

Nellie didn't take them. She put the kettle on to boil. It was permanently on the stove, and the water inside it only ever went cold overnight. Chase didn't press for coffee, feeling it would have been ungracious. Tea was as necessary as air, an appreciative nod to visitors, and he was slowly gaining a taste for it. Alongside, something sweet to eat appeared, arranged on a painted ceramic plate. Hospitality wasn't monopolised by the Berbers; graziers were just as welcoming.

Perhaps isolation, rather than race, bestowed that especial importance upon visitors.

'Now, before I show you what I brought you here for, I want to fill you in on what happened after Sylvia Golding arrived.' Her hands braced against her thighs, she sat down next to him with a groan.

'We buried Jim alongside his great-grandfather, over there'— she pointed vaguely south—'down past the cattle yards, under a stand of stringybark. I'll show you the plot, if you're interested.'

He nodded at her and she seemed pleased.

'After the funeral, Miss Becky got very sick, not just in her body, but in her mind too. One day, right out of the blue, she turned to me and said that she'd heard about Aborigines who had the ability to will themselves to die, and did I know how they did it? Lord, I was worried sick. I'd heard about it too, I'd even seen it happen.

The old folk, they knew how, they had their way. Of course, I never knew how they did it. Even if I had, I'd have never told her.

'Now you can understand why I was desperate enough to write to Sylvia Golding. I never said a word to Miss Becky about having written to her, or that her mum had written back to me asking for directions to Glen Eira, because she couldn't find it on any map. When I got that letter, I couldn't wait for her to arrive. While we waited for Sylvia, I did the same as I'd done for Mrs Sandra, back when she was sick. I made her all kinds of little bites to tempt her, I taught myself to make pizzas just like they have in New York, doughnuts and even them big pretzels dipped in lye. There was nothing I wouldn't have done for her and Jim's baby.

'I remember the day I first clapped eyes on Sylvia Golding. My word, but that woman was stylish. She got out of old George's truck looking like a beauty pageant winner… A beauty pageant winner who had just lived through a tropical cyclone, that is.' She chuckled at the image. 'I don't blame her, you know, but she looked a fright. She wasn't ugly, mind, not a bit. That woman was a real stunner—reminded me of that president of yours' widow—with her big sunglasses and her lovely clothes—but she'd crossed the whole of America, the Pacific Ocean and then come up from Sydney looking like a fashion catalogue, just so she could steam away in George's old truck for hours. The stink of his BO must have been horrendous. Poor thing! You have to love someone a lot to do that, that's for sure.

'I'd tried to do everything I could to help her, but Miss Becky really needed her own blood. There's real comfort in a mum's embrace, I reckon, and Sylvia Golding was better than any tonic a doctor could give her. Nothing was ever going to stop the pain, but at least her mum could give her a bit of support. I left them there so they could talk for a while, and that night Miss Becky slept inside the homestead, right next to her mum.

'I never knew what Sylvia Golding made of me, but she said that she was grateful that I had written to her. She wasn't happy that Becky and Jim weren't exactly married, and she asked me why I forgot to mention that in my letter. I asked her what she would have done if she'd known, and she never answered me.'

Nellie stood up abruptly, took three tea cups out of the cupboard and a plate filled with petit fours and placed them on the table. After that, she hovered.

'After a while, they began having some terrible rows. I tried not to listen in at first, but I couldn't help but overhear. I reckon everyone must have heard them. Back then, it was a big shame to be an unwed mother. I heard of girls who went all the way down to Brisbane to have their babies. I heard tell that there was a special part of the hospital down there, the Royal Brisbane, for girls who'd got themselves in the family way. When they were due, they were put into a hidden room and tied up to the bed, like they were criminals who might escape. I heard that they gave the girls pills to keep them calm, and then the midwife delivered them and took away the baby. They never saw their babies again. And not just girls went through that, but I heard that that's what happened to Gladys MacGregor and her baby, too.'

She filled the pot with three spoonful of leaves and topped it up with water.

'Shameful what the Queensland government did to blackfellas and bastard children, ay?'

She wiped a trickle of water from the side of the pot and sat down again. 'Anyway, at first Sylvia insisted that Miss Becky go home with her, but Miss Becky said she wasn't leaving Jim. They had made a promise to each other. How could she leave, anyway, now that Glen Eira was hers? So, then Sylvia asked her to leave Glen Eira, before her condition became obvious, so no one would know she was having a baby. She'd heard that Miss Becky could have the baby in Brisbane, have it adopted out, and come back to Glen Eira and nobody needed to know. Miss Becky said that she was never letting her baby go. People were bound to notice a baby at Glen Eira anyway, so what was the point of hiding her pregnancy?

'In the end, Miss Becky went into town to deliver, and she came back with her baby straight away. Exactly as I predicted, she had a girl. She named her Constance, because she said that that was how her love for Jim was. When she brought her home, Constance was a tiny little thing, pale as a skinned rabbit. Sylvia said she'd stay on for a while, to help her settle in.

'A week or two later, it was clear to me that Miss Becky wasn't coping. She wasn't herself. I know of plenty of women who have had the baby blues, and we know all about it now, but back then we just thought she was being selfish. You just told them to snap out of it, and mostly they did. Except Miss Becky didn't. She went to bed again and stayed there, and when she was up, she took to staring out into space. For hours at a time. I never saw anything like it.

'Sylvia and I tried to get her to take care of her baby, but she just wouldn't. I pleaded with her, but she'd gone deaf. She didn't want to feed her, and just as well I had bought tins of formula, in case her milk didn't come through, or the poor baby would have starved. Nothing either of us said made any difference, Miss Becky was in another world. About a month later, I heard her tell her mother that she was scared she'd hurt the baby, and wanted it gone. She'd made a terrible mistake. She couldn't take care of a baby. It was barely a week after that that Sylvia Golding left Glen Eira and took Constance away.

'I was too frightened to ever ask Miss Becky exactly what happened after that, and she never breathed a word to me either. She just got up one day out of bed and she began running the station. She mustered and drafted the cattle along with the ringers, she did the books, and she ran the station. It was as if the baby suddenly never was. At first, some of the men tried to put her in her place, but she stood up to them, just like Jim would have if he'd been there. She said to them not to call her dear, or darling, or sweetheart. They could call her Miss Golding or Boss Lady, from then on. I watched her go from being a little girl to a tough grazier, I suppose, because she had to.

'When the family company sold out, she took her share of the money and helped Mr Cal and Mrs Sandra buy themselves a farm up north. I know they did okay there, until Mrs Sandra died a while ago, after that cancer came back. Miss Becky kept in touch with Mr Cal until he retired to the Gold Coast. As for the rest of them, well, I guess they spent what they got, because I heard that they all ended up pretty much bankrupt.

'I'll never forget the day Gladys MacGregor drove up the road in her old Land Cruiser, unannounced. I thought I was seeing a ghost. I hadn't seen her in at least ten years, and time wasn't kind to her. To be honest, she looked like a slapped bum. What did she come to Glen Eira for, I wondered? Well, money, of course. Seems she and her husband were about to get kicked out of their house. Out of nowhere, here she was, begging Miss Becky to help her and Mr Donald out. Then she got all uppity when Miss Becky asked Maurie Crowbar to toss her out. She got back into that Land Cruiser and spun the wheels.' She sniggered at the thought. 'I saw Gladys once more, in Barkers Hill, years later, taking things out of a St Vinnie's bin, but she put her nose in the air and acted like she didn't see me. I never saw any of the MacGregors again after that.'

Nellie glanced away. The spectre of the fallen dynasty hung around them like a fog. 'A big pastoral company bought out the family company, and it runs the rest of the old MacGregor stations now. Thank goodness Glen Eira was never part of that. It's all Droughtmasters and Brahman now, and I reckon that they don't make as good eating as the English breeds. In the eighties, Miss Becky took on a manager to help her run Glen Eira, but she still did everything the men did. They finally learned to respect her. Some of the ringers would have even died for her. It's not that long ago that she'd still go out riding, you know.

'I don't know if Miss Becky ever wrote to her mum after she left. I was too scared to ask her, or to write to Sylvia again myself. To this day, I never knew what became of either Sylvia Golding or to baby Constance.'

Nellie poured out two cups of tea but left the third cup empty. Then she covered the pot with a cosy crocheted out of multi-coloured wool, like a rastacap. She walked over to the dresser adjacent to the door, opened a drawer and pulled out a package. She sat back down with a huff, and unfolded the paper bag. Out of it, she produced a hospital tag, a tiny pair of white kid-leather shoes and a pale pink knitted layette.

'These,' she remarked, 'were Constance's.' She pushed a small bundle of photos secured with an elastic band over to him.

Chase thumbed through the photographs of a young Miss Golding, of a stylish older woman, and of a baby, alone and in various combinations, with and without Nellie.

Nellie scrutinised his face. She said, 'It's now time for you to fill in the gaps.'

Chase cleared his throat. He glanced at his palms. 'How did you know?' he asked her.

'How wouldn't I know? I know your walk and the set of your shoulders. I've seen them before. You're Jim's...'

He was nodding. 'My mother was that baby.' He glanced away from the photograph, frightened of the knot developing in his stomach. 'After Nanna—that's what I call Sylvia—left here, she went straight back to New York with Mom. She told everyone that she and Pop had had a change of life baby, and that she hadn't realised she'd been expecting when she'd gone to visit Becky... Miss Golding... I don't know what to call her anymore...'

He frowned, picked up his cup and took a sip, as if the tea might help him solve his dilemma. Having found no answer there, he resumed his story. 'If anyone asked her, she said that it was such a long trip, that she'd decided not to risk flying back, so she stayed in Australia until she'd given birth. She said to Pop that with every-thing that had happened, weren't they lucky to have the chance to bring up another child? I mean, they'd felt as if they'd lost both of their children, and Nanna could never understand why. Pop went to his grave never knowing exactly what became of Sam.

'My mom was a new beginning for them. I don't know if anyone suspected that Mom wasn't their child, but if they did, Nanna never heard about it. I guess it wasn't that hard to pass Constance Golding off as their own. You know that Becky's full name is Rebecca Sylvia Golding, and Nanna's is Sylvia Rebecca Golding, right?'

'No,' said Nellie, 'I didn't.'

'Anyhow, Pop eventually sold his business in Manhattan, and he and Nanna moved to New Jersey. Oh, Mom grew up knowing vaguely about Sam and Becky—I guess it would have been too hard to hide them from her entirely—but as far as she knew, she had a brother and sister, they were much older, and anyway they had nothing to do with Nanna and Pop. Nanna told me that Constance had been a blessing. It was like she and Pop had been given a second chance to get things right. All of her life, Mom never knew that Nanna was really her grandmother, and not her mother.'

Nellie scowled. 'All of her life?'

Chase glanced away. 'Mom died last year.' He threw it out as if he was disconnected from it.

Nellie could tell that he wasn't. She looked devastated. 'Oh, I'm so sorry,' she muttered. She took a sip, as if to steady herself. 'How did you find out the truth about your mum?'

'Mom was diagnosed with lung cancer, and she died about ten months later. She never even smoked, you know?' he added, his eyes quizzical, as if he was looking to Nellie to explain it to him, searching for some justification.

He resumed. 'Mom and Dad were divorced a long time ago, so I was filling out the paperwork after she died. I studied Mom's birth certificate for the first time. I mean, I really studied it. First up, it was weird that Mom was born in a country we had no connection to. At first, Nanna tried to make out that it had something to do with Sam, but I didn't buy it. As I read her birth certificate, I realised that the location of her birth, and the way Mom's mother's name was swapped around, weren't the only things that didn't make sense. Although Nanna had reported Mom's father as Walter Golding when she registered my mom's birth in Queensland, Mom's mother was described on her birth certificate as only being twenty-two years old.

'I asked Nanna about it at Mom's funeral, and she said she didn't want to talk about it. I kept hounding her until eventually she told me everything she knew. She said she never knew who my real grandfather was, but she gave me Becky's address. Once I had that, I knew that I had to come out here. After graduation, there seemed no reason to delay it any longer.'

He had just finished speaking, when there was a rap on the door.

Nellie turned towards the sound. 'Thank goodness,' she said, bustling away.

Chase expected to see Miss Golding in the doorway, but he saw a young woman with a luminous face and long-lashed amber eyes instead. He quickly bundled up the photographs and the clothing, and slipped them back into the paper bag.

'This is my granddaughter, Lily,' said Nellie proudly, filling the third cup and tipping in some milk. 'She's come down from the university in Townsville to visit me. I've been expecting her.' She glanced at Chase's face and added, 'She's studying to be a nurse, you know. She won't let me eat those caramels of yours, in case I get diabetes.' She pushed the tin across to Lily. 'So I guess she'd better have them.'

Lily glanced at the tin and smiled. Her teeth dazzled white against her satiny skin, the exact shade of Nellie's milky brew. She flicked back an errant strand of hair and shook Chase's hand. 'Pleased to meet you.' Her voice was velvet. 'Yeah, she has to be careful: it's in the genes. Sorry. Gran knows that I've got a bit of a sweet tooth,' she giggled. 'I'll enjoy eating these.'

He had spent so much time in the company of men and horses, that he'd almost forgotten the pleasure of the company of a young woman. He caught a hint of her perfume when she leaned forward to take his hand, and again when she sat down next to him—the green, heady scent of woodland, unpretentious and subtle.

Nellie grinned stealthily as she sipped her tea and listened in to their chatter about their studies, station life and their thoughts about the future. Talking to Lily was easy: she was clever and immediately engaging. He was drawn to her cool elegance, the glitter of her marcasite earrings catching the light as she turned her head, the gloss of her raven hair. Even under the harsh fluorescent globe, she was radiant.

He would have gladly talked to her all night, but about an hour and a half later, his eyelids heavy and the struggle to keep them open tougher, he gave in to his fatigue. He had to be up again in seven hours to muster cattle on the far side of the ridge, past a chain of rock pools. It was a fair ride, and he still considered himself a beginner.

He turned to Nellie as she showed him to the door and murmured, 'What should I tell my…grandmother?' He hesitated as he said the word, as if there was disharmony in calling Miss Golding that.

Nellie blew out her breath. 'I don't know if there's any use telling her anything at all. You've probably noticed that since she had that turn, she hasn't been all that well. Oh, she's recovered physically, all right. Given the pain she's in, she's still pretty strong in her body, but I'm not too sure where she is in her mind. She won't come into the kitchen anymore. She was pretty vague earlier tonight when I took her her coffee. If you do tell her, I'm not sure if she'll understand and, even if she does, she'll most likely forget it again.'

'Hmm,' he began, lost in thought, 'I have to tell her. She deserves to know.'

'Well,' she replied. 'It's totally your call.'

*

In the morning, Miss Golding was sitting alone on the verandah on an old chair that someone a long time ago had painted bright yellow. The rests where her arms lay were worn through to bare cane the colour of toffee. Her eyes settled on the horizon, the milky hue of dawn tinted rose, a warning to shepherds perhaps, but not to northern Australian cattle folk.

Chase glimpsed her as he walked towards the ringers' quarters after breakfast, and he took a detour, climbing the steps towards her, smiling widely, his hat in his hand, silhouetted in the halo of the rising sun.

Miss Golding started, as if she'd seen a ghost.

'Do you remember me?' he asked gently, crouching low.

She blinked, adjusting her focus, and said, 'The American boy. Of course. We haven't met up for coffee for a while. Where have you been?'

'Chase Miller. I've been right here all along, although I think that maybe you haven't been having your coffee in the kitchen lately.'

'What nonsense,' she replied.

She seemed sharp enough to him. 'Do you mind if I sit next to you?' He pulled up another of the cane chairs and sat down. 'I'd like to talk with you, Miss Golding.'

'Go right ahead.'

He chose his words. 'I suppose you still remember what Glen Eira looked like the first time you saw it. Was it the same as it is today?'

'Oh yes,' she said. 'I haven't changed anything really. I hear they use quad bikes and helicopters on cattle stations these days, but Mr Stewart and I believe that the old ways are sometimes best.'

'I'm sure you're right.'

She was oriented, at least to place. He rubbed the blisters on his hand where the reins had chafed them. It was time.

'I need to tell you something that might be a little hard for you to hear,' he ventured.

She frowned. 'If it's hard, then I don't want to hear it. Don't tell me.'

'I think I should.' He took a breath.

Miss Golding's eyes were misted with tears, as if she anticipated what he was about to say.

He leapt in, without testing the waters any further. There was no place for artifice now. The opportunity of that moment might never recur.

'Miss Golding, I haven't told you who I really am.' He watched the panic rise in her eyes. 'Oh, I'm Chase Miller, all right, but I'm not a backpacker who just happened to come by here. I came here on purpose, just to find you.'

He watched her suck in a breath, as if she half-expected it to be her last.

In his dreams, he had imagined a homecoming, the comfort of kin, warmth, acknowledgement and acceptance.

'You see,' he continued, 'I'm your daughter, Constance's, son. I'm your grandson, Miss Golding.' His words shredded the still morning air. He heard them reverberate in his ears.

She heard them too and looked frantic, her eyes darting. 'No, no,' she garbled, 'no, I was never married. You're mistaken. I had no daughter.'

He leaned towards her, his posture open, trying to reason with her. Gently, he began, 'Yes, fifty years ago, you had a daughter. You and Jim MacGregor had a baby, remember, and you named her Constance? Your baby girl was my mother.'

Miss Golding clapped her hands to her ears and made a sound like an injured calf. 'Lies,' she wailed, 'all lies. No baby, no grandson. No, no, no, no!'

The horses in the paddock inclined their heads towards her, ears twitching, acknowledging the distress of a wounded animal.

She rose from her chair. 'I don't know who you are! Get out!' she cried. 'Get off my land!'

Chase searched her face for clarity, but the book that had briefly been open before had snapped shut again. He hung his head and walked away. It hadn't gone as well as he had hoped. The only saving grace to their conversation was that she would probably soon forget that they had ever had it.

*

Chase and one of the contract ringers rode out towards the ridge that morning to check the fences and tag any cleanskins. They rode out over the stony downs which had long ago been a wooded field, poisoned since to open up the land. Where there were once copses of ironbark, box and ebony trees, there was desolation, some clumps of African buffel and subterranean clover. It sustained the cattle, but even to unaccustomed eyes, the landscape looked wrong.

They turned towards the river, just as the downpour started. Chase was sweating underneath an old japara coat Mr Stewart had lent him—it stank and it didn't allow the perspiration to evaporate—but he needed some sort of barrier against the stinging rain. He tugged his hat low on his forehead as the water trickled over its rim and down his collar. His horse, a tidy mare named Sarah-Jane, seemed unperturbed by the flash of lightning over the distant, ashen hills and the din of the storm. She picked her way along the path, following the gelding, head bowed, waiting for the weather to clear so she could stretch her legs.

They trotted along the near bank for another kilometre, turned off onto a four-wheel-drive track that led away from the river again, and then followed the ridge line. They found the cattle amidst the tufts of kangaroo grass, grazing quietly. The cattle, some solid red, some roan, lifted their eyes without turning their faces away from the pasture. The approaching horses didn't worry them. Miss Golding had persisted with the line of Shorthorn cross that she'd inherited from Jim, where just about everyone else had switched to Brahman cattle.

Chase stopped close to the herd and slid off his horse. He walked among the cattle loath to move as he pushed past them, running his hand over their backs, feeling the tightness of their skin over muscle, the wet dust clinging to their smooth coats, the bestial, bovine smell filling his nostrils. It was as foreign and strange as it was familiar, an echo of a forgotten past, rekindled through the vibrancy of his senses. He had never been on a farm, much less dealt with any stock, so there was absolutely no rational reason why he should feel that he was in his element. But he did.

They tagged three heifers and two mickey bulls, and coaxed them back out of the scrub towards a fenced paddock of barley Mitchell. Chase glanced skyward. Patches of blue had begun to punctuate the endless grey. He took off the coat and revelled in the freshness of the draught kicking up from the river as it kissed his bare arms. The rain clouds had disappeared entirely by smoko.

Chase's phone rang just as the billy had started to boil.

'Yes, hello,' he answered, lifting the billy off the fire and tipping in the tea leaves.

It was Nellie. Even before she said a word, he knew she was troubled from the snort of her breath as she held her phone too close to her face.

'I can't find Miss Becky anywhere,' she spluttered. 'I've been looking for her, but she's disappeared. That old mare of hers is missing too.'

'Maybe she's just gone for a ride?' he suggested. 'Could that be it?'

Nellie paused. 'Well, she hasn't ridden Chrystobel for almost a year, and she hasn't gone anywhere in a long time, but I suppose she might have. She's pretty arthritic, but she really can do anything she sets her mind to.' She hesitated again, her voice doubtful, 'It's just that she usually lets me know if she's going anywhere.'

Chase retraced their conversation. He wondered if the catalyst for her disappearance was what he had said to her. He knotted his brow. 'Maybe she just forgot to tell you. We could keep an eye out for her. Do you know where she might be?'

'Not really.' Deep in thought, she let out a sigh. 'Would you do that for me please? I'll phone you the minute she comes home.'

The sun had replaced the overhead clouds and the rain that had settled on the ground was steaming. They drank their tea in the shade of a brigalow, the atmosphere clammy still, then they saddled up and headed back towards the homestead. They had barely gone two kilometres when the telephone rang again.

'Is she back?'

Nellie's voice was even more urgent this time, trembling and fearful. 'No, she's not, but Chrystobel is. She just walked into the yard a few minutes ago. There's no sign of Miss Becky. I hope she hasn't thrown her.'

He was worried. 'Think hard, Nellie. Any idea where she might have gone?'

She stuttered, 'She had a special place, she never told me exactly where, but I know it wasn't very far from where you were today. A waterhole, I think.'

Chase reflected on the route they had taken. He reran the terrain in his mind. There were waterholes along the creek that fed the river; he was sure of that. He had seen them delineated in an old survey map of the station that adorned one of the walls in the ringers' quarters, so familiar that it had become invisible to every eye but his own.

They had already descended almost as far as the river plain. He sent the ringer on ahead, as he turned the mare around. Further along, he spotted an old, overgrown track, running parallel to the one they had taken before. As he approached, he observed that the spinifex had been flattened, the juvenile softwood scrub broken where it had been pushed aside.

He followed the stream, ascending through patches of wiregrass and spinifex, and African buffel grass that had spread on the wind and the livestock, and had taken seed. The track snaked past some small falls, the lowest one barely a dribble, the highest above a thickly wooded glade. Water thundered over rocks close by, and he was certain that the last waterhole had to be just past the senna bushes.

He got off and led Sarah-Jane, scouring the vegetation for any sign of recent tracks. Beyond that, the grass was untouched. He was certain that Miss Golding's horse had gone no further.

He strode towards the waterfall, combing the undergrowth for signs of Miss Golding as he proceeded, waiting for his eyes to adjust from the brilliance of daylight to the sheltering shadows under the stand of tall rivergums.

He found her sitting under a casuarina, propped up against its hoary trunk, listing gently to her left.

'Miss Golding,' he called out.

She didn't move.

He called again, and then he crouched down and shook her gently.

There wasn't a mark anywhere on her, and if it hadn't been for the coldness of her hands and legs, he might have believed that she was asleep and not dead.

He called Nellie to let her know he had found her, and to phone the police. There was no hurry, he was certain she was gone. He wondering if anything he'd said to her that day had passed the fortification she had erected. Her face was smooth and untroubled. She was at peace with the world and there was no awkwardness between them.

Once it was confirmed that she had died of a stroke that day, Chase obtained official permission to bury her at Glen Eira, alongside Jim.

Nellie entered Miss Golding's bedroom the following day. She had put it off, reluctant to disturb her last private space, but she needed to check it over and to tidy up. The undertaker had demanded a dress for the funeral, and she had to find Miss Golding's papers for Chase.

The entire room was sombre, the walls untouched in decades, the paint yellowed, hints of black mould in the corners where neglect had allowed the damp to settle and proliferate. The heavy curtains were drawn against the sun. It was as if Miss Golding had wanted to banish the light from every part of her life.

Nellie threw open the curtains and let in the day. She flung the window ajar to take away the pervasive dankness. She checked the tiny, cedar secretaire, lifting its honeycoloured lid, shuffling through the papers in its depths, taking out and piling to one side anything she thought Chase might require. She felt like a voyeur. Death had deprived Miss Golding of her right to privacy and the authority to protect the essence of her being against prying eyes. In death, she was utterly exposed.

Nellie had begun to strip the bed when something fluttered off the top of the bedside drawer and drifted to the floor. She picked it up, took her glasses out of her pocket and put them on. At first she believed it to be nothing but a chit of paper, torn from a larger sheet. She turned it over and studied it again.

Cut roughly from a leaf of printer paper was a photograph of Chase, smiling, arms akimbo, that someone—presumably Miss Golding—had printed from his Facebook page. Nellie placed it in her pocket for safekeeping. As she lifted the feather duster, a second photograph caught her eye, this time still lying on top of the same bedside drawer. She adjusted her glasses and studied it carefully: a young man standing in the identical posture, smiling at the camera. For a moment, she thought it was another photograph of Chase, except that this one had been reproduced on glossy, thick, white-rimmed, photographic paper.

And it was at least fifty years old.

The End